SO-ARO-218

Volusia County Public Library
LIBRARY SUPPORT CENTER
1290 Indian Lake Rd.
Daytona Beach, FL 32124
www.volusialibrary.org

CHASM CREEK

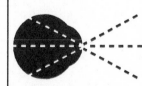

This Large Print Book carries the
Seal of Approval of N.A.V.H.

CHASM CREEK

A NOVEL OF THE WEST

PATRICIA GRADY COX

THORNDIKE PRESS
A part of Gale, a Cengage Company

GALE
A Cengage Company

Farmington Hills, Mich • San Francisco • New York • Waterville, Maine
Meriden, Conn • Mason, Ohio • Chicago

Copyright © 2017 by Patricia Grady Cox.
Thorndike Press, a part of Gale, a Cengage Company.

ALL RIGHTS RESERVED
This is a work of fiction. Names, characters, places, and incidents are either the product of the author's imagination or are used fictitiously, and any resemblance to actual persons, living or dead, locations, and events, is entirely coincidental.
Thorndike Press® Large Print Western.
The text of this Large Print edition is unabridged.
Other aspects of the book may vary from the original edition.
Set in 16 pt. Plantin.

LIBRARY OF CONGRESS CIP DATA ON FILE.
CATALOGUING IN PUBLICATION FOR THIS BOOK
IS AVAILABLE FROM THE LIBRARY OF CONGRESS

ISBN-13: 978-1-4328-5753-0 (hardcover)

Published in 2018 by arrangement with Patricia Grady Cox

Printed in the United States of America
1 2 3 4 5 6 7 22 21 20 19 18

Dedicated to my family — parents, sister, brothers, sisters-in-law, and son, in appreciation for years of support and encouragement.

ACKNOWLEDGMENTS

Thank you to Mary Todacheenie Black for her help with Navajo translations; Deborah Whitford for being there from the very beginning; Sue Tone for never refusing to read and read again; Janet Cooper and Jock MacIver for answering unending questions about goats and reading my drafts; Navajo guide Adam Teller for his enlightening tour of Canyon de Chelly; Janice Russell for her technological skills; Jim Sallis and all members of the Thursday night creative writing workshop at Phoenix College; and Thomas Cobb for excellent advice and encouragement

CHAPTER ONE

Rubén tightened his hold on the pack mule's lead rope and waited. The horses, flanks frothed white with sweat, kicked dust and huffed while Rubén held up a hand against the glaring sun. A small herd of scrub goats blocked a rutted path turning off the wagon road, cutting through cactus and dried-up bushes, and leading down a slight incline to a battered adobe cabin. The goats lifted their devil faces, jaws working. Rubén stared through the shifting pickets of their long, narrow horns. What caught his eye was the mesquite tree, thickly leafed, behind the cabin. A tree of that size meant a spring.

His friend beside him sat so hunched over that the brim of his hat touched his horse's mane, one hand white-knuckled around the reins, the other shaking at his side. Eyes closed, jaw clenched, tangled hair straggling over his shoulders in damp tendrils.

Rubén shaded his eyes and looked again toward the cabin. Past a stone barn, behind a rock wall, a woman straightened from a cloud of dust. Children ran for the cabin, dropping shovels and hoes, while the woman walked through an opening in the wall and picked up a shotgun that had been resting against the rocks. She stood, waiting.

"Morgan, we will stop ahead."

His friend raised his head, looking toward the cabin. "That woman plans to shoot us."

Rubén knew the possible truth of that statement. But the promise of water beckoned.

"It will not hurt to ask for some water."

"Not if she kills us with the first shot."

Rubén yanked the pack mule's lead and his friend's horse fell in behind. The goats parted to let them through, bleating their annoyance. Their demon eyes bored into Rubén's back and he glanced over his shoulder. They followed along behind Morgan.

A boy came from the cabin with a rifle and crossed the yard to stand by the woman.

Rubén reined to a stop in the yard, the pack mule and Morgan behind him, and she aimed the scattergun, one hammer cocked.

The boy, tall as a man, stepped forward.

"We don't want no Indians around here."

"Shush." The woman kept her eyes on Rubén.

"*Señora,* my friend is sick and needs a place to rest —"

She stepped back and pulled the boy with her.

Rubén shook his head. "No, no, you will not catch anything. Please do not worry. *Por favor,* allow us a rest in the shade of your trees, perhaps some cool water from your spring? Until the heat of the day has passed."

She cocked the second hammer and the sound brought Morgan's head up and his hand to hover over his sidearm. The woman swung the barrels toward him. Morgan said, "Let's go."

Rubén nodded. His seventy-year-old bones felt brittle in the heat, as if they would crack and turn to dust without rest and water, but he did not feel like getting shot. He turned his horse back toward the trail, the mule following.

The boy lowered his rifle, and the woman uncocked one hammer.

"You'll come to a creek a few miles down the trail, before you reach town," she said. "Plenty of shade and water there."

Morgan had reined his horse around when

11

the second barrel of the shotgun fired. The goats bleated in panic and scattered, flushing quail from nearby bushes. Morgan fell off his horse and landed with a hard thud in a cloud of dust. His hat fell away and he rolled onto his stomach, spots of blood already seeping through his shirt on his shoulder and upper arm. He crawled through the dirt, reaching for his hat while the horses and mule stomped around him.

Rubén struggled to dismount and hang on to the reins and lead rope. The woman said, "Oh, my God," over and over. The boy stood to one side, mouth hanging open and eyes riveted on his mother.

Morgan got to his knees and pushed Rubén away. "I can get up." He lifted his hat and dirt fell into his wet hair. Rubén crouched beside him and looked up at the woman.

"I'm so sorry." Her voice was barely a whisper. "It just went off."

Rubén helped his friend pull the hat down to shade his eyes. A quick look assured him most of the buckshot had missed although blood was now streaming. "*Señora,* it is not serious but it needs attention."

"Take him over to the ramada." She nodded toward the open-sided shelter jutting out from the barn.

The boy raised the rifle again. "Ma, I don't think —"

"Richard, help them."

"Ma, I don't think —" the boy tried again, but she pulled the rifle from him and gave him a shove.

"Help them. Then get James, and you boys take care of their animals."

Esther Corbin watched the old Indian settling his friend in the ramada. She slipped her hand into her apron pocket, fingering the extra shotgun shells she always kept there. Willing her legs to stop trembling, she broke open the gun, emptied the discharged chamber, and reloaded.

She fetched a bucket of water from the spring. The sick man gagged and vomited in the ramada and, by the time she reached him, he sat breathless in the shade, leaning against the barn wall. His hand went to his sidearm but his gunbelt was out of reach, on a pile of belongings unloaded from the mule. His eyes narrowed. "You shot me."

"It was an accident." She held out the bucket. He took it without looking up and put it by his legs, dipping his hands in it to rinse his face and mustache. He wet his hands again and pressed them against his forehead, covering his eyes. The water dripped over a ring on his left hand, a wide silver band inlaid with dark malachite, and ran down his arms, diluting the blood that soaked through his sleeve.

The Indian came from the corral and dropped two sets of saddlebags on the ground. He unrolled a blanket.

"Can I do anything to help you?" Esther asked him.

"You have done enough, *Señora*."

The cabin door slammed. Her youngest daughter Mary ran across the yard and wrapped her arms around her mother's legs. Esther tried to pry the girl off. "Go back in the house with Millie."

"I want to stay with you, Mama."

"Then stay close."

The girl hid her face in her mother's skirts. Esther stepped back as the Indian bent over his friend and helped him to lie down. A crucifix swung out from inside the Indian's shirt; an intricate silver Jesus suffering on a wooden cross suspended from a rawhide cord. The old Indian closed his hand around it and tucked it back in his shirt with a practiced movement before he slowly straightened, a hand pressing into his lower back, and turned to her.

"I am called Juan Rubén Tellez de Santiago. Most of the time simply Rubén."

He was dressed like a Mexican, in light, loose-fitting cotton trousers and white blouse, a carved leather scabbard at his waist that sheathed a large knife. His black eyes were deep-set in creviced leather skin, and shoulder-length gray hair hung from a wide-brimmed straw hat and framed his broad face. He didn't look Mexican. He didn't look Apache either. She wondered why he was riding around the Territory with a white man, but she kept her curiosity to herself.

"This is my friend, Morgan Braddock. We will be on our way as soon as I tend his wounds and he is feeling better."

"I'm Esther Corbin. This is Mary, my youngest."

At the mention of her name, Mary grabbed one of her long braids and stuck the end in her mouth, still hiding her face.

The Indian began to remove his friend's shirt. "How far is it to town?"

"Chasm Creek? About three miles." She pointed east, along the wagon road. "It's not a place for someone who's sick. Or for you."

"I see." He looked toward the wagon road. "So, for now, may I build a small fire? To brew some medicine?"

"There's kindling next to the woodpile."

She pointed to the far side of the barn.

He looked at her for a moment, then nodded. *"Gracias, Señora.* I shall get a fire now. *Gracias."*

She took Mary's hand and turned away but the child pulled loose and knelt down next to the sick man. She leaned close to his ear, her long dark braids brushing his arm. "Mister, are you gonna die?"

Her voice startled the barely conscious man into awareness. His eyes opened and he looked at the girl. *"Shi yózhí,"* he whispered. "What are you doing here?"

"Dios mío!" Kindling wood flew across the dirt as Rubén rushed back to the ramada.

Morgan reached for the little girl. *"Shi yózhí."*

Esther pulled her daughter away. "Don't touch her!"

Rubén fell to his knees, put one hand on his friend's chest to keep him from sitting up. The other arm, palm up, he held out toward Esther.

"He will not hurt her, *Señora.* He thinks she is someone else. He is sick, he does not know where he is."

"Is he gonna die, Mama?" Mary asked.

"No, he's sick." She let go of the girl. "You leave him alone, and maybe he'll get better. Hear me?"

"I think he's gonna die." Mary's eyes filled with tears.

"Don't cry. All you've done for three days is cry. Go in the house. I'll be there in a minute."

Esther glanced down to make sure the man, quiet again, wasn't dead, then started toward the corral to check on the boys and the strangers' animals. Maybe it would be a good idea to stop working on the irrigation ditch for the day and keep the children quiet. Maybe if that man got some rest he wouldn't die in her yard.

At the edge of the garden, a coyote poked his head out into the opening in the rock wall and squinted against the sunlight, his slitted gaze following the chickens as they scratched and clucked in the yard. James must have left the gate to the chicken house open again. Esther picked up a rock, flung it, and it landed with a puff of dust near the coyote's front paws. He didn't run but instead sat on his haunches, panting a smile, staring at her with golden eyes. Ragged fur lay draped across his ribs. When Esther bent for another rock, he got up and trotted back into the garden, disappearing into scorched leaves, reappearing at the far end. He turned his head and looked back at her before leaping the wall and fading into the desert.

She went to the corral and grabbed James by his shirt. A fringe of curly brown hair shielded his eyes. "You! Get those chickens and lock them up. Right now!"

Later, long after dark, Esther sat by the open window and kept a watchful eye on the deeper blackness under the ramada, taking comfort in the weight of the scattergun across her knees.

She knew nothing about those men. The memory of the old Indian's knife — which grew larger as the night wore on — drove her to recheck the gun's chambers, and she felt in her apron pocket for the extra shells. Howard had been gone less than three full days and already she doubted her ability to keep her children safe.

Voices drifted from the yard. She drummed her fingers on the gun's stock as she considered the way that man had looked at Mary. Who had he mistaken her for? What ghosts haunted him? She thought of her precious baby Ida, in the little grave behind the house.

One of the children coughed, followed by the soft sound of bodies shifting on pallets in the loft above her. Did they hear the coyotes yipping from the ridge behind the cabin or the frogs' rattling trill at the spring?

One more muffled cough from above before the cabin fell silent. When did she last enjoy such peaceful sleep? She prayed for the day when she would spend less time regretting her decisions than making them. She blew out the lamp and rested her hands on the scattergun.

A glow on the horizon brightened and spread over the hills, heralding a gibbous moon's ascent into a star speckled sky.

CHAPTER TWO

The next morning Rubén let the reins slide through his fingers so his horse could lower its head and drink from the turbid waters of the Rio Verde. The river, little more than a shallow seep, oozed downhill toward its junction with the Salt River. A small movement of the horse's hooves raised clouds of mud in the stagnant pool.

"This plan is too complicated," Rubén said. His horse twitched its ears back and nodded as if in agreement. "We have been fine without such a scheme so far." He shook his head, thinking of the plan Morgan had come up with — the reason they were in this God forsaken desert instead of headed to California as Rubén would have preferred.

"I'm tired of working for others. Someone always ends up dead. Next time likely one of us."

The set of Morgan's jaw told Rubén the conversation was over.

Sunlight crept from behind jagged mountains looming over the opposite bank. Even his horse did not want to cross, and Rubén was about to point that out but Morgan was already riding away. Rubén grunted and nudged his horse into the riverbed. He glanced back to see his partner headed south toward the fort, the mule plodding along behind.

After splashing across the muddy stream, Rubén urged his horse up the bank. They maneuvered around cactus and thorny brush and switch-backed up the steep slope, headed for a saddle between two peaks. The ground was thick with prickly pear, and stands of saguaro cactus towered above him.

Mounds of brittlebush dotted the incline. The stems that once held flowers were burned naked and stabbed through clusters of gray-green leaves to threaten the horse's legs as they passed. Waxy creosote glistened in the harsh light while the sun climbed to the apex of the sky's bleached dome.

Cicadas and birds abruptly quieted when the horse's hoof released a miniature rockslide to rattle down the mountainside.

Rubén spurred his horse the last few yards to the crest of the hill, only to face a maze of ragged mountains, each higher and more formidable than the one preceding. No wonder the renegade Indians had chosen such a location to hide. It would be a long time before greedy miners ventured into such countryside; these mountains would be daunting even to soldiers bent on blood.

He rode downhill with painstaking slowness. Talons of black volcanic stone slashed the mountainside and formed a lustrous ridge above him. A hedgehog cactus poked its spiny nose from a crevice in the ebony rock.

He stopped in the shade of a ravine. The cooler air carried the scent of creosote, and he took a deep breath before lifting his canteen to his lips. Four Apache materialized before him in the time it took him to swallow twice. He lowered the canteen. A horse broke the silence with a snort as it pawed the ground.

Two Indians turned and rode away. The others indicated with a jerk of the head, pointing with pursed lips, that he was to follow.

For the rest of the day they wove through cactus and brush, up and down hills until the sun sank low in the sky and they followed long, narrow shadows into the renegade camp. Rubén sat his horse and waited in the growing gloom, flanked by two of the young men who had ushered him into the camp. The other two hopped off their horses near three more Indians sitting around a fire. A short, muscular man got up and approached Rubén. He wore only a lengthy breechcloth, knee-high moccasin boots, and a long rag tied around his broad forehead.

"You are from the reservation far to the north?" He spoke in the language of the Apache.

Rubén knew the man referred to *Diné-tah,* the Navajo reservation. In the Apache tongue he introduced himself in the traditional way, to gain the man's trust. "Greetings. I am Juan Rubén Tellez Santiago. I am meadow people, born to the within-his-cover people," referring first to his mother's family, *haltsooí din'é,* and then to his father's, *bit' ahnii,* and continued in Spanish, "I am called Rubén." He eased himself down from his horse and looked toward the fire; its smoke carried smells of cooking meat and grease. His stomach rumbled.

"Very well, Rubén. Come, eat, then we talk." The Indian replied in Spanish. A relief, since Rubén preferred Spanish to his native tongue or the related Apache.

When the food was gone the others left them alone by the fire. As the last vestiges of daylight ebbed, the Apache asked Rubén what had brought him to seek their camp.

"My partner and I want to buy horses from you."

"Why not get your own? There are wild herds east and north."

Rubén sighed. "I am too old."

The embers of the fire glowed brighter in the thickening darkness. Sparks and smoke blew into their faces and both men waved their hands until the breeze shifted again.

"What would an old man do with these horses?" the Apache asked.

"We will break them to saddle and then sell them at Fort McDowell. To the army."

The Apache's eyebrows shot up and he gave a sharp laugh. "You want us to catch horses for you to sell to the Blue Coats? So they have good horses to chase us?" He shook his head and laughed again. "You are crazy!"

"They do not chase you as long as you live here quietly."

The Apache stopped laughing and grunted his agreement. He picked up a stick and poked at the fire. "They are tired of war, like us, and afraid to come into these mountains. But when the gold seekers move closer, they will chase us again." His eyes narrowed. "The army would not buy horses from an Indian."

"My partner is a white man."

The Apache was quiet for a long time, poking the fire. Then he said, "You trust this man?"

"I trust him. I do not always agree with him, but I trust him."

The Apache asked a few more questions regarding the plan. Rubén assured him of the money and that all he had to do was deliver captured horses to an agreed upon location. Then they both stared at the remnants of the fire, a bit of red glowing through the ashes, each thinking their own thoughts.

"If I agree, there are no long promises."

"We understand. We will pay as long as you bring the horses. You can stop any time. No promises and no questions."

The Apache smiled. "It would be good to take the white eye's precious money without them knowing. We will answer in the morning."

J.C. Dugan liked to keep an eye on the sky this time of day, both to ponder tomorrow's weather — even though he'd been in the

Territory long enough to know tomorrow would be the same as today — and to enjoy the sunset.

The hospital window above the sink where he cleaned his surgical tools offered a clear view of the parade grounds and surrounding buildings. This evening he watched a civilian ride in from the direction of the Verde River, turning at the hog pens and heading toward the stables. J.C. put down the scalpel and rubbed enough dirt off the window pane to get a better look.

He watched for another minute, assessing the way the man sat his horse, then called to the sergeant who served as his assistant. "I'm leaving for a while. I might not be back tonight." He stepped out onto the porch. Enlisted men hurried to the mess hall, and the smells of their dinner — warm bread, greasy salt pork — hung in the air.

Walking across the parade grounds, he passed a few cavalrymen still putting their horses through their paces. He removed his hat to wave the dust away. When he reached the stables, nobody was there except a private mucking out stalls. J.C. cut back to the parade ground, past the sutler's store and the guard house.

He spotted the man's horse and mule tied outside the Quartermaster building.

25

Inside the civilian and the Quartermaster were shaking hands. J.C. hesitated in the doorway. When he'd seen the man riding onto the post, he was sure he knew him but now he was not positive. The man had the same tall build but was thinner, the same dark hair but it hung down to his shoulders.

"Morgan? Morgan Braddock?"

The man stiffened, turned his head toward the door. A streak of silver hair seemed to flow from an ugly raised scar at his temple. His eyes, guarded and full of suspicion, showed no sign of recognition and his hand moved to rest on his sidearm as he turned.

"I'm sorry. I thought you were somebody I —"

"J.C.?" The hard expression disappeared and the eyes, tired and older than J.C. would have expected, crinkled with a familiar half-smile. "J.C.? What the hell are you doing way out here? I thought you'd have gone back east."

"Hell, man, I thought you were dead."

Morgan grabbed J.C.'s shoulders and made a show of inspecting his uniform. "Captain?"

"Finally. I'm the post surgeon." J.C. slapped Morgan on the back as they moved toward the door. "What brings you to the Territory?"

"Business. Selling horses to the Army."

"Come to my quarters. We can have dinner and you can spend the night before you head back to . . ."

"Chasm Creek. I'm setting up a business out of Chasm Creek."

"That little gold-mining town northwest of here? I know it. Some of the men head up that way when they have leave."

J.C. tried to calculate the years since he had seen Morgan, and he wondered if he had aged as much as the man whose gaunt features he now assessed. Probably, he thought, and found himself smiling.

"It's good to see you, Morgan."

He found a soldier to take care of the horse and mule, keeping them at the Quartermaster's corral, and he and Morgan walked across the parade grounds, followed by the sounds of the enlisted men in the mess hall — loud talking, an occasional laugh, dishes clanking.

"You said something about dinner?"

J.C. laughed. "Yes. But let's stop by the hospital first. I'd like to show it to you."

They entered the hospital, an adobe structure with inside walls plastered smooth, a canvas tarp for a floor, and several doors that led to other rooms with cots. J.C. pointed to the examining table. "Sit there

27

and take off your shirt."

"I thought you just wanted to show —"

"You're bleeding."

Morgan sat down, unbuttoned the cuffs and collar, and pulled the shirt over his head. "It's nothing. It's been tended to."

J.C. brought a lamp to the table and lit it. "I can see that. Whoever cleaned this up did a good job, but this area could use a dressing." He got some bandages and took a bottle of carbolic acid off a shelf. "Lucky for you he was a poor shot."

"It was a woman."

"And she shot you in the back? Not sure what that says about your skills with the ladies." He wrapped Morgan's upper arm and carried the bandages and bottle back to the shelves near the sink.

Morgan pulled his shirt back on and stood. "Claimed it was an accident."

J.C. got two glasses and a bottle of whiskey from a cabinet against the wall. He poured and handed a glass to Morgan.

"To old friends."

"Yes, old friends." Morgan took a sip.

Memories were never far from J.C., and seeing Morgan again had stirred even those most deeply buried. Battles where "doctoring" consisted of hacking off limbs before gangrene set in. Trying to pour enough

28

laudanum into the gut-shot to ease the pain of inevitable death. During that first big battle, the dead had piled up by the thousands below a cloud of circling buzzards, revealed when the smoke from the cannon cleared enough to see the sky. He tossed back the rest of his drink and refilled his glass. The army had been J.C.'s life since 1863, when he'd joined the 16th Vermont Infantry Regiment straight out of medical school and marched into Gettysburg, Pennsylvania, where Morgan had taken him under his wing. He lifted his glass again to stave off the groans, screams and sounds of cannon exploding that always hovered near, threatening to overwhelm him.

Morgan watched him with a look of compassion, as if reading his mind. "Those were hard times."

"We did our duty."

"Our duty." Morgan finished his drink. "Our Goddamned duty."

"I heard you volunteered to go west after the war. Your family thinks you died fighting the Indians."

"I did go west. I was assigned to Fort Sumner." He took the whiskey bottle and poured himself another drink. "Where we held the Navajo. Marched them three hundred miles, those that could keep up. The

Bosque Redondo, 'twas called. Bad water. No shade or shelter. No food eventually. For the Indians, of course." Morgan put his empty glass on the table. "We had plenty."

J.C. watched the lamplight play across the scar near Morgan's temple. He hadn't gotten that injury in the war and if he wasn't fighting Indians, where then? "I don't know what to say."

"There's nothing to say. Orders from Washington. Everyone did their duty. Funny thing, though. It was General Sherman himself who came out to sign the treaty that sent them home. I'd hoped never to see that man again, but on that day I was glad to hand him my resignation in person."

"And since then?"

"I've kept busy." Morgan stood at the window, looking out at the parade grounds. With his trousers tucked into military boots and his straight posture, he still looked the officer J.C. remembered. But the pistol and holster, the extra cartridge belt loaded with shells, the second gun tucked into his waist, spoke of a hard life on the frontier. He wondered what exactly it was that Morgan had been doing to keep busy.

Rubén spread his bedroll near the dying fire. His body creaked as he lowered himself to the ground. Rocks poked his back. He got to his knees, moved the blankets, lay down. Rocks poked his legs. He moved again, finally finding a space where he could fit his bones between the rocks. He stretched to reach his saddlebags and took out his Rosary beads, pulling a blanket up to conceal them. He began to pray, but his thoughts drifted to the day he, as a small child, had been watching his clan's herd of sheep. This memory often intruded, right before sleep, on nights he was especially tired or uncomfortable. He would see again the riders that bore down upon him and the other children. He felt again, more than six decades later, the pain as a screaming Comanchero grabbed his arm and hauled him up onto a galloping horse, holding tightly as he squirmed. He looked back one last time at his homeland. Sheep scattered like goose down across the red earth and children screamed. His best friend Anaba ran toward the hogans, long hair streaming behind her.

Eventually they delivered him to a Spanish family in Mexico City.

He plotted escapes from the hacienda's walls, but they always caught him and brought him back. Eventually he learned their language, and the last time he ran away

Señor Tellez had asked, "Why do you want to leave?" Dressed in his white suit, seated in a fine leather chair, he spread his arms wide. "Such a beautiful place."

"I want to go home, to my family."

"Those savages do not want you back!" *Señor* Tellez laughed. "They sold you for ten sheep and a horse."

Even now, remembering, Rubén had to press his fist against his chest as the words pierced him. That explained why nobody had followed to rescue him. Why nobody had come for him.

He'd stopped running away. He became quiet, compliant. The family treated him more kindly. On Sundays and Holy Days of Obligation, they allowed him to sit with their children in the beautiful cathedral, beneath tall windows made of colored glass, where the Blessed Mother held her baby in gentle arms.

Every Sunday he attended Holy Mass, kneeling beneath statues of the saints, gazing up at the giant crucifix behind the altar. Jesus Christ with open wounds at hands, feet, side. The anguished face beneath the crown of thorns. Sacred Heart exposed, dripping blood. The smell of incense, bells ringing.

On the day he accepted the sacrament of

Holy Communion, they dressed him in white. He joined the other children in the procession to the holy altar.

The priest held up a golden chalice and spoke in Latin. "The Lamb of God who takes away the sins of the world."

Bells chimed. The congregation murmured. "Lord I am not worthy to receive you, but only say the word and I shall be healed."

The priest's long robes brushed along the altar where the children knelt, heads tilted back, mouths open.

The priest lifted the host. "The body of Christ."

"Amen." The papery wafer touched Rubén's tongue. Such a feeling of peace, of love, flowed through him. He bowed his head, and tears flowed down his round cheeks. When he returned to his pew, *Señor* Tellez put a hand upon his head and looked deep into his eyes.

"That is grace you feel. You have been blessed."

That day he sat with the family at the celebratory feast and they gave him his name, Juan Rubén Tellez Santiago. From that day, he went to school with the Tellez children. At home he sat at the dinner table with them.

Every week he and the Tellez children spoke of their sins to the priest. Rubén knelt in the dimly lit confessional booth and breathed in the scent of lemon mingled with incense. The priest muttered whiskey-laced prayers from the other side of a small screened window. Rubén's sins usually involved the tenth commandment. He coveted the other children's clothing and books — new while his were handed down. He coveted their home, even though they allowed him to share in much of it. Most of all he coveted their parents, the love of the *Señor* and *Señora*.

Rubén shifted on the hard ground which seemed to be sprouting sharp pebbles. His coveting days had ended long ago. When he reached adulthood he began to wander, aware he belonged to no family, to no place. His heart had dried up and sat, black and impenetrable, in his chest. Until last night, camped at Esther Corbin's farm. Night had fallen and, he'd gone to fetch water from the spring behind their cabin. He knelt to lower his bucket and caught a glimpse of the family through a window. *Señora* Corbin kissed the children goodnight as they climbed a ladder to their sleeping loft. That night, a well of loneliness opened within him.

Deep inside, something had shifted.

These memories ruffled the edges of his mind. Sleep eluded him for hours but then, as he grew drowsy, fields of corn waved in the sunlight, herds of sheep grazed near a stream, a canyon's tall red cliffs towered into a deep blue sky. Peach trees hung heavy with sweet, sticky fruit. The frayed fragments could not be brought into focus, and he fell into a restless sleep where shadows flitted like ghosts and no birds sang.

In the morning he stretched his aching body and shook the dirt from his blankets. The young men brought his horse and the Apache leader handed him some jerky wrapped in a cloth and a skin filled with water for his trip back to the river. "Tell your partner Eleven will trade with him."

"Eleven?" Rubén glanced at the small group of Apache, much less than a dozen men.

"The white eyes gave me a number when I was their prisoner on the reservation. On a metal tag they hung around my neck." The Apache put his face close to Rubén's. "Since I escaped, I have made my own number. That is how many white men I have killed now. Eleven. Maybe someday I will change my name to a higher number."

One of the men who had led Rubén to

the Apache camp guided him back to where they had found him the day before. He found his way from there and, tired and still feeling the indentations of rocks in various body parts, saw Morgan at the river's edge, holding his horse's reins and the mule's lead while the animals drank. He looked up as Rubén approached.

"You look like you had a rough night."

"I thought often of you — drinking fine whiskey and smoking good cigars with the officers at the fort," he said. "It added greatly to my pleasure while I attempted to sleep outside a filthy wickiup."

Morgan took Rubén's canteens, stepped into deeper water, and held them under the surface. "Did they agree to do business with us?"

Rubén nodded. "And the army people will do business as well?" He waited for a response.

"I ran into someone at the fort, someone I knew a long time ago."

"How long ago?"

"Jeremiah Culbertson Dugan, J.C. we called him. Our families knew each other. He joined the army a couple years after I did, in sixty-three. He's a captain now."

"It disturbed you to see him again?"

"Said everyone had written me off as

36

dead. He wants to let my parents know I'm still alive. Said he'd write to them back in Vermont."

In all the years Rubén had known Morgan, this was the first time he had mentioned parents. Rubén had assumed they were dead. "I did not know you had family back in, what did you say? Vermont."

"My family's in New Mexico," Morgan said. "They —"

"And now —" Rubén interrupted before the conversation went any further in the direction of New Mexico. "What do we do about this horse dealing?"

Morgan pulled the last canteen out of the river. "Now we need a location. I have one in mind."

"It does not have anything to do with the *señora* back in Chasm Creek?"

"She's got a good place with water and empty corrals. Away from town." Morgan threw the canteen to Rubén.

"*Si.* And that is the only reason we are going back?"

"You got something to say, say it."

"I just do not know, *mi hijo,* if it is a good idea." He had seen the way Morgan looked at that woman on the farm. And the children. What memories would those children, especially the little girl, stir up? "It is not

37

your responsibility to look after them. Her husband will return."

"I know that."

"Perhaps we should not get too close to that family. I have a bad feeling about it."

"You have a feeling." Morgan swung onto his horse. "We should spend weeks clearing out desert scrub and building corrals because you have a feeling."

"I suppose you are right." But Morgan had already ridden off. Rubén directed the rest of his comments to his horse. "If truth be told, I think we should have gone to California." He clucked and put some heel on its flank. He had to yank on the mule's lead to get it to follow. "Do not be stubborn. One stubborn mule in this company is enough."

CHAPTER THREE

Esther drove the wagon into Chasm Creek, lurching over ruts and trash scattered in the road. Millie and Mary sat beside her. They hung on as best they could. The herd of goats, except for the billy and a few nursing does, followed, shepherded by Richard and James.

The road ran between the creek, which flowed at the base of a sheer cliff, and the town's array of adobe and wooden huts, one of which was the jail. Her brother came out and shooed his goats off the boardwalk, stood combing his fingers through his beard while he waited for her to pull up. When she reached him, he squinted at the load of sacks and trunks.

"What the hell you doing, Essie?"

He stepped off the boardwalk and lifted Mary from the wagon. The girl wrapped her legs around his waist and hung on his neck.

"I rented out the farm. We're going to stay in your house until Howard gets back."

As she expected, his expression changed from suspicion to surprise to delight. He hated the thought of his sister out on that isolated farm, just her and the children.

Then the suspicion returned. "Rented it to who? It ain't exactly usual for someone to wander by and want to rent a farm."

"Two men did happen to wander by the other day. They came back today and wanted to use the corrals but I convinced them to take over the whole place."

"Came by from where? What do you know about them?"

"I know they had the first month's rent in cash."

"Howard ain't gonna like you leaving that place in the hands of strangers."

"I'll have the rent money to show for it. He won't care how I got it. Do you want me to move into town or not? You've been saying it long enough."

Jacob had his eyes on Millie. "Stop smiling at those men!" He pulled on his beard and narrowed his eyes. "You're gonna have to keep an eye on that one," he said.

Esther put a hand on her older daughter's arm. "Millie, be a lady, please." She turned back to Jacob. "They're even going to finish the irrigation ditch and take care of the animals I left behind."

"Move along," Jacob shouted at two miners who had stopped panning to gape at Millie. He started to hand Mary back up into the wagon, then stopped.

"What's that in your hand?" He pried her fingers open. In her palm lay a small quartz stone laced with gold. "Where'd you get this?"

"From Pa." Her fingers shut tight over it and she tried to pull her hand away.

"Your father gave you that?" Esther asked. "When?"

"Afore he left."

Jacob gave Mary a little shake. "Where'd he get it?"

"I can't tell." Mary's eyes filled and her chin quivered. "Pa said never to tell! Don't

40

you tell nobody, he said!"

"You can tell me, Mary. He didn't mean you couldn't tell Uncle Jacob."

Tears spilled down her cheeks and she started to wail.

"Okay, okay. Shush, child, shush." He put her back in the wagon.

"All she's done is cry since Howard left. And tell this ridiculous story about him having a gold mine," Esther said.

"Ridiculous?"

"Do you think he would have gone off to California if he had a mine to work?"

She knew what Jacob thought: any normal person would be hard put to figure out why Howard did anything, but at least he didn't say it in front of the children. Jacob's gaze and attention were now on the hills to the east of town, where he liked to prospect when he wasn't working his own mine at the far end of town.

Esther left her brother to his daydreams and continued on to the last building on the town road, the house he never lived in. He had built and furnished it for his future wife, the one who took one look at Chasm Creek and had her driver take her back to Maricopa where she could catch the next train back east.

A small stream meandered from the hill

41

behind the house, crossed the yard and road, and drained into Chasm Creek. A trickle; it muddied the road and pooled in the grassy yard and nourished a pair of Palo Verde trees and a cottonwood. It spread a moist coolness through the yard, freshening the air as the breezes drifted down the canyon.

The coolness reminded Esther of that morning at the farm. While the three older children worked at their chores, she and Mary had headed for the shade of the big mesquite, where its low, thick branches leaned over the spot where the spring water pooled behind the irrigation gate. They pulled off their shoes and stockings, held up their skirts, and waded into the water. Soon they were splashing and laughing. Esther unraveled Mary's braids and removed the pins from her own hair. With their skirts and aprons tied up around their waists, they bent over, rinsing their hair in the cool, clear water.

They sat at the edge of the pool, and Esther cradled Mary on her lap, their feet dangling in the water. While she rocked her daughter back and forth, she thought of the last time she'd held her baby Ida, how she had clutched the tiny body in her arms on the day she died. It had been more than a year ago, almost two, yet only yesterday in her heart.

Mary patted her arm with hands that, at four years of age, were losing their baby plumpness. "Don't be sad, Mama."

Mary always had a sense about people's emotions. Esther hugged her closer. She sang a quiet lullaby, one she'd learned from her mother.

"Hush, my babe, lie still and slumber,
Holy angels guard thy bed,
Heav'nly blessings without —"

A soft huff, a horse close by — she twisted around. Morgan Braddock sat his horse, looking down at them.

"It seems you've snuck up on me, Mr. Braddock." She lifted Mary off her lap and pulled down her skirts. He saw her glance at the scattergun, left just out of reach, leaning against the base of the cottonwood.

"You weren't planning on shooting me again, were you?"

She felt heat rising from her neck into her face. She was glad that he didn't seem angry about the incident, but his tone was almost taunting. "Probably not today." She picked up her weapon with one hand, her stockings and shoes with the other.

"I didn't mean to startle you, ma'am. I was waiting for you to finish your song. You've a pretty voice."

"You do, Mama! A pretty voice."

Esther's wet hair hung loose down her back, and she brushed at the few dry strands that floated around her face in the breeze. "Mary, get your shoes and stockings on."

Braddock had been looking away but now he turned to her. "Rubén and I wanted to talk to you about a business proposition."

"You'd like to buy some goats?" She tried to get Mary's stockings and shoes on, dropping a shoe in the pond.

"Let me help," Braddock swung down from his horse. With his longer arms, he was able to grab the shoe. "Shall we go to the house and talk?"

He scooped the girl up into his arms. Esther caught the scent of soap and tobacco. They headed for the house.

"Mama!" Mary was not the least unhappy about being carried. "My feet are still wet!"

"That's okay, sweetie. We'll dry them properly after our company has gone."

"Mister, Mama says mushrooms grow in dark, damp places. There was lots of mushrooms in the woods where she grew up. Do you think mushrooms will grow on my feet?"

He smiled. "Your mother can check when you get inside."

"If we find some, can we pick them off and eat them? Mama says they used to eat mushrooms. Have you ever ate a mushroom?"

"Yes, I have, but the tastiest ones would surely be the ones from your toes."

"Mary," Esther said, "stop plaguing Mr. Braddock."

"I don't mind, ma'am. My own daughter was about this age, last time I saw her."

Thinking back on the conversation, Esther wondered how long it had been since Mr. Braddock last saw his daughter. He looked so sad, somewhat lost, when he spoke of her

"Mama?" Millie waved a hand in front of Esther's face. "Are we going to sit here all day?"

Esther slapped the reins to hurry the horse and keep from sinking in the mud patch in front of the house. She pulled to a stop as close to the deep, covered porch as she could get. She climbed down and held up her arms for Mary. After assigning the older children to unload the wagon and settle the goats in the fenced area on the far side of the house, she held the little girl's hand as they climbed the wide staircase to the

45

porch. She lifted the latch and pushed the front door open.

A thick layer of dust covered the wide plank floors and rugs. She started pulling sheets from the furniture, making it into a game with Mary. Sunlight streamed through the two front windows and one on each side. They waved the sheets in the air until the room was full of flying dust motes and they began to cough. She went to the kitchen and threw open the window, hoping for fresh air. More dust blew into the house than out. She shut the window.

The stove had been hauled at great expense from the docks in Yuma where a steamer originating in San Francisco had unloaded it. No more bending over a crude fireplace to cook or heat water. Maybe those men would rent the farm for a long time. Maybe when Howard returned he'd agree to live in town, here in Jacob's house. Maybe Jacob would let him.

She walked as if in a dream through the parlor, ran her hand along the sofa, touching each table and lamp. Two doors on the back wall opened onto bedrooms — the empty one would do for the children. They wouldn't mind sleeping on the floor. But the other door — that one opened onto a room with a four-poster bed, a feather mattress on metal springs instead of ropes, a wardrobe and a chest of drawers. And a mirror!

She pulled off the sheet that covered the mirror and took a moment to look at her reflection. The girl that had traveled across country seemed to be gone, replaced by an older, tired woman. But she leaned close and looked hard and caught a hint of herself lingering.

Soon after his sister had ridden away, Jacob started out for the farm, his herd of goats trailing along behind him. It was yet a cool morning, and the goats were frolicsome. He enjoyed looking back to watch them; he loved his goats. Over the years Esther had given him wethers when they were still babies. He bottle-fed them so they followed him everywhere. Of course, he suffered a lot of ridicule about the goats in the beginning, and then worse abuse when he fashioned miniature panyards for them and started using them to haul his prospecting supplies. But in a short time, other miners began to see the sense of it. Unlike a mule, the goats needed no lead rope, foraged for their own food in the desert, could get into smaller spaces and climb steeper hills, and they grew nice sharp horns to ward off predators. He'd been approached by others about buying a wether from Esther. So far, his explanations about what was involved in bottle-feeding a kid day and night, a newly castrated baby that missed its mother, had put them off. But the taunts had subsided.

He dismounted in Esther's yard and tied his horse to the porch railing before the two men came out into the covered dooryard. Jesus Christ, an Injun? Esther rented her house to an Indian? What the hell? He directed his comments to the tall white man.

"Name's Jacob Tillinghast. This here farm belongs to my sister."

"Morgan Braddock." The man nodded toward the Indian who stood with a hand resting near, too near in Jacob's estimation, the knife at his waist. "My partner, Rubén Santiago. What can we do for you?"

Jacob hooked his thumbs through his braces, careful to push back his vest enough to reveal the town marshal's badge.

"I wanted to introduce myself, and let you know if you need anything to come on in to town." He wiped dust from his teeth with his tongue and spat by the porch post. "Not him, though." He glanced at the old Indian. "You ain't sleepin' inside my sister's house, are you?"

Braddock started to take a step forward,

48

but the old Indian put a firm hand on his arm.

" 'Tis not worth it, *mi amigo.*" The glinting black eyes were on Jacob's badge. "I sleep in the ramada, *Señor.*"

"What all are you needing this place for?"

Braddock pulled some papers out of his vest. "We've got a contract to provide horses to Fort McDowell." He handed the papers to Jacob.

It looked official enough, a contract with amounts entered that would be paid for horses, broken and delivered. Jacob gave the papers back.

"You know the rental terms might change when her husband gets back."

"We'll be happy to discuss it with him."

The way the man kept saying "we" seemed almost a challenge, but there wasn't much more to be said unless Jacob wanted a fight. It was two to one, so he climbed on his horse and rode back to town.

Still troubled but not knowing what, if anything, to do about the situation, he sat in the jail and watched the children playing in the creek. There was just the mining office between, and he could see his house from the jail. The children played in the creek and smoke curled from the chimney. He laughed to himself. He knew Esther'd

49

always been jealous of that stove. Now she had a fire cranked up in the house and it must be a hundred degrees out.

He hoped nobody in town found out about that Indian living at her farm.

Dusk came early in the canyon, and Jacob was still sitting at his desk wondering if he should do something about that old Indian running loose. Shadows cast by the window bars faded into the dirt floor as darkness fell. He held a match to the lamp, then leaned back in his chair and loosened the cartridge belt around his waist with a sigh. He pulled the bottle of mescal out of the lower right-hand drawer before propping his feet up on the desk, one long leg crossed over the other.

Yawning, he glanced over at the strap-iron cage he'd salvaged the last time the prison wagon from Yuma had come through town. The wagon was too broke down to make it back to Yuma, but there was nothing wrong with that cage. It served well for locking up an occasional drunk or brawler. He'd put a cot in it and the cot was comfortable enough; he'd slept on it himself many a night, when he wasn't staying at his claim up on the hillside.

Something about that Braddock bothered him. Was it that the man looked so sullen and ready for a fight?

He yawned again and thought about riding to his claim so as to get an early start in the morning. One more quick swig from his bottle and he smacked the cork back into place.

He started to return the bottle to the drawer when he sat up, his boots hitting the dirt floor with a thud. Reaching farther into the drawer for that pile of bulletins he kept, some so old they were yellowed and cracked, he pulled them out and studied each one in the circle of light from the lamp until he found what he was looking for.

Morgan Braddock. The description was accurate enough. Wanted for murder. Issued in Muddy Springs, New Mexico, November of 1870. Ten year ago come fall. A reward — two hundred dollars. Why, he could make more than that in a good week at his mine, and nobody shooting at him. He wiggled the cork back off as he stared at the faded print.

Lifting the bottle to his lips he wondered if he was expected to go lock up this criminal, but he knew Mr. Snapp, the big mine owner, had only hired him to make sure the employment pool providing a steady supply of ore didn't decrease due to shootings and brawls.

If he locked up Braddock and ran off the Indian, Esther would move back out to the farm.

He put all the wanted posters into the drawer and pushed it shut, then hoisted his feet up onto the desk again. He lifted the bottle. The sharp tang of the liquor cut through the lingering dusty odor of the old papers.

A smart man knew when to mind his own business.

Morgan looked away from the clouds on the eastern horizon to take the cup of steaming coffee Rubén offered. His old friend eased down beside him on the bench in Mrs. Corbin's dooryard. Morgan's thoughts were on the little girl's sweet voice. She had been full of life and questions, light as a feather when he picked her up.

"The sky is beautiful," Rubén said. "It is a good sunset."

Morgan nodded. The streaks of gold and red in the western sky made him think of Mrs. Corbin's dark hair hanging damp past her shoulders, the way wisps of it had floated like a halo around her face, flashing those same colors in the sunshine. How pretty she'd been when she smiled, her copper eyes shining under straight brows.

He had wanted to brush those flames of hair away from her cheek, and now he burned with guilt.

A sharp pain at his temple erased all thought for a moment. He closed his eyes and waited until the spasm subsided to a dull throb. He sipped his coffee and turned again to the east where distant hills faded into layers of translucent purple beneath pink-tinged clouds. He wondered how long it would take to ride to Muddy Springs, but he couldn't seem to focus on the thought. "Do you think she still waits for me?"

He sensed Rubén's sudden straightening on the bench, heard his breath stop, imagined in the moments of silence that his friend debated whether to say anything, then what to say.

"Why do you bring up such foolishness?"

Why, indeed. Morgan knew, of course, that she waited for him. He could feel it, always, in his heart. He thought again, with another twinge of guilt, of Mrs. Corbin smiling at him in the sunlight. Perhaps the memories were no longer enough to fill the empty spaces inside of him. "Maybe it's time I went home."

Rubén stood up and waved an arm toward the eastern horizon where a slice of dark red illuminated the black tips of the farthest mountains. "You cannot go back! You know you cannot!"

"Maybe things have changed." Morgan watched the play of emotions across his friend's face. "I should be with my wife. With my family."

Rubén leaned down so their eyes met. "You cannot mean that. Do not speak of it again. Please. Those who want to hang you are waiting. *Sí*, that is what waits for you." He sat down hard.

Silence hung between them as the sky turned black and stars winked to life. Morgan let the throbbing in his head swallow the vague memories. Sometimes he forgot how old his friend was; he should try harder not to upset him. He stood up and stretched.

"I think I'll turn in."

"Good," Rubén got up stiffly. "There will be no more foolish talk tonight."

CHAPTER FOUR

Esther took comfort in the rhythmic pounding of the stamp mill. Perched on the top of a hill overlooking Chasm Creek, it ran twenty-four hours a day, seven days a week. Ten iron cylinders, weighing a quarter of a ton each, dropped ten times a minute within the wooden framework. The constant banging rattled the canyon walls. Soot from its wood-fired steam engine sifted into the canyon as a steady shower of grit.

To Esther, after the isolation of the farm, it seemed a giant, soothing heartbeat echoing through the canyon.

Soldiers from the fort, coming into Chasm Creek to work their claims when they had two or three days off duty, reminded her that all the Apaches were not contained within the boundaries of the San Carlos reservation. Another reason to be glad her family now lived in town. Rumor had it that renegades camped north of Chasm Creek, on the other side of the Verde.

Esther unlocked the door of the mining office and let it swing open. Dust sifted from the rafters of the small adobe shack onto an oak desk that almost filled the back half of the room. To the right were brand new filing cabinets, opposite the one window which faced Jacob's house.

The cabinets had sailed from San Francisco, around the Baja California, up to the mouth of the Colorado River in Yuma. Then a friend of Jacob's who worked at the territorial prison hauled them to Chasm Creek in a prison wagon, so no need to wait for a freight wagon. They arrived yesterday, and

Esther thought they were beautiful. She had brought a jar of her linseed oil, beeswax and turpentine solution and some rags to polish them. It would be her first official act as the new filing clerk for Mr. Snapp's mining operations.

When she finished polishing the cabinets, she squeezed around the desk and cleared a space so she could get to work.

Halfway through organizing one pile of mining claims, Esther sat back and stretched her arms overhead. Almost right outside the window, Millie and Mary sat in the grass by the stream, sewing dresses for their dolls while Richard sprawled across the porch steps. Something caught his attention — he looked up, then gathered his gangly legs beneath him and stood as Morgan Braddock rode right up to the porch. The girls went to greet him, and as soon as he dismounted he picked Mary up and held her while he spoke to Richard. Her son looked very interested in whatever Mr. Braddock was saying.

She pulled herself away from the window when heavy footsteps on the boardwalk stopped at the door before it flew open and crashed against the wall. Otto Schmidt filled the doorway, a big man, red hair bushing out from under a filthy hat and covering almost all of his face except for his nose and the area around his eyes. Jacob had pointed him out once and said to stay away from him.

"Where is Snapp?" One step brought him to the desk. His hand slammed down and her papers flew.

"Probably at the stamp mill." She tried to sound calm as she grabbed at the papers. "Is there something I can help you with?"

"He cheated me," Otto bellowed. "I sold him my ore, and he cheated me!" He swept his arm across the top of the desk. Her neatly piled papers, pens, and the inkwell spilled over the edge of the desk like an avalanche.

"Hey! What are — you can't do that!"

The hair on the lower half of the man's face parted to reveal a mouth with two yellow teeth. Otto leaned over the desk. She turned her face away from his sour breath. "This ain't the first time that old bastard has done this to me! Don't you tell me nothin' except where to find that cheatin' son of a bitch."

She started around the desk, hoping to bolt for the door, but he blocked her way, grinning at her. She retreated back behind the desk.

"Perhaps if you give me your name and a

detailed account —" She picked up a pencil and dropped it, her heart pounding, as a huge hand reached toward her. She leaned back. "I could speak to Mr. Snapp the next time —"

They both heard the click of a pistol being cocked. Otto's hand stopped in mid-air. The leering opening in his face closed back into solid hair. She caught a glimpse of Braddock standing behind Schmidt.

"Get out." Using the barrel of his pistol, Braddock prodded the man to the door and out into the street.

Richard ran into the office. "Are you all right, Ma? We heard him yellin' all the way to the house . . . Ma?"

"Yes, son, I'm fine, perfectly fine." She fought the shakiness in her voice. "Mr. Braddock, please, come inside. No harm was done." She lowered herself into the chair. "He's just a bully."

"Don't underestimate a bully, ma'am." Braddock lowered the hammer and slid his pistol into its holster. He turned away from the door. "If he comes after you like that again, shoot him."

She forced an overwrought laugh. "Mr. Snapp might have something to say if I shot every miner who came in here with a complaint."

"That man meant to hurt you, Mrs. Corbin." He glanced around the office. "Don't you have a weapon?"

"No. I guess I should have brought the shotgun. I didn't think —"

He pulled the extra pistol held at his waist by his cartridge belt. "It's a Colt 45. You know how to use it?"

She nodded. "I'm not that good a shot with a pistol, but then Mr. Schmidt is a pretty big target." She liked the way the lines around his eyes crinkled when he smiled. "I've never shot a man, though. I mean, not on purpose! Maybe I'd prefer to let you save me."

The smile faded to a grim line. He touched his hat and his eyes disappeared in the shadow of the brim. "I'm afraid I'd make an unreliable savior."

He went out the door, brushing past Jacob who was pushing his way in.

"What the hell happened? I heard Schmidt in the saloon yelling about the mining office."

"He threatened me, but Mr. Braddock chased him away and left this in case he ever comes back."

She held up the pistol.

"I'll arrest the son of a bitch."

Jacob turned to go but Esther pulled on

59

his arm.

"No, don't bother. It's over now. I doubt he'll be back — he's probably off looking for Mr. Snapp, God help him."

She settled herself behind the desk. Jacob slapped dust from his clothing and launched a projectile of tobacco juice past the front steps where Richard sat scratching a goat's head.

"When are you heading out to prospect again, Uncle Jacob?" Richard asked.

Jacob looked toward the hills. "Soon, I hope. Damned good colors in those hills. Not to mention some float in an arroyo."

"I wish you wouldn't go that way. They say Apaches are in those hills."

"Last time I climbed up a hill and come across maybe fifty buzzards. They was flappin' around, squawkin', scared the goats half to death." He took off his hat and waved it in front of his face. "Something was rottin' up there. Stench of it was God awful."

Richard laughed. "Uncle Jacob, you're not making it sound like much fun."

"Who said fun?" He scratched his head and put his hat back on. "But hittin' a vein and gettin' rich would be fun, I reckon."

It was Esther's turn to laugh. "The world is full of people hoping to hit a vein." She went to the door, stood looking past Richard. "What brought Mr. Braddock into town today? What was he talkin' to you about, son?"

"He wants me to work for him at the farm."

Jacob's head snapped up. "What?"

"He wants me to take care of the animals we left there and the gardens. Help out, you know. It'd be just like doing my old chores, only I'd get paid."

"That sounds like a great idea," Esther said.

"No it ain't! You both wait here. I'll be right back."

Esther and Richard stood on the boardwalk and watched Jacob push his way past the miners and mules and wagons in the road. He rushed into the jail and in a minute was out again, hurrying back to them and thrusting a folded paper into Esther's hand.

"What's this?" She unfolded the cracked and stained paper. "Richard, go home."

"But, Ma!"

"Go home, I said!"

When they heard the door slam at Jacob's house, she looked at the paper again. Wanted for murder. Out of the corner of her eye, she saw Jacob fold his arms across his chest.

61

She forced herself to read the details: November of 1870. Two hundred dollar reward. As she held the poster, it ripped halfway apart on the fold. "This doesn't mean anything." She shoved the poster back into Jacob's hands.

"Look how old it is, and look at the paltry reward. You could make that in less than a week of hard work at your mine."

The smugness drained from his face. "For God's sake, Essie! It says murder!"

"He's not a killer. Why would a killer rescue me from Otto Schmidt and give me his pistol? And if you think he's a killer, why haven't you locked him up?"

"Don't think I haven't thought of it."

"What stops you?"

"Besides the fact that his Indian friend would probably slit my throat with that big knife of his? To keep you in town. Now I'm not so sure. Damn!"

She waved the poster. "It's old. No doubt it's groundless. But I guess it must be considered where Richard is concerned."

Jacob tucked the poster inside his shirt. "I could send a telegram from the fort. To this Muddy Springs and ask for confirmation." He headed for the door. "If I go now, I can be back before dark."

Alone again in the small office, Esther

pulled the top drawer of the desk open and looked at the weapon. Had she stayed in Rhode Island she wouldn't have a job, or a gun, or an absent husband. It was she who encouraged stodgy Howard to come west. She, driven by the thought of seeing her brother again and, she admitted at least to herself, the lure of adventure. She remembered the glee with which she'd tossed her corset into the darkness beyond camp one night as everyone slept. She had danced in her shift, twirling in the moonlight, drunk with the freedom of that first week on the trail west, even though they could still see the lights of a town through the trees. She had laughed, wondering what the next wagon train would think, seeing that corset hanging from a trailside bush.

What would her life be like had she never left Rhode Island? Ida would still be alive. The familiar pain stabbed her heart.

Maybe she should have been more like her mother, a lady, always aware of her behavior and comportment, dressed in fine clothes and living in a fine house, doing things that ladies do. If she had stayed and become like her mother, her children would be safe.

But just thinking of all the grass and trees and houses crowded together on manicured hills under clouds and fog and rain brought on that old feeling of suffocation. She could never see the sky there. She looked out at the dusty street of Chasm Creek, where rough men crowded the water's edge, greedy men with no pretense and heads full of schemes. If she rode a quarter mile out of town, the canyon opened up to a wide expanse of desert, not a tree to be seen between town and the spring in her farm's back yard. The air didn't sit in puddles on your skin and blue sky went on forever. Her breath eased.

With one last look at the pistol, she pushed the drawer shut and went home to fix the evening meal.

After supper, Richard pushed away from the table and stood over her. "You can't tell me no, just because Uncle Jacob says so. He ain't my father."

"Isn't." She cleared the plates from in front of the other children. "Go outside and play, please. Your brother and I need to talk." She waited until they were out in the yard. "I said we'll wait until Uncle Jacob gets back from the fort."

"It's the perfect job for me."

"Richard, stop it."

"You let James get a job."

"Yes, he sweeps the floor at the saloon.

64

He's home every night."

"Fine. Then I'll get a job in the mines. They're always lookin' for swampers."

"No, you won't. It's not safe in those mines."

"Ma, I'm almost sixteen years old. I'm not a baby." He pushed past her and ran outside, almost colliding with his uncle who was tying his horse's reins to the porch railing.

Jacob came in and sat at the table. He made a show of looking around. "Nice place you got here."

Esther put a cup of coffee before him. "So what is the answer?"

He shook his head. "I never sent the telegram."

"Why not?"

"There's still no telegraph at the fort — they got turned down that last time they requested one. I didn't feel like riding all the way to Phoenix. Besides, that town, Muddy Springs, probably has no telegraph either. It's nowheres near even a fort. One of the soldiers showed me on a map."

An image of Richard hauling trash rock from some dark hole stole into her mind. "So what now? Are you going to arrest Mr. Braddock?"

"Essie, I don't know what to do."

This surprised her. She poured herself some coffee and sat down across from him.

"There was this soldier at the fort. Spoke up when he saw the poster. Turns out he knows Braddock from the war and even before; they're both from Vermont. So happens he ran into Braddock just a few weeks ago. He said the poster must be a mistake."

"Really? Do you hold his opinion to be reliable?"

"Well, he's a captain. He's the post surgeon."

"An officer."

Jacob nodded. "He had nothing but praise for Braddock. To hear him tell it, Braddock finished the war decorated like a Christmas tree. The man practically walks on water."

She started to get up. "Well, that should settle it."

"People can change, Essie."

"Not that much."

"That's what that Captain Dugan said. As far as he could see, the man hadn't changed a bit. Was there making a deal to sell horses to the army and his terms were more than fair."

"Well, good. Richard will be happy." She looked out the window. James was chasing the girls, hunched over with his arms extended, pretending to be some kind of

66

monster, while they ran in circles, screaming and laughing. Richard sat alone by the
stream, looking sullen as he flung his
pocketknife into the dirt by his feet. He had
grown so much, especially in the last two
years. He was more like a man now than a
child, with a tall, lean build like his father's.
How could she expect him to be satisfied
hanging around town with his sisters and
little brother? Now he could take the job
out at the farm and have some indepen-
dence. She turned back to her brother. "It
seems the United States Army is vouching
for him. That should be enough for us."

Jacob scraped his chair across the floor.
"Soldiers are trained to kill people. Don't
you think there might still be a few unanswered questions?"

"My life is full of unanswered questions.
What's one or two more?"

"That poster did say murder."

"You know you're not going to arrest him.
You would've done it already."

"I won't, if you'll stay away from them."

"They're my tenants. I might have to
check on the property on occasion."

He gulped down his coffee and got up.
"I'm going to Muddy Springs. Send Richard to the saloon to tell Will he's deputized
until I get back."

"Jacob, who cares what happened ten years ago? It'll be a long, hard trip for nothing except to satisfy your curiosity."

"It's more than curiosity. Dammit, you're a pretty woman and he's . . . well, you stay away from there until I get back."

"I can't stay away. I might need to kill a chicken or butcher a goat. And I'm not paying Mr. Osgoode's prices when I've got the same food in the root cellar." She followed him as far as the porch and watched as he climbed onto his horse.

"Don't let him take the job," he said. "Not before I get back."

"If you were that worried, you'd stay here with us."

He grunted as he turned and rode away.

That night, after the other children were asleep, Esther and Richard sat out on the porch and had another talk. "There are things about Mr. Braddock you don't know. Your uncle fears he may even be dangerous. We should wait until we find out more."

"Dangerous? That's crazy, Ma."

"You'd be all alone out there with them, and we don't really know anything about him or that Indian."

"Ma, we don't know anything about a lot of people."

"Go to bed now."

She went outside and watched the stream trickle across the yard into the creek, watched the creek flow into town. It was too dark for the placer miners to pan for gold, and she sat listening to the sounds from the saloon. She resented having to make another decision without Howard until she remembered that she seldom agreed with his decisions anyway. A chorus of yapping howls echoed through the canyon. Coyotes. She checked on the goats in their enclosure and then went inside.

After checking on the younger children, she stood over Richard. He was so tall, he almost stretched the width of the small room. And his upper lip was dark — soon he'd be shaving. She knelt beside him and gently shook his shoulder. When he opened his eyes, she said, "I'll give it some more thought."

"Thanks, Ma."

She pushed his hair back from his forehead and kissed him goodnight.

CHAPTER FIVE

On Sunday Esther got the children up early. Too early for them: they fell back to sleep in the bed of the buckboard, snuggled into hay and blankets, as they rattled along out of Chasm Creek and toward the farm. Dawn splashed the sky, gray when they left town, with shades of red, pink, and yellow. After so much time living in town, the open spaces and the big sky gave Esther an airy feeling.

The morning light glistened on sheer cliffs and jagged peaks to the north. Due west, the desert plain extended to the horizon where more hills piled up in purple layers, their tips golden where touched by the rising sun. Alongside the road, thick silver bristles of jumping chollas glowed in the early light. The clopping hooves and wagon wheels crunching the rocky trail drove scurrying quail in and out of prickly pear and brittlebush, and a roadrunner darted across the road. She inhaled the fragrance of creosote. It loosened the dust of Chasm Creek in her lungs.

Considering the resentment she'd been holding toward her life there, the depth of her delight at seeing the cabin surprised her. She and Howard made each adobe brick with their own hands. It had been home for five years. Some of them had been happy years. A couple, anyway.

"Children," Esther said. "Wake up. We're here."

James crawled over the girls, and Richard

sat up, yawning and stretching. James and the girls hung over the side of the wagon, staring at the corral and the half dozen horses milling around inside it as they rode past the barn.

"Are they ours, Mama?" asked Mary.

"No, sweetie. They must belong to Mr. Braddock and Mr. Santiago."

"Can we ride them?" asked James. "Look at that one!"

"The spotted one is pretty," Millie said.

"No, I want the spotted one!" Mary said.

"Children, they're not ours! You'll have to ask permission to ride them, and don't carry on if the answer is no."

They came to a stop in front of the cabin. Nobody was home.

Mary, James, and Millie piled out of the buckboard and ran for the corral to look at the horses.

Esther went inside and slipped into a chair, a visitor in her own house. She saw everything with fresh eyes. The worn table, big enough to seat the whole family. The sideboard and shelves, a few pieces of china on display. The fireplace with only embers left to heat the enamel coffee pot sitting on the fire ring. She had always wished for a stove, but Howard said it was too expensive to have one shipped. At the thought of

Jacob's stove she smiled.

The bed, dresser, and a trunk filled the other half of the cabin near the ladder that led to the children's loft. Sunshine streamed past faded calico curtains and brightened the rough adobe walls and packed dirt floor. The light illuminated her collection of small bottles on the windowsill. Some of the bottles held tiny bouquets of dried flowers, some held naked stems with colorless petals scattered on the dusty wooden sill.

Through the window she could see the children hanging on the corral fence. James offered some oats to one of the horses. The horse must have grazed James' palm with its teeth because he yanked his hand back, the horse bolted, and Richard fell off the fence.

Laughter danced across the yard. How long had it been since they had all laughed together like that? The horse came back, looking for oats, and Millie stroked the horse's neck to soothe it. They were talking about something; they kept looking toward the house and then, all at once, they came running. The door banged open.

"We're going fishing, Mama!" James exclaimed.

"Can we go, Mama?" Millie pleaded. "Please?"

She did want to go through the trunks in the loft, gather some canned goods, tend Ida's grave. She could get her chores done faster with all of them gone and maybe they could head back to town before those men returned. "Don't be gone for very long."

"Just to the creek, Ma."

"Fine, then! Go!" Esther said. "You'd best bring back enough fish for dinner."

Richard and Millie tacked up their ponies and, with the younger children riding double with them, they rode off.

With the children away, a sweet blanket of silence fell over the yard, broken only by the faint cooing of quail as they bobbed and pecked near the rock wall and chickens clucking. She breathed in the quiet, until the quail beat the air with their wings and took off in heavy flight. She turned to see what had alarmed the birds. A coyote, shadowy even in the sunlight, its head and tail hanging low, at the edge of the yard.

"Get! Go away!"

The coyote, panting, held her with half-closed yellow eyes. In its own good time, it loped off into the desert scrub.

Rubén followed Morgan along the quiet path to the creek. Dust lay thick on the trail and muffled their horses' hooves.

Giant saguaros guarded their passage on both sides. Ripened fruit pods clung to the crowns and tips of the saguaros, opened like little mouths revealing crimson centers. The dried remnants of spring's creamy flowers hung from their lips like scabs. Some of the fruit had already fallen to the ground. The horses tramped through them, leaving scarlet clots scattered along the trail.

They passed a steep hill of jumbled rocks. Opposite the big boulders, the ground dropped off in a sharp incline dotted with cactus and rocks and Rubén's horse was skittish and stepped close to the edge. He pulled the reins hard to bring the horse's head around and get him back on the trail.

Morgan glanced back. "You're jumpy today."

"I had bad dreams last night. And woke up wishing we had gone to California."

The murmur of water came from ahead. As if someone had drawn a line with a stick, the land suddenly became lush. Cactus and creosote gave way to brush and mesquite trees. Silvery cottonwood leaves shimmered above them. An ancient sycamore with smooth bark, blotchy green, olive, and cream, curved heavy branches low across the trail. Its leaves brushed against their faces as they passed. A breeze rustled the foliage and seemed to banish the dust from their skin.

At the creek, a mantle of leaves filtered the sun which dappled the water while the current eddied and swirled, intensifying the hues of the rocks that lined the creek bed. Rubén's mood lightened.

Morgan reined in and dismounted. "Looks like this is the place. Plenty of branches." His boots crunched dried leaves on the side of the narrow trail as he checked the trees for a likely fishing pole. He looked up at the sound of voices and horses approaching.

"Children." Rubén's ugly dream last night had been of children, but these voices were filled with laughter. The children, two to a pony, rounded the bend in the trail and reined in sharply, surprised to see the men by the stream. "Mrs. Corbin's children."

"This here's our fishin' spot." James leaned around his older sister. "Who said you could use it?"

"James, shut up." Richard pushed his hat back. The little one, Mary, sat in front of him. "That ain't polite. Sorry, Mr. Braddock. Rubén."

"I'm sure there's enough fish for everybody." Morgan helped the girls to get down and he and Rubén fashioned their own fishing poles. The children retrieved the ones they had stashed there on previous trips. But Morgan's words proved to be wishful thinking — there were no fish for anybody.

"I've got an idea." James pulled his fishing line from the water and wrapped it around the pole. "Let's quit this fishing and go to Haunted Hill!"

"We told Ma we were goin' fishing." But Richard was also pulling his line out of the water.

"Haunted Hill?" Rubén shook his head. "It does not sound like a place I would care to visit."

The children all spoke at once, describing, explaining, and begging.

"The children want to show us their secret place, Rubén." Morgan dropped the branch he was stripping to make a fishing pole. "What harm is there in that?"

"Ma lets us go to Haunted Hill," Richard said. "I guess she wouldn't care."

It was decided. Rubén, the only dissenter, grudgingly followed the others across the creek and up a series of switchbacks until they were atop a low cliff that bordered the far side of the creek. Again a line had been drawn, and the oasis was left behind for another world of tumbled sandstone formations interspersed with squat barrel and prickly pear cactus.

Richard reined his horse to a stop and pointed over Mary's shoulder to the top of the hill before them. "There it is. That's Haunted Hill."

At the summit, shaded by a passing cloud, stood a jumble of rocks. Only after several moment's scrutiny could Rubén discern that the jumble was not capricious. The rock piles evoked primitive buildings with windows, doorways, and walls.

In the thick silence, the wind fluttered past his ears. He whispered, "Jesus Christ," and made the sign of the cross, letting his hand rest on the crucifix hanging beneath the thin cotton of his blouse. "The Ancient Ones."

"Don't be afraid," Millie said. "It's not really haunted."

"We come here lots of times," James added. "Nothin' bad ever happens." They dismounted and tied their horses to bushes.

Rubén was not consoled. A miasma surrounded those piled rocks; he could feel it all the way to his bones. He took what comfort he could from the crucifix hanging warm against his chest. Glancing at his hands he was surprised to see that they were still. His trembling was internal.

This hill, he knew deep in his soul, was the resting place of many dead souls. He could feel them all around. But the children seized his hands and dragged him, pulling him along while they talked and laughed.

Their laughter reminded him of other children, long ago in Mexico, who had also laughed at his fear of the dead, a fear it seemed he had been born with. What danger could there be, here, where children played? He prayed silently and allowed the children to lead him up the hill.

By the time they reached the top, the clouds had dispersed. Thin wisps hung in the sky, permeated by sunlight and turning shades of pink and green before dissolving. At the crest of the hill, several stone and mortar buildings stood in various stages of disintegration. Decaying wooden beams supported doorways and ceilings. Some of the buildings had been two stories high and wooden ladders still led up to a second floor; others were nothing more than slopes of rubble.

Rubén clung to Mary's hand. "Stay with me, little one," he said. Morgan and the older children explored, pointing out to each other what they spotted: circular cooking areas surrounded by soot-blackened stones, clay pots and bowls, water drainage pipes made of clay, courtyards with metates for grinding corn. All untouched for centuries, as if the residents had stepped away for a moment.

Rubén hesitated at the edges of the crumbling ruin. Everywhere shadows flitted through doorways, hovered in corners, disappeared when he turned his head. Why did none of the others notice this? Why were they not feeling the presence of spirits in this place?

The children climbed in and out of the low window openings. They called back and forth to each other, and soon the air filled with young voices and laughter. Morgan wandered around by himself, touching a stone wall or stopping to examine a clay pot. Rubén's tension dissipated somewhat; the sunlight seemed to chase the shadows away.

Mary suddenly pulled her hand from Rubén's and ran halfway up a half-rotten ladder as if headed for the sleeping loft at home. He called to her. "No, little one. It is too dangerous!" She climbed through a hole to what remained of a second level, a small outcropping no more than a ledge.

Beside the wall a pile of rubble sloped to where Morgan was exploring.

"Mary, get down from there."

"I am getting her," Rubén said and, pushing back his dread, climbed the ladder to retrieve the child. He poked his head through the opening. Mary, giggling, scrambled away from him, crawling on the rubble toward Morgan. "Come back here, *travesa!*"

Mary's mischievous laugh ended in a small squeal. She turned back toward Rubén, her eyes wide with terror. Rubén heard a click-click-click growing faster and louder. He rushed to snatch Mary, and Morgan drew his gun. The rattling reached a piercing level as Rubén leaped for the little girl. He grabbed her arm and yanked her to him as the snake coiled itself into striking position, mouth open, fangs showing. At the same moment, a shot rang out from Morgan's pistol, and the snake flew over the edge in a hail of shattered stone.

Rubén swung Mary around so he could put her safely down on the level section of ledge. His legs felt unsteady, and he thought perhaps he had exerted himself too much, maybe he should sit down, then realized with a jolt of panic that the ground was giving way beneath him. He waved his arms as he pitched backwards, and the edge of the outcropping crumbled under his weight. Before he hit the ground he heard Morgan yell his name, and the little girl's high-pitched scream rang in his ears as all turned to blackness.

Chapter Six

Rubén opened his eyes. He lay on the ground. There was the ladder Mary had climbed. Above was the hole through which she reached the ledge. Yet none of it was the same. The ladder was sturdy, the hole symmetrical. The ceiling above him was solid. He rolled onto his stomach only to find himself staring at a small woman, hair as white as his own pulled into a tight bun, colorful scarf draped across hunched shoulders. Over a long skirt she wore a multicolored tunic woven of wool fastened with a silver belt.

"Grandmother?"

He rubbed his eyes, blinked. He remembered Grandmother issuing the list of chores first thing in the morning. He remembered her soft voice waking him before dawn. Get up, sleepy one! Go and get the horses! We must take care of the animals.

She spoke. "Yes, my child. I am your grandmother."

Rubén trembled, afraid of this apparition that stood before him. Surely Grandmother was in the Spirit World or wherever heathen ghosts lived! How could she be here?

He got to his knees, then stood, with intention to run from this ghost but his body did not respond. As if he inhabited it but did not, he could not make it move as he desired. Grandmother waited, patient and quiet. She looked not into his eyes but beyond him, tilted her head as if expecting to hear words. He managed to cross himself, pleading with God to protect him from this apparition. Yet his mouth opened, almost against his will, and out came the question that had burned in his soul all his life.

"Why did you not come for me?"

The tears he had cried as a child fell again from his eyes.

Grandmother's soft voice spoke the language he had not heard since he was ten years old. "My child, you were taken far away, deep into the homeland of our enemies. That does not mean I did not want to find you."

Tears glistened in her eyes — tears of guilt! — and gave Rubén courage. "You sold me! You sold me to them!"

"We did not sell you, my child. The Spaniards stole you!"

Rubén sought the crucifix that hung from his neck and closed a hand around it while Grandmother continued in her gentle voice.

"When they took you away, I grieved as if you had died. I knew you would no longer grow in the beautiful way of the *Diné.*"

82

"You gave up," Rubén cried. "My family said the Navajos gave up, whipped like dogs." He remembered how the Mexicans rejoiced when the Americans moved the long-hated Navajos to a reservation. The priests at the mission where he worked held a special Mass to give thanks.

Grandmother began to sing, a song that filled the air. Although Rubén had not heard the words in sixty years, he recognized the story of the emergence of the *Diné* into the Fifth World, this world.

Her haunting chant lifted them high above the earth, into the clouds. Without fear he floated upon the song as it carried him far from the haunted ruins. When the clouds parted the desert's drab browns and greens had been replaced with splashes of red, vermillion, ochre, olive, yellow. Flat land, soaring rock monoliths, all a rainbow of colors. Directly below him the ground opened in a deep gash. A clear turquoise stream ran through it and a spindly rock formation towered almost to the top of the surrounding cliffs.

He whispered the name the Spaniards had given that place. "Canyon de Chelly."

He and Grandmother descended from the clouds. The canyon sheltered hogans made of branches and plastered with mud, doors always to the east. But the fields, the peach orchards, the gardens, were not as he remembered. Not green and lush, full of waving corn and branches weighted with fruit. Now all was smashed, smoldering, charred. Dead bloated sheep, horses and cattle lay with stiff legs pointed skyward and swollen bellies blanketed with buzzards. A forest of blackened stumps remained where the peach orchards once grew.

At the mouth of the canyon a line of people stretched as far as he could see. They cried as they walked, old and young, mothers and grandmothers, old men and children, thousands of them, from horizon to horizon.

"The Americans, the *Bilagáana,* brought war to our sheep and horses, to our gardens and orchards, mothers and children. Our leaders surrendered to keep the *Diné* from starving. Or so they thought."

The *Bilagáana* rode horses and carried rifles. They taunted The People, laughed at them, prodded them to hurry. Rubén and Grandmother joined the people trudging along. They hovered near those who struggled to walk while laden with belongings and crying children. Rubén longed to help them. A few wagons rolled by, filled to overflowing with supplies for the soldiers.

People clung to the sides, tried to climb up, begged to be carried. A man fell and rolled toward the wheels of a passing wagon. Despite calls to the driver, the wagon continued. It rolled over him, never slowing. The man's screams stopped abruptly when his bones cracked against the hard, frozen ground. A woman shrieked but other women gathered around her and then led her away. Some tried to stop and help the fallen, but the soldiers prodded or struck them with rifles and quirts. They walked on, leaving the weak behind, not turning when gunshots rang out behind them. Dead and dying littered the trail.

Rubén and Grandmother floated above the carnage. A hundred feet ahead a woman fell and her husband stopped to help her up. A soldier yelled and raised a shotgun, fired both barrels. The explosion echoed in Rubén's ears as the woman's gaunt body accepted the blast with arms flung wide before she sank against her husband and crumpled to the ground. With a shout the bloodied man charged. A sharp report, this time a rifle, and his body fell upon the woman's.

The line of people trudged past where they lay. Blood darkened the red earth of *Diné-tah.* Rubén's heart broke into many pieces. He turned to his grandmother's spirit, searched her mournful face.

"Yes, they are your parents, my child. They did not give up. You are the one who gave up."

His grandmother's eyes were black and deep and grew larger. He fell into her eyes, spun and twirled and flew through darkness, through muffled sounds, chanting voices. Somewhere a drum beat fast and hard but then it slowed. Slower and slower. Ghostly images of ancestors rained tears upon his face. They mingled with his own.

Morgan's voice. "Bring the canteen."

Children's voices.

Water on his face.

"Please do not cry," Rubén whispered. "I cannot stand any more sorrow."

"Rubén!"

He opened his eyes. Morgan leaned over him.

Rubén raised a hand to his forehead and winced. The pain was real, not a dream. His fingers came away bloodied. He tried to sit up. "The snake! Mary!"

"She's fine." Morgan motioned to Mary. "Come here and let Rubén see you're okay."

The little girl leaned down and kissed Rubén's forehead. "That will make it better."

86

Rubén let his friend help him to sit up and rest against a rock wall. Morgan rinsed the wound and tied a rag around his head. When it was time to leave, Morgan helped him up and brushed the dirt off his clothes until Rubén pushed him away. "I can still — I'm not a child!" Several times during the slow ride back, Morgan asked if he was all right. Each time, Morgan's voice brought him back from his reverie, lost again in the world he had just visited.

"*Sí*, I am fine." But he did not really know. He wanted only to wipe the look of concern from his friend's face.

The children rode ahead of them but, as the cabin came into sight, Richard waited for them to catch up and then rode beside them.

"I don't think we better say anything about that snake to Ma."

"Don't you think we need to tell her what happened?" Morgan asked.

"She will ask." Rubén felt a thin stream of blood trickle down his face.

"Yeah, we can tell her. Just leave out the snake. You hear that, Mary?" he said to the child riding in front of him. She nodded. Richard kicked his horse to a lope and caught up with Millie and James.

"It will be my pleasure," Rubén muttered, "never to mention the cursed snake."

CHAPTER SEVEN

Esther glanced out the window and, seeing her children riding toward the yard, she quickly went outside. They had been gone too long and now they were with those men. She grabbed the shotgun, rested it against the dooryard railing, and waited in the shade of the overhang.

"Mama!" Mary exclaimed, as soon as they were within earshot. "We went to Haunted Hill and Mr. Braddock shot a snake!"

"Mary!" Richard said. "I told you —"

"The snake wanted to bite me, Mama, but Mr. Braddock shot it. Then Mr. Rubén fell off the —"

Esther heard not a word after "snake." For a moment she couldn't breathe, but then her breath burst from her chest. "Oh, my God!"

"Shut up!" Millie yelled. "Mama doesn't need to hear about it. Shut up, Mary!"

Esther pulled Mary from the pony and searched for puncture marks, pushing up sleeves, pulling stockings down.

"Let me go! Mama, stop it!" Mary managed to twist away and run into the house, followed quickly by Millie.

Mary was fine, unhurt. Alive. Esther shot an angry look at Richard. "Haunted Hill? Do they have fish there now?"

"I'm sorry, Ma. We wanted to show —"

"Leave me!" Rubén sounded annoyed. "I can get down by myself!"

Morgan was trying to help his friend, who had a bloody rag tied around his head and, indeed, looked as if he needed assistance.

Esther ran to help and they each held an arm and guided Rubén into the house. They sat him down at the table and Esther sent Millie to get some fresh water from the spring. "What happened?"

"*Por favor, Señora* Corbin. I fell. Fortunately I landed on my head. No harm has been done."

"Is that a joke? You're bleeding. What happened?"

"He climbed up a ladder at those ruins," Braddock said. "Some rocks gave way, and he fell. That's all, Mrs. Corbin."

Above them, Mary hung her head over the edge of the loft. When she saw her mother looking at her, she disappeared. Esther was pretty sure there was more to the story. She was also pretty sure nobody was going to tell her.

Millie brought the pitcher and quickly left

it on the table then scampered up into the loft. Esther poured some water into a bowl and cleaned Rubén's forehead.

"It's not bad," she said. "Just a lot of blood from a little cut."

"See? I told you." Rubén pushed her hand away.

"But a big bump. You need to rest now." Esther glanced up. "When I thrash these children, I'll make sure they don't yell too loud." The girls' faces disappeared from the edge of the loft.

"I'll go help the boys with the horses." Morgan headed for the yard. He looked as if he were trying to avoid being thrashed along with the children.

Esther tied a fresh bandage across Rubén's forehead. "I think he's going to warn the boys." For the first time, Rubén smiled. Esther patted his bony shoulder.

But Rubén's smile faded and tears filled his eyes. He lifted the rawhide cord over his head and handed his crucifix to her.

"Take it." He closed her fingers around it and held onto her hand, his own shaking slightly. "I ask that you hold on to this for me. Will you do that?"

Braddock had returned from the corrals and stood in the doorway. "Come on, Rubén. I think you better get some rest."

Esther pulled the rawhide cord over her head, tucked the crucifix inside her dress, and Rubén nodded to her before he let Braddock help him from his chair and out to the ramada.

She was gathering the things she wanted to bring back to town when Braddock returned.

"Are you going to tell me what really happened today?" she asked.

"Well, the children wanted to show us that Haunted Hill —"

"I don't mean that."

"You mean about the rattler? It never got that close to Mary. Rubén pulled her away and I shot it — Mrs. Corbin? Are you all right?"

"I don't want to hear about the snake. I meant what happened to Rubén."

"You know what happened. He fell."

"He gave me this." She pulled up the rawhide cord and showed him the crucifix.

Braddock seemed surprised. "I don't know. I'm glad it's not the snake that's bothering you. The color went right out of your face."

"I've been told I'm overprotective."

"Is that why don't you want your son to work for me?"

"Well, I just need to think about it."

She remembered where Jacob had gone, and why. Maybe he would come home with some answers that would help her decide. "I have to be going. Could you help Richard hitch up the rig while I get the children?"

"Rubén and I need the help. He's not as young as he thinks he is; you can see that. And I — well, I hope you'll be finished thinking about it soon. Your son seems like a fine young man."

"I need to get back to town. I don't want to be on the road after dark."

He was standing close to her. He touched her hand, but she pulled it away.

"I really must go."

By the time she loaded the wagon and gathered the children, it was dusk. Morgan tied his horse to the back of the buckboard and climbed up beside her. She didn't protest when he took the reins from her. It would be safer to have a man beside her on the trail. "What about Rubén? Maybe you should stay with him."

Morgan slapped the ribbons and the wagon lurched forward. "He's the one who said you shouldn't be going home alone this time of night. His whole life has been taking care of other people. He doesn't know how to be taken care of."

And now he takes care of you, Esther thought. She suspected that Mr. Braddock had no idea how Rubén cared for him when he was sick. She remembered that day the two men had ridden into her yard, how sick he had been. How she made it worse by shooting him.

"Wait," she said.

He pulled on the reins.

She felt him watching her as she sat staring out at the darkening desert. Mr. Braddock talked so kindly about his friend. The way the two men watched out for each other, the way Mr. Braddock had protected her from Otto the other day in town, the way they had looked out for her children that very day — everything she had seen told her these were good men. Deep in her heart she knew they would never harm her or her children.

"Richard, climb down and go on back."

Richard leaped out of the wagon and started for the cabin, then came back. "Does this mean I can stay? I can take the job?"

"Yes."

Richard took off like a shot, yelling his thanks over his shoulder. She turned to Braddock. "I don't think Rubén should be by himself. And the two of you could use some help."

Braddock slapped the ribbons again and they headed for town.

When they reached the house, Braddock helped Esther carry the two youngest inside. She watched from the doorway as he gently lowered the soundly sleeping James onto the bed. He carefully tucked the coverlet around him and smoothed the hair from his forehead.

She went to the kitchen and poured a glass of water from the pitcher. "Mr. Braddock, would you like something to drink before you head back?"

He came out of the children's room, hat in hand. "Much obliged. I am a little thirsty."

She was about to thank him for watching out for the children but her throat tightened. Tears stung her eyes.

Morgan put his glass down and his arms went around her and she let herself lean against him.

"I'm sorry. I feel so foolish."

"Nothing foolish about worrying over your children."

"Thank you for understanding." She moved out of his embrace, tried to smile.

He brushed a tear from her cheek. "Mary reminds me of my daughter."

"Was it long ago you last saw her? You must miss her terribly."

He took her hand and his fingers tightened around hers. When he looked down at her, hair fell across his face, obscuring the ugly scar at his temple. "Please don't ask any questions."

He lifted her hand to his lips.

A tear slipped down her cheek and she brushed it away.

"I'm sorry." He let go of her and stepped back. "Forgive my rudeness."

She crossed her arms over her chest. "You'd best go now. It's late."

He picked up his hat and said goodnight.

She went to the window and watched him descend the porch steps, untie his horse, and swing up into the saddle. He saw her at the window and touched his hat and nodded. She raised her hand and he turned and rode away. Her breath made a circle of fog on the glass.

She went to bed but tossed and turned the whole long night, giving herself plenty of time to reflect on the way he had looked at her before he left. It was almost dawn before she finally slept, Rubén's crucifix resting at her breast.

CHAPTER EIGHT

Jacob wiped sweat from his face and shifted to sit his horse without touching a blister on his ass. He had found a place dustier than Chasm Creek — called the Territory of New Mexico. Should've given it back to Old Mexico, far as he was concerned.

That night he drank coffee and ate jerky by a small fire that flared and faded in the light wind. He hoped Muddy Springs wasn't very far because he was out of mescal. He threw the empty bottle into the scrub and laid his current misery at the feet of one Miss Essie Corbin. Clearly this trip was all her fault. Just because she was a couple years older didn't make her a man, and a man knew how to handle situations like the one back there.

Ever since they were kids, she had tried to boss him around. He'd thought maybe she'd come to respect him when she talked Howard into moving out west. After all, he was successful with his gold mine and held a responsible position, even if the marshaling was only part-time. But it seemed she was more of the mind that he needed her there to look after him.

He had to admit it was nice to have family around, especially when his fiancé bolted.

Until little Ida. Then Essie had needed him.

But only because she'd married an ass-hole who made everything worse. Howard must have looked good in that uniform right after the war, was all he could think. There wasn't much else to recommend him, except Pa was dead and Ma pushing Essie into it. He hoped Ma was happy now, sitting back there in her fine house on Narragansett Bay, Rhode Island — all by herself.

And so was Essie all by herself. Except for the kids. Millie and Richard were old enough to be a help, James almost. But Richard was not yet a man no matter how much fuzz he sprouted on his upper lip. Jacob guessed it would fall to him to teach the boy how to shave, since his father was off God-knows-where.

Jacob spread his bedroll and his last thoughts before drifting off to sleep involved blame and resentment directed at Essie, which slowly turned to worry which led to a good-sized portion of blame and resent-ment being parceled out to Howard. It took some time to fall asleep.

The next day he rode into Muddy Springs, a town hunched in shadow and even shab-bier than Chasm Creek. The sky hung heavy with clouds snagged by the nearby Zuni's ragged peaks. A hot wind blasted dirt down the main street and rickety shutters banged against sand-scoured buildings that looked mostly deserted.

He rode up to the first place showing any signs of life. A family of skinny Injuns loitered on the boardwalk under a sign nailed to what used to be the crossbeam for a porch roof. Under a few broken and spaced out boards providing a poor amount of shade, the hand-painted sign said "Trading Post" in faded red letters. Smaller letters added underneath, in black and a different style, said "Indian Agency."

Jacob went straight to the counter. "You got any mescal?"

The clerk, an old man with an accumulation of local dirt ground into the cracks of his face, glanced over at his only other customer: a young Injun holding a pile of striped wool blankets.

"We trade with Indians here. You know there ain't no liquor allowed."

Jacob slapped a half eagle onto the counter. "Do I look like a redskin to you?"

The man scurried through a doorway into the back and returned with a small bottle of mescal and put the coin in his pocket.

"Five dollars for this puny bottle?" Jacob asked.

"Supply and demand. Don't like it — go somewhere else."

Jacob pulled the cork and took a drink, worth every penny as it cut through the dust in his throat and warmed his stomach. "You better bring me a couple more bottles for the trip back."

While the clerk was in the back, Jacob pulled out the wanted poster and smoothed it on the counter. The young Injun glanced at the bottle and yelled something, was still yelling when the clerk returned and shut him up with a look.

Jacob pointed to the bulletin. "You know anything about this?"

"I'm afraid I don't. I just got assigned to this here post a few months ago."

"There a marshal or a sheriff here?"

"There ain't been any law here except once every few weeks a U.S. Marshal rides through. Things are pretty quiet in these parts."

"I can see that."

"You might want to try the saloon. I hear the barkeep has been here forever. If some-one around here was to know anything, it'd be him. Last building before the south edge of town."

Jacob left the clerk and the Injun to argue over the blankets in a foreign tongue. Hadn't we beat the Injuns? Seemed they ought to at least learn to speak English. He put the bottles in his saddlebags and walked his horse to the end of town.

A sign's faded lettering spelled out half an "a" and then "loon." It hung sideways from one nail driven into the wall near the door where two horses waited, tethered to a broken post that might have once been a hitching rail. Jacob tied his horse next to them and went inside.

Weak sunshine seeped through the window's layer of greasy soot. At midday oil lamps burned, although little light actually penetrated their blackened chimneys. Two tables crowded the space between the bar and the door, and two men sat hunched over drinks at one of them. They didn't look up when Jacob entered. Neither did an old Indian on the floor, slumped against the wall under the window. Jacob had to step over his sprawled legs.

The barkeep leaned across the bar and slapped a dirty rag at a fly.

"I was told you been here over ten years. Have a question for you."

"You wanna talk to me, you gotta buy a drink."

"Sure. Mescal," Jacob said.

"No mescal, mister. Whiskey's all we got."

"Well, whiskey then." Jacob threw his money on the bar and reached inside his shirt for the poster. He smoothed it and turned it so the barkeep could see.

The barkeep's eyes shifted between the poster and Jacob, then narrowed. "Yeah?"

"I'd like to know what this is about," Jacob said. "You know what the story is?"

"Ain't no story to it. He kilt a man."

Jacob swallowed the brown liquid that had been placed in front of him and the barkeep refilled his glass.

"He was convicted?"

The barkeep looked at him with suspicion. "Never heard of no bounty hunter who cared about con-vick-shuns." Drops of spittle landed on the bar. The fly returned.

"The poster says he committed a murder. There was no trial?"

"Hell, no! He stabbed that poor bastard right out there in the street. Plenty of people seen it. I seen it myself." He leaned over the bar and stretched his lips across black stumps of teeth. "He was already covered with blood when he got to town. God only knows who else he kilt. Crazy, that's what he was. I seen him come into town. Crazy all right."

A young man emerged from a darkened doorway at the far end of the bar, his head down, carrying two plates of steaming beans and greasy tortillas. The barkeep stopped talking and polished one spot on the bar. The young man let the plates bang onto the table in front of the two men, then vanished back into the gloom.

The barkeep looked up, a smile creeping onto his face. "Some people here still remember that day. Not a good idea to be bringing it up."

Jacob folded the poster and put it back inside his coat. With great effort, he managed to get one more swallow past the sudden tightness in his throat.

"Besides, we ain't seen Braddock around here since then and that's, what, almost ten year ago. He busted out of jail and run. Goddamn renegade Injuns helped him. So the sheriff put out that notice. Nobody ever heard nothin' more about him. You're chasin' a cold trail, mister."

Jacob's stomach knotted painfully. He put down his glass, dropped another coin on the bar, and walked out. As he untied the reins, there was a tug on his coat. The old Indian he'd seen slumped on the floor had woke up and followed him outside. A gnarled finger hooked onto Jacob's sleeve.

"It ain't true," the Indian said.

Jacob tried to pull his coat free. "Get away from me."

The Indian pushed himself up close to Jacob's face. "That man lies."

Jacob pried the fingers from his arm. The old man's putrid breath held the scent of alcohol, and Jacob turned away from the rheumy eyes sunken in the bony, crackled face. The man's long white hair whipped in the wind.

"Look, old man, I'm in a hurry." Jacob pushed him away.

"That man deserved to die."

"Braddock didn't have no right to decide that."

"My people would have wiped out this town and everyone in it." He threw his arms wide, indicating the expanse and the swiftness with which they would have obliterated it. "But Mr. Braddock killed him and we were satisfied."

"Oh, Jesus. I ain't listening to any more of this. Being a friend to you Injuns is hardly a recommendation. Besides," Jacob nodded toward the saloon, "He says Braddock killed others —"

The old man shook his head. "Lies. Lies!"

"Hey!" The barkeep dashed into the street, flapping the dirty rag. "Git! Go on

103

back where you belong. Sorry, mister. God-damn Injun–drunk agin. Don't you pay him no mind, mister."

The Indian ducked and held up a hand. The rag slapped his head and he snatched at it but missed. With an angry wave of his arm, he stalked off.

Jacob swung onto his horse, nodded to the barkeep.

"You gonna keep lookin' for Braddock?"

Jacob turned his horse and started to ride away. The barkeep headed back inside but yelled from the doorway, "Never heard of no bounty hunter who cared about court trials!"

When the door slammed behind him Jacob stopped and looked back at the saloon. Someone had rubbed a spot clean in the sooty window. For a moment he thought he saw a face but it disappeared.

He nudged his horse and loped past the trading post, where the Injun was emerging with no blankets and several bottles of mes-cal, the woman of the group doing the yell-ing now. This place made Chasm Creek look like paradise. He was in a hurry to get back but as he rode away he felt uneasy, felt eyes on him. He stopped and turned, looked at the town, small below the looming moun-tains, and picked out the saloon. That young man who had come from the back room, whose back had been to him — he wished now he'd gotten a look at the face.

CHAPTER NINE

James drew the broom carefully along the floorboards of the saloon. He didn't want any of the dirt to fall into the cracks where it would disappear into the muck underneath. He wanted to pile it up and scoop it into the sack he brought for that purpose. Mr. Will didn't care how long it took him to sweep. In fact, Mr. Will didn't care whether the floors got swept or not, so James could proceed in any fashion he preferred. And he preferred to be careful with the dirt. Occasionally, he found a coin that had fallen from one of the gaming tables, and that went into the other sack, the one Mr. Will kept for him behind the bar.

"Come on boy. We heard you was a card player." Three men were taking a break from placer activity along the river, and one had called out to him. Cards and coins moved quickly from one hand to another, drinks and smokes rising from table to lips.

They all waved for him to join them; one even pulled out a chair. He knew they wanted to take his money, but sometimes he could win a pot because they never suspected he knew what he was doing. He leaned on the broom and considered the offer. He had to be home by the usual time or Ma would come looking for him.

The thought of his mother coming looking for him again made his face hot.

He'd been playing cards one time not long after he started working there when she came tearing in, having heard him cussing from out in the street. She was so mad she grabbed him by his shirt collar and dragged him out of the saloon, yelling all the way home about the bad habits he was picking up. He was lucky she'd let him come back to work.

He couldn't finish the sweeping and play cards and be home on time and wasn't sure he could win more than the dirt was worth, but the dirt would still be there tomorrow.

He grabbed his sack of coins from behind the bar and climbed into the empty chair. One of the men plopped a bowler hat onto his head. The miners laughed when the hat sank so far down it would have covered James' eyes except that his ears, bent under the weight of the brim, held it up.

"All he needs is a cigar in his mouth." Immediately a cigar appeared. He let it hang from the side of his mouth like the men in the saloon did.

"Don't light it. We don't want him pukin' on the cards!" Somebody blew out the match that had been headed his way.

"Your Ma's workin' at the mine office, right? She ain't gonna be comin' in here raisin' hell?" The men all laughed.

The man who owned the hat, his bald head shining, shuffled and dealt. Several hands later, James was losing, but now he held a king high straight. "I'll meet that." He threw the coins on the table. "And raise it four bits."

"Reckon the kid's got a good hand this time?" the cigar man asked. The men exchanged glances.

"That's horse shit," the bald one said. "He wouldn't know a good hand if it whomped him on the ass. I see yer four bits, kid."

"I'm out," said another. "Good luck, sonny." He put down his cards, picked up his money, and walked away.

James laid down his cards.

"Shit." The bald man slapped his cards onto the table.

The miner who left had gone through the door to the cook tent, shoving his way past Miss Hildie, the woman who cooked for the miners. James hoped she was bringing leftover biscuits like she did sometimes —

maybe even with that jam she made from the prickly pear fruit. But she wasn't carrying anything. She pushed her way between the tables like she was in a big hurry and stopped right by his chair, an angry voice following her through the door.

"I told you I ain't putting up with it no more!"

"I didn't do nothin'! I swear, Fred!" Miss Hildie was a smallish woman with a high-pitched voice. Her husband ain't never gonna hear her unless she speaks up, James thought, as he pulled the winning pot into his sack. Especially over all the banging and crashing pots that was going on out there.

She grabbed the back of his chair, and James offered his advice, since he felt well practiced in the art of defending against accusations of misbehavior. "Miss Hildie, you gotta speak up. He can't hear you back there."

Fred, the husband, appeared in the doorway. He carried a shotgun, and all the men in the saloon jumped up from tables and the bar and ran for the front door so fast the bald man forgot to take his hat. James stretched for the rest of his money. When he had slid it all into the sack, he looked up from under the brim of the bowler to see that Fred had lumbered to a stop right in front of him. Hildie had let go his chair and was slowly backing up.

"Hildie, get your cheatin' ass back in that cook tent. I ain't done with you."

Fred stank of sweat and urine and whiskey, his gray face lined and mean looking. "What you lookin' at, boy?"

James gripped the seat of his chair so tightly the rough wood dug into his skin. Fred swiped his shotgun across the table, scraping cards and coins onto the floor.

"Fred! What the hell do you think you're doing? You drop that weapon!" Mr. Will pulled out the rifle he kept behind the bar.

James peeked from under the hat brim at Fred's shotgun, inches away. Behind him, Miss Hildie screamed. "Leave the boy alone!"

Fred's finger, with its black-edged fingernail, hooked through the trigger. Long hairs grew out of his knuckle. James put his hands over his ears. A shot rang out from Mr. Will's rifle and the shotgun exploded. James looked up in time to see a hole opened up in Fred's forehead, spewing blood and splinters of bone onto James' borrowed hat.

On the floor beside him Miss Hildie lay in a heap like one of Mary's rag dolls with half the stuffing took out. He couldn't tell what was skin and what was shredded dress. She twitched a few times as blood spurted up in little fountains from the biggest hole. She stopped twitching and blood spread in a puddle beneath her, spreading out fast toward the legs of his chair.

He tore his eyes away to see Fred sink to his knees, then pitch forward and hit the floor with a sharp crack.

The hat fell down over James' eyes.

People crowded into the doorway. He could hear them pushing, shoving, making comments. His mother's voice came from the boardwalk. He lifted the hat enough to see her squeezing through the doorway packed with miners, her scared face searching until her eyes found him. She pushed chairs and tables away, stepped over the bodies and, ignoring the blood on the floor, knelt in front of him.

He leaned away from her to spit out the rotten taste that had come up into in his mouth, and everything in his stomach retched out as well. Even though his mother had not picked him up in years, she did then.

She scooped him up into her arms as if he were as small as Mary, and she carried him out of the saloon into the bright sunlight. She carried him all the way down the street to Uncle Jacob's house, not stopping even when the hat fell off into the street.

Rubén carried another lantern from the cabin out to the corral, illuminating the struggle as Richard and Morgan tried to get a half-broke horse let them lift his hoof to see what caused a limp. Even long after sunset, the air remained hot and dusty. Morgan had refused to quit, and now they worked in the dark except for lanterns and moonlight.

Over the horse's annoyed whinny and stamping hooves, Rubén heard a wagon approaching. He motioned the others to look toward the path leading to the wagon road.

Ma!" Richard yelled as Esther drove the wagon right past the corral.

Mary yelled out of the wagon bed as they rattled by. "Miss Hildie got kilt in the saloon right in front of James!"

Richard and Morgan broke into a run, and Rubén urged his tired legs to go as fast as he could make them. The wagon stopped in front of the cabin. Millie climbed down and held out her arms for Mary, still talking. "And then Mr. Fred got kilt. And his blood got all over James. Look you can —"

"Mary, shut up!" Millie slapped Mary's finger that was pointing at James, who sat, eyes red-rimmed and swollen, on the seat next to his mother. Rubén reached up to help Esther down.

"I didn't know where else to go." She clung to Rubén's hand for a moment. "Jacob is out of town."

"You and the *niños* will stay here tonight. Morgan can join me at my little camp at the ramada, and you will all have the comfort of sleeping in your own beds tonight."

He held out a hand to the boy. "Would you come sit with me for a while, *niño chico*? Let your mother go and have some coffee." He nodded toward the cabin. "Go ahead, *Señora* Corbin."

James nodded and climbed from the wagon.

"Oh, thank God. I thought he was permanently deaf!"

"I can hear, Mama."

Rubén sat on the bench outside the door and patted the space beside him, inviting James to sit. "Leave the door open," he said to Morgan, "so the boy can see his mother inside if he wishes."

James sat with his head hanging. Rubén waited, listening to snatches of *Señora* Corbin's story of what had happened, and after a few moments the boy spoke. "Mama said Miss Hildie's in heaven now."

"And who is this Miss Hildie?"

"She's the lady that cooked at the saloon. For Mr. Snapp's miners. Fred shot her dead. Fred was her husband."

The boy had witnessed this? Rubén made the sign of the cross. "That is true, then. She is in heaven with the angels."

"But Fred's dead, too. If they're both in heaven he can still hurt her." The boy's eyes filled with tears.

"No, no, this *Señor* Fred would not be in heaven. People that kill people do not go to heaven, *muchachito*. That is a mortal sin. All the people in heaven are safe forever."

"But then Mr. Will can never go to heaven. He killed Fred!"

Morgan came out of the cabin. "Whoa, whoa." He smoothed the boy's hair and wiped the tears off his cheeks. "Will didn't set out to kill Fred. He was trying to keep Fred from hurting anybody else."

"So someday Mr. Will can go to Heaven, and see Miss Hildie again." The boy wiped away the last of his tears with his shirt sleeve. "She's probly singin', too. She was always singin' in the cook tent."

Esther came to the doorway. "Come on, son. Mary and Millie are already asleep. I think it's time for you to go to bed, too." She led the boy inside.

Morgan eased himself onto the bench and

113

leaned back against the cabin wall, his face drawn and pale, his jaw clenched the way he did when in pain. Rubén crossed himself again and considered making another pot of coffee. He feared he would be up most of the night.

Esther took the coffee pot from Rubén. "Let me do that," she said, and sent him back outside. "I'll bring you both a cup when it's ready."

The children slept upstairs in the quiet loft, and Esther's muscles began to relax as she poked the fire and raised fresh flames. She'd been tied in one big knot ever since she'd heard the shots coming from the saloon, but now, with the children asleep and something helpful to do, the knot loosened. She was grateful to the men for the way they had talked to James, comforting him with their words and, she thought, by their attention. Maybe he would sleep through 'til morning. Please, no nightmares tonight.

Rubén came inside. "Morgan has a headache.

She remembered how sick he had been when they first rode into her yard. Even before she shot him. "He should sleep in my bed then. Not outside at the ramada. I can go to the loft with the children."

Rubén went to the doorway. "Morgan, Mrs. Corbin has kindly offered to let you sleep in the bed tonight. Perhaps you should come in now and get some rest."

"There's no need to fuss over me. Shut the damn door."

"I'll bring you both some coffee." Esther smiled, hoping to ease some of the worry from Rubén's face. "Before we shut the damn door."

"I think I will turn in then, for a while, if you don't mind sitting with him. He will be much worse later. Call me when you need me." He went outside and stopped next to Braddock. "Give me your pistol, *mi amigo.*" He waited for Morgan to take off his gunbelt and hand it over, then trudged off toward the ramada.

Esther brought a cup of coffee to Morgan. Remembering light could hurt his eyes, she lifted the lantern from its hook on the porch post and turned down the wick until it went out. The sharp scent of kerosene floated into the darkness on a wisp of smoke. She hung it back on the post and started to go back inside.

Morgan said. "James isn't the only one who had a bad day, is he?"

She felt tears well up in her eyes. "It's a bad day when your child comes close to being murdered."

"That's what family does. Causes pain."

She stopped in the doorway, looking down at him. "Not always."

"No, not always. I wish you could meet my wife. And children."

"Children? You have more than the daughter?"

He looked up at her. "Two sons, younger. Although they are all half grown by now." He took her hand and she let him pull her down beside him. How could he stand to go so long without seeing them? He must have seen the sympathy in her eyes, because he said, "See? Pain."

"Because you miss them. That's not a bad thing. Maybe you could send for them."

"No. No, I don't think so." He twisted the malachite ring on his finger. "I think I will have to go to them."

He seemed so sad it made her heart hurt. But when he spoke again, there was an edge in his voice.

"Tell me about your husband. Why he's gone away and left you and your children alone."

She didn't want to talk about Howard. For almost two years they had hardly spoken, and she was glad he was gone. It would be hard to explain that to a man who so missed his wife.

"There's not much to tell. He works on the farm, he goes off like the other men around here — looking for gold — when he gets a chance. Oh, and, of course, once a week he went into town."

"For supplies?"

"No, for the Bible Study."

"Bible study?"

"Howard insists on holding a Bible Study class in town on Sunday evenings." She smiled. "He holds them in the saloon so he can save a few souls from the evil of drink for an hour or so. He won't let Will serve anybody while the class is going on. You should see those poor men, sitting there, full of hope —"

"Hope that he'll shut up and they can go back to drinking?"

"Yes!" She laughed. She should feel guilty. She and the children had poked fun at Howard — that was okay. But not ridiculing him with another man.

"Sounds like a dangerous occupation." Morgan suppressed a smile but she could see it in his eyes.

"Oh, it is dangerous! Several times they threatened to shoot him if he didn't stop!"

"But nobody ever did."

"Will always stopped them. He liked having Howard come and preach! Said it increased his business. Howard aggravated everyone so much that they drank even more after he left."

"He should be here with you. What kind of husband is he to leave you alone like this? To care for those children all by yourself? Doesn't he realize what could happen?"

"It doesn't matter what kind — he is my husband."

Braddock got up and walked away from her, out from under the canopy of the porch, and stared up at the stars. "He's no worse a husband than me, with my own wife and children abandoned."

"Don't say that." Nobody could be as bad a husband as Howard.

The farm was peaceful in the night. The barn, a dark silhouette against the starry blackness, sheltered her goats; all was quiet in the chicken house. The dirt trail out to the wagon road, two ribbons of lighter ground laid across the desert scrub and grasses, glowed bright in the moonlight. The new horses in the corral stood three legs, one leg resting, and flicked their tails. The goats shuffled in the hay in their stalls in the barn. Frogs sang at the spring behind the house.

Morgan held onto the porch railing and

lowered himself back onto the bench.

"I thought you were feeling better," she said.

"I'm fine — don't be worrying about me. Rubén does enough of that."

"Can I get you anything?"

"Just stay with me."

The frogs fell silent as somewhere out in the hills a pack of coyotes yapped and howled, their sounds so like human screams they sent a chill up Esther's spine. Then one long howl came from a different direction and the others fell silent. The lone coyote howled again, a high-pitched, undulating song almost like a wolf.

The horses in the corral snorted and stomped but the howling stopped and all was quiet until the frogs started up again.

Morgan leaned back against the cabin and pressed both hands against his forehead. She touched his arm and felt his pulse pounding through his sleeve.

"Shall I get Rubén?"

"No. I'll go on out to the ramada." He stood, then stumbled, and took hold of the post to keep from falling. "God damn it."

She helped him back to the bench, then ran for the ramada. When she returned with Rubén, Morgan sat bent over holding his head, and Rubén had to pry his hands away.

"Let me help you." Rubén lifted Morgan's arm over his shoulder, struggling to stand with the weight of the taller, bigger man leaning against him.

Esther and Rubén helped him into the cabin and onto the bed. Esther retreated to the kitchen area, busied herself with washing coffee cups and refilling lamps. She sat at the table and stared at the half-melted candle on a cracked plate in the middle of the oil cloth. She thought about lighting it. She let her head drop for a few minutes, then put her arms on the table and rested her head on them and slept fitfully, watching the men during the moments her eyes were open.

The oil lamp on the nightstand cast a yellow circle of light on her bed. Whenever Morgan leaned over the side of the bed, the old man jumped up and held a bucket ready. He spoke soothing words and patted his friend's back, offered wet cloths for Morgan to wipe his face and held out a cup of water that was pushed away.

When Morgan settled and appeared to be asleep, Rubén carried the pail outside. She heard him rinsing it out by the spring. When he came back he placed the pail on the floor next to the bed and sat himself in the chair, arms folded across his chest.

Esther pushed herself up from the table. She pulled a handful of small pieces of wood from the kindling box and stuck them under the cast iron fire ring that held the coffee pot. Crouching before the hearth, she blew gently until the embers flared. A hot cup of coffee was what Rubén needed.

She sat on her heels in front of the small fire and wrapped her arms around her knees. She thought about the two men, how they watched out for each other. She thought of Howard, and of a time when she had needed caring for, when she had been as helpless as Morgan was now, after Ida died. Her thoughts dwelled in that dark time until the coffee hissed in the pot.

She refilled her own cup and poured one for Rubén. He came over and sank into the chair across from her.

"Muchas gracias." He gestured toward the bed. "He sleeps now. He will be better tomorrow."

She held a match to the candle. The light accented Rubén's wrinkles. Shadows deepened the lines on his forehead and alongside his mouth into crevices. His half-closed eyes were heavy as he raised the cup and sipped.

"You should sleep now, too," he said. "You have had a trying day."

"No worse than anyone else."

"The little ones sleep well."

"Yes, not a peep out of any of them. You were so good with James tonight. How can I thank you?"

"No need. The poor *muchacho*."

"And Mr. Braddock, too. James and Mary have really taken to him. It's a shame he's separated from his own children."

Rubén lowered his cup to the table, sloshing coffee. "He told you that?"

She reached for a rag near the wash pan and wiped the oil cloth. "Yes, he told me he has three children and a wife."

"He hardly ever speaks of them."

"Have you met them?"

Rubén's shook his head.

"In all the time you've been friends, you've never met his family?"

"It is a long story, *Señora* Corbin."

"Tell me."

"I cannot. It is not my story to tell."

Esther looked toward the bed, at the man stretched out upon it. Her innate courtesy told her not to pry, that it was none of her business, and Rubén had just politely told her the same. Yet she wanted to know. "Then tell me how you met. Your story."

Rubén had been leaning back in his chair, resting, but now he rested his elbows on the table and when he opened his eyes the

122

candle flame danced in them.

"I had gone to a saloon just over the border from Mexico but the owner would not serve me. I had money, money I had earned working for the priests in Mexico. This saloon looked very poor. Even so, no Indian could be served, but I was able to convince him to sell me a bottle to take outside.

"There I was, seated against the shady side of the building, drinking, content, when a man came around the corner and stumbled and fell in front of me. Sat up. Drained what was left in his bottle. Passed out.

"I continued to drink my whiskey and enjoy the shade. I paid little attention to the gringo at my feet until he lifted his head up from the dirt. Then he spoke to me — in the language of the *Diné*."

"What did he say?"

Rubén made a soft laughing sound. "It is not easy to translate directly into the English but he said, 'Get me more whiskey.' "

Esther put her hand over her mouth.

"Yes. Those were the first words I heard in my native tongue since the age of ten, and out of the mouth of a white man. And so, of course, I was curious. I did not get him more whiskey. Instead I prodded and pushed and pulled until I got him onto the

123

horse he pointed out as his. I led him and my pack mule out of town where I made a camp and built a fire. I put on a pot of coffee and encouraged him to drink until he came to his senses."

The small fire crackled; the coffee pot hissed; outside the frogs continued their chirping night chorus; a child coughed.

"I have often been sorry for that." Rubén said.

"For sobering him up?"

Morgan stirred, groaned, turned onto his back.

"Wait, *por favor.*" Rubén pushed up from the table and hurried to lean over Morgan, pulling up the sheet that covered him. He turned the lamp lower, then came back and sat down. "Sometimes when he is sick, he has bad dreams."

"Please, Rubén, continue your story."

"I have told you how we met."

"But not how you became friends. And why you were sorry."

He nodded. "*Si*, very well. He said he was from New Mexico and must get back soon. Things to finish, he said. I asked him how he had learned to speak Navajo, and he told me he had been at the Bosque Redondo, when he was in the army. He said it was an

evil place where the *Diné* had been imprisoned.

"But the more sober he became," Rubén
continued, "the less inclined he was to talk.
He grew surly and demanded that I go to
town and get another bottle of whiskey. I
refused and did not tell him of the whiskey
left in the bottle I had purchased.

"He was quiet for a while. Then he started
to talk again." Rubén's voice trailed off. "I
have said too much."

"You're right. It was rude of me to ask. If
he wants me to know about his past, he'll
tell me himself. I'll say goodnight." She got
up to join the children in the loft, but Rubén
spoke again and she stopped at the bottom
of the ladder to listen.

"I will tell you this much, because it
explains how we became friends, which is
what you had asked. People died. He felt
responsible. He said he should have died
with them."

"Who, Rubén? Who died?"

"Indians. Navajos that lived on his ranch
in New Mexico. They were murdered by
white men from the nearby town."

"But why would they do that?"

"It is a long and complicated story."
Rubén hesitated, as if deciding whether or
not to continue. "I do not know this for

myself. This is what Morgan told me that night. When the *Diné* returned from the Bosque Redondo, their reservation was only a fraction of what their lands had been before. Many simply settled where they had lived before, where their mothers and all the grandmothers before had always lived. They gave little thought to the *Bilagáana's* arbitrary borders. They lived peacefully, tending their flocks and their gardens and, for the most part, were left alone by whites in the area.

"But when renegades from the reservation attacked the New Mexicans, those living peacefully outside the reservation became easy targets. Retribution from the whites."

"But why would Mr. Braddock feel responsible for this?"

"He allowed many Navajos to live on his ranch. One day, while he was away, the white men attacked."

A lump rose in her throat. He had tried to help them. She imagined him ten years younger, working side-by-side with his wife, offering sanctuary to these Indians. Her grip tightened on the ladder rung.

"Morgan killed one of those white men."

This was the murder. This was what the wanted poster was all about.

"And now he is a fugitive." Esther sat

again at the table. "That's what keeps him away from his family."

Rubén stared at the steam rising from his cup. "I should not be telling you this."

She had to lean toward him to hear his words.

"He told me a terrible story, so cruel it was hard to believe. After a while I was getting ready to turn in when I heard the sound of a hammer being cocked. I was able to deflect his hand, but not enough." Rubén raised a clenched fist and then, perhaps remembering the sleeping children, slowed his arm before he struck the table with any force. The candle flickered and shadows shifted on the walls. He bowed his head and his hair fell forward, hiding his face. "I should have left him drunk."

She covered his leathery hand with her own.

Through the open window a bright sliver of moon hung above the hills. The small stampeding hooves of a javelina herd stopped at the spring, as they did every night at this time. From the barn a goat bleated in response to their slurping grunts. Then the splashing stopped, the hoof beats receded back into the desert, and once again the silenced frogs raised their voices.

"He was unconscious for over a week. He

was very sick for many months. It was almost a year before he spoke."

"You took care of him, until he recovered. And then you were friends."

"I don't know that he has recovered, *mi amiga,* but we have traveled together since then. He is my friend, the first and only friend in my life." Rubén looked up at her. "*Por favor,* do not tell him we have spoken of this. He does not remember all of what happened. He talks sometimes as if . . . as if those people were still alive."

"It's a blessing then, that he can't remember."

"*Si.* But I believe he knows the truth, deep in his heart. He tries to remember but gets very sick. Then he dreams of what happened. When he has such dreams, I wake him."

"Why?"

Rubén pulled his hand from hers and leaned back. "I do not wish to lose my friend. When he gets sick, I take his pistol away, just in case. It used to make him angry, but now he hands it over. He thinks it is some strange quirk of mine, to not let sick people have weapons." Rubén's face twisted with sadness and fear. "Someday he will remember all of it. I do not see how to stop it."

She looked away. She knew what it was like to be overcome by blame, unable to forgive the harm done to another because of one's own failings. She whispered, "Those poor Indians. He must have cared for them very much."

Rubén reached across the table and touched her cheek. "He could care that much again, *mi amiga*."

CHAPTER TEN

At first light Esther sent Richard out to hitch up the wagon, then herded the younger ones in their bare feet, quietly and quickly, to the wagon. She went back in for their shoes. Both men were sleeping soundly, Rubén snoring on a pallet on the floor next to her bed. She held her breath when Morgan shifted his position, but he remained deeply asleep. He looked peaceful and younger than when he was awake. His hair was spread across the pillow and falling onto his face. One hand rested on his chest. The beautiful malachite ring, loose on his finger, evoked images of him on his wedding day, young and robust, before the tribulations of war and sorrow and illness. When he moved again, she clutched the shoes tightly and hurried from the house.

She drove the wagon back to town, approaching a group of miners gathered at the cemetery. Mr. Osgoode from the mercantile and Will stood closest to the fresh mounds of dirt. Others directed glances at her wagon, and a man in a bowler waved at them. James waved back.

Esther stopped the wagon in the middle of the road and handed the reins to Millie. "You children stay here."

She made her way to Mr. Snapp, who stood out among the roughly dressed men, his frock coat hanging open over an ample stomach contained by a tight brocade vest.

"I'm sorry about yesterday, Mr. Snapp. I locked up everything before I left."

"Not a problem, not a problem, Mrs. Corbin." He took her hand and patted it kindly. "I heard about the boy. Just terrible, witnessing that. He's not more than ten years old, is he? So young to see such violence. How is he?"

"He's fine today, thank you. But Will looks upset. I didn't think Hildie meant that much to him."

"No, probably not. But Fred meant a lot to some of those miners." He nodded toward a group of rougher looking men, standing to one side of the graves with hats in hand. Esther quickly looked away when she saw Otto Schmidt among them.

"They wanted Will arrested for killing Fred, but your brother was nowhere to be found. Will's the deputy. He can't very well arrest himself."

"I'm sure Jacob will be back in a few days. Not that Will should be arrested."

"Well, I knew he must have left town because his goats are penned up in the livery. I reckon by the time he gets back this will all be forgotten, but Will's afraid they'll come after him on their own."

Mr. Osgoode moved to the head of the graves, Bible in hand. With a tight smile, he nodded at the assemblage and cleared his throat.

"Too bad Howard ain't here. He's always good with the Word of God." Another cough, then he opened the book and read, " 'Yea, though I walk through the valley of the shadow of death, I will fear no evil: for thou art with me; thy rod and thy staff they comfort me —' "

"I'm sure gonna miss that Hildie's biscuits," someone said.

"Yeah, and Fred. You could count on him to lose at poker," another shouted out, and there was laughter.

Mr. Osgoode gave up on reading scripture and cleared his throat again. "Well, it's too bad they're both dead now, and we'll miss 'em. Ashes to ashes, dust to dust." He slammed the book shut and put his hat on.

"Free drinks at the saloon," Will said.

"Ah, a stroke of genius." Mr. Snapp took her elbow and steered her away from the gathering. "Mrs. Corbin, may I speak with you for a few minutes, as long as we are both here?"

A couple of men stayed behind to shovel dirt into the graves. Thudding clods followed the scraping of shovels.

"I want you to know how much I appreciate all your work. I stopped in the office earlier and it appears the filing is almost complete."

"I still have that pile that was stained with ink. You know, the day Mr. Schmidt came in."

"Yes, no doubt it will be difficult to decipher the information on them. But my thought was that there is no need for you to be in the office all day. I could post that the office is open only in the mornings. You'd get the same pay, of course. You've been a great help to me."

"Why, thank you. That's very generous."

"Tell your brother to see me when he gets back. Unlike you, he owes me some extra hours." He squeezed her hand again before walking back to town.

Esther climbed back into the wagon and took the reins from Millie. They headed down the slight hill into town. "Did you children say a prayer for Miss Hildie?" Behind them, men piled rocks on the graves, and James and Mary leaned over the wagon's tailgate, watching with great interest, whispering to each other.

"James?"

"Yes, Mama, I said goodbye to her in my prayers."

"Do you think they piled enough rocks?" Mary asked.

Esther turned to look at her daughter. "Enough?"

"To keep the dead people in them graves."

"I think it's to keep animals away from the bodies." Esther was sorry right away that she had conjured such a grisly image for the children. "Try not to think about it."

"So they can get out? The dead people can get out?"

"Mary, please, stop being silly."

Then Millie asked, "Why did they bury them together like that, Mama?"

"Because they are husband and wife."

"But he killed her."

"Well, I guess he was still her husband."

"I can't see praying over a man who killed

his own wife. People should be glad he's dead."

"That's enough, now."

As they drove by the saloon, James started to ease himself over the side of the wagon.

"Hey! What do you think you're doing?" Esther slowed the wagon.

"I gotta go to work. Mr. Will's expectin' me."

"Get back in the wagon!"

"But Mama, I have to sweep!"

Esther reined the wagon to a stop, trying to think amidst all the traffic and dust and shouts from the street and the creek. "You shouldn't be in there, a child. You've seen what can happen. You didn't even know enough to run!"

"Mama, I'll go with him," Millie said. "I was thinking maybe I would ask Mr. Will if I could have Miss Hildie's job."

"Oh, dear God." Esther shook her head. "Absolutely not! I won't have my daughter working in a saloon."

"It's not the saloon, it's the cook tent. And you know nobody would bother me with Uncle Jacob being the marshal."

"Uncle Jacob isn't here."

"But Will is. He'll look out for me, like he looked out for James. I'm sick of babysitting Mary all the time."

"I'm sick of her," Mary said. "She's mean!"

"The answer is no." Esther slapped the reins.

"Mama! Please!" James yelled.

Her thoughts were a jumble. Mary was crying. Millie was pouting. James was angry. She couldn't think.

"Mama?" Millie said. "I'll go in with James to make sure he's okay, and then I'll come home. He wants to go to work. You should let him. He ain't scared. Why should you be?"

"Isn't!" She stopped the wagon at the livery. "Don't you dare move out of this wagon," she said to James, who was still hanging half over the sideboard. "Millie, you go with him and tell Mr. Will that if James sits at a gambling table again, he's to take him out back and whip him with a stick. Then you come home."

"Can't I just ask Mr. Will —"

"Absolutely not. I won't have my daughter working in a saloon. Or next to it!"

James rocked back and forth on the sideboard until she told him to go ahead. "Behave!" Millie hung her head. "And you go with him, but only to tell Mr. Will what I said, nothing else, understand?"

CHAPTER ELEVEN

The long ride home left too much time to think, and Jacob was happier to see Chasm Creek than he thought possible. The solid adobe buildings, the people crowding its one street, and the placers splashing in the creek spoke to an aliveness sadly missing in Muddy Springs. That town spooked him. All the way home, day after day, he'd been uneasy, the kind of uneasiness that felt like eyes on his back, that made him keep turning around. With a sense of relief, he dismounted in front of the livery and tied his horse to the railing.

Inside, dust motes floated in shafts of sunlight streaming down through cracks in the shingled roof. The noise of the street faded, the only sounds coming from animals boarded in their stalls, a huff or a snort, crunching hay, a water pail sloshing. He waited for his eyes to adjust, breathing in the smell of hay and manure, until one bleat led to another and pretty soon six goats banged horns and hoofs on the walls of the horse stall that had been their home since he left town. They knew he was back.

"Okay, okay, calm down." He raised the latch and they pushed the door wide, gathering around him. They climbed on each other in their desire to get closer, sniffing and nibbling at his clothes. "Okay, enough!" They looked well fed and reasonably clean. He pushed his way through to the street, and they fell in line behind him, already accepting that life had returned to normal, already forgetting their weeks of confinement.

Jacob had to pass the saloon to get to Esther's, and the cool, dark interior called to him. He made his way past tables that were unusually crowded for this time of day. James, busy sweeping, didn't notice his uncle coming in.

Jacob stepped up to the bar. "Will, business looks good."

"Where the hell have you been?" Will reached for a shot glass.

"You know, I'm powerful thirsty. Maybe a beer."

Jacob lifted the mug that Will placed in front of him. "To home sweet home," he said, and took a long drink. He slammed the mug down and slapped his hands to his forehead.

"Cold, huh? You gotta drink it slow." A smile stretched across Will's big face. "I ordered ice from the ice house in Phoenix."

The searing pain in Jacob's forehead subsided. "You should warn a person."

"Nothing like a cold beer in this heat. It was your niece Millie's idea."

Jacob laughed. "Since when are you taking business advice from a fourteen-year-old girl?"

Will's eyes shifted toward the door to the cook tent and back again. "You ain't seen your sister yet?

A young man entered the saloon and leaned against the far end of the bar. "Hey! Get away from me!" The goats, having followed Jacob inside, sniffed and nipped at the stranger. He shoved one of them away. "This here animal's chewin' on my shirt!"

"That's my uncle's goat. Don't you hurt him," James yelled. "Hey, Uncle Jacob!" The boy ran over and threw his arms around Jacob's waist.

Jacob didn't care for the way that stranger had shoved the goat, harder than necessary, but he was tired and didn't want trouble. The young man wasn't much older than Richard, and he looked trail weary, covered with dust and dried sweat.

"Don't know why a person would bring goats into a saloon. Don't nobody complain about this around here?"

Will put a beer in front of the boy. "This'll cool you off."

"Is this a saloon or a Goddamn barn?"

Jacob put his mug down on the bar and stepped back.

"Look, mister," Will said to the boy. "Those goats belong to Mr. Tillinghast here. We don't pay them no mind."

"That's right," James yelled. "Because my uncle is the marshal!"

The boy could see his complaints were pointless so he shut up and lifted his mug. Jacob put a hand on James' head and left it there while he finished off his beer. "I guess I better go see Esther." He reached into a pocket for some money. "You stay here, son. I need to talk to your mother."

"On the house, Jacob. You give my regards to Mrs. Corbin."

"Thanks. I'll be back directly. Just have a few things to take care of."

He found Esther in the mining office. As soon as he came through the door she jumped up and ran over to give him a hug. "God, you need a bath."

Mary wrapped her arms around his legs. He laughed as he bent and picked her up. "How's my baby?"

"I ain't no baby, Uncle Jacob."

"I'm glad you're back. I've been dying to show you something." Esther pulled a sheet of paper out of one of the filing cabinets. "Look at this."

"Esther, I need to talk to you about what I —"

"I know, I know. He killed a man, but he had a good reason. Rubén told me all about it."

"You know what Braddock did? You don't know all —"

"I told you your trip would be a waste of time. Now look at this."

She held out a paper, shaking it at him until he took it from her — a form to file a mining claim. Howard's mining claim.

"So he did find gold. Son of a bitch —"

"You used a bad word," Mary said.

Jacob put the girl down. "Weren't you practicing your letters over there?"

"Mama's gonna file them when I'm done." She went back over to the corner where she had dropped her papers and a pencil. She squatted on the floor and resumed scribbling.

"Esther, I need to talk to you about —"

"Yes, but look." She pointed to the section that described the location, covered by a blotch of black ink. "From that day Otto came in here. The ink spilled."

"God damn!"

"Uncle Jacob!" Mary looked up from her letters and wagged a finger at him.

"There couldn't be much to it," Esther

said. "He wouldn't have gone off to California again if he'd struck a good vein."

"Who knows why Howard does what he does."

Esther took the form and sat down, staring at it.

"Essie, about Braddock —"

"Jacob, please. It was a long time ago."

"I'm still going out there to talk to them."

"Go ahead, if you must."

"I suppose I'll find Richard out there."

"Yes, you will. And you'll find Millie working for Will, as if you haven't already stopped there."

Jacob sat down on the edge of the desk. His niece was working at the saloon? Good God, she was a young girl. Esther had lost her mind. "I knew I was gone too long. What the hell is happening around here?"

"Don't be so dramatic. She's working in the cook tent, just breakfast and dinner — not at night. Will practically begged me after Hildie got killed."

"Hildie's dead?"

Mary looked up from her papers again. "Mr. Fred kilt her. Right in front of James. He said some of her guts got on him."

"Mary, please!" Esther said.

"Some of Mr. Fred's guts, too!"

"Fred's dead, too? Who killed him?"

"Will."

"Good Lord."

"You should have been here instead of off on your wild goose chase. Not that you could have stopped it, but the children and I were all alone. It would've helped to have you here."

He wanted to grab that mining claim out of her hands and point out to her that she could make mistakes, too. To start with, there was the idiot she married. But he held his tongue and left, letting the door slam behind him.

He rode out to the farm, slowly so as to give the horse a rest and so the goats could keep up, and give himself time to think about what he was going to say to those men. He felt he had to at least make it clear that he knew the story and would be keeping an eye on them.

He turned off the wagon road at the edge of Esther's property. There was green growth in the garden. He rode along the rock wall and saw damp furrows and irrigation ditches. A couple of new corrals on the far side of the barn held about a dozen horses each. Inside a brand new round pen, Braddock was working with a horse, and two men — he recognized them from around town, a squat Negro with coal black skin and a tall, skinny white man, red-haired and a permanent sunburn — sat on the top rail along with Richard.

Richard yelled, "Hey, Uncle Jacob! When'd you get back?"

The two men twisted around to watch him ride past, and Jacob waved. The goats headed for the spring and Esther's old buck goat complained with a long, loud bleat, then butted his stall gate a couple of times. Jacob rode up to the house and dismounted as the old Indian came out, wiping his hands on a rag.

"Welcome, *Señor* Tillinghast. I was making some preparations for dinner. You will join us?"

"I doubt it." He pulled the wanted poster out from where he had tucked it inside his shirt and unfolded it.

"Where did you get this *cartel de se busca*?"

The old Indian actually looked nervous.

There was a loud whinny followed by hooves stomping and men yelling and laughing. Jacob looked over and saw Braddock picking up a saddle from the ground, dust flying all over and the horse doing a high-legged dance around the inside perimeter of the corral. Richard jumped off the fence and helped Braddock settle the horse.

"Señor?"

Jacob turned back to the old Indian. "Well, I am the marshal. I get wanted posters. This seems to indicate we have a predicament here."

"It can be explained."

"Yeah, I know. Heard the story myself from a barkeep in Muddy Springs."

Jacob had expected a reaction from the old Indian — a look of suspicion or anger. Maybe even some appreciation for the lengths he had gone to in his investigation. He was not expecting fear.

"You went to Muddy Springs?"

"I did. Heard an interesting story, too."

"How much of a story, *Señor*?"

"I was left with a few questions." He pictured Braddock coming into town as the barkeep had described: covered with blood, who knows who else he kilt . . .

"*Por favor, Señor,* do not bring this up now, I beg of you."

"I need to talk to Braddock. I might have to be convinced of why it's okay for my sister to rent her place to a killer."

Out of the corner of his eye, he saw Richard headed their way.

"Killer?" Richard asked. "What are you talking about, Uncle Jacob?"

"You go on back to the corral, son."

The boy gave him a look before he dragged his feet and slouched across the yard back to the pen. He climbed onto the fence, looking over his shoulder to give his Uncle an angry stare.

"Your sister is a kind woman and knows when someone needs compassion, not threats," Rubén said. "Morgan did this murder, *si*, but he had reasons."

"Reasons. Such as?"

The old Indian put his hand on Jacob's arm. "Leave that *cartel de se busca* in the past. Tear it up. No good will come of speaking of this to him. He is not a well man."

"He looks well enough to me."

Braddock had climbed onto the horse and for a few seconds it looked like the mustang would allow it, before it exploded into a flurry of bucking and twisting. Braddock flew off, hitting the ground hard and sliding into the fence. Richard ran to help him to his feet, all the while talking. Braddock, covered with dust, limped over toward the cabin with Richard tagging along behind. When Braddock got close, he nodded to Jacob.

"Something we can do for you, Marshal?"

Richard stood beside Braddock. "I ain't gonna quit my job here, Uncle Jacob."

"The boy's been helpful," Braddock said. "We'd hate to see him go."

"Jesus, Richard. I ain't here about you."

This time it was Braddock who sent the boy away. "What, then?"

"Well, I thought I'd better check on a few things, seeing as how this is my sister's place." He held the wanted poster so that Braddock could see it.

"So this is what brings you out here?"

"I understand you murdered a man by the name of Miller, back in this Muddy Springs."

Braddock hardly paid attention to him; instead he watched the old Indian. "Rubén, is the heat getting you?"

"I am fine. I think the heat is getting *Señor* Tillinghast. He should go back to town and get a cold drink. I hear the saloon has ice now."

Braddock seemed surprised at the suggestion, but when he turned back to Jacob there was a hint of annoyance in his voice.

"I recall a man by that name. A hateful son of a bitch, but then that town was full of such men."

"You sayin' you didn't do it?"

"I'm saying if someone killed him, they should be thanked for it. You planning on arresting me?"

"It crossed my mind to do so, yes. Before I saw what you've done with my sister's farm." He folded the wanted poster and slipped it back inside his shirt.

"She's been out several times to see for herself. She seemed satisfied."

"She's married, you know," Jacob said.

That wasn't exactly what he'd planned to say, but the words came out. Now Braddock's eyes narrowed, and the silence stretched out too long.

"I know you're her brother." Braddock turned his head and spat. He wiped a hand across his mustache. "So I won't take offense at what you have suggested."

Jacob patted his shirt where the wanted poster was soaking through with sweat. The Indian stared at him, fidgeting with the rag and looking like he was going to maybe say something — but before he could, Jacob said, "I guess I'll be headed back to town."

"Gracias, señor, gracias!"

"Rubén, what the hell is wrong with you?" Braddock said.

Jacob untied his horse and pulled himself back into the saddle, whistled, and the goats came running from behind the house. "I'll be keeping an eye on things from now on. There won't be no more need for my sister to come out."

He waved at Richard as he rode by the round pen and the boy waved back, a big smile on his face.

Plodding toward town, dog-tired through to his bones, Jacob's thoughts swirled, thoughts about what he should have said or what he should have done, but they slowly sank into a daydream of a warm soapy bath and a soft bed. He went from wishing there was a hotel closer than Phoenix to almost wishing he hadn't given his house over to Esther. It occurred to him that she had commented on his need to bathe. She might be so grateful that he hadn't thrown Braddock in jail that she'd actually heat the water and let him take a bath in the copper tub they'd all been enjoying while he was off on his important legal business.

Much cheered, he stopped at the saloon again, on his way to Esther's.

"Give me another one of them cold beers." He took the mug to the table nearest the bar and winked at Will. "What do I gotta do to get some food around here?"

"Ordinarily you gotta go out to the cook tent. Your sister don't allow Millie in the saloon, but we might could make an exception." He called for Millie who came to the doorway and, when she saw her uncle, darted back into the cook tent.

"It's okay, Millie," Jacob yelled. "Your ma told me you're working here."

She came to his table and stood there, shy and nervous, her blond hair pulled back except for a few damp tendrils clinging to flushed cheeks.

"What're you making back there?" he asked.

"Pork and beans."

"So Will finally got sick of those hogs hangin' out in the street?"

Millie laughed. "One of 'em, anyway. I made biscuits, too."

She must have seen the pained look flash across his face, because her smile disappeared and she looked hurt. Millie was famous for her biscuits — not in a good way. Either burned and uncooked or hard as rocks. Esther had tried her hardest but the girl didn't have biscuit-making in her blood.

"Uncle Jacob, Mr. Rubén showed me how to make them so they come out right."

Jacob took her hand and gave it a quick squeeze. "You go get me a plate, honey. I'm sure it's right tasty." Once again he wondered how much time Esther and the children spent out at the farm. Enough for that old Injun to be giving cooking lessons? He was formulating the words he would deliver on the subject upon seeing his sister when Millie returned and put a plate in front of him. "My God, this looks delicious," he said. The biscuits were golden brown, light and flaky, and he forgot all about lecturing Esther.

At the table nearest the cook tent door sat the weasel-faced young man who had insulted Jacob's goat. When Millie walked by, he reached out and took her hand. She smiled at him, and the boy said something. Jacob wondered if he had positioned himself there in order to intercept his niece. Millie stopped laughing when Jacob got up, kicked out a chair, and sat across from the young man.

"You can let go my niece now, boy."

"His name's Danny, Uncle Jacob, and he was just —"

"I was placin' an order. You seemed pleased with what she brought you."

"She don't wait on tables. Millie, get yourself to the cook tent right now." He turned back to the boy. "I ain't seen you around before. Where you from?"

"New Mexico."

"That's funny. I was just in New Mexico."

"That so. You spend a lot of time in other territories?"

"No, I don't, as a matter of fact."

"Why would a marshal be traveling so far away from his town? You trailin' somebody?"

"You're pretty nosey, ain't you?"

"A little curious about what'd take you away from them goats you think so much of."

Jacob started to get pissed off. "What're you doing in Chasm Creek?"

"Passin' through. Seems like a nice town. Nice people. Maybe I'll be lookin' for work."

"What kind of work?"

"Well, workin' with horses is what I do best, but the bartender says there ain't much call for wranglers around here. He said I could probly get a swamper job in one of the mines."

Jacob leaned back and balanced his chair on two legs. The boy had dark hair and dark eyes and there was a miasma of darkness all around him. Something about him made Jacob's skin feel crawly. He wondered how someone so young could get so mean looking.

"I don't think you'd like swampin'," Jacob said. "You might consider moving on."

The boy looked toward the cook tent door. "Well, I don't know. I kinda like it here."

Millie brought out a plate and placed it on the table. Her cheeks were scarlet, and she risked her Uncle's wrath by smiling at the boy before hurrying away. The boy dug into the food, watching Jacob with eyes as cold as a snake's.

"You any good at breakin' horses?" Jacob asked.

"Yes, sir, I'm real good at that."

"Well, now, you might be in luck. There happens to be an outfit outside of town that could use someone good with horses."

CHAPTER TWELVE

Danny followed the road west for three miles, like he'd been told, and came to the turn-off to the farm. Wasn't that just like a lawman, buttin' in where it was none of his business, telling people what to do. He'd wanted to stay in town, keep an eye on that pretty yellow-haired girl in the cook tent. He didn't need a job. He'd be collecting reward money soon enough. But he couldn't say that, not to someone who thought they was gonna be the one to collect.

He rode up to a couple of corrals holding horses. Two men looked up from their work, repairing tack. One of them had red hair, as red as a ripe tomato, and the other had skin black as midnight.

"I'm looking for the boss of this outfit."

The Negro pointed to a cabin about a hundred feet away. Danny rode up to the cabin and tied his horse to the porch railing. A wrinkled up, gray-haired old Indian came to the doorway.

"Are you looking for someone, *señor?*"

Danny pulled his canteen from his saddle, unscrewed the top, put it to his lips, swished a mouthful around to wash out the dust, and hawked out a wad of spit right next to the Injun's feet. "I need to see the boss."

"You are looking at the boss."

Danny laughed. "Look, you old coot, I ain't got all day. Go get the boss."

He hit the ground hard, all the air knocked out of him. Through the dirt in his eyes he could see the Indian crouched over him. He went for his knife, but the old man pinned his arm to the ground. He tried to reach around with his right hand and felt steel against his throat.

"I, too, have a Bowie knife, *muchacho,* and I am not having a good day. It has made me impatient, I'm afraid."

Another man had come out of the cabin and stood over them. "What's going on, Rubén?"

The old man released him and stood up.

"Are you hurt?"

Morgan Braddock! Danny went for his

153

knife again but the Indian stomped a foot down on his arm.

"Ow!"

"The young man does not show the proper respect."

"What's your problem, boy? What're you doing here?"

Calm down, calm down, Danny told himself. Don't do nothin' stupid. There's two of them. "The marshal sent me, the one in Chasm Creek. For a job."

He was only answering a question, but once he spoke he realized what the words meant. The marshal had sent him. The man who had that wanted posted, had come all the way to Muddy Springs, so he knew what Braddock had done. Yet here was Braddock, standing over him, and this is where he got sent to find a job. The marshal was friends with Braddock?

Think. He had to think. What the hell was going on here? His plan had been so simple. Follow that bounty hunter from Muddy Springs, get to Braddock first, kill him.

But the bounty hunter turned out to be the law. And Braddock was his friend.

He had to change the plan. "I weren't expectin' no Indian to be running the place, that's all. I didn't mean nothin'. I'm looking for a job breakin' horses."

"You're a mite young for a contract bus-ter."

"I can do it."

The Indian took his foot off Danny's arm but he didn't put his knife away. While the two men talked, Danny rolled over and stood up on shaky legs.

"We don't need another hand," the Indian said. "We have Roy and Al already. And Richard."

"None of them know how to break a horse," Braddock said.

"You can do it."

"I'm tired of getting thrown."

"How can we work with someone like that?" Rubén pointed the knife at Danny. "He is like a snake. He hates Indians. I do not want any trouble from our suppliers."

"There's plenty for him to do around here."

"I do not trust him."

"Better his young bones getting bucked off than mine. Unless you want to start breaking the horses yourself."

The old Injun was annoyed — Danny could see it plain enough. "Look, I'm really sorry. I won't cause no more trouble. I need a job."

"What's your name, son?" Braddock asked.

155

"Danny. Danny Lee."

"My name's Braddock. This gentleman is my partner, Rubén Santiago."

Partner? An Indian? "Pleased to meet you." He kept his eyes down.

Braddock looked at the Injun. "It's up to you."

"It is not like *Señor* Tillinghast to do us a favor."

"True."

The Injun kept his eyes on Danny as he slowly slid his knife into its scabbard. "We should find out what he can do first. Perhaps he is all talk."

Danny followed Braddock over to the far corral where the red-head and the Negro man were trying to rope one of the horses.

"Roy, throw me that rope and you and Al get out of there."

The men jumped for the fence and climbed over. The red-headed one handed a rope to Braddock who tossed it to Danny. "Pick one out and bring it over to the round pen."

Danny fixed in his mind where the round pen was, in case things got wild, and saw the tack waiting on the top rail.

He looked the stock over. He could tell some of the horses had been worked with; they were less spooked. A couple even had

156

halters on. He figured they'd expect him to pick one of them, an easy one, but he chose a piebald mare that looked like a real snorter. He eased into the corral. It took a few minutes to get a rope on her. Roy and Al yelled encouragement and, when he finally caught her, they held the gate open so he could move her to the pen. He hung on the rope, dragging her, while the two men came up by her flanks to help move her along.

Braddock and Santiago followed them over. Danny haltered the horse without too much trouble. He fashioned rough reins out of the rope and snubbed her so he could cinch up the saddle. He climbed on, Roy and Al hanging on the halter until he signaled to let her go.

The horse tried to throw him off, bucking and crowhopping across the pen. Each time the stiff legs hit the dirt, Danny felt his spine coming up through the back of his head. Then she slammed him into the railing. He yanked on the rope until her face was almost at his boot and they circled a few times before the horse broke loose of that and reared up. Pure meanness kept Danny on the mare.

By the time Danny wore her out and jumped off, the Indian was on his way to the cabin.

Braddock, leaning against the fence, said, "Pay is twenty dollars a month plus food." When Danny nodded, Braddock pointed toward the far corral where a boy was working on the gate. "Go put your bedroll in the barn. Then report to Richard over there. Do whatever he says for the time being."

Braddock turned away, but he stopped and looked back at Danny. "You show respect to Mr. Santiago. He's the boss."

"Yes, sir." Danny watched Braddock go into the cabin before he untied his own horse and headed for the barn. His heart gradually, finally, slowed, and his breath came easy for the first time since he saw Braddock standing over him. He couldn't stop smiling. He would find a way to kill Braddock and not have to answer to the marshal, even if it took a while to figure it all out. He'd enjoy killing the old Injun, too. Kill him first, maybe, and make Braddock watch. Then they'd know who was all talk.

Roy caught up with him and slapped him on the back. "That was some good riding, kid."

Al took his reins. "I'll put your horse up for you. Good ride!"

"Pick an empty stall and put your stuff in it," Roy said.

"Where's that old Indian sleep? He don't sleep in here with us, does he?"

"He's got a little camp set up for himself in that ramada next to the barn," Roy said. "Rubén's okay. You'll get used to him. He ain't bad for an Apache."

"He ain't no Apache."

"No?"

"He's a Nava-joe. There was a nest of 'em used to live right outside my town."

"Not on no reservation or nothin'?"

"Nope."

"That don't seem right. Just one maybe, though, like old Rubén."

"So Braddock stays in the house by himself?" Danny asked.

"Yup, Mr. Braddock sleeps in the house. Except, of course, when Mrs. Corbin comes out. She owns the place, you know. Jacob's sister. Then he camps out with Rubén."

Danny threw his bedroll into a stall. So the marshal's sister owned this farm. That would be the yellow-haired girl's mother.

That might mean he'd get to see the girl again after all.

CHAPTER THIRTEEN

Every afternoon clouds piled up in the east, white and dense in the heavy air. The dampness increased each day. Esther could hardly wait for the clouds to turn dark and open up, drenching them with late summer storms. In the meantime, she opened the window that overlooked Jacob's yard and waved at Mary. "Stay out of the mud!" But she knew there was no way to keep the children away from the banks of the creek. She propped the mining office's door open with the big rock she kept for that purpose, and prayed for a breeze.

She continued putting claim forms in alphabetical order and looked up when a shadow fell across the room. Otto Schmidt filled the doorway, glaring at her with his beady eyes and holding a broken shovel in his hairy hand.

"What can I do for you, Mr. Schmidt?"

"I'll tell you what you can do for me."

With one step he reached the desk and slammed the shovel's blade onto it, sending papers flying. While he raged on about what he was going to do to Snapp when he found him, he jabbed the shovel toward her, threatening her with harm if she didn't tell him where Snapp was.

Esther pulled the desk drawer open. She raised the pistol Morgan had left with her.

Otto took a step back. "You don't want to be threatening me."

She cocked the hammer. "I'm not threatening."

"Ain't you the bold little lady. I bet a bold little lady like you is good at other things besides pointing that shooter."

She squeezed the trigger. The warning shot, aimed over his shoulder, hit the wall above the door. Dust sifted down from the rafters.

"You think you're something, don't you? Working here like a man, living in a nice house. Marshal for a brother. But I tell you something. I know you are nothing but a whore. I see you going out to those men at your farm, and I seen that man coming to your house. You wait 'til your husband gets back, then everyone will know you ain't nothin' but a whore."

He slammed the shovel into the door frame on his way out. The cracked handle broke off below the blade. He threw the pieces to the floor, then left.

A few seconds later, Mary stuck her face in. "Mama, what's a whore?"

Esther fell into the chair. With shaking hands, she laid the pistol in the drawer and pushed it shut. The smell of gun powder lingered.

"It's a bad word, sweetie pie. Don't ever say it."

Hard footsteps drummed down the road, and Jacob plunged through the doorway, pistol drawn.

"It's okay, it's okay," she said. "Put that away."

He picked up the broken shovel and held the pieces out toward her with a questioning look.

"Otto Schmidt. He threatened me so I scared him away. That's all."

"That's it. I'm gonna run him out of town."

"You do that, Jacob." He should have done it a long time ago, she thought. "Come on, Mary, we're going home."

Esther sat on the porch, sweating. The sun had finally moved beyond the canyon rim and cast the town into shadow, which brought no discernible relief from the heat. Her chemise and drawers were damp and stuck to her skin. She rolled her stockings down to the tops of her shoes and removed her apron, letting her dress hang free. She hoped a breath of air would touch somewhere, anywhere a stretch of naked skin could enjoy. She considered propping her legs up on the porch railing until she realized what a sight that would present to anybody happening by and settled for unbuttoning the top two buttons of her dress and her cuffs, pushing her sleeves to her elbows. Her mother always said, "Horses sweat, men perspire, ladies glow." Well, the glow was dripping down her back. She put her glass of water on the small table beside her and picked up a copy of last week's Salt River Herald.

The children played in the little stream, the water so low it was more like a mud puddle which they walked in with bare feet. She wondered if that would be a good way to cool off or if even the mud was hot. The town, quiet as a tomb, looked empty. The placers had pretty much given up for the day and were cooling off in Will's saloon.

Sweat dripped into her eyes, stinging them so she couldn't read. She folded the newspaper and used it as a fan. Jacob came up the street, his goats lined up and trotting along behind him. When he reached the porch he threw himself into the chair on the other side of the little table.

"When's it gonna rain?" He took off his hat, soaked through at the band, and wiped his face with a rag.

Down at the creek, James and Millie were lifting Mary onto the back of one of the goats. "Don't do that!" Esther yelled. "You know those horns are dangerous."

They pulled Mary off and all three flopped down at the water's edge, as if now there was nothing left in the world to occupy them. Then Millie suddenly jumped up and raced across the yard. She pounded up the steps in her bare feet, creating a short-lived but welcome breeze in her wake.

"Shit." Jacob watched a group of riders approaching. "What the hell are they doin' here?"

Morgan, Richard and a young man rode toward them. Esther grabbed her apron from the porch railing and put it back on, hurrying to roll down her sleeves and button them. She went to smooth her hair but she felt Jacob's eyes on her and dropped her hand.

The riders stopped in front of the porch.

"How come you ain't been out for a few days, Ma?" Richard asked.

"There ain't no need for her to be riding out there," Jacob said. "You want to see your ma, you can come in to town."

"That's what I'm doin', Uncle Jacob."

James and Mary ran up from the creek. Morgan dismounted and swung Mary up into his arms.

Esther again felt Jacob's eyes on her.

James plopped down on the bottom step and looked up at Danny. "I seen you at the saloon. You's the one was mean to Uncle Jacob's goat."

"His name's Danny. We hired him to break the horses," Morgan said.

"I know who he is," Jacob said. Evidently this young man annoyed Jacob even more than Morgan.

"He's been a big help," Morgan said. "He says you sent him out to us, so I guess I should be thanking you."

"It looks like you men could use a drink." Esther enjoyed the sudden smile that Richard tried to not have, obviously surprised to be included in "the men." She was about to call Millie to bring them some water when her daughter appeared in the doorway, in a fresh dress with her hair combed, carrying a tray of glasses. She carefully balanced the tray as she went down the steps, not stopping to offer any to her mother or uncle.

"I brought home a chunk of ice from the cook tent. It wasn't all melted yet." She stayed next to Danny's horse, looking up at him.

He took a glass and swirled it, clinking the little chunks of ice before raising it to his lips. "This is right refreshing." He smiled down at her.

"Richard, you gonna get down and visit with your mother or not?" Jacob was still in

165

his chair, one foot braced against the porch railing. "No need for everyone else to waste their time hanging around here."

"Jacob, there's no need to be so rude," Esther said. "Please, everyone, get off those hot horses. Danny, isn't breaking horses dangerous? Don't you get thrown a lot?"

Richard swung down from his horse. "He don't mind. The meaner they are, the more he likes it."

"I don't mind it, ma'am," Danny said.

"Rubén says better Danny's bones than anyone else's." Richard came up the porch steps. "He don't like him much."

"Goes both ways."

"Why is that?" Esther looked at Morgan. He put Mary down and tied his reins to the porch. Millie, never looking away from Danny, held the tray towards him and he took a glass.

"I've got Sunday off," Danny said. "Why don't I bring a nice saddle horse into town and you and me can go riding."

Jacob dropped the front legs of his chair to the porch floor with a bang. "Wait a minute here."

Morgan stepped close to the porch. He held out his glass to Esther and, when she went to take it, their fingers touched. He leaned toward her and spoke quietly. "Mrs.

166

Corbin, you say the word and there won't be no need for him to have a day off."

She couldn't hold his gaze because Jacob was staring at them. "Thank you, but there's no need." She took the glass and stepped around Morgan. "Danny, that's very nice of you, but she's too young to have callers."

"Damn right she's too young," Jacob added. "You stay away from her, you hear?"

Millie let out a little shriek and stomped into the house, slamming the door.

Danny dismounted and placed his glass on the tray Millie had left on the porch steps. Red blotches spread up his neck to his cheeks, and he climbed back up on his horse, sat looking away from everybody.

"I guess we should get back," Morgan said. "Richard, you stay and visit with your ma as long as you want. Danny and I can manage the supplies."

"That's okay, Mr. Braddock. I'll come with you." He gave his mother a hug. "Come out to the farm again, Ma. You'll be happy with what we've been doing out there."

"I will, son. You all go on now, and take care not to over exert in this heat."

The three rode off but were probably not out of earshot when Jacob said, "That little guttersnipe needs to stay away from my niece. How much time did you spend out there anyway while I was gone?"

"Hush, now. They'll hear you." Esther picked up the tray of glasses. "What put you in such a good mood?"

"One of 'em sniffin' around Millie, the other sniffin' around you."

"I can't believe you are being so crude in front of the children." James and Mary were watching intently from the bottom step. "You two go find something to do."

The children ran back down to the creek, scattering goats as they rushed through the small herd.

"You're a guttersnipe!" Mary said to James.

"No, you are!"

Esther went inside and put the tray down on the table where Millie sat, her face streaked with tears.

"You tell me to act my age, and then you treat me like a baby."

"Millie, that boy is too old for you."

"He's not! He's only a couple years older than Richard."

"That makes him four years older than you, and he looks like he's been around. For once I agree with your uncle."

"Father was five years older than you."

She couldn't very well explain to her

daughter that marrying Howard wasn't the smartest thing she'd ever done, or that she often wished she hadn't. "That was different. My family knew his. We don't know anything about that boy."

"This isn't Rhode Island, Mother. People don't come with pedigrees around here."

"No, this certainly isn't Rhode Island." It's a place where husbands disappear for months at a time and others shoot their wives dead in saloons and even a million miles away from anyone who would actually judge you, you still can't do what you want, have what you want, love who you want — and after not doing or having anything that you want, you get called a whore.

The glass she'd taken from Morgan was still in her hand. She threw it against the wall, and shards exploded across the floor.

"Mother!"

"Everything okay in there?" Jacob yelled from the porch.

She closed her eyes and took a deep breath. "Yes, everything is fine. I dropped a glass."

She picked up the larger pieces and pushed Millie's hand away. "Please, Millie, just go to your room."

"Why? What did I do?"

"You were disrespectful. I don't feel like

arguing right now."

"Neither do I!" Millie ran to the bedroom. The door slammed.

Esther finished picking up the broken glass, cutting a finger. "Damn it." A trickle of blood ran down her hand and dripped onto the floor.

Jacob's chair scraped across the porch. He came inside and helped her up from her knees. "Here, sit down. And why are you crying? It's just a little cut."

He took a rag from the sideboard, ripped off a strip, and tied it around her finger.

"You don't know how much it hurts," she said

"I do, Essie. It's all over your face every time you look at him."

"Regret is an awful thing."

"You don't want him, Essie."

"It wouldn't matter if I did. His family is back in that town you went to. Someday he'll go to them."

"Hell, Essie, his family is long gone and he don't even know it. If there was a family in that town it was well hidden. That place ain't nothin' but a ghost town. That's where he's from. A ghost town. You'd best leave him be."

CHAPTER FOURTEEN

Rubén rode along behind Roy and Al on the narrow trail that penetrated deep into the foothills near the Verde River. Every rustled leaf, scattered stone or chirping bird caused the two hired hands to jump, so much so that now their horses shied and danced sideways at every shadow. Morgan must have been drunk when he hired those two, Rubén thought. After all, he said he met them in the saloon.

The last time Rubén had come to collect the horses, he told Eleven that he was too old to keep making the long ride and handling all the animals by himself. The heat was hard on a man of his age, with brittle bones and tired muscles. When Eleven suggested that Rubén's partner take over the chore, Rubén explained that his partner's health was also unreliable. Eleven agreed to meet the hired hands, Roy and Al.

God knew they were not good for much else now that the irrigation system and extra corrals were complete. At least with this chore they could earn some of their pay.

"Just around the next bend. We shall go down into the wash and ride north a little ways, to where it widens. That is the meeting place we have arranged." At Rubén's words they looked even more nervous, a condition Rubén would have thought impossible.

"Remember, do not put your hands anywhere near your weapons." All they needed was some fidgety reflex of theirs being misinterpreted by the Apaches. They would all end up dead. "If you cannot manage that, then hand them over to me right now."

"We'll be careful, Rubén," Al said. "It's just that we ain't never been around no wild Indians before."

"You sure they won't scalp us?" Roy asked, a question that must have weighed heavy on his mind. He had been taking off his hat and running his fingers through his red hair repeatedly since they left the farm.

"They are going to take our money and then give us the horses. That is all. It is quite simple." The plan was simple. The men were simple. At least they were merely afraid and not filled with hatred like most white men.

They rounded the bend and came upon the clearing. Eleven, riding a piebald pony, emerged from behind a mesquite thicket. He raised a hand in greeting to Rubén, and three mounted men leading a string of seven lean mustangs appeared behind him.

When Eleven and his men saw Roy and Al, they reined in, backed up, and murmured among themselves, glancing at the men. Eleven spoke forcefully and the Indian who held the lead rope approached and held it out as if he were afraid to get too close.

Al handed a sack of eagles and double eagles to Eleven with a hand shaking so badly that a few of the gold coins fell out. Roy dismounted and when he bent over, his hat fell off, causing a ripple of comment by the Indians about the flaming orange color. Roy jammed the hat back on his head, handed the coins and a good amount of dirt to Eleven, and scrambled back into his saddle. He and Al turned toward home immediately, and Rubén reined his horse to follow.

"We will meet yet again, Rubén Santiago," Eleven called out.

"Did you see how they was dressed?" Roy said to Al as Rubén caught up to them. "They was nigh onto naked."

Their own shirts were so wet the grimy trail dust turned to patches of mud on the wettest areas. Rubén's loose cotton clothing, equally damp, stuck to his skin. All their horses were soaked as well, hot under heavy saddle blankets that left outlines of salty sweat on the horses' flanks. Rubén thought of the Apache's sparse clothing and light tack, and surprised himself by thinking how practical they were.

"They wasn't so scary after all," Roy said, now that they'd left the Indians far behind.

"Downright puny," Al said.

"You had best be looking for landmarks to guide you. I will not be coming the next time." Rubén stopped at a point a few miles north of the farm. "Go south from here until you arrive at the wagon road, then turn west. You will know your way from there. Do not forget — if anybody questions you, you caught those horses yourselves."

Roy and Al were in high spirits now, having survived their encounter with the wild Indians, and did not complain about this abandonment. Rubén watched until they disappeared behind a hill. He nudged his horse and turned toward the ruins on Haunted Hill.

At the bottom of the hill, he tied the horse to a bush, and took his canteen. He climbed to the remains of the ancient village. Sweat puddled in the wrinkled crevices of his face and turned his gray hair dark where it hung on his shoulders. At the top of the hill, the only sound his own rasping breath, he waited for his heart to slow. The desert spread below for miles, a brown expanse dotted with cactus and scrub. To the south a long, winding oasis of leafy trees marked the creek. To the north, mountains loomed. Rocks, bleached by mid-day glare, lay scattered around him.

Without the children or Morgan for company, the eerie silence fed his fear. Lizards skittered away as Rubén walked past the crumbling walls. He thought he saw shadows — how could that be at this time of day? — and when he turned his head they were gone. Like the last time he was here. The wind fluttered against his ears.

He tread carefully, keeping an eye out for snakes, and found a spot near a wall where a Palo Verde tree cast a circle of dappled shade. He bent to brush away rocks, smoothing a place upon which to lower his brittle old bones.

He sat and made the sign of the cross. "*Por favor,* my Lord Jesus Christ, I pray to you, in the name of the Father and the Son and the Holy Ghost."

Reciting the Lord's Prayer, he waited for the peace doing so always brought to his soul.

"*Padre nuestro que estás en los cielos . . .* Amen."

He waited, eyes closed, then drank from his canteen and wiped sweat from his eyelids with his shirt sleeve. A whirl of dust sprouted in the valley below, wandered through clumps of dried brittlebush and raced toward the northern mountains. Clouds piled up behind low hills to the east.

He should have listened to the stories Morgan had tried to tell him about the Navajo people, instead of walking away in anger, saying, "They are not my people." His friend stopped talking about the *Diné* many years ago. He stopped talking about the conditions at Fort Sumner, at the place called Bosque Redondo, where the soldiers imprisoned the *Diné*. About Indian children sneaking into the barn to pick through manure piles. They searched for undigested kernels of corn. These they would eat. About women who contracted syphilis from the soldiers with whom they lay in order to obtain food vouchers. Stories such as these only indicated what a degenerate race he came from.

Now he remembered the pain his comments had caused his friend. He remembered the pain his accusations had caused his grandmother. He wanted only to see her again, to tell her he had been wrong.

He waited, eyes closed. He waited a long time. His grandmother did not appear.

He squinted about for any sign of snakes. Whatever had possessed him to come back to this dreadful place? All for nothing.

A fly, large and heavy and slow, buzzed near his face. He waved it away.

It had been, after all, only a dream. He had not been with Grandmother. A dream. He should be sitting in the shade by the creek, drinking cool water. Or back at the farm with a smooth brandy at his lips. He thought longingly of the bottle in Mrs. Corbin's cupboard.

He turned to grab the stone wall and pull himself up. A coyote sat not ten feet away, watching him. Rubén fell back against the wall as it trotted by, so close he heard the pads of its feet on the dirt. He could have reached out and touched the gray brown fur. Its lips pulled up to show fangs and a long, panting tongue. As it passed, it twisted its head to look at him.

It had human eyes!

The coyote hurried down a narrow footpath leading away from the ruins. Another appeared and followed the first. Then another and another. Dozens. Hundreds. Some whined as they passed, others growled. All looked at him with those eyes. Yellow tears fell from their haunted eyes and hardened to nuggets of gold as they fell.

Rubén dropped to his knees. "Jesus Christ, have mercy on me!"

Still they came. They trotted past him and

disappeared down the footpath, only to re-appear farther away. They formed a long line snaking toward the eastern horizon. Thousands of them stretched across the desert to the far hills.

He awoke in darkness. Clouds blotted out the stars but, to the east, the full moon's diffused glow penetrated the black sky. A rumble of thunder brought him to his senses. Out of habit, out of superstition, out of fear, he made the sign of the cross. "In the name of the Father, and of the Son, and of the Holy Ghost." He looked toward heaven. "May the sacred heart of Jesus pour its blood upon me and protect me."

He must have fallen asleep, but the coyotes with their bewitched eyes had not been a dream. They had been as real as the hard ground upon which he lay — he knew that to be the truth. He got to his knees and scooped up a handful of the stones that had fallen from their eyes, held them up to the sky. Even in the dim light of the obscured moon, they did not glitter or shine. They were only stones. He opened his fingers and let them fall thudding to the ground.

He carefully picked his way down the hill, listening for the rattle of snakes, and found his horse. He rode toward the fishing creek. Its gentle water sighed over smooth rocks, and his shoulders relaxed as he crossed the stream; his breath eased.

Bolts of lightning illuminated his way back to the farm.

Chapter Fifteen

Esther opened her eyes wide, heart pounding, and tried to determine what had awakened her. Thunder rumbled, but it was far away. No lightning. Yet something —

A shadow in the door. "Mama," Millie whispered, and crawled to her bedside. "There's someone in the yard."

"Shush. Here, get in here and be still." Esther eased slowly out of bed, picking up the Henry on her way to the front of the house. She tripped over something in the middle of the parlor floor and fell toward the window, grabbed the sill, and caught herself. Sliding the window open, she stuck the rifle barrel out as a bolt of lightning illuminated Otto Schmidt not fifty feet from the house. He had been watching the house but, seeing the rifle aimed at him, turned and ran toward town.

Esther hobbled over to the lamp and struck a match. A rock in the middle of the room and shards of glass on the floor. The window next to the door was shattered.

Sudden flashes of lightning blinded her and thunder cracked right above the house.

"He's gonna get us! He's gonna get us!" Mary screamed.

Esther grabbed the lamp and raced to the children's bedroom. James knelt on Mary's pallet, hugging her. "He can't get you. He's buried!"

Mary rubbed her eyes with balled fists.

"Remember?" James asked. "At the cemetery? How they piled up those rocks? Them dead people can't get out from under the rocks."

Mary lowered her hands. "You're sure?"

"What are you children talking about?" Esther asked. "Who's going to get you?"

Mary opened her mouth but before she could speak, James said, "A monster. It's a monster she dreams about."

"Oh, dear. There are no monsters, Mary." She joined the children on the floor and pulled Mary into her lap.

"He's buried under the rocks." Mary snuggled into her mother's embrace.

The children settled down, and Esther left their room to clean up the broken glass. For the rest of the night she shared Jacob's unused marital bed with Millie and her Henry rifle. Lying in darkness, she strained to hear any sound. The children were quiet, no noise from the goats. Twice she convinced herself she heard footsteps and got up, creeping from window to window. Nobody there.

The last of the distant thunder finally faded and the soft light of dawn glowed at the window. She gave up on sleep. Throwing on a dress, she went outside to get kindling for the stove, the Henry tucked under her arm. It must have rained somewhere in the hills because the creek was running fast and sparkled in the sunlight breaking over the rim of the canyon.

She dropped the kindling by the stove and checked on the still sleeping children. She decided against starting the fire and walked into town, intending to let Jacob know what had happened last night, her anger at her brother growing with each step so by the time she banged the jail door open she was screaming like a banshee.

The angry pounding on the jail door woke Jacob with a start. His eyes shot open and he scrambled for his pistol before he realized it was only Esther yelling at him. In the middle of the night? He pulled the bolt and jumped away from the swinging door and his wild-eyed sister. "What the hell, Essie — it's barely daylight."

"I thought you said you were going to get rid of Otto Schmidt!"

"I told him to leave town."

"Didn't it occur to you to check?"

"Essie, please. I just woke up." Even her normal voice would have given him a headache. This morning she was in rare form. His head would explode if she didn't quiet down.

"Do you ever wake up? You're always saying it's safer for us to live in town but nobody ever broke our windows at the farm. That's what he did. Threw a rock through one of your windows in the middle of the night. Can't you do your job and protect us?"

"Essie, please —"

"I know. You just woke up. I'm taking the children out to the farm, right after breakfast. Maybe by the time we get back, the law will be able to guarantee our safety."

"What is it you expect me to do?"

"I want you to lock him up or get him out of town! Before another rock comes flying through my window! He's at the saloon. I just walked past him."

"He bother you?"

"With me carrying this?" She lifted the Henry. "He ran back inside like the coward he is."

She slammed the door behind her.

Jacob rolled off the cot and hobbled over to his desk. Just one sip, to dull the headache before he headed to the saloon. Only a freight wagon headed south out of town traveled the deserted street. He found Will on the boardwalk with a pile of boxes the wagon had delivered. "Mornin', Jacob."

"I'm lookin' for Otto."

Will put down the box he'd been holding and straightened up. He pushed his hands into his lower back and flexed his knees. "Well, he was here but he ain't now. Probably afraid I'd ask him to help with these crates." He looked from the stacked crates to Jacob and back again, but Jacob pretended not to notice.

"Well, thanks. If you see him, let me know."

"Wait, don't go." Will pulled an envelope out of his pocket. "The driver left this. Addressed to Howard. You want to give it to Mrs. Corbin?"

Jacob took the envelope. No, he didn't want to give anything to his sister. The last person he wanted to talk to right now was Esther, being unable to assure her that Otto was either gone or incarcerated. He started to stuff the envelope in his vest pocket when he noticed the feminine penmanship. And a

183

return address of a hotel in San Francisco.

With the headache threatening, he went to the jail, sat at his desk and uncorked the bottle of mescal before he opened the envelope. Delicately penned words flowed across the hotel stationery.

Dearest Howard,

I've not heard anything since your letter of three weeks ago. Knowing the slowness of the mail, I expected your arrival shortly thereafter but all this time has gone by and you are not here. Where are you, my dearest?

I know if you was able, you would send word as to why you are detained. You said in your letter that your mine continued to be profitable so lack of funds is not keeping you away. I can only then believe that something terrible has befallen you. Perhaps an accident or an illness that has left you unable to contact me.

I am going to cash in the rest of the rent you paid for my room and use the money to come to you. As soon as I can make arrangements I will be on a steamer for Yuma and then a stage coach to Phoenix. Even if I have to walk from there I will come to your side. Whatever is wrong can be righted, and we can begin our lives together as you promised.

All my love,
Your Victoria

Jacob smoothed the letter against the rough wood of his desk. He read it again. He drank some more mescal. He held the proof that justified his low opinion of his brother-in-law. Somehow it didn't bring him the satisfaction it should have. He put the letter back in its envelope, folded it over and over and tucked it deep into his vest pocket.

When Esther got to the farm, Morgan was working a horse, a pretty grey mare with black stockings, in the round pen. The children ran to watch and hung on the railing and, as soon as she climbed from the wagon, she joined them. Morgan let go of the horse's halter and let her rest while he came to the fence.

"Where is everyone? I'd hoped to see Richard," she said.

"They're at the creek. Well, Rubén and Richard. Fishing. Roy and Al went to get some more horses. And Danny's taking a string to the fort."

The mare came up to the children, searching their hands. Morgan gave them each a piece of carrot.

"She's a gift for Captain Dugan at the fort. He's a friend of mine." He tied the horse's lead to the railing. "I plan to take my time with her. When I give her to him, she'll make every soldier there jealous."

"She's a beautiful horse. He'll be proud to ride her."

"I'm getting her used to a blanket today. When I'm done here, we could take the children to the creek."

"You can go. Take Millie and James. Mary can stay with me. I think she needs a nap."

In the bright and clear day, Esther relaxed, happy to be out of town, happy to see her children enjoying themselves, and sleepy after the restless night. She folded her arms on the top railing and rested her head. She was the one who needed a nap, and the prospect grew more pleasant by the minute.

James watched Ma's eyes slowly close. She looked like she was sleeping standing up and Mary beside her looked about to have a hissy fit. She didn't look like she wanted no nap. He whispered. "Let's go to the creek. We can walk there."

She stepped away from the railing and, when they were both about six feet back, they took off running, laughing.

"Where are you going?" Ma yelled. She sounded pretty much awake.

He grabbed Mary and they both skidded to a stop. "No place, ma'am."

"Don't you leave the yard!"

They slowed to a walk, scuffing their shoes in the dust, which allowed them to notice a lizard squashed flat inside a wagon track. Forgetting about the creek, they squatted to study the small reptile, only as long as James' index finger, which he used to poke it. "Dead," he said. Mary touched the tiny, black dot of an eyeball at the edge of its flattened face.

"Must've got run over by a wagon wheel," James said.

Mary pushed at the eyeball. "It's stuck on there good."

James nodded. He picked up the lizard by the tail.

"What're you gonna do with it?"

"Come on." They ducked behind the barn. He studied the ground for a sturdy stick which he used to scratch out a hole in the dirt. He laid the lizard in it.

"A grave," Mary said.

James nodded. They both crouched on their heels, contemplating the dead lizard. Mary started to scrape sand on top of it, but James pushed her hand away.

"No, not sand." He scurried around on his knees and gathered a handful of little stones which he piled over the grave.

"Just like Hildie," Mary said. "And Fred."

"Yes, just like all of 'em. Next time we come out, we'll check and see if it's still here. Then you'll see. Then you can quit them nightmares."

Esther held Mary's hand as Morgan, James and Millie rode out, headed for the creek. "Wave goodbye, Mary." She'd promised her daughter a bowl of canned peaches, enough of a bribe to settle her down, although it didn't completely remove the pout from her face. Morgan was the only one who looked back to see them waving.

"I think we left some cans of peaches in the cupboard." Esther took Mary's hand and they went inside.

"Mama! What happened to our house?"

Sunlight through the open door illuminated a floor covered with wooden planks. A staircase replaced the ladder to the loft.

"Oh, my goodness! This must be why Richard wanted us to come out."

"How'd they do this, Mama?"

"I'm not sure. I think it's the wood from behind the barn, you know, that your Pa got to build an addition."

188

Mary pulled her hand free and ran up and down the stairs.

"Be careful!"

Mary yelled from the top of the stairs. "Will they will bring some fish, do you think, Mama?"

"Well, we can hope!"

"Green beans! We need green beans to go with the fishes. Can I help snap them?" She banged down the stairs.

"We'll have to check if any are left in the garden, sweetie."

Esther turned to look for a basket and jumped, her hand flying to her heart. A man stood silhouetted in the doorway. Instinctively, she pulled Mary close and held her.

"Is that the little girl's name? Sweetie?"

Esther pulled Mary behind her. "What do you want? You better go before the men see you."

Otto pulled a pistol from his belt. "There ain't no men here. I watched 'em all ride away. What's the matter, Miss High-and-mighty?" He came into the house. "You look a bit peaked."

How long had Morgan been gone? Would he hear her scream? She drew in a breath but Otto's pistol slammed against the side of her face and knocked her to the floor. She felt blood running down her cheek, tasted it in her mouth. Then he grabbed Mary's arm and lifted the little girl into the air. Mary's face contorted in pain. She struggled and cried out.

"Don't hurt her. I'll do whatever you want — don't hurt her." Esther struggled to her knees, reaching for her crying daughter.

He put the girl down and pulled his neckerchief off and handed it to Esther. "Tie it around her mouth so she shuts up. And if you scream, she dies."

"Come here, sweetie. Don't be scared. Be quiet, please?" She tried to smile, to re-assure her daughter, as she tied the dirty rag around her daughter's small, tear-stained face, all the while maneuvering herself between the open door and Otto. "Run, Mary! Run as fast as you can!" She pushed the girl toward the door, through the door, started to follow but a big hand grabbed her arm and hauled her back. Otto kicked the door shut. She threw herself at him. She tried to hit him but he easily fought her off and pinned her arms at her sides.

"You think you're smart, don't you? Now you get what's coming to you, whore." He threw her down on the floor and climbed on top of her, straddling her. She thought her legs would break from his weight. She tried to squirm out from under him but he grabbed her hair and jerked her head so she was forced to look at him.

Clenching her teeth, she turned her face away. Otto pressed his pistol into her breast and cocked the hammer. "Don't you move." He lowered his mouth close to hers and she gagged as brown drool dripped onto her face. Otto moved up her thighs. She struggled to get a breath and struck at him, scratching his face.

"Whore!" he yelled. He yanked her hair and slammed her head against the floor. He pressed the barrel of the pistol against her while he pulled at her dress.

She screamed as loud as she could.

"You bitch — I told you —"

She fought him. Kicking, biting, pushing him away and screaming the whole time. She bit his hand, and he hit her. She closed her eyes and kept screaming and thrashing beneath him.

The door swung open and slammed against the wall. Bright sunlight flooded into the cabin. She screamed, "No, Mary! Run!" Otto hit her again, and the room spun and grew dark. Otto's pistol discharged; the explosion made her ears ring; another loud bang and then all was quiet. She fought against the darkness engulfing her and suddenly the awful pressure on her legs was gone. She scrambled away, pulling her legs up and her dress down. Morgan was in the room but she couldn't think about that, only look for Mary and pray, "Please, God . . ."

She started for the door — she had to get to her daughter — but Morgan held out an arm and stopped her. "Mary! Where's Mary?"

Morgan hung onto her. She caught a glimpse of Mary outside the open door, standing in the dooryard, crying and rubbing her eyes.

"Oh, thank God. I need to hold her, please, I need to hold her."

Morgan let her go and she ran outside, pulling Mary into her arms.

Jacob heard the shots as he turned off the wagon road. He galloped into the yard to find his sister kneeling in the dirt, holding her daughter, both crying.

Esther, her face bruised and bleeding, nodded toward the cabin's open door. Jacob ran inside. Braddock struck Otto with his pistol, a blow that sent the big man sliding down the wall to the floor, then dragged Otto to his feet and held him against the wall. He slammed his pistol into the man's face and drew back to hit him again, but

Jacob grabbed his arm. He remembered the Muddy Spring's barkeep. "Crazy. He was crazy — killed the man in front of the whole town." Morgan shook Jacob loose and struck Otto again. Otto's blood spattered Braddock's shirt. "Covered with blood . . . who knows who else he kilt!"

"Stop!" Jacob struggled to pull Braddock away from Otto. "Don't kill him!"

"He needs killing."

"No! I'll arrest him."

Braddock turned his head and stared at Jacob. "Arrest him?"

"Yes. Arrest him. Throw him in jail."

Braddock continued to pin Otto against the wall but he stopped hitting him. He hung his head for a moment, catching his breath.

"Where's Esther?"

"She's outside. Her and Mary are outside. They're all right. Go on out and see for yourself. Go on, I say."

Braddock let Otto go and the big man slumped to the floor, picking at a bloody hole in his shirt sleeve. "He shot me. Son of a bitch shot me."

Rubén appeared in the doorway, knife in hand.

"It's all over," Jacob said.

Braddock and Rubén went out to the yard

where the other children had gathered around their mother and Mary.

"Get up," Jacob said to Otto. "You son of a bitch."

"You told me to leave town. I left town."

"I didn't tell you to make any stops along the way." He dragged Otto outside, away from the others, and took shackles out of his saddlebags. "I figured you might head this way. If it'd took me a little longer to think of it, Braddock would've kilt you before I got here. Too bad."

Esther knelt in the yard, pressed Mary's face to her chest as Jacob dragged Otto past them and shoved him up onto one of the horses in the yard.

A hand squeezed her shoulder, and Morgan spoke close to her ear. "Here, let her go, Mrs. Corbin."

Rubén insisted Morgan come and sit on the bench. He ripped the trousers above the knee, revealing a bloody gash, and sent Millie into the cabin for a clean rag. She handed it to Rubén, and he tied it around the wound.

"It is deep but only a flesh wound. This will do for now," Rubén said. "I will clean and bandage it properly later."

Esther got to her feet, still hanging on to

Mary. "Oh, Morgan. I'm so sorry!"

"It does not even bleed that much. It is nothing." Rubén adjusted the rag a little tighter.

"It still hurts," Morgan said.

"How can you joke about this?" Esther asked. "You could have been killed."

"Here. Let Mary go." He opened his arms and Mary ran to him. "Rubén, can you take Mrs. Corbin inside and tend to her? I'll look after the children."

"Are you all right, Ma?" Richard asked.

She wiped her face with shaking hands, smearing blood and tears together. "Yes, I'm fine. Millie, help Mr. Braddock with the children." She kissed Mary on the top of her head. "Are you okay, sweetie?"

"I'm okay, Mama."

Esther went inside with Rubén, managing to reach a kitchen chair before her legs gave way.

Rubén rummaged through the open trunk and pulled out a light shawl which he draped over her shoulders. "You are shivering, *mi amiga*." He inspected the cut on her cheek.

The sadness in his eyes touched her, and she tried to smile but the fear was still within her. He filled a bowl with water, brought soap and a wet cloth. "This will sting a bit, but it must be done." He tenderly cleaned the wounds on her face. "Morgan should have killed him."

She wished she had killed him, when he was running from her house in the dark last night.

"There was no harm done."

"You cannot see your face."

She smiled at that.

"And there is this —" He lifted the shawl and pointed to her ripped dress.

"Oh, yes, definitely harmed."

Rubén smiled when she laughed.

"I can take care of it. Here, hold this against your face." He put her hand over the wet cloth pressed to her cheek, then took a wooden box out of the cupboard and removed a needle and thread. "Take this dress off and get into your bed. You need to rest, and I will sew."

"Oh, Rubén, no! I couldn't let you —"

"Please, do not be alarmed. I am going to sew your dress, not your face!"

He went again to the cupboard. This time he returned with a bottle and two glasses. "This will help you relax. Drink up and then get into bed."

"Thank you."

They downed the brandy, and he turned his back while she took off the dress and laid it at the end of the bed. She slipped in under the quilt, pulling it up to her neck. Rubén brought her a refilled glass when he came to get the dress and patted her head as if she were a child.

"Enjoy your siesta, *mi amiga.*"

She drank. Her face ached and she savored the softness of the pillow when she lay her head upon it. It smelled like Morgan.

Her last thought before she drifted off —
He sleeps in my bed.

CHAPTER SIXTEEN

A pleasant glow lingered although details of her dream disappeared as soon as Esther opened her eyes. She stretched, slowly becoming aware of darkness in the cabin. She turned onto her other side, ready to sink back into sleep, ready to leave awakened thoughts to some other time. Her awareness felt a quiet presence, someone standing nearby, and then a gentle touch on her shoulder.

"Oh!" She pulled the quilt back up to her neck.

"Didn't mean to scare you. Rubén said to wake you up after a few hours." Morgan stood at the edge of the bed, looking down at her. "How are you feeling?"

A candle burned on the kitchen table. Enough light to show her damaged face according to the concern in his eyes.

"Where are the children?" She touched the spots on her face that throbbed now that she was fully awake.

"Rubén took them home."

She sat up. "He shouldn't go into town alone!"

"He said Jacob wouldn't let anybody shoot him in front of the children. Besides it would've been dark by the time he got there. They won't notice him."

"I should get back. Could I . . . could I have my clothes, please?"

He handed her the mended dress that Rubén had left draped across the foot of the bed and went outside so she could put it on.

She ran her fingers over the stitching. Rubén had done a better job than she could have. She took the candle over to the dresser across from the bed and stood in front of the mirror. In the flickering light she could see bruises. The cut on her cheek was puffy and red. After inspecting her face, she ran a brush through her hair, pinned it back in place, grateful for the darkness.

She finished the last few buttons of her bodice and opened the door. Morgan stood leaning against a porch post, staring off across the yard.

"You can come back inside, if you'd like."

He followed her in and pulled out a chair for her at the table. "We left some dinner for you."

"I don't feel like eating."

"Maybe something hot to drink?" He picked up the pot that usually held coffee and put a cup in front of her. As he poured, steam rose up carrying the rich aroma of strong, black tea.

"How did you know I liked tea?"

"It was in the cupboard."

"Aren't you having some?"

"No, ma'am. I am not." He poured himself a glass of the brandy that still sat on the table.

She lifted her cup and winced when it touched her swollen lip, and the hot tea stung. She put the cup down and put her hand over her mouth. "Ouch."

Morgan leaned across and poured brandy into her tea. "Don't let Rubén know I let you drink any more of this. It's his private stock."

The candlelight accentuated the hollows beneath his cheekbones and the lines around his eyes. He grunted as he stood up, favoring the wounded leg. Otto could have killed him, or her, or Mary. She was grateful that this man had come into her life, grateful he had shown up in time. Grateful that Rubén kept good brandy in the house.

She drank her tea, fighting the tears threatening to well up. "You don't have to keep watching me. And there's no need to look so sad. It could've been worse."

He emptied the water bucket into the dishpan and rinsed his glass.

"That was the last of the water?" She got up and checked the pail — empty. "Come with me, down to the spring — if your leg doesn't hurt too much?"

"Didn't you hear Rubén? It's nothing."

He took the pail from her and offered his arm.

Down at the spring, the motionless pond reflected a starry sky that shook and wavered when Morgan lowered the pail. He filled it and started back to the house.

"Wait," she said. She stopped at the grave, righted the cross and pulled a weed.

"My youngest daughter. My baby Ida."

"I'm sorry — I didn't realize. It's so small I thought maybe — a dog . . ."

"She'd be almost three now. I wonder sometimes what she'd be like. Would her hair still have curls like Millie's? Maybe it would have gotten darker, like Mary's did."

"You've had a shock today. Maybe you shouldn't be thinking about this."

Unsteady, she reached for his arm. A portal opened in her mind, a door which she always kept locked against certain memories. But suddenly she found herself there, in that morning more than a year ago.

"We were all outside. I was doing laundry, Howard and the boys were in the garden." He kept yelling at them for little things. Missed a weed or stepped on a tomato. Each time, she just scrubbed the clothes harder.

Sweat ran into her eyes. Her clothes were soaked through. "I put Mary and Ida on a quilt. Mary was playing with a doll and Ida tried to grab it. She was just a baby. She didn't want the doll but Mary knocked her over. She was just a heap of howling flour-sack ruffles and thrashing pudgy legs. Then Mary started to cry when she saw me coming 'cause she thought she was getting a spanking."

"Did she?" Morgan asked.

"No, I just handed her to Millie. I picked Ida up and kissed her. She liked it when I kissed down her arm, down to her chubby little fingers. I would pry them open and kiss her palm. She always laughed when I did that."

"You're shaking. Are you cold? We should go inside."

"It was such a hot day. I moved the quilt over there." She pointed to the mesquite tree near the pond. "Before I got back to the washing she screamed. I never heard a scream like that before."

"Please don't talk about this now."

She didn't talk, but that didn't stop the memories stampeding on.

She'd dropped an armful of wet clothes to the ground and run. It had felt like trying to run underwater. Like a nightmare. Slow. Everything became slow, even the snake as it crawled away.

"The snake never rattled. It should have rattled."

Morgan's arm went around her. He tried to move her away from the grave but she didn't let him.

Ida had struggled in her arms, the little hand swelled up. Esther put her mouth to the red circles the fangs had left, tried to suck out the poison but the swelling moved to the crease at Ida's wrist, to her elbow, her shoulder. Then the cries stopped. Ida lay in Esther's arms, her breath whispering through a froth of pink bubbles. Esther had fallen to her knees, holding her baby, rocking back and forth, screaming.

The child limp and heavy in her arms, Esther had laid her across her lap. Ida stared at her with dull, unseeing eyes.

"She died in my arms." She wished she'd felt her soul leaving, felt her going to God. Felt something. She'd heard other people say that. But she felt nothing.

Her other children had gathered around but she could hardly see them, ghostly figures bent over her, wavering through heat and tears. Then Howard's contorted face, shouting, shaking her.

"Howard pulled Ida from my arms and walked away, yelling at me. Blaming me."

Esther put her hands over her eyes, squeezed them shut, but the images kept coming. She fell to her knees by the grave. Morgan got to his knees beside her. He put an arm around her but nothing would stop the memories that had broken free.

"She looked like a little doll in his arms, her legs dangling, her curls bobbing up and down."

"Go ahead, Mrs. Corbin. Cry. Cry it all out."

She fell against him, clung to him. "I should have known, I should have seen it, should have looked before I put her on that quilt."

When her sobs slowed, he helped her to

her feet, turned her away from the grave. She stumbled along beside him.

The day Ida died someone had put her to bed and she'd stayed there for more than a week. Never cried, never mourned. In her mind she was not in the Arizona Territory but curled up in her childhood bed, beneath nine-paned windows framed with starched curtains and lace panels. Coastal fog pressed against the gray glass and waves thumped the shoreline. She was a child again, safe, nothing to do but sleep and dream. Jacob's voice whispered to her from the edges of the shore. She pulled the covers up over her ears. She would awaken now and then to see him trying to make her drink something or changing the sheets or washing her face. She would awaken to him sitting on the edge of her bed, talking. Always talking. He reminded her, over and over again, that she had four other children who needed her. "Come back, Essie. Come back." He'd talked until the booming surf grew quiet and she heard him. "It wasn't your fault."

She leaned against Morgan. Just as on that day when she finally got out of bed, her strength came back into her. The candle they'd left burning on the table inside cast a faint glow through the window and guided them toward the house.

At the door, Morgan asked, "Are you all right?"

"I want to go home. I want to be with my children."

"I'm sorry. I'm sorry you lost your baby like that."

She tried to smile a little, to ease the pain she saw in his eyes. "She'll always live in my heart."

"In your heart. That would be a nice place to live." Morgan leaned down and brushed his lips against her forehead. "I'll go get the horses."

She went inside for her shawl. Rubén's bottle of brandy glinted in the candle's light. She lifted it from the table to her lips. When she heard the horses in the yard she put the bottle back in the cupboard.

They rode through a desert softened by moonlight, past cactus with glistening spines and mesquite and Palo Verde trees fluttering in the breeze. Saddle leather creaked. The horses' hooves thudded along the dusty road. Clouds had rolled in, a roiling heap of darkness piled up against the hills beyond Chasm Creek. Now and then a flash of inner lightning set them aglow. A bolt broke through, seared the sky, chased by deep rumbles. Morgan's horse shied and whinnied, and Esther almost slid sideways off her saddle. She grabbed the pommel.

Morgan leaned close. He looked at her with narrowed eyes. "How much of Rubén's brandy did you drink?"

Just as she thought nothing could be worse than falling off her horse, because she was too inebriated to hang on, she not only hiccoughed but followed it with a loud belch. The little ball of brandy-induced heat that had rested comfortably in her stomach crawled up to her face and, she was sure, turned it as red as a New England barn.

She covered her mouth. From behind her fingers, she mumbled. "Oh, my God, what you must think of me —"

"I think you're drunk. A drunk beautiful woman."

The wind picked up and the first drops of rain plopped onto the road. She urged her mare to a lope then rode faster and faster. Her hair shook loose and streamed behind her. Heavy raindrops cooled her face. Morgan caught up with her, and they raced through town to the house.

Rubén stood up in the darker shadows of the porch as they approached. Esther reined in her horse, sat as straight as she could in the saddle, catching her breath, and waited for Morgan to help her down, but Rubén reached her first. She slid into his arms, and he looked over at Morgan. "She has been into my brandy."

Morgan swung down from his horse. "She was upset."

"Thank you for taking care of the children," Esther said.

"It was no trouble at all. They are all asleep."

"Otto?" Morgan asked.

"In the jail — I sent Richard to check. He seemed to have a few more cuts and bruises than the ones you gave to him."

Esther watched Morgan and Rubén exchange satisfied looks. If Jacob had finished the lesson Morgan started, she was glad of it, too.

Rubén went inside to get Richard, who gave his mother a hug. Then they untied their horses and swung up into the saddles, except Morgan. Rubén looked at him.

"I'll be along in a while," he said.

"Do not linger too long. This storm will worsen."

They rode off and Morgan took her arm. "You don't mind, do you? I want to make sure you're settled."

She let him follow her inside to the parlor where she sank onto the sofa. "There's whiskey in that cupboard. Why don't you pour us each a glass?"

"Why, Mrs. Corbin, I never suspected you enjoyed spirits so much."

"It's Jacob's, not mine!"

Morgan poured the drinks, handed a glass to Esther and sat down beside her. She gulped down the liquor.

His eyebrows went up. "More?"

She nodded. "It'll help me sleep. I'm afraid of storms. Of the lightning."

"And here I thought you weren't afraid of anything."

"I am afraid. Often. I'm not like you and Rubén."

He looked at her for a long moment. "Rubén and I are also afraid. Often."

He returned with her glass, and she took a little sip before setting it on the table, next to the lamp. She turned down the wick, pulled her feet up and stretched out on the sofa.

"I think I'll sleep here tonight." She pulled the quilt from the back of the sofa and arranged it over her lap. "You can go. I'm fine. You'll want to get back before the rain gets worse."

He nodded, but instead of leaving he sat by her legs and took her hand in his. He turned it over and examined her palm, then ran a finger along each of hers. A flash of lightning illuminated his face, revealing a sad half-smile and haunted eyes when they met hers. "After all this time," he whispered. "I didn't believe I could feel this way about anyone."

The words, their emotion, pleased her, but the very pleasure also frightened her. They called for a response, but she could only say his name. She wanted to say she had grown fond of him. But she felt more than fondness, and she dared not put it in words. "You are such a good man."

"There are things about me that you don't know. You wouldn't think much of me —" He took a deep breath and rubbed his temples.

"A headache?"

"It's just the weather, it's nothing."

"Rubén told me what happened."

"Told you what?"

"About New Mexico, about the Indians who were killed. How you came to be in Arizona. All of it."

He turned his face away. "I don't know what you're talking about."

"Please don't turn away. I told you about Ida tonight. I know what it feels like. You think it's your fault. You wish you were dead, but how would your wife and children feel, if you had died as well?"

He buried his face in his hands. "Someday

I'll go to them."

She wanted to comfort him, wanted to hold him in her arms. It was her turn to look away, so he wouldn't see the tears spilling down her cheeks. "It'll be raining hard soon. You should leave."

He raised his head from his hands and looked into her eyes. "Let me hold you a while. Then I'll go."

His arms went around her and he pulled her close. She rested her head on his chest and listened to his heart beating. She brushed his cheekbone gently with the back of her hand. When he made no move to stop her, she traced the line of his jaw, stroked his mustache.

He sat still, his head resting against the sofa, eyes closed. She thought he had fallen asleep, but when she ran a finger gently along his lips, he took her hand and kissed it.

"I shouldn't have let you drink so much." He pressed her hand against his warm cheek, and the side of his mouth twitched, a smile suppressed.

"It's not the whiskey."

He pulled her close, pulled her until her mouth merged with his. She pressed the length of her body against him.

He caressed her arm, upward to her

shoulder, slowly slipped his hand between their bodies. His fingers trailed down the front of her dress. His lips moved down her neck, her shoulder, until he pressed his mouth against her breast. The heat of his breath penetrated her thin clothing. She wanted him to rip through her dress and shift so she could feel his tongue against her skin. Then his mouth was on hers again.

Her breasts were crushed against his chest, and she gasped at the pain from the places Otto had bruised and Rubén's crucifix digging into her skin.

"Stop. Please."

He lifted himself away from her. "Am I hurting you?"

"Yes. Yes, you are." She began to cry. "You're breaking my heart."

He pulled his arm from behind her. He got up and stood looking at the door, his hat in his hand.

"You should wait," she said, wiping the tears away. "Until the storm is over."

He brushed his hair from his face and put his hat on.

"When do you think that will be, Esther?"

The sound of his boots crossing the wooden porch disappeared into the rain that, in a sudden roar, drummed against the roof.

Chapter Seventeen

Danny hit the hard-packed dirt of the round pen and rolled over, cursing the mustang that had thrown him there, and got to his feet. He brushed off, still swearing under his breath, while the horse stomped and snorted at him from the other side of the pen.

Lightning threatened to split the air that hung heavy and damp. Horses, ready for delivery to the fort, circled inside the other corrals, whinnying and shaking their heads. They milled around, stopped to paw the ground and, now and then, nipped or kicked at each other. Squealing when thunder reverberated in the hills.

But Danny's attention was on only one horse. "Get the hell over here, you God-damn piece of —"

"Maybe you should take a break." The old Indian was watching him from across the yard.

Danny muttered a few more curse words, this time under his breath and directed at the wrinkled redskin who thought he was the boss. 'Course, it wasn't any worse than taking orders from Braddock. What did either of them know about breaking horses? Everyone knew you tied them up long enough to strap on a saddle and rode 'em hard until they knew who was boss.

"I'll be back, you piece of shit nag!" He headed to the barn. He'd take a break. If that's what the old Indian wanted, he was happy to oblige. He plumped up a nice pile of hay and spread his blanket over it, then eased himself down with a contented sigh.

No sooner had he started to drift off than he heard a wagon pulling into the yard. He lay still, half asleep, wondering if it was that Mrs. Corbin. She hadn't been out for a while, not since that day when the man from town attacked her.

Danny had wanted to see Millie again but, in a way, he was glad she hadn't been around. She was starting to crowd out thoughts of Braddock.

Hell, that damn Indian being around all the time was the problem. They'd had words more than once, and the old redskin always kept an eye on him, didn't trust him. The stinking Injun might be old, but he was quick and pretty smart.

It should've been simple — kill Braddock and collect the money. Nobody would fault him for killing somebody with a price on his head, a dead-or-alive price. It would be legal and profitable. But Chasm Creek was a very small place, hardly a town, and

Danny had grown up in such a place. Killing a friend of the marshal wasn't smart, bounty or no. Maybe he wouldn't even pay the reward.

And he hadn't counted on Millie, another problem. She smiled at him and talked to him. He wanted to kiss her and she had let him do so more than once. He couldn't sleep at night sometimes, thinking about what else he would like to do to her.

Millie liked Braddock. Her whole damn family seemed to like Braddock and the goddamn Indian. Once he killed them, Millie might be mad enough to not let him kiss her anymore or squeeze her tits as he planned to do, and that was a consideration.

He lay on his back and pulled his Bowie knife out of its sheath. He turned it, catching a shaft of sunlight on the blade.

A scorpion cut across the stall toward his toes, and he threw a handful of dirt at it. Half buried, it wriggled and thrashed its pincers, until it unearthed itself and scurried away.

Voices came from the yard. He had one foot shoved back into its boot when he heard a giggle from outside the stall.

"Millie!" He scrambled over and grabbed her hand, pulling her down into the hay with him. "What're you doing here? Your ma will whip you if she catches you in here with me."

"She's working. She doesn't even know I'm here. I hitched up the buckboard and came out with the children. Want to go for a ride?"

"I can think of better things to do." He pushed her onto her back.

"Hey!"

"You like me, don't you, Millie? I sure do like you."

He rolled on top of her. She giggled and squirmed underneath him, until he started kissing her. He figured she liked it as much as he did. But after too few moments of enjoying the taste of her, she started squirming again, talking into his mouth, pushing him away. He was getting really annoyed until he realized she was pointing behind him, her eyes opened wide, and then something hit him hard, square in the middle of his back.

"Get off my sister!"

He rolled off Millie. "What the —"

Richard held a shovel, ready to swing again.

"What the fuck are you doing? You can't just —"

"You'll get worse, you ever touch my sister again!"

"Son of a bitch." Danny put his hand on his knife as he got up, moving out of the stall, into the barn.

"Danny! Don't hurt my brother!"

He held the knife at arm's length, keeping an eye on the shovel. Millie grabbed for his wrist but he shook her off and she stumbled back, falling against the stall's door. Danny turned back to Richard but a hard shove from behind knocked him down.

Braddock, who'd been sick for days with one of his headaches, stood over him looking about as mad as he ever had. Why did he have to pick today to get better? That little shit Richard had been asking for a good licking for a while now.

Richard tried to whack Danny again with the shovel, but Braddock grabbed his arm and held him back.

"He was messin' around with Millie!"

Millie got up quickly and brushed the hay off her dress, her face turning red and her eyes cast down.

"You better get outside," Braddock said to her, and she broke and ran. Braddock turned back to Danny. "She's a little young for you, don't you think?"

"It ain't your concern."

"She's my sister. It's my concern!" Richard yelled and swung the shovel, but Braddock stopped him again and took it away from him.

"You boys get back to work." He threw the shovel into a corner and walked out.

"You're gonna get yours, you son of a bitch." Danny said it to Braddock's back, low enough to not be heard, but Richard heard him. "What are you looking at? You're gonna get yours, too, you mess with me again."

Richard picked up the shovel and walked out.

James held Mary's hand and motioned her to stay quiet. They pressed themselves against the cool stones of the barn wall until the yelling inside was over. James peeked around the corner, saw Mr. Braddock and then Richard leave. "Okay," he said.

He crouched by the lizard grave, and Mary knelt down beside him. One by one, they lifted the little stones from the dead lizard.

The skin had shrunk back revealing tiny white bones. The black seed of an eyeball had fallen away.

"See?" James said. "It can't get out when you pile stones on."

"Is that what Hildie looks like now?" Mary asked.

James nodded. "And him. That's what he looks like now, too." He felt a sudden nervousness and looked around to make sure nobody was nearby. "Let's cover it back up, quick before anyone sees."

When they were almost finished covering it, James arranged one bony front leg of the lizard so that it protruded from the stones. "There," he said. "Now it looks just like him. You see? Once stones is piled on a dead person, they're done. They can't get out."

Mary nodded. She took the tiny stone laced with gold out of her pocket and placed it on top of the pile. "Here. You can have it back."

James hoped Mary's nightmares would now end.

They both jumped when they heard Millie pleading. Her whining voice carried across the yard. "Why do we have to go back? We just got here. It's not my fault they were fighting."

"You wait here while I get the little ones." Mr. Braddock sounded angry.

They scrambled to their feet and turned quickly when they heard his voice close behind them.

"What are you children up to?"

"Nothin'," James said.

"Well, get in the wagon." They ran past him and climbed into the buckboard next to Millie, and Mr. Braddock handed her the reins. "Don't come out here again without your mother."

"She says she isn't coming out here again 'til Father gets home," Millie said.

Mary looked up, scowling. "Then we ain't never coming! Pa ain't —"

James slapped a hand over her mouth. "Shut up, Mary!"

She shrieked and jabbed an elbow into her brother's side, and he let go. She settled herself back onto the seat with her arms folded across her chest, her lower lip protruding in an angry pout. Millie slapped the reins. The horse shook its head and then pulled forward, and the wagon creaked along toward the road.

Morgan waited until the wagon was out of sight, then set his intentions on the bench near the cabin door. This was his first day out of bed in several, and he felt shaky and more than a little dizzy. The business in the barn was not what he needed or wanted, and now he'd sent Esther's children back to town with every one of them upset.

He made it halfway to the cabin when

219

Richard came up and said, "I'm finished in the barn. What now?"

"Start on the railings." He pointed to the new corral they were building. "Get Danny to help you."

"Danny?" Richard's mouth dropped open.

"You both work here, don't you? Go get him."

Rubén yelled from the porch. "You don't need to take it out on the boy."

Turning toward the house brought a wave of nausea. "Don't you have anything else to do but stand in the shade and make comments nobody wants to hear?"

"I heard the little *señorita* say her mother would not come out again."

His head pounding, Morgan gave up on reaching the bench and headed to the nearest corral. He leaned on the fence for a few moments. When his head stopped spinning he singled out a horse, bridled it and led it out of the enclosure. He headed for the tack shed with Rubén following.

"What happened in town the other night? You never told me."

Morgan could still feel Esther's body pressed against his. He could still smell her skin, taste her lips. The horse acted up and he yanked hard on the bridle. "Ho," he said, startling the horse who was not used to

220

harsh words. He felt badly then and stroked the horse's neck and made soothing sounds.

"Something must have happened," Rubén said. "You came back sick and your temperament has only worsened since."

He threw the blanket on, then the saddle. He lifted the stirrup leathers and reached under the horse for the latigo. "What do you think happened? Nothing. I'm married. She's married."

"And her husband is gone for months."

Morgan looped the latigo and cinched it snug.

"I'm gone from my family. That don't mean anything. Her husband will come back some day, just like I'll go home. Some day."

Rubén touched his shoulder. "If you cinch that saddle any tighter you will cut that poor horse in two."

Morgan leaned against the horse, resting, waiting for another spell of dizziness and nausea to pass. But Rubén's sorrowful, troubled face penetrated the thickening fog in his mind.

"You know you can't go back, don't you?" Rubén's voice was gentle, as was the hand he rested on his friend's shoulder. But the words seemed harsh. "You will never go back."

Morgan's breath tightened in his chest and anger welled up within him. "They're waiting for me."

"Do not talk like this!"

Morgan shook his head. They were waiting for him; he knew that. But his mind clouded and he couldn't clear it and he didn't know how to get back to them.

"You've kept me from them." It had been a fleeting idea, a feeling, but the shocked look on Rubén's face, the way he pulled his hand away and stepped back, told Morgan he had guessed correctly. "You don't want me to go to them." His head began to throb in earnest.

"Perhaps I have been wrong," Rubén said. "Perhaps —"

Morgan swung up into the saddle. "Perhaps? You've always told me they're safe. Have you been wrong about that, too?" He pulled on the reins harder than he needed to. He kicked the horse and rode until Rubén's voice, calling his name, faded beneath the sound of horse's hooves. He slowed. Above him the sun was a flat white disk glowing weakly through a curtain of gauzy clouds. It hung low in a sky so colorless it seemed to merge with the gray horizon he rode toward, no clear border between the shadowless earth and the darkening, stormy sky.

CHAPTER EIGHTEEN

Esther watched from the mining office as the children snuck toward the house. Bent over, walking on their tip-toes, they no doubt thought the few trees and scrubby bushes hid their progress as they disappeared around the far side of the house. She leaned away from the window for a few seconds, then looked again to see them racing up the porch steps and into the house.

New claim forms awaited filing even though the stamp mill no longer ran as many hours a day as before. Companies from back east were buying up the mines, according to Mr. Snapp, some even as far away as England. The new owners weren't mining but speculating, holding the claims until prices went up or they could flimflam someone else into buying them at an inflated price. She took a stack from the desk and returned to the filing cabinets, making sure to stand where she'd spot any action at the house. Sure enough, within a few minutes, they all came out and pulled up chairs around the little table on the porch. Cards and pebbles appeared; they were playing poker.

"Good God." She placed the rest of the papers into a neat pile and slid the roll-top closed.

Outside, the breeze smelled like wet dirt and so full of electricity it made her hair stand on end.

"Here she comes," Millie warned, unaware of how clearly her voice carried across the yard in the humid air. The children huddled around the little table on the porch, trying to block any view of their activities, glancing over their shoulders as she approached.

They scooped up the playing cards and pebbles from the table, shoving them into James' hands.

"I'll get the rest of your money next time." James rushed into the house to hide the evidence.

By the time Esther reached the porch, the girls were sitting on the steps, giggling. James hurried down the stairs to give Esther a big hug. "Hi, Ma!"

Relieved that all her children were home safe, that she didn't have to drag James out of a saloon, and they weren't fighting, she ignored the poker playing, but she couldn't ignore them taking her wagon out to the farm without her permission. And she would have to speak to whoever was running the livery these days to make sure that didn't happen again.

"Did you all enjoy your ride?"

"You knew?" Millie asked, the smile falling from her face.

"Millie, I can see the livery from the mining office."

"Mr. Braddock yelled at Millie so we had to come home," Mary said.

"Shut up, will you?" Millie pinched her sister's arm, making her cry.

"Why did Mr. Braddock yell at you?"

"I don't know! He was in a bad mood."

Mary stopped crying long enough to say, "You was in the barn with Danny. We seen you run out."

"Shut up!" Millie's face turned red. She looked at her mother and then stared at her shoes.

"I should have known. I've told you to stay away from him, Millie."

Millie dared to look her in the eye. "Well, it's our home! It's been almost a week since we was out there. Just 'cause you're never gonna go again is no reason not to let us. Mr. Braddock didn't like it either, when I told him you said that."

"You have no idea what Mr. Braddock likes or does not like. You are a child, and you'd best start remembering it. You are to do what I tell you, and I'm telling you again to stay in town!"

Millie let out a little squeak and folded her arms across her chest.

"I'll put a padlock on the wagon if I have to."

James and Mary stood behind Millie, holding hands, looking at Esther with big eyes. Mary's chin quivered.

"Go inside."

All three opened their mouths as if to speak, but Esther spoke before they could say a word. "I don't want to hear anymore. Get in the house. Now."

She walked across the road to the creek. The northern sky had darkened from gray to almost black. Farther out in the southwest hills, toward the Verde where the canyon opened up, the wind whipped the trees. Canvas flaps that hung over dugout openings next to the mines waved and cracked as, here and there, a miner scurried to haul his retort and other supplies into his cave or shack. By the time she returned to the porch, the wind screamed down the road and turned the creek frothy.

Within seconds dust choked the canyon. Men ran down the wagon road, rushing for shelter in the saloon, bandanas held to their faces. Dry weeds and trash wedged under wagon wheels of rigs abandoned in the street. Horses whinnied in their traces and tried to turn their backs to the red-tinged gale.

Esther needed all her strength to push the door shut once she was in the house. She and the children raced through the rooms, closing windows as gusts buffeted the walls. Sand rattled down the chimney and shot out of the hearth. The door banged in its frame, threatening to pull the hinges and latch right out of the wood. Esther and the children huddled on the sofa and watched the creek turn crimson as it lathered and foamed with each new blast of wind.

The storm abated, but only momentarily before it resumed full force, and they sat in growing darkness as flying dirt blocked the sun.

Slowly the world quieted. The winds diminished then dwindled to an ominous calm. Esther pulled the door open, and she and the children stuck their heads out. Chasm Creek, scarlet with silt, washed over the road as far as the boardwalks and lapped at the edges of her yard. Beyond the hills, the sky remained black.

"It must be raining hard up north," Esther said.

"Will it come this way?" Millie sounded nervous.

A bolt of lightning sliced through the clouds. "I don't know, but it doesn't have to rain right here for the creek to flood. James, why don't you go over to the jail and ask Uncle Jacob if he thinks we need to go to higher ground."

"Yes, ma'am!" James ran off, puffed with pride because his mother trusted him for this mission.

"Stay out of the water!" Esther yelled after him, already too late. James headed straight for the wettest part of the road and his boots splashed the water high as he ran.

Esther and the girls righted the chairs and small table on the porch. She thought about the extra cleaning the house would need when thunder of a different kind approached — horses at the gallop. Soldiers tore by, mud flying from hooves, and came to a stop down the street. They milled around near the jail, ten soldiers and two officers, soon surrounded by curious miners venturing out of the saloon. Jacob, shadowed by James, came out of the jail. As he talked with them, his expression turned serious. He glanced up the street toward the house and leaned down to say something to the boy.

228

"Mama, why is the cavalry in town? What's wrong?" Millie asked.

"I don't know."

James headed back to them, legs pumping. He shouted from the road. "Indians!"

The two officers entered the jail with Jacob, leaving the soldiers to stand around in the wet road by their muddy horses and answer questions from the miners.

Esther gathered her children around her on the porch, fighting the feeling of panic the word had caused. Most of the Indians were settled on reservations by the time she arrived in the Territory, and she'd never encountered any wild ones, only Rubén and the few Apaches that lurked around Fort McDowell, looking tired and hungry and not dangerous. But she'd heard stories from people who had been there during the bad times and remembering those gruesome stories fanned her fear.

Jacob left the jail and headed to the house, trying to hurry as the mud sucked his boots with each step. He stopped at the bottom of the stairs. "Seems some renegades are on the warpath. Stole some horses from the fort, right out from under their noses. Happened last night — they didn't hear a thing."

"No one was hurt?"

"Just their pride. They've got several

scouts out looking around. Major Whitehall, he says they're going to report back here.

"They don't want to leave the town unprotected. Just in case, Essie. It ain't nothin' to be worried about."

"Richard's out at the ranch."

"I know. One of the scouting parties went out that way. They'll be warned."

She wanted to ride out there and get her son, but Morgan and Rubén would be with him. She convinced herself he would be all right as she counted off household weapons in her mind: the scattergun, the pistol Morgan had given her, a couple of older pistols.

CHAPTER NINETEEN

Danny kept himself busy the rest of the day, especially after Braddock returned on a lathered up horse, looking as angry as when he left. Then, not long after, soldiers rode right into the yard. Braddock spoke with them, and Danny noticed Richard had stopped working and was watching and waiting too.

The soldiers all rode off at a fast lope, and Braddock watched them ride away, standing there like Danny and Richard weren't waiting to hear what was going on. Danny let his hammer drop to the ground, pulled off his work gloves.

"What do you think you're doin'?" Richard asked. "We ain't done with this corral yet."

"We're done, asswipe. Look at Braddock's face. Whatever those soldiers had to say, we ain't gonna be spendin' time building no fence today."

Braddock walked over to them. "Some horses were stolen from the fort. They think it was renegade Indians."

"Why would they do that?" Richard asked.

"They wouldn't."

"You don't think it was Indians?" Danny asked.

"Whoever did steal those horses may come after ours next. Could be comancheros, could be anyone." All the while he was talking, he was getting a big bay they knew was fast out of the corral. "Danny, I want you to go meet up with Roy and Al. They should be on their way back with the horses. Head north of the creek and you should run into them."

"Where are you going?" Richard asked.

"Into town to make sure your mother and the children are safe."

"I'm goin' with you." Richard put his saw on the pile of boards and pulled off his work gloves.

Braddock looked around. "Where's Rubén?"

"I ain't seen him." But he had seen the old Indian ride off after having words with Braddock that morning. He hoped he'd fallen off his horse and broke his neck, but he kept that to himself.

"He said he was goin' fishing," Richard said.

"He shouldn't be out there by himself. I better go get him."

"What about Ma?"

"I have to find Rubén. God only knows what'll happen if the soldiers find him first."

"I'll ride into town, then, to check on Ma."

Braddock put his hand on Richard's shoulder.

"Wait 'til I get Rubén, son, and we'll both go into town. I won't be gone long if he's at the creek. I really need you to keep an eye on things here. Get your Henry and keep it handy."

"Yes, sir, Mr. Braddock."

Danny waited until Braddock was out of earshot, then leaned close to Richard. "Yes, sir, Mr. Braddock!" He made his voice a sneering imitation of Richard's.

"Shut up!"

"Why do you let him call you son? You got a father, ain't you?"

"He's being nice. Ain't nothin' wrong with that."

"He don't ever call me son."

"Yeah, wonder why."

"Danny! We don't have all day," Braddock yelled, leading his horse toward the tack shed.

Danny rode toward the creek, watching Morgan's dust far ahead of him, amazed that such a stroke of good luck had come his way. He wasn't used to such occurrences. Usually his luck was always bad. Before a bend in the trail he came to the place the children called "the boulders." He rode behind the tall jumble of rocks and tied his horse to a mesquite tree.

At the top of the hill a flat area opened up, surrounded by more large rocks. Perfect view of the trail, perfect rocks to hide behind. Again he marveled at his luck. From this vantage point he would hear anybody coming from the creek before they came into sight around that bend.

He sat with his back against rocks and checked the load in his Winchester. Then he fell to imagining how it would all go. He'd get both of them, of course, when they came riding back from the creek, and the wild Indians would get the blame. So perfect.

He couldn't keep the smile from stretching across his face. Nothing to do now but wait.

He pulled the wanted poster out of his shirt pocket, unfolded it, and laid it on the ground. Holding the point of his knife between thumb and forefinger, he flipped it through the air. The blade sliced through the paper and stuck in the sand. No use hanging on to it; wasn't likely he could've gotten the marshal to pay it anyway. This way, he can kill them and still keep Millie. She might even need some comforting, since she liked them both so fucking much. Again and again he flipped the knife until he heard a horse coming down the trail.

He grabbed the rifle and positioned himself behind the rocks. Calm down, calm down, calm down. For some reason, now that his plan was about to be realized, his hands shook. He feared his aim would be off.

Braddock rode into sight. Where's the Indian? Danny's heart slammed against his chest — where's the Goddamn Injun? Braddock approached, right in front of him now — he couldn't hear any other horse. Now or never. Stop thinking. He squeezed the trigger.

Too nervous, too soon. Damn! At least he hadn't missed completely. Braddock leaned forward, his right arm hanging limp, his hand bloodied, unable to pull his gun, unable to control his horse. Hurry, hurry. He cocked the rifle, aimed, fired again. This time Braddock pitched over the horse's withers and landed in the dirt with a satisfying thud. The horse ran off into the hills.

Pure joy replaced the nervous feeling in Danny's gut. He jumped to his feet and danced around in a circle, waving the rifle in the air, laughing. It had been so easy.

He climbed down and stood over Braddock, lying face down and motionless beside the trail. He grabbed a shoulder and pulled him over. Dark red seeped from a hole in Braddock's side; the bottom of his shirt was blood soaked but he was not dead. The shirt rose and fell with each wheezing breath. He raised his rifle and took aim to finish him off, then remembered he didn't know where the old Indian was. "Guess we'll do this the old-fashioned way." He grinned as he kicked Braddock, harder for each grunt of pain he heard.

Then he heard riders fast approaching. Soldiers. He dragged Braddock over to the side of the trail and with one more hard kick pushed him over the edge of the steep slope. He ran across the trail and hid behind a rock in time to see the mounted soldiers charge past, headed toward the creek at full speed.

Had they heard the rifle shots? Danny's anxiety returned. His stomach hurt so bad he was forced to pull his pants down quickly and take a shit right there. His hands shook as he pulled them up and buttoned them. By then the dust had cleared.

He walked across the trail and looked down at Braddock. Was the bastard dead? He raised his rifle and took aim, but the thought of the soldiers stopped him again. They'd hear the shot. Come back and find no Indians, just him standing there with his rifle.

No reason not to leave Braddock there and let animals do the rest. As he untied his horse, he wondered what it would be like to lie helpless while buzzards picked at your eyes or javelinas and coyotes chewed your legs off. The thought brought a happy smile.

He nudged his horse to a jog and rode into the cactus.

Close to the farm, he ran into Roy and Al a short distance before the wagon road, but they had no horses. "Damn Indians never even showed up," Roy said. "No sign of 'em. We figgered we better head back and check with Rubén."

Danny told them about the renegades and

the soldiers out on scouts.

"I thought I heard shots a while ago. We better hurry," Al said.

"Storm coming." Roy pointed toward town. The black sky hung over swirling red dust. Thunder rumbled.

When they got to the farm, there was no time to unsaddle their horses. Richard had seen them coming and held the barn doors open for them, and they rushed inside, pulling the heavy wooden doors shut against the stinging sand.

"Thank you, Richard," Danny said.

"Well, ain't that something?" Roy said. "Danny — in a happy mood."

"What's tickling your fancy so?" Al asked.

"Oh, nothin' like a good storm. Clears things out. You can start fresh."

"Did you see Mr. Braddock or Rubén out there?" Richard asked.

"I wasn't in that direction," Danny said. "I got sent to find these two, remember?"

"We didn't see nobody," Roy said.

"I need to go to town to check on my Ma."

"You ain't going nowhere right now," Roy said. "This storm has to pass first."

They sat in the darkened barn with the nervous horses and listened to the wind banging the doors. Dirt sifted down from the shake roof and the horses shied at each booming roll of thunder. They waited for rain that never came, just wind and dirt. By the time it passed, Roy and Al were busily checking their weapons and counting their rounds of ammunition, having convinced themselves that at any minute they would be under siege from hostiles. It was all they'd talked about the whole time. And Danny encouraged it.

"Can't never trust an Indian. Not even that Rubén," he said. He waited for Richard to give him an argument but he didn't say a word. Probably too worried about his mother and his favorite person, Mr. Braddock, sir. Danny almost laughed out loud.

Full sunlight streaked in through the cracks in the doors before Roy and Al allowed the boys to pull them open. Weeds and sticks and shingles lay scattered around the yard, and a single horse drank from the water barrel near the corral.

"That's the horse Mr. Braddock was riding." Richard ran to the house, called out, checked the privy and the ramada.

Roy ran a finger through sticky blood on the horse's neck. "This horse was grazed by a bullet."

"He must've run into them renegades he was so sure wasn't out there," Danny said.

Richard snatched the reins from Roy and

jumped up into the saddle but Roy grabbed his shirt with one hand and the bridle with the other. "Where do you think you're going?"

"To find Mr. Braddock."

"We can't let you go — you're just a boy," Roy said.

Al's eyes got big. "You ain't saying we oughta go?"

"Somebody's gotta," said Roy. "What if he ain't dead?"

"There's wild injuns out there!"

"That's right," Danny chimed in. "I think we oughta wait 'til the soldiers come through again. Let them handle it."

"And look at that sky." Al waved toward blackness coming at them from the northern hills. "It's gonna be pourin' buckets any minute."

Richard tried again to wriggle loose from Roy.

"God damn it," Al said. "I'll get our horses — you check those weapons again."

Roy nodded.

"I'm goin', too," Richard said.

"No, you ain't." Roy shook his head. "You stay here and tend to this horse." He looked at Danny, as if he expected him to offer to help search for Braddock. Finally, Roy said, "You and Danny stay here."

"Mr. Braddock went to get Rubén down by the fishin' creek," Richard said, and Roy and Al took off at a lope.

"Ha, they ain't gonna find him," Danny said.

"They'll find him." Richard loosened the latigo. "Why wouldn't they?"

"If injuns got him, they'll cut him open and pull out his intestines and stretch 'em out for the coyotes to eat. Or maybe they'll cut off his eyelids and bury him out in the desert up to his neck. Or maybe they'll stake him out in some wash and let the javelinas have him. Even if Roy and Al find him, there won't be enough to bring back and bury."

"You shut up, Danny!"

Danny walked off to the barn, still laughing.

CHAPTER TWENTY

Esther sat in the window, looking down Chasm Creek's deserted street, thinking of the time a few years ago, not long after Jacob had dug his first mine, when he had taken her to see his progress. It was toward evening and he had to light a lantern for them to see their way deep into the hillside. Then, to be funny, without warning, he blew the flame out. She thought of that sudden blackness and the fear that had clutched her. This evening, with the town crouched on the banks of the river, she remembered that fear. Soon night would descend upon them, maybe not as sudden as Jacob blowing out a candle, but once it fell there would not even be shadows on this stormy night to warn them of what might be lurking in the darkness.

She turned away from the window and tried to reassure herself by recounting all the firearms and ammunition spread over the dining table. She clutched the extra rifle Jacob had brought.

The deserted street lay hushed but for a random hog grunt or occasional bleat from a goat. The miners huddled in the saloon, no music or laughter or even talking. Esther knew that some of them had memories of the Apaches running wild. The thought of even a few renegades on the loose sent even the most swaggering miner running for fellowship. The town squatted in mute watchfulness, soldiers posted at either end of the canyon.

Millie sat in the doorway between the parlor and the children's bedroom, cradling the shotgun, her eyes darting to each window. James and Mary, relegated to the sofa, teased each other, poking and pushing, whispering with an occasional giggle. James pointed his forefinger at Mary and imitated the sound of a gunshot.

"You're dead!"

Millie jumped out of her chair, and Esther spun around, shushing them as loudly as she dared.

"No, I'm not!" Mary slapped James' hand.

"You're dead, I killed you!"

They wrestled on the sofa until Esther yanked them apart. She smacked each of them on the leg which stunned them into silence. They stared at their mother with wide, frightened eyes, holding their arms over their faces.

"Be quiet!" Esther spoke through clenched teeth.

The sound of a single horse pounding into town came through the open window and Esther ran to look, the children pressed behind her. A rider leaped off his lathered mount at the jail and hammered on the door until Jacob opened it. Light flooded through the doorway as Jacob put his arm around the rider and ushered him into the jail. Richard.

"I'll be right back — don't move." She ran out to the street.

"Mamma, don't leave us!" Millie cried.

"I'll be at the jail. I can hear you if you call me."

"And I don't know where Rubén is —" Richard was saying as she pulled the jail's door open. The words came hard as he struggled to catch his breath from his fast ride into town. Jacob was strapping on his sidearm and two officers moved out of her way as she pushed through layers of cigar smoke to get to her son.

"What's that on your shirt? Is that blood?" Her legs suddenly felt weak.

"I'm fine — it ain't my blood, it's Mr. Braddock's."

"Morgan?" She let go of Richard and grabbed the edge of the desk.

Otto let out a loud laugh. "Somethin' happen to your boyfriend?"

"Shut up!" Jacob banged the strap iron with a rifle butt, and Otto lay back down on the cot, muttering.

One of the officers pulled over a chair. "Mrs. Corbin, please, have a seat."

"I can't — I must get back — I left the children in the house —" She sank into the chair.

"I'm J.C. Dugan, a friend of Morgan's."

"Captain Dugan? The post surgeon?"

"Yes, ma'am." He put on his hat and picked up his rifle. "What happened, son?"

243

"His horse come back without him after the storm. Roy and Al, they found him. I was gonna go to the fort, for you," Richard said. "But when I saw all the soldiers in town I came here to check with Uncle Jacob."

"Found him? His horse threw him?"

"No, sir. He's been shot."

Captain Dugan opened the door and called out to an enlisted man to bring his horse.

"Rubén sent you for the doctor?" Esther realized Morgan must be badly hurt if Rubén couldn't manage on his own.

"No! We don't know where Rubén is. That's where Mr. Braddock went — to get him after the soldiers come through." He started for the door, following Captain Dugan.

Esther grabbed his arm. "No! You're staying with me!"

"Ma, I'm going back to the farm."

"Go hitch up the wagon, then. We're all going."

"Essie, you can't be out on your own —"

"Ma'am," the officer behind her said. "I can order some soldiers to accompany you to your farm."

"Essie, this is Major Whitehall. He's the commanding officer at the fort."

"Thank you, Major. Yes, I think we'd like to go home."

Quickly the children and the guns were loaded into the buckboard, and Jacob and Captain Dugan rode up with six soldiers.

"Please go on ahead, Captain." Esther checked that the children were settled. She gathered the ribbons. "Don't wait for us. Jacob can show you the way."

"Essie —" Jacob started to protest.

"There are no Indians between here and the ranch. Richard never would've gotten through if there were. We've got these soldiers to protect us. Go!"

Captain Dugan, Jacob, and Richard took off down the wagon road. Esther prayed that what she had said was true; the men entrusted to guard her and her children looked hardly older than Richard. With no moon it was a long, dark ride to the ranch in the old wagon, and she was afraid of what she would find when she got there.

When they arrived, she rushed across the yard into the cabin. The sickly sweet smell of blood filled the air. When the children pushed in behind her, she held out her arms to stop them.

"Millie, please take the children upstairs. I want you all to get into bed and stay there."

"Yes, Mama."

Esther pushed her way past the men standing around near the bed.

"Maybe you should go up with the children," Jacob said.

"I'd like her to stay." Captain Dugan spoke from a chair next to the bed.

Morgan lay on his side, a sheet pulled up to his waist. The captain motioned for her to sit down. "I think he'll feel better with you here."

"I fell off my horse." Morgan's blood-matted mustache muffled his words. "Cut my lip."

She tried to smile. "It looks like you did more than cut your lip."

"He's a little groggy. Morphine." Captain Dugan placed a square of gauze over one of the wounds. "Hold this. Press on it. Lightly."

"Tell her how you got here so quick, J.C.," Morgan said.

"Well, I have this really fast horse." The Captain rummaged in his medical bag. "A pretty gray dun mare. Best trained horse in the territory."

Esther had always enjoyed the way Morgan smiled, how his eyes crinkled and the side of his mouth turned up. But when Captain Dugan smiled, his eyes lit up and his smile spread across his whole face. He looked almost boyish. His affection for Morgan was obvious.

"What's this?" Captain Dugan held the sheet aside, indicating a neat bandage above Morgan's knee.

"Gunshot," Jacob offered. "Happened a few days ago. The man who's in my jail waiting for the Yuma prison wagon is who done it."

The captain snipped the bandage off the stitched, healing wound. "I thought you didn't have a doctor in Chasm Creek."

"We don't," Esther said. "Rubén tended that wound."

"Rubén?"

"A friend of Morgan's. Our friend."

Captain Dugan removed a leather case from his medical bag. It held his surgical instruments. "Another slug hit that hand." He looked at Esther with kind eyes. "I'll do my best to save it."

"I know you army doctors." Morgan's voice faded to a whisper. "First thing you want to do is amputate."

Esther felt her stomach lurch.

"Lay still, Morgan. And be quiet. I told you I wouldn't do that." Captain Dugan smiled at Esther, not the smile he'd had over the horse Morgan gave him, but the kind doctors used to try to reassure worried people. "His breathing's clear so far. He was pretty lucky although there was a lot of blood loss. But this," he pointed to dark bruises. "These broken ribs — with so many bone fragments there's always a danger one may yet puncture a lung." He rinsed his hands in a bowl of water on the night table. The water turned pink. "It looks like I'll have to resect at least two ribs; they're too shattered."

"What does that mean?"

"Surgically remove them. To keep the broken edges from perforating any vital organs or blood vessels."

"Are you all right, Esther?" Jacob asked.

She was trying to take a breath; she pressed a shaking hand to her chest. "It's hard to believe a bullet can cause so much damage." Her voice shook.

"It didn't. It must have been the fall down that cliff. Or he was kicked maybe."

"Would Indians do such a thing?" She looked from one man to the next. She could tell by their faces that they believed it to be so — Indians could do this, and worse. "Indians wear moccasins. How could they kick him that hard?"

"I seen Indians with boots on," Danny offered. "Hell, Rubén wears boots."

"I'll be back in a minute." The captain

wrapped his instruments in a cloth. "I've got water boiling outside. I'm going to clean these."

Morgan said, "Millie was — she said you —"

"Don't talk now. Rest." Esther pushed damp hair back from his face. "Jacob, hand me that rag." She wet it in the bowl of water on the nightstand and began to wash the blood from his mustache and the side of his face.

He pushed her hand away. "They won't look for him."

"Look for who?"

Jacob answered. "He wants us to go find Rubén. He thinks something happened to him."

"I left him at the creek." Morgan closed his eyes until a spasm of pain eased. "He would've heard the shots, would've come —"

"He's right." Esther looked at Jacob. "Something must have stopped him."

Captain Dugan returned with a pail of hot water and his instruments. He put everything down by the bed, then leaned close to his friend. "Don't you quit on me, Morgan. I'm not going to have you be the first man I lose since I got to the Territory. You stay with me." He put a hand on his friend's forehead. "Look at me!"

Morgan opened his eyes.

"We're going to fix you up. You have to hang on. Do you hear me?"

The captain dug around in his medical bag and took out two tin flasks.

"Didn't anybody go to look for Rubén?" Esther asked. The men avoided her eyes.

"I wanted to but Roy and Al wouldn't let me," Richard said.

"You can't expect us to risk our lives for an Indian," Jacob muttered.

"Is that what you all think?" Esther glared at the men. "We're talking about Rubén!"

Captain Dugan glanced up from his preparations. "Rubén's a renegade?"

"He's our friend," Esther said.

"How do we know he ain't turned?" Roy asked.

The captain sprinkled some chloroform from one of the flasks onto a square of cloth. "Mrs. Corbin? Would you hold this over his mouth and nose for me?"

"I'll go get him myself," Morgan whispered. "In the morning."

"Shush. He'll be back in the morning. Don't worry about Rubén now." She held the cloth, stroked his forehead and watched his eyes close. "It's going to be all right."

"Mrs. Corbin? Take that away now. We

want him to wake up when we're through."

The men all went outside when Dr. Dugan picked up the scalpel. Esther turned away at the first incision. Captain Dugan worked efficiently, removing bone fragments, then sutured the deep gashes and bullet wounds. He rinsed the entire area with carbolic acid from the other flask, then bound everything tightly with clean bandages. "Hold that cloth again for a moment, please, ma'am." Then he moved over to Esther's side and repeated the process on Morgan's hand. While he was fashioning a splint, he asked, "Did your husband leave behind any of his shaving gear?"

"I believe there's a razor in the trunk."

"Could you shave off his mustache, then? And I'll sew up that lip while we're at it."

When they were finished, Captain Dugan washed the blood from his hands and arms. "You're a good nurse. And a good barber."

She didn't feel like a good nurse. She felt sick, and she wished Rubén would come home.

The doctor cleaned his instruments and packed them all into his bag. She followed him out into the dooryard. Someone had started a fire out at Rubén's camp in the ramada and for a moment her heart leaped. But he was not among them. Only Jacob and Richard and the hired hands. The soldiers were waiting by the corral. The doctor's horse was tied to the porch railing, and he secured his medical bag behind the cantle.

"You're not leaving, are you?"

"I have to get back. I've been gone too long already. Major Whitehall is not a patient man." But he came to stand with her near the door and rolled a cigarette. He raised it to his lips with a trembling hand.

"Is Morgan going to be all right?"

"I don't know, Mrs. Corbin." He exhaled smoke. "I hope so."

"You seem to know a lot about me, Captain. My name, that I'm married, that my husband is away."

She noticed again how kind his eyes were, thought again how she could understand why Morgan would be friends with such a man. He seemed to have the same compassionate heart as Rubén, the same strength and loyalty. "Morgan mentioned you. Maybe once or twice."

"You've been friends for a long time?"

"We're from the same town. During the war, he sort of adopted me as a younger brother, watched out for me." He drew on his cigarette again.

"Do you know his wife?"

The captain looked surprised. "He's married?"

Millie called from the top of the stairs. "Mama. Mr. Braddock is awake."

Captain Dugan tossed his cigarette into the yard, pulled a small bottle and a syringe from his bag and hurried into the house. "Morphine." He injected the medicine and Morgan eased back into sleep.

Esther felt a rising panic. "What if he wakes again?"

"Keep him still. I left a bottle of laudanum on the table, but I don't think he'll awaken before morning. I'll be back as soon as I can get away again."

"Maybe we should take him into town, or to your hospital at the fort."

"Don't move him. Those wounds could open up and he'd bleed to death. Keep him quiet. If he wakes up, put a few teaspoons of the laudanum in some water and get him to drink. However much he needs. I'll be back."

"When?"

"I hope in the morning but I don't really know, ma'am."

The captain and the soldiers rode off toward town and, even though Jacob and the other men came to the house and checked their weapons and put spare rounds

253

near at hand, she felt alone. And very afraid.

"Essie, why don't you turn in," Jacob said. "You look tired. Go on up in the loft with the children."

Instead she gathered some quilts and made a pallet for herself on the floor by the bed, as she knew Rubén would if he were there.

CHAPTER TWENTY-ONE

Sunrise pushed back the darkness, revealing the thrown-together greythorn fence that imprisoned Rubén and maybe fifty men, women and children. Most seemed to be sleeping, huddled together under blankets while soldiers patrolled on foot outside the perimeter of their make-shift stockade. Rubén sat by himself while daybreak slowly illuminated his plight. Tired from a sleepless night, still damp from the rains that had soaked him during the night, hungry. He longed for the tender fish fillet left sizzling in his frying pan by the fishing creek.

During the long night he had revisited, again and again, his last conversation with Morgan, when his friend had come looking for him. He had been crouched by the stream, using a flat rock as a table on which to clean a small fish, when Morgan had ridden up. Rubén had kept his eyes on the fish.

"What do you want?"

"You need to come back with me. Now."

He knew Morgan did not even remember they had argued. Did not remember the crazy things he had said or the crazy things he'd threatened to do. Sometimes Rubén envied that distorted memory, but his friend paid a high price to keep the horrible memories at bay. Rubén washed off his knife in the creek and dried it on his shirt before he stood and turned toward his friend. "Not until we have said words that need to be said."

Morgan looked surprised at the impatience in Rubén's voice. "I didn't come out here to have words. I came to tell you the army is out looking for renegades."

"What happened?"

"They say horses were stolen from the fort. That it was Indians."

"They are quick to blame the Apache. Now everybody will be angry and nervous. Anything could happen."

"Exactly why you better come on back to the ranch."

"I have other plans for tonight. I'm going to the haunted hill."

Morgan had looked impatient. "Wait until it's safer."

"No." He had felt drawn to the ruins from the moment he had looked up at the overcast sky during his prayers earlier in the day and saw a rainbow encircling a milky sun. "Nobody will bother me. I am an old man and I have no stolen horses." He pulled his small frying pan out of his saddlebag. "I shall return in the morning."

"I don't feel good about this."

"You do not need to feel good about it. Go home."

He placed the fish in the pan and rinsed his hands in the creek. "Go!" He swatted at the air as if shooing a fly.

His friend made no move to go. Ignoring Morgan, he bent to gather kindling for a cookfire. "What do you wait for? Are you sick again?"

"No."

"Well, what is it then? Can you not see I am busy?"

It occurred to him now, too late, that if the conversation had gone differently, if he had agreed to go back to the farm, he would not be shivering in the mud, a prisoner. He would not have spent the previous night regretting his harsh words and worrying about those rifle shots ringing out so soon after Morgan had ridden away.

When he heard them, he'd leapt on his

horse and galloped up the trail, rifle in hand, right into the soldiers.

They made him dismount. They took his weapons. He tried to explain in his best English that he was not a renegade Apache. "I am looking for my friend Morgan Braddock! Have you seen him?"

Sudden pain answered him. From where he lay on the ground, holding his throbbing and bleeding head, a soldier stood over him, grinning and wiping off the stock of his rifle with his hand. They hauled him to his feet, threw him on his horse and tied his wrists together . . .

He'd ridden in a fog of pain and dizziness until long after dark when, in a hard rain, they had tossed him into this stockade.

The sun grew stronger, warming and drying the ground. People stirred, prisoners and soldiers. Voices carried in the early morning stillness, children cried and mothers made soothing sounds. Rubén sat in the mud, wrapped in his serape. His head ached; his stomach growled; he worried about Morgan.

Around him, light moved down the harsh mountainsides that surrounded them, illuminated the cactus and scrubby trees. Groups of Indians watched the soldiers walk around and around the outside of the fence, rifles resting on their shoulders. Other enlisted men, beyond the barbed branches, played cards and smoked. Small campfires burned near them, but no such comfort existed inside the stockade. Instead, the fragrance of coffee boiling and bacon frying tortured them.

From behind him, a familiar voice spoke in Spanish. "Good morning, Grandfather."

Rubén twisted around. "Eleven!"

The Apache sat down beside him.

"What have you done, to cause so much trouble for so many?" Rubén asked.

"We did nothing! The stupid white-eyes must have lost their horses. Why would we steal the same horses we sold to you?"

The sun began to warm Rubén's bones, and he pulled off his serape and spread it on the ground to dry. "Perhaps you wished to increase your business. If you stole their horses, they would need to buy more."

Eleven's angry face broke into a wide smile. "A good idea. I wish we thought of it. At least we would hang for a reason."

"They intend to hang us?"

Eleven pointed outside the thorny branches to where an officer tended one of three injured soldiers. The officer gently pulled on a bandage. The soldier groaned in pain as the cloth stuck to his wound. Another soldier turned to his side and pulled his legs up, moaning, arms wrapped around his abdomen.

"My men shot those soldiers." Eleven got up and brushed the mud from his high moccasins. "We were on our way to meet your men, to deliver the horses, when they came after us. They shot at us and we shot back."

Rubén wondered what it would be like to hang. When he at times contemplated the end of his long life, that was not how he pictured it.

"At least we will die quickly," Eleven continued. "Better than drinking or starving to death on a reservation, or dying of a white man's disease."

The officer, accompanied by two soldiers with rifles at the ready, entered the enclosure and knelt beside one of several injured Indians. He opened his medicine satchel. Rubén guessed he must be Captain Dugan from the fort, the post surgeon, Morgan's friend.

A white-haired Indian sitting near the wounded Indians began to chant. The haunting sound sent chills through Rubén. "Who is that?" he asked Eleven.

"Who do you mean?"

"That man. He seems to fancy himself

some kind of medicine man, singing like that." Rubén snorted. "Nothing will save those men except the doctor and his medicine."

"Warriors," Eleven said, "do not believe in the white man's ways."

"They do not have to believe in a doctor for him to heal them. He does not use foolish magic." Rubén wished the old man would stop singing. It was giving him a headache.

"You judge harshly."

"I have read books on science and medicine. I have seen doctors and their medicine heal people. I do not rely on superstition."

The chanting continued until Rubén felt his head would explode. "When will that man be quiet!?"

The old man stopped his song and twisted slowly to meet Rubén's gaze. Rubén wanted to look away but could not. He knew those eyes. Within them he saw the faces of his ancestors — the ancestors whose tears had washed over him when he was in his spirit vision. He saw light ebb and flow around the old man, an aura the colors of a rainbow.

The old man spoke to him. He heard every word clearly as though all other sound had stopped. "Your past is still within you, more than you know. You would be wise, old man, to honor your ancestors."

Rubén's hand went to his chest but the rawhide string and crucifix were not there.

Pale light at the window grew brighter. Esther had not slept but lay awake on her bed of quilts on the floor by Morgan's bed. The men had patrolled outside all night, and a few minutes ago she'd heard Jacob near the window telling Roy that he was going back to town. Morgan stirred and she got to her knees beside the bed.

He was awake. He shifted, as if trying to get up.

"Lie still."

At the sound of her voice, he forced the pain from his expression. "What're you doing down there on the floor?"

"Where else would I be?" She went to the table and poured a spoonful of laudanum into a cup of water. She cradled his head and held the cup to his lips. "Here, drink this."

He swallowed. "What did you do?" he asked.

She put the cup down. "What?"

He touched his swollen lip, ran his finger over the catgut stitches and the bare skin where his mustache had been. "Did you do this? Delilah."

261

If he could make jokes, surely he'd be all right. "Now isn't exactly the time to rob you of your strength."

She held the cup again and he drank. After she'd helped him settle back onto the pillow, she said, "Jacob wanted me to ask if you remember anything about what happened."

"I was coming back from the river —." He lifted his splinted arm a few inches and quickly lowered it. Perspiration glistened on his forehead. "Where's Rubén?"

"We don't know. Here, drink the rest of this. Captain Dugan said he'd be back this morning; maybe he'll have some more morphine."

She helped him sit up enough to take another drink. When she braced her hand on the bed, the blanket felt damp. She thought she must have spilled the water but pulled the covers back to find the sheets stained with blood. The cup dropped to the floor.

"I'll be right back." She hurried to the doorway. Roy leapt up from the bench, rubbing sleep from his eyes.

"Go into town and get that doctor, that Captain Dugan."

"He's supposed to be back this morning, ma'am," Roy drawled. "I don't know if —"

262

"For God's sake, Roy. Go get him. Now!"
Roy ran for the corral.

Esther did what she could to make Morgan comfortable. She changed the bandages and the sheets. She bathed his face with cool water. She made him drink. He clung to consciousness, asking at each sound from the yard if Rubén had returned. And at each sound from the yard, Esther hoped Captain Dugan had arrived.

Millie fixed breakfast and brought a plate for Esther. She rearranged the lamp and Morgan's gun and holster to make room on the bedside table. After the children and the men finished eating, she came back for the plate. "You didn't touch your food, Mama."

"I ate some. Thank you, dear."

They both turned to the window as a horse galloped into the yard. "Please God, let that be the doctor. Millie, stay here with him." Esther ran to the doorway only to find a sweat-soaked Roy dismounting from his lathered horse. Her younger children sat on the bench, and she rested her hand on James' head.

Richard ran up and took the reins. "I'll walk him."

Roy held his hat in his hands and stared at Esther. His face was shining, wet and flushed in the bright sun. He ran his shirt sleeve over his forehead.

"Well?" Esther asked. "Where's the doctor? When is he coming?"

"He ain't, ma'am."

"What?"

"Jacob says all them soldiers left town before dawn. I rode all the way to the fort, but they ain't there either. I tried my best, ma'am, to find 'em —"

She lowered herself onto the bench. James and Mary moved over to make room for her. A hot breeze stirred Mary's hair and Esther, unable to comprehend what Roy's words would mean for Morgan, instead thought of the need to comb and braid her daughter's hair neatly — such a tangled mess. She reached out to smooth it and Mary looked up at her, all round cheeks and big, serious eyes.

"Mr. Braddock's gonna die."

"No he's not. I don't want to hear that again, Mary."

Roy eased away toward the barn, waved to Al who positioned himself at the round pen, rifle in hand. Danny leaned against the corral's gate nearest the barn, smoking a cigarette, watching the road. Richard turned Roy's horse into the corral and came toward the house, scuffing his boots in the dust, head down.

James said, "If Pa was here, he'd tell us to pray."

"Yes, that's right." Howard, she thought. She would be grateful now even for Howard's presence. "That would be a good idea."

The children knelt in front of the bench, resting their elbows on it, eyes closed, heads bowed over clasped hands.

She left them to their prayers. She pushed herself up from the bench and walked slowly back into the cabin, Richard close behind her. She motioned Millie out of the chair and sat down next to the bed.

Morgan moved his lips, formed one word, "Rubén."

"I'm sure he'll be here soon. Don't worry, please. Be still. The bleeding is less if you're still."

"Something's happened to him." He braced himself up on his elbows, as if he would get up, and Esther threw her arms around him to keep him from falling off the bed.

"Richard," she cried. "Help me!"

They lowered him back onto the pillows. Sweat streamed down his face. Fresh blood leaked through the bandages.

"Ma?" Richard looked scared.

She fought panic, remembering the doctor's warnings. She took a cloth from the bedside table and pressed it against him, watched the red stain creep to the edges. She took another cloth and did the same, pressing harder. She would hold the blood inside him. She bore down on the cloth until her hands shook from weariness. The bleeding stopped.

"Oh, God, please, help him," she whispered, and lowered her head to the mattress.

"Ma?" Richard tapped her shoulder. "He'll die, won't he? If Rubén don't come back."

"No!" She got up and wrapped her arms around her son. "You're not looking for Rubén! The soldiers will catch the Indians and then Captain Dugan will be back."

Richard pried himself from his mother's arms, then left the cabin and hurried across the yard. James and Mary finished up their prayers and ran after him. "Go back and sit on the bench," he said, but they followed him to the saddle shed. He got his tack and carried it to the corral, the two children sticking to him like shadows.

Danny moved to the other end of the corral, smoking and shaking his head.

266

"Where you going?" James asked his brother.

"None of your business." Richard opened the gate, caught a horse and slipped the bridle on it.

"He's going to look for Rubén." Mary swung from the gate until Richard pushed her off so he could pull his horse through and tie it to the railing. "Be quiet, Mary. For once." Richard eased the blanket and saddle onto the horse and cinched the latigo, letting the stirrup leather drop.

"Mama said no," James said. "We heard her."

"So don't tell her."

"I can keep a secret," Mary said. "I can, can't I, James?"

"Yeah, I guess so."

Danny threw his cigarette to the ground and stepped on it. "Those Indians are gonna get you next."

Richard walked the horse out to the wagon road, then swung into the saddle and hit a full lope, riding fast in case his mother tried to call him back.

The fishing creek was the last place anybody had seen Rubén, so that was where he headed. Near the boulders, he spotted Mr. Braddock's hat beside the trail, beat up and covered with dust. He reined in, slid down

267

and picked it up, slapped it against his leg a few times, and put it on. Marks in the dirt, dried blood turned black and footprints. He thought this must be where Roy and Al pulled Mr. Braddock up from the hillside. Riders had trampled the trail with too many marks to make sense of. Maybe he'd get some notion of where Rubén had gone if he climbed to the top of the rocks and took a look around.

The easiest way up the rocks was from the back and he led his horse around and tied it to a bush. Climbing to the top, he looked up and down the trail but there was nothing out of the ordinary. A brightly colored lizard did push-ups on a sunny rock.

"Did you see anything? Know where Rubén went?" Richard asked, but at the sound of his voice the lizard disappeared into a dark crevice between the rocks. On the ground were two spent shells and a piece of paper. He picked up the paper and smoothed it open. When he saw its contents, his jaw dropped, and he knew he had to talk to Uncle Jacob. He folded the tattered sheet and put it and the shells in his pocket, then climbed down the hill and rode toward the fishing creek.

Danny waved at flies and pulled his hat

down against the glaring sun. It was stupid to be standing watch for Indians, but he had to act like he was as scared as everyone else. The buck goat was chomping on hay in his pen outside the barn. The old goat stunk. Danny picked up his rifle and was about to move to another location when Millie came out of the house carrying some food wrapped in a towel.

"You make good biscuits, Millie." He shoved one in his mouth and took a couple more.

"They're left over from breakfast. Seems everyone is either too tired or too scared to eat."

"Not me." He wiped crumbs from his mouth with his sleeve. "Where's your Ma?"

"Inside. With Mr. Braddock. She won't leave him."

He grabbed her hand and pulled her around the barn, into the stall he used for sleeping. He pushed her against the wall and pressed his body against hers, kissing her, then pulled her down into the hay and lay on top of her. "What's the matter with you?" he asked. He put a hand on her breast.

She sat up, brushing straw out of her long blonde hair. "I'm worried about Mr. Braddock."

"What the hell are you worried about him for?"

"I don't want him to die. He's been good to us. He lets us ride the horses."

"He's a killer."

"No, he ain't."

"He made his living shootin' people for money for years."

"How would you know such a thing?"

"People would pass through town — I'd hear stuff. He used to live near me before he —"

"You're making that up. You're jealous."

Danny laughed. "He's a little old for you, ain't he?"

"Maybe," Millie snapped. "Maybe not."

"What's that mean?" Danny asked, shoving her back down into the hay. Millie squirmed under him, but he pinned her shoulders and stuck his face close to hers. "You want Braddock to be good to you? Good to you like this?" He pressed his mouth down on hers and forced his tongue past her lips.

"Stop fighting, Millie. Let me be good to you. Someday I'll take you away from here." She still fought him, and he slapped her. She cried out and her eyes got wet.

"I'm gonna tell my Uncle you hit me!"

"You won't tell nobody. Not unless you

want your uncle and your Ma to find out about my little visits to the cook tent. And what are you going to tell them about being in here with me?"

He kissed her again.

The prisoners lined up, filing through the opening in the fence under close watch of the soldiers. As Rubén left the makeshift stockade, he overheard the doctor talking to another officer.

"I'd like to head back by Mrs. Corbin's farm."

"We have our own wounded to look after now, Captain."

"Yes, sir, Major, but I told Mrs. Corbin —"

Rubén moved closer and dared to interrupt. "Are you talking about *Señora* Corbin? Her farm is outside of Chasm Creek? Esther? Do you know her?"

A soldier, not yet old enough for more than a stubble on his chin, shoved his rifle into the small of Rubén's back. "Keep moving," he barked, but the captain motioned for the soldier to stop.

"You know Mrs. Corbin?" the doctor asked. "Are you Rubén?"

"Has something happened to Morgan?"

"Ha! As if you didn't know!" The young

soldier pushed Rubén again with his rifle.

"Private! If you touch this man again, I'll have you arrested." The soldier walked off, muttering under his breath, and the captain turned back to Rubén. "He was shot. We assume by some of these renegades." He nodded at Eleven, standing at Rubén's side.

Eleven pulled on Rubén's arm. "What is he saying?"

"He thinks you and your men shot my partner."

"We did not shoot anybody except crazy stupid soldiers," Eleven shouted in Apache.

The major waved at two nearby enlisted men. "Restrain this prisoner."

The soldiers rushed up to grab Eleven's arms. He twisted in their grasp and continued to yell. "Crazy white men who try to murder us!" The soldiers dragged him away. Other prisoners stopped to watch, and one broke out of the crowd and ran towards the remuda of horses. A rifle shot rang out and he fell to the ground. A woman screamed. Soldiers moved quickly to surround the prisoners.

The major moved off, shouting orders to get the prisoners under control and back into line.

"What was he saying?" Captain Dugan asked Rubén.

"He said he didn't shoot anybody. Even if they did, I was not with them. I am not Apache."

"Who cares?" a soldier yelled. "You're an injun, ain't you?"

The captain looked embarrassed. "I'm sorry."

"Is my partner alive?" His heart sank at the worry in the officer's eyes.

"If he is, he needs a doctor."

"Release me! I did not participate in any horse stealing!"

"Nobody stole the horses," the captain said. "The night guard left the gate open and let them wander off."

The major came stalking back, his hand on his saber. "I've heard about enough of that theory, Dugan."

"It's no theory. You could smell the whiskey all over him when you questioned him about the damn horses."

"Whiskey or no, he said Indians took them. Didn't we catch this bunch with them?" He pointed to some men that Rubén recognized from Eleven's camp.

"Sir, those weren't our horses. They weren't even shod!"

"Then you tell me," the major said, leaning into the captain's face. "What were those Indians doing wandering around this close to the fort with a dozen horses on a lead?"

The major yelled to the soldiers who had taken Eleven away. "Get this old man in line with the others."

"Our own wounded take precedence over a civilian. You know that."

"The Indians are dead, two of our men are dead. The others' wounds are not serious."

"Orders, Captain!"

Captain Dugan turned his back, started to walk toward the remuda to get a horse. "The hell with your orders."

"That's insubordination, Captain."

Rubén broke free and ran for the nearest horse. The soldiers scrambled after him and wrestled him to the ground. His mouth filled with dirt until pressure from a knee in his back painfully blasted it out. He choked.

"Leave him be! Can't you see he's an old man!" Captain Dugan shoved the soldiers away and helped Rubén to his feet.

"I'm sorry," he said. "Please, do as you're told. The sooner we all get back to the fort, the sooner I can go to Morgan. I don't see any other way."

But Rubén heard the hopelessness in the officer's voice. The soldiers tied his hands in front of him, hauled him to his horse, and shoved him up into the saddle.

Chapter Twenty-Two

Morgan squinted against the bright noonday light at the window. Esther sat at the edge of the bed, watching him.

"You're shivering." She pulled a quilt up to his shoulders.

He slipped back into his dream, buttoning his heavy wool coat and pulling on his gloves. His horse exhaled puffs of vapor into the pine-scented air.

He rode down out of the hills, his mule loaded with freshly killed and gutted meat. Snow sparkled on the peaks of the Zuni Mountains, and he turned away from them, headed west, toward home.

The tall and tawny grass of the high plains undulated around him. The tips, weighted with seed, brushed against his stirrups. To the horizon, in every direction, nothing but grass, shining like gold. He took off his gloves, then his coat, and felt the sun against his shirt.

In the west, beyond the crest of a hill, thin spires of smoke billowed into the sky. As he rode closer, the black smoke thickened and churned; the sky turned red, smoke and sky swirling together to create a vortex that pulled him faster and faster toward his ranch.

His horse raced past the long shadows cast by the framing timbers of his unfinished house. The smell of fresh sawdust mingled with smoke hanging over the rounded huts at the far end of the cornfield, beyond the dried stalks rattling in the breeze. He gripped his holstered pistol.

When he got to the hogans he slowed his horse to a walk. Blue smoke and the smell of sulfur hung thick in the air. He rode past trampled gardens and knocked down fences and dead bodies.

Flies buzzed and vultures held up their wings and waddled aside, as if one dark conjoined clump, when he passed. He held his scarf over his mouth and nose to block the smell of charred wood and a stench he had hoped to never encounter again after the war. Burned flesh.

Grandmother sat slumped at her loom. Her head rested on the blackened wooden frame near embers still glowing, and her hair had burned down to her scalp leaving only a few strands matted with tissue and blood against her face half gone, cheek and jaw hanging open, a seeping wound. The blanket she had been weaving smoldered, tendrils of smoke rising from the tattered yarns.

As he rode by, she twisted her head. Beneath dead eyes a mouth, half human, half monster, moved.

"Do not go in."

But he was already standing at the doorway.

"Turn back!" the monster screamed from behind him.

A flock of ravens perched on the roof, heads turning, a dozen pair of obsidian eyes among rustling, blue-black feathers.

He touched the rough woolen fabric hanging in the doorway, closed his fingers around the edge of it.

In one loud rush of beating wings the ravens took flight.

He called out from his dream. "Rubén!"

Behind the cabin, Esther leaned over the wash tub, squeezing sheets and bandages, watching eddies of blood pirouette through the water and rise up against her submerged arms. She scrubbed until Millie yelled from the doorway. "Mama! Come quick!"

Racing to the cabin, she found Morgan restless, pulling on the bedclothes, muttering in his sleep. He called for Rubén.

She wiped the perspiration from his face

and neck. "Please, lie still — you'll be bleeding again." Please, God, please. She talked to him and stroked his hair and prayed until he quieted.

Lost in his dream, Morgan stood at the doorway and fingered the edge of the blanket. For a moment, it had begun to fade beneath his touch. He had almost turned away, almost heeded Grandmother's words, almost let himself be soothed out of this nightmare. But the blanket hung in the doorway, vivid colors and intricate patterns bright in the sunlight. From above, circling ravens cawed, their voices echoing.

They had left his half-finished ranch house standing. They hadn't dared to destroy this home either. They would not dare to hurt his family. He would find them huddled together, afraid to call his name or come out, not knowing he had come back to protect them.

He closed his fist around the blanket and pulled, letting it fall to the ground. A heavy rush of beating wings and fluttering shadows blocked the sun. When they dispersed, light flooded into the open doorway.

His legs gave way. He sank to his knees. Doubled over, unable to take a breath, so much pain. He put his hand down to keep from falling into the river of blood on the floor, still warm.

At Morgan's anguished cry, Esther dropped the lid onto the pot of stew she'd been stirring and hurried to the bedside. "Millie, please take the children outside." Millie took their hands and went out.

Esther tried to wake Morgan. He wouldn't wake up, he wouldn't lie still. He would bleed to death. He shivered as if cold but when she pulled the covers up, he tore them away.

"Richard! Richard, come and help me!" Where was that boy?

Morgan groaned, then exhaled sharply, a sudden grunt as his whole body stiffened. His eyes opened and rolled back until whites showed and then spasms wracked his body and shook the bed.

She threw herself across him, afraid the seizure would kill him. She dug her fingers into his shoulders and screamed at him. "Stop it, Morgan! Stop it!"

Bloody saliva foamed past his clenched teeth. Minutes seemed an eternity until his convulsion finally ended and he lay motionless except for labored breathing. She knelt on the bed beside him, crying, and after a while his breathing slowed and she wiped the blood from his lips.

Flame scorched Morgan's eyes. He tried to catch his breath, tried to see where he was, tried to get up, but a hand held him down.

"It's all right." Esther's voice. Light flared from the lamp by the bed. "You had a seizure but it's over now." Esther's touch on his shoulder. "Lie back, stop this!"

He tried to shove her away, tried to shove away the images uprooted by his dream.

"What's wrong? What's wrong?" she cried. "It was a dream!"

No, not a dream.

Doubled over by pain, unable to stop his own groans or the pictures in his mind, the memories crashed over him, the memory of kneeling in his hogan, the blanket he'd ripped from the opening still in his hand. His wife, on the floor. Her throat cut open, scalped, blood covered. They'd spread her legs wide, left her that way with her feet facing the door.

He'd crawled around her, wrapped her in the blanket. He picked her up and placed her on their sleeping skins.

His daughter and young son lay nearby. He crawled across the floor and picked up his son, laid him next to his mother.

He went back for his daughter. He knelt

beside her, leaned down and slipped his arms underneath her, lifting her gently to his chest, where he held her close. He let his head drop to rest against hers.

"*Si at'eeyazhi,*" he said, over and over again. My precious little one.

He knelt for a long time, holding his daughter, rocking her. The sun was fading when he carried her, crawling on his knees, and laid her beside her brother.

He found the empty cradleboard, then found the baby tossed against the far wall. He started to lift the tiny body, then stumbled to the door. He leaned against the mud exterior, gagging and retching. When there was nothing left to vomit up, he went inside. He carefully held the baby's head to its body as he picked him up and put him in the cradleboard, then placed it next to his wife. He covered the children with a blanket.

He went outside and took the monster's hand and she walked with him into the hogan. She lay down next to the children and he covered her.

Then he lay down next to his wife. He caressed her face, brushed her eyes closed. He ran a finger over the knife wounds on her arms.

"I know you didn't see our children die.

They would've had to kill you to get to them."

One thick strand of hair remained hanging from the side of her head. He rested his cheek against it, then kissed her forehead. He kissed her lips before pulling the blanket up over her head.

Taking a jar of kerosene, he poured it over the bodies, the floor, the children's pallets.

From the doorway, he lit a match and tossed it in.

Smoke poured from the hole at the top of the hogan. The heat built up inside, and he stepped back from the flames. The interior timbers caught fire. He watched, waited, until the beams burned through and collapsed. The outer layers of dried mud and straw fell with a loud thud and extinguished the flames.

Ravens returned and circled overhead, their shadows dancing across the smoldering hogan before they took flight.

Morgan fought to catch his breath. In his memory, his dream, he had fallen to his knees but now he lay in a bed. Someone's lips close to his ear. He felt the warm breath. Esther's arms around him, her words in his ear. "It's just a dream, it's alright now."

No, it would never be alright. "Dead.

They're all dead." He struggled to get up, to get away from the grotesque images that still played before his eyes.

She spoke but he couldn't understand her words. She eased him back into the pillows, but he fought through pain for air. "Their throats were cut. Scalped —"

"Oh, God."

Her cool hands pushed the hair from his face.

"I could have stopped it," he gasped. "I should have been —"

Pain engulfed him, so intense he could do nothing but lie with teeth and fist clenched, wishing for death. I should have been there. The pain grew, but he no longer stood outside the smoldering hogan.

His head fell back into the pillows. Air found its way into his lungs. His vision cleared.

He turned away from Esther's sadness, the tears that ran down her face. He rolled away from her and tried to push the memories back to wherever they had been for ten years, but they would not be banished. All he could see was his family, lying lifeless as he anointed them with kerosene and watched as fire incinerated their mutilated bodies.

Esther knew this was the memory Rubén had told her about, this was the death of his Indian friends. "It wasn't your fault." She leaned over him and whispered those words over and over again, the same words Jacob had once whispered to her.

She checked to make sure Morgan's gun-belt was out of reach before she stretched out on the bed, pressed herself against his shivering body and rested her cheek against his back. When she put her arm around him, his hand closed over hers, held it tight against his chest. His heart pounded. Then his shoulders began to shake.

Weeping silently, her tears dampened the bandages across his back. As the cabin grew darker he grew still. His heartbeat steadied and his breathing slowed. The setting sun painted the windows red before his hand fell away from hers.

CHAPTER TWENTY-THREE

Richard ran into the Chasm Creek jail and pulled the shells and poster out of his pocket before Jacob could lower his feet from the desk to the floor.

"Richard, what —"

"It wasn't no Indian that shot Mr. Braddock!" He gave Jacob the evidence. "It was a bounty hunter!"

"Shush! Keep your voice down." Jacob took Richard outside, away from Otto's curious ears. "If it was a bounty hunter, why didn't he make sure Braddock was dead instead of riding off and leaving him out there? Why didn't he bring the body in to prove his claim?"

"Uncle Jacob? Did Mr. Braddock murder someone?"

Jacob put a hand on Richard's shoulder. "The law in New Mexico says he did."

"Maybe it ain't true."

"It's true. I've already checked it out."

"You knew about this? Ain't it your job to arrest him?"

"Richard, you're too young to understand. Not everything is black and white. Braddock's broken no laws here. I decided to leave it be."

"But don't this mean even if you find whoever shot him, there's nothing you can do?"

"That's right."

Richard folded the paper and stuck it back in his pocket. "I think he's gonna die."

"Good," Otto yelled from the strap-iron cell.

285

"You shut up," Richard yelled.

Jacob's hand squeezed his shoulder. "Rubén never came back?"

Richard shook his head. "That's where I found this stuff, when I went to look for him. I went as far as the fishin' creek. Rubén's frying pan was there with a burned black fish in it. Nothin' else."

"Wait. Does your mother know you're gone?"

Richard didn't want to answer that, but the hand tightened on his shoulder. "Ouch!"

Uncle Jacob's voice grew louder. "You went looking for Rubén? Did you stop to think what could happen to you?"

Richard pushed the hand away. He didn't care if his uncle was angry. All he could think of was his mother leaning over Mr. Braddock, crying. He raised his own voice. "Did you stop to think what would happen to Mr. Braddock? When you wouldn't look for Rubén?"

Jacob stepped back. For a minute, Richard thought his uncle might hit him for his mouthing off, but his uncle asked, "You really think that old Indian can save his life?"

Richard nodded.

"All right, then. I'm making you my deputy." He pulled the boy into the jail and

286

put a Springfield carbine in his hands. "Sit at my desk here and keep an eye on the prisoner." He dropped some extra shells on the desk. "Just in case."

Otto was in the strap-iron cage, grinning. "How's your whore of a mother, boy?"

Richard sat behind the desk. He pointed the barrel at Otto.

"Now, try not to shoot him unless he gets out of that cage. I'll tell Will to bring you over some supper later on." Then Uncle Jacob was gone.

Richard put a thumb on the hammer and pulled until it clicked. "Call my mother a whore again."

The soldiers and their prisoners trudged along beside the Verde River. Rubén's hunger had gone past pain into weakness. The pain moved from his stomach to his left hip, which throbbed with every step of the horse. The rope chafed his wrists. He tried to stay alert yet his head kept dropping down to his chest and his eyes would close until the sensation of falling off the horse awakened him with a start and he would grab for the worn saddle horn.

That morning the soldiers herded the captives past the hasty graves of the dead Apaches. Women and children wailed and

287

cried but, after a few miles of marching, all fell silent. Wrapped in blankets, the two dead soldiers hung draped over horses. Now and then a child's voice or cry, quickly hushed, punctuated the shuffling footsteps and creaking saddle leather. Soldiers yelled orders and taunted prisoners as the column marched through the heat of the day.

They entered the shadow of a westward hill, and the breeze off the river suddenly cooled. Rubén wished he could get to his serape, stuffed into a saddlebag behind him. He twisted and stretched his bound hands to no avail.

He gave up, sat his horse while his head spun from hunger, pain and exhaustion. The aged Navajo healer he had seen at dawn in the stockade rode up beside him.

"Get away from me, old man."

"Ha'át'ée gosha' naaháchi', Shisóí."

"Speak English if you wish to talk to me!"

"Hey! You shut up back there," a soldier yelled from up ahead. "Crazy old man."

The Navajo spoke again, in the soft, lilting tones of the *Diné.* "I asked only why you are angry with me." He pulled the serape from the saddlebag and draped it over Rubén's shoulders. The weight of wool on his thin blouse brought immediate warmth, and Rubén's strength returned.

"You do not know me," Rubén said. "Why do you bother with me?"

"You are Yiska."

It could not be. Nobody knew the name except his parents and the singer who blessed him with it as a child because he had been born at dawn. His name meant Night has passed. Blessed! It had been a curse!

The present faded away and long forgotten images crept into his mind, a flash of ceremony — men in headdresses made of animal skin helmets and feathers. Drums. Singing. A family gathered in their hogan. The fire smelled of burning juniper mingled with tobacco and sage. He shook his head to clear the unbidden memories.

The images faded and again he rode among the soldiers and prisoners. They emerged from the shadows into bright sunshine. Rubén squinted to see if the old man still rode beside him but a wave of dizziness overcame him. When the spinning stopped the desert had fallen away, and juniper-studded plains surrounded him and other children herding sheep on a warm summer day. They ran and played, carefree and happy. He walked near grazing sheep and held the small, soft hand of the girl he had especially loved. Anaba smiled at him

— sparkling brown eyes, silky black hair shining in the sunlight.

He wanted to stay in that place but his horse stumbled and with a jolt he was back in the real world. Real except a ghost rode beside him. A ghost he spoke to. "Yiska is dead. His family sold him to the Mexicans."

"Is that what they told you? How clever of them. If you had no hope, you would not try to escape."

Despite himself, Rubén's heart felt a twinge of hope. Could it be true that his parents did not sell him? It was what his grandmother had said at the ruins. Had it been not a dream but a vision of truth?

The crevices in the *hataalii's* face deepened and lips spread in a toothless smile. "You have lived in two worlds long enough. Spirit is showing you the way. You need only follow." A leather pouch, larger than a canteen and with long straps, hung across the *hataalii's* chest. He lifted it over his head and handed it to Rubén.

"Your medicine bag?" Rubén asked. "Why give this to me? I would not know what to do with it."

"Many times you heard me at *hatáál.* You will know what to do."

"Heard you? I have never seen you before.

It matters not. They will hang us all tomorrow."

"You will need it. Remember, the white man's medicine does not come from here." He tapped a boney finger against Rubén's chest. "Only ours."

Rubén felt as if he were riding through a dream. A faded song, an image of ritual stole across the edges of his memory, but he could not hold on to it or bring it into the light. "This will not work for me. It is foolish superstition. You keep it."

The *hataalii* smiled again. "You will need it. I prepared the pouches especially for your friend."

An officer ordered the column to an abrupt halt. Word spread that a rider approached from the direction of the fort. Rubén pulled the straps of the bag over the saddle horn and when he looked up the *hataalii* was gone.

Jacob reached the crest of a hill and looked down on soldiers and prisoners. They moved south beside the Verde River, trailed by a cloud of dust that made them easy to spot from miles away. Jacob nudged his horse to a lope, searching the column until he spotted Captain Dugan.

Dugan rode to meet him. "Marshal, what

291

brings you out here?"

"I'm looking for an Indian. Looks like you found yourselves a few."

"Let me guess. Rubén?"

Jacob nodded. "You know he ain't no renegade. But he's been missing since the army came through."

"He's here. How is Morgan?"

"I don't know. Haven't been back out there today. My nephew seems to think he's doing poorly. You'd best get over there."

"I wanted to go back this morning. I promised your sister I would. But I have orders."

"Well, if you can't come, I guess I really need to bring Rubén. Where is he?" He looked at the column of prisoners plodding through the dust. He thought he spotted Rubén but couldn't be sure. Just an old Indian riding with his head hanging.

"The major won't let you ride off with one of his prisoners. He's bent on hanging every Indian he can get his hands on."

"Look, I have to bring him back —"

"I already tried to get him released. You can't reason with the major."

"Son of a bitch." Jacob leaned and spat.

The column of prisoners slowed and bunched up, then erupted into chaos as several Indians broke and ran for the river.

Above the yelling from all the Indians, the major shouted his commands and the soldiers aimed their rifles. Shots rang out. Several of the fleeing Indians fell to the ground, but one continued to run. The major pulled his own rifle out, levered a shell into the chamber, lifted it to his shoulder and took aim. The last fleeing Indian fell as the gunshot sounded over the screams of women and children and soldiers shouting. The prisoners yelled threats at the soldiers. Others rushed to soothe those who were falling to their knees and wailing. "Get these prisoners under control!" he shouted at the soldiers.

Jacob tried to figure out what he could tell Esther if he showed up at the farm without the old Indian and without even Captain Dugan. The situation didn't look promising. Captain Dugan took hold of his arm and leaned close. He spoke with urgency.

"Listen. You'll have to give him a reason he can understand."

"What? What does that mean?"

"Tell him you're here to arrest Rubén. Say he's suspected of trying to murder Morgan."

"Rubén? He would never hurt Braddock!"

"We know that. But they must have captured him near the creek. That's where Morgan was ambushed." Dugan leaned closer. "Tell the major. He'll believe it. He might let you take him — into custody."

Jacob greatly admired such devious thinking, especially when it seemed likely to get him what he wanted.

The major crossed the line of prisoners, allowing his horse to trample any who were in the way, and finally noticed Jacob. He rode up and joined the two men. "Marshal Tillinghast, what brings you out here?"

"He's investigating the murder attempt of Braddock."

Jacob cleared his throat, then followed the captain's lead. "Um, well, I hear an Indian was captured by your soldiers near the scene of the crime. I'd like to put him in my jail, if you don't mind."

"I see. Which one is it? Do you see him here?"

"It's Rubén Santiago," Dugan said. "The old one."

"The one you wanted set loose?"

"Yes, sir."

The major laughed. "Good judge of character you are!" He turned to Jacob. "The captain here wanted him turned loose so he could tend to Mr. Braddock's injuries, and all the time he's the one who shot him. Ha!"

Once again, Jacob had cause to admire Dugan. The man sat his horse and didn't defend himself. He met Jacob's eyes briefly and there seemed to be a hint of a smile there.

The major yelled to a soldier riding by. "Go get that old white-haired aboriginal. The one on the horse." The soldier wheeled his mount and rode toward the column, returning in a few minutes leading Rubén's horse. The old Indian sat slumped over, his bound hands clutching the saddle horn.

Dugan nudged Jacob's arm.

"You're under arrest, Rubén Santiago, for the attempted murder of Morgan Braddock," Jacob said. "You'll have to come to town with me. Don't give me any trouble, now."

Rubén's head sank deeper on his chest.

The soldier held up a rifle. "It's the Indian's. You want me to give it to the marshal, sir?"

Jacob took the rifle. He nodded to the officers as he accepted the reins from the private, then he and Rubén headed west toward the hills, toward Chasm Creek.

Captain Dugan broke away from the column and caught up with them. He took two bottles out of his medical bag. "Quinine." He stuffed it into Ruben's saddlebag.

"You might need it. It's good for fever. And this one is more laudanum, for pain." He patted Ruben's shoulder. "I'll be there as soon as I can. Please tell Mrs. Corbin."

Rubén lifted his bruised and swollen face and watched Dugan through squinted eyes.

"Rubén, snap out of it!" Jacob said.

"He'll be alright," Dugan said. "He needs water and some food. Make sure you're out of sight before you turn toward the farm." Dugan wheeled his horse around and rode back to the column.

"Let's go," Jacob said. "I'd thought you'd be in a hurry."

But Rubén didn't move, just sat his horse and watched the Indians. "In a hurry." His spoke in a dry whisper. "To get to your jail?"

"Rubén —"

"How little has changed." Sadness deepened the lines and crevices of his face. "Years go by, decades, yet all remains the same."

"Come on, we better go. You need to get out to the ranch, and I need to get back to town."

Rubén looked up. "What are you —"

"Come on!" He turned, leading Rubén's horse until they were on the other side of a hill, out of sight of the fort and the soldiers. He dismounted, unsheathed his knife and cut the ropes that held Rubén's hands.

"Here, get down, for Christ's sake."

Jacob helped Rubén off his horse but when the old man's feet found the ground, he kept going down until he was sitting in the dirt.

"Jesus, what did they do to you?" Jacob dug around in his saddlebags and found some jerky and hardtack. He handed it, along with his canteen, to Rubén.

He crouched beside the old Indian, watched him eat and drink. "I'm not really arresting you, don't you know that? That was just to get you away from that crazy major. You have to get back to the farm and take care of your partner."

Rubén wiped the crumbs from his lips. "How is Morgan?"

"At death's door, according to Richard."

"Help me up."

Jacob held out his hand and hauled Rubén to his feet and assisted him in mounting his horse. He gave Rubén the rifle. "You better hurry."

"Are you not coming?"

"I left Richard at the jail, guarding Otto. I reckon I should get back there."

"What if I run into more soldiers?"

"The soldiers at the fort said everyone is back except the ones bringing in the prisoners. You won't run into none of them. They're finished with rounding up Injuns for now."

"*Gracias, Señor* Jacob. I shall always be grateful for what you have done."

Impulsively, Jacob held out his hand and the old Indian, looking surprised, shook it. Then he kicked his horse and rode off at a fast lope. Jacob watched him go and wondered, after all, what harm these Indians had done. Rubén wasn't such a bad sort. And all those prisoners headed for the fort — God only knew what would happen to them. Some had shot those soldiers, of course, so they'd have to hang. But what about the rest of them? What had they done, other than want to be free, live where they chose. Wasn't that the same as he wanted? Bah! He leaned over and spat. If he wasn't careful, he'd start sounding like those bleeding hearts back east. Or Braddock, or Essie. He spat again, then got on his horse and headed back to town.

CHAPTER TWENTY-FOUR

The knife, the one Morgan had found in the doorway to his hogan, glowed. He felt its heat surging through his hand as he extended it to the sheriff of Muddy Springs.

298

The sheriff's face billowed outward, like a sheet in a breeze, his smile flapping. His laughter swelled until it filled all the space within the jail's adobe walls.

Morgan was sure the sheriff didn't understand what he was saying. He rubbed the knife against his shirt to remove more of the blood, to display the name engraved on the blade more clearly. Touching it to his shirt caused a sharp pain through his body. He held the knife out again.

"Can't you see the name? Look!" He tried holding it at a different angle. "Right there, the name!"

Words floated out of the sheriff's wide, smiling mouth.

"That man did you a favor. Removed the vermin from your land. No law against controlling lice."

Morgan stared at the glowing knife. He picked at the dried blood and dry flakes fell to the floor. Whose blood, he wondered. His wife's? The baby? The memory of the walls splashed with blood clawed at his mind, the memory of picking up the lifeless body of the baby and seeing his small head fall backwards, hanging by a piece of skin, his soft, small neck almost completely severed, his body black with dried blood —.

"Hey! Quit scraping that knife like that.

You're making a mess in here. Get out!" The sheriff had shrunk down to size. Instead of billowing, he was small and hard and dark. "I seen Miller down at the saloon. Maybe you better give him back his knife, before I arrest you for thievery."

Out in the street, ghostly people stared and pointed at him when he passed. They whispered to each other and hurried away, disappearing into flames that lined the street.

Men came out of the saloon. They stood on the boardwalk and their images shimmered in the heat.

The sheriff's voice boomed out. "He's got your knife, Miller."

Daniel Lee Miller appeared, his mouth moving, but Morgan couldn't hear him because his ears were full of women's screams, children's cries, the sounds of bones breaking and flesh tearing apart, flames crackling and then roaring. Ravens flapping above his head.

Sweat stung his eyes.

Slowly, Miller's voice broke through, stretched out, a low roar that coalesced into words.

"Did you like your new welcome mat? The rest of the little presents we left you? I think the ladies call it a tableau, everything all arranged to make a pretty picture to —"

Morgan plunged the knife into the man. It went in easily, smoothly, no effort at all. The man's mouth stopped moving and became round and all his words compressed into one. "Oh!" Morgan pulled the knife out and stabbed again, then again. Each time Morgan stabbed, Miller said, "Oh!" as if he were surprised. The man fell to the ground. Morgan dropped to his knees and grabbed the man's hair, pulling his head back, exposing his gulping, pulsing throat.

Rough hands yanked Morgan to his feet, and he dropped the knife. They dragged him away. More men poured out of the saloon and stared at the bloody man thrashing on the ground. Morgan fought and kicked but the men held fast.

Footsteps coming. Light, fast footsteps. A young boy ran from the alley beside the saloon and threw himself next to the wounded man.

"Pa, Pa!" He knelt in the spreading blood and waved his arms helplessly.

Blood foamed up past Miller's teeth, turned them red. He grabbed the boy's shirt and pulled him close, spewing blood-tinged spit onto the boy's face. "Kill him! Fucking Injun lover." His voice strangled as blood filled his mouth. "Kill him." Then his words turned into gurgling, choking noises.

The boy picked up the knife and charged at Morgan.

One of the men in the street reached out and swung the boy off his feet.

The men argued, making comments about the boy's spunk, while Morgan fought to break free. All around the town flames raged, turning the sky red. The boy hung in the air in front of him and blood from the knife sprinkled Morgan's face, sizzled and evaporated.

"Turn the boy loose. Let him kill the son of a bitch!"

"String him up!"

"Indian lover!"

"He's crazy! Look at him!"

"Miller's dead!"

They dragged Morgan away, toward the flames. He was on fire. His lungs filled with smoke, and he choked and coughed and gasped for breath. The knife was in his hand again and the name engraved on the blade glowed red. Daniel L. Miller. Danny Lee.

Chapter Twenty-Five

Esther gave the stew another stir, then carried a bowl of fresh water over to the nightstand. Millie sat by the bed, keeping an eye on Morgan for her. "Excuse me," Esther said to Danny, making it clear he should get out of the way. Can't stay away from my daughter for more than an hour, Esther thought. But she had other things, more worrisome at the moment, to occupy her. "Don't you have anything to do outside?"

"Not right now, ma'am. I thought I'd see how Mr. Braddock was doing."

She put her hands on her hips and leaned backwards, trying to ease the tightness in her back, then bent forward to turn up the lamp. "You'll hurt your eyes reading in the dark," she said to Millie.

Millie slapped her book shut. She smiled at Danny. "Poe should always be read in dim light."

"It's not dim, it's dark! I'm going out to get James and Mary," Esther said. "Supper's so late it'll be time for bed as soon as they eat. Have you seen Richard?"

"No."

"Keep an eye on Mr. Braddock for a few more minutes, please."

Morgan lay with his back to them, as she had left him earlier. She hoped his sleep was peaceful. "You know to call me if he wakes up."

"Okay, Mama." She opened her book.

■ ■ ■ ■

At the bottom of a deep, dry well, the sides closed in on Morgan and heavy, smoke-filled air seared his throat. He gasped, desperate for fresh air. A hand touched his shoulder, and Millie's voice came from the top of the well. "Are you all right, Mr. Braddock? Do you want me to get Ma?"

He attempted to speak, but it was all he could do to breathe. He started to slip away again to flames and thick smoke and burning hogans.

"Mr. Braddock?" A cloth, cool and damp, touched his forehead.

He drew in a breath and tried to answer but pain shot through his chest. He coughed. His whispered words scraped his throat. "Get your mother." Had she heard him? He rolled onto his back and opened his eyes. "Millie." But she was gone; an empty chair by the bed, a book dropped on top of his gun and holster on the bedside table.

Millie was gone and in her place Danny stood over him.

Morgan tried to reach for his pistol. Danny gently kicked the table a few inches away.

"I see from the look on your face you figured out who I am." He leaned closer, close to Morgan's ear. "I am my father's son. You can bet on that. Biding my time."

Then he was gone.

Gone. Everyone is gone.

Cool, soft hands pushed damp hair from his forehead.

"He's burning up." Esther's voice floated above him. "Get some sheets from the trunk upstairs and soak them in the spring."

He tried again to speak. "The children . . ."

Strands of Esther's hair brushed against his face; her skin smelled sweet. "What about the children? Morgan?" whispered a voice next to his ear.

"Take them to town." Pain shot through him again. He shut his eyes tight until the vise around his chest began to loosen. "It's not safe. Not safe here."

A wet cloth pressed against his forehead, and Esther's voice kept him from slipping back into darkness.

"We're not going to town. We're staying here with you."

"No!" A whispered word when he wanted to shout. He tried to rush a warning out, while he still had breath. "He's like his father." You have to get Jacob, you have to

305

take the children and get out of here. "He'll kill everyone."

"What's he saying, Mama?" Millie's voice sounded far away.

"It's the fever talking."

Esther's hand brushed his cheek.

"We're going to put this wet sheet over you, Morgan. To cool the fever."

He coughed again. He couldn't breathe. "The knife . . ." His father's knife, the knife that killed my family. He'll use the same knife his father used, leave you and the children lying bloody on the floor. "Tell Jacob about the knife." He wasn't sure if he spoke the words or if they remained in his head, but their frightened eyes told him that they must have understood. Their voices faded, became wind whistling in his ears. The room began to spin. He rolled onto his side, pressing his hand against his chest, coughing. He'd done all he could, done enough. He tasted blood and thought he would soon be dead. He welcomed the blackness that would end his pain and reunite him with his family.

Rubén kept his eyes on the glow from the cabin window as he turned off the wagon road. His horse dragged its hooves through the dust and Rubén stroked its neck under the matted mane. "Just a little farther. You can make it."

Halfway between the turn off and the cabin the horse stopped. When Rubén nudged with his heel, it hung its head lower. A pack of three coyotes ran in front of them. The horse did not spook, did not move. Foam dripped from its muzzle. The scrawny coyotes showed skin through patches of fur missing after the long hot season. Rubén was afraid to look at their eyes, but they never lifted their heads, intent on whatever prey they were seeking.

He waited a few minutes, watching the cabin's lighted window, hoping the horse would move forward. A kick to the flank produced no result so he eased himself to the ground, took the reins and pulled until the horse followed him down the trail. Rubén limped along, his hip throbbing, his legs weary and aching. The light drew him onward even as cold dread grew within him.

A rifle levered in the deeper darkness within the barn.

"Who goes there?" Al stepped out of the shadows. "Oh. Rubén."

"Will you see to my horse?" Rubén handed him the reins. He unwrapped the straps of the medicine pouch from the pommel and pulled his saddlebags off. They weighed him down and made the trek across the yard long and difficult.

The children crowded in the doorway to greet him.

"Rubén, where have you been?" James asked. "We was worried!"

Rubén forced a smile. "I was captured by the army."

"You was?"

"*Si,* and then your uncle came and freed me." He pushed past their astonished faces and hurried to the bed. He dropped his dusty bags on the floor by Esther's chair and placed a hand upon her shoulder to steady himself. She leaned into him and rested her head against his arm.

"Thank God, you're here. Now everything will be all right."

He eased himself onto the edge of the bed, not sure his friend was even among the living until he laid a hand on Morgan's forehead and felt the heat of fever. He did not see how anything would be all right.

"I am so sorry, *mi amigo.* I could not get here sooner."

He was sorry for many things, especially the harsh words of the previous morning, which he feared would be the last words he ever said to his friend.

He pressed his ear to his friend's chest,

listening to the unsteady heartbeat. Too fast, too weak. The smell of blood and sweat rose from the soiled bandages as Rubén pushed himself up, taking care not to meet Esther's gaze.

Mary had climbed onto the bed. She jabbered away to Morgan, asking him why he was still sleeping and did he feel better yet, and pressed a damp cloth against his face. Esther got up and took the cloth. "Come, Mary. Let's get out of Rubén's way." She lifted Mary down but the child wriggled from her arms and turned back to the bed.

"Look, Mama. Mr. Braddock's awake."

Esther glanced at Rubén, a smile starting on her face, as if to say I told you so, but Morgan's eyes were glassy and sunken in deep purple shadows, the feverish flush of his cheeks the only color in his ghostly face.

"Shi yózhi," he whispered, his gaze searching the room.

Mary leaned against the bed. "Hello, Mr. Braddock."

He reached out and Mary put her tiny hand in his.

"Rubén!" Esther said. "He knows her."

" *'Anaa ni daa stah' nisin nahee'h,' "* Morgan said. *"Shi yózhí."* He looked from Mary to Esther. A tender smile played across his lips. " *'Ałk'id,,àà ch'ééh Shiba' sédá. K'ad naa*

309

nísdzá,' " he whispered before his eyes closed.

Esther's voice filled with hope. "Was he speaking Apache?"

What was he to say? Rubén took so long to answer that Esther twisted in the chair to look at him. He realized his fingers were digging into her shoulder.

"Rubén!"

He eased his grip. "No, not Apache. Navajo."

Mary pulled on his sleeve. "What did he say to me, Mr. Rubén?"

"He said he knew he would see you again, and he called you his precious little one."

"I'm precious, Mama." She ran to the table, announcing her preciousness to her brother and sister.

Rubén took a deep breath. He dreaded the question that was coming.

"And what did he say to me?"

She had asked. Now he must answer. There was nothing left but to tell the truth.

"He did not say it to you."

"What do you mean? He was looking right at me."

"He said, 'You have waited a long, long time for me. Now I come to you.' "

"Why would — that doesn't make any sense. I've been here all along. Why are you frowning like that?"

"He has mistaken Mary for his own daughter. And you — he thought you were his wife."

She fell silent. Rubén watched her begin to understand what he had said, what his words meant, the words that had wiped the smile from her lips.

"His wife." Her voice was a sad whisper. "That look was not for me. But why would he speak to his family in — oh. Oh, my God. His wife — was Navajo?"

Rubén nodded. *"Sí."*

"They were in the hogan — his wife and children!" She looked over at her own children, gathered at the table. "Not the Indians he was trying to help, from that fort. He found his own wife, his own children. Dead." She twisted one of the clean bandages she was holding.

"He told you what he found?"

"I tried to wake him up, but —" She covered her mouth and looked as if she would be sick.

"Mama, are you okay?" James called from the table. "Why are you crying? Is Mr. Braddock —"

"No, it's okay. Don't worry." She took a deep breath. "Eat your supper." She lowered her voice. "He spoke of the children, and the blood, and he said . . . He said . . ."

311

When she did not continue, Rubén whispered, "Their throats had been cut. I pray to God he did not tell you any more than that."

"His family. That's the part of the story you didn't tell me. Why, Rubén? Why didn't you tell me?"

"Because Morgan himself does not know they are dead." The pain in her eyes cut his heart into a million pieces. "It was a blessing that he could no longer remember, after he told me the story that first time. After he shot himself. Who would want to remember that? I thought I was doing what was best for him, waking him up, so he would never remember again." He confessed his selfishness. "And what was best for me, since I did not want my friend to kill himself again."

"But now he knows."

"No." Rubén shook his head. "He will not remember when he wakes up. He never does."

"Listen to me!" The children turned in their chairs and she lowered her voice again. "He told me about it while he was awake." She stared at him with eyes round and hard.

He knew too well what she was seeing in her mind — the same ugly scene he had seen when Morgan had first told him the terrible story.

312

His shoulders sagged as the tension of holding Morgan's memory for ten years suddenly seeped from his body. "I feared he would remember soon. The headaches had gotten much worse since we came here."

"He said he would go to her. And he knows she's . . . dead." The tears fell down Esther's face and he could do nothing to ease her anguish.

Her quiet sobs tore at his heart. "We will not let him die. It will not be the first time he has not gotten his way."

He helped her up, told her to get some rest, eat. He felt her sink in his arms and tightened his hold around her. When she saw her children at the table, she wiped her face and stood steady.

"Thank you, Rubén. I'll have Millie bring you some supper. You must be hungry."

He shook the dust out of his serape and spread it over the end of the bed. He placed his saddlebags upon it and removed the tin of quinine powder and bottle of laudanum Captain Dugan had given him. Then he picked up the medicine pouch and put it on the bed.

"A memento," he said, when he saw Esther looking at the leather bag. "From a place I have not been to in a long, long time. A gift."

"It's beautiful."

For the first time he noticed the beadwork that covered one side of the bag — an intricate design, colorful, scene of red rocks and spires and cliffs under blue sky. In the middle stood a coyote.

Its eyes were not beads but two small nuggets of gold.

CHAPTER TWENTY-SIX

Esther dropped into a chair and Millie put a bowl of stew in front of her. "Please fix some for Rubén, dear. He must be hungry." Mary and James, across the table from her, shoveled food into their mouths. It was past their bedtime. Dark shadows under their eyes and pale faces. What kind of a mother was she? "You children finish up and get to bed."

She turned to Millie. "Have the others eaten? The men? Richard?"

Millie, at the sideboard washing up some dishes, nodded. "Danny took a pot out to the barn earlier."

It was a tremendous relief to have Rubén back. Morgan would stop asking for him, stop worrying about him. And Rubén would take care of Morgan, like he always has.

"I need someone to help me," Rubén said.

"I must lift him to change these bandages."

"Mama, you're too tired," Millie said. "I'll help him." She picked up a towel to dry her hands.

"You're not strong enough." Esther hung onto the edge of the table to pull herself up, but her arms and legs shook and she fell back into her chair. "James, go get your brother. Richard can help."

The boy stared at her, eyes opened wide, as he slowly laid down his spoon.

"Didn't I tell you to do something?" Esther's voice rose and cracked but James remained rigid in his chair. For a moment nobody spoke.

"Richard ain't here," he finally said.

"What?"

"He went out this morning. Lookin' for Rubén."

That meant he'd been gone all day. It was way past dark now and he still wasn't home. She pushed the bowl aside and laid her head down on her arms. "The Indians got him." She'd thought she had no tears left, but she was wrong.

James ran to her side. "I'm sorry, Mama. I'll go look for him."

She grabbed his shirt. "No!" She shook him. "You'll not go anywhere!"

Rubén hurried over and pulled the boy

away from her. "Richard is at the jail —
Jacob told me he left him there. There are
no Indians out there." He held her shoulders. "Richard is with Jacob. In town. Do
you hear me?"

"Yes. He's with Jacob." She wiped the
tears from her face. "No Indians. Richard is
in town, with Jacob. Safe." She tried to
believe that was true.

Rubén nodded. "Go up to the loft and lie
down for a while. You have spent all night
and all day worrying and taking care of
everyone. Let me worry now."

Esther felt as if Rubén's steady hands were
all that held her together. She pulled
strength from him. "I will, after we see to
our patient."

Rubén helped her up.

Mary dipped her spoon into her bowl. "Is
Mr. Morgan gonna die?" she asked, her
mouth full of food.

Rubén's hand tightened on her arm. She
had no answer for her daughter.

James shrugged. "Whoever shot Mr. Braddock is a bad man." He shook his spoon at
Mary. "If I ever find him, I'm gonna kill
him."

Mary, stew dripping down her chin, nodded in agreement.

"Hasn't there been enough killing, enough

death?" Esther asked, as Rubén guided her toward the bed.

"I hope so, *Señora,*" Rubén whispered.

Long after Esther and the children went upstairs, Rubén lingered in the chair next to the bed, elbows on knees, resting his head in his hands. He stared at the coyote on the medicine pouch deep into the dead of night. The one candle threatened to go out with each slight breeze through the open window. He could not remember a time in his adult life when he had felt more disheartened, helpless to do anything except recall the events of the last few days over and over again. He cursed the moment he had ridden off to go to those damned ruins. If he had only come back to the farm with Morgan, none of this would have happened.

He let his chin fall to his chest.

"Is he better?" Esther asked, startling him awake.

She put a hand on Morgan's forehead. Her eyes accused him.

"The quinine did not work," Rubén said. "Nothing has worked."

"You said you wouldn't let him die! How can you be so quick to give up?" She pulled the quilt off the bed.

"What are you doing?"

317

"Help me! Help me get him to the wagon. We'll take him to the fort, where that doctor is. I'm sure that —"

He got up and grabbed her arms, putting his face close to hers. She had lost her senses. He spoke slowly, as if talking to a child.

"He will die before we get there."

"No!" She fought him, but he held tight.

"Everything that can be done has been done. He is my friend! I am angry, too." At his words, the fight went out of her. Her face sagged with resignation.

"I wish I'd never met him. I wish I'd never met either of you." She shoved him away and went to stare out the window. A coyote howled in the distance, answered by a chorus of barking and yipping closer to the cabin. She rested her forehead against the window frame and closed her eyes.

"I am sorry, Esther." Rubén had never been more sorry. What would he do without his friend, his partner?

A rider approached. They waited to hear if Roy or Al, still standing guard, would take any action. There was no sound other than the hoof beats right up to the cabin, then Richard's voice calling out to one of the men. Esther hurried to the door. She held it open and hugged Richard hard as he tried

318

to get inside.

"Thank God you're all right!"

The boy seemed content to let his mother hold him, at least for a few seconds. "Sorry, Ma. Uncle Jacob didn't want to let me ride home in the dark, but I told him you'd be worried."

"That's okay. It's okay. You're home now, you're safe. That's all that matters."

Richard dug into his shirt pocket and pulled out a ragged piece of paper. "I found this where Mr. Braddock was shot."

Esther snatched it from him and, after she looked at it, held it up so Rubén could see it. He knew his lack of surprise caused the anger now sparking from her eyes.

Richard kissed his mother on the cheek. "I'm going to sleep out in the barn."

She pulled him close for another hard embrace. "Goodnight, son."

After Richard left, Esther smoothed the poster on the table. "We thought Indians had done this, but he brought it on himself."

"How can you say such a thing?"

"He killed a man. And so someone came to kill him. And where is this bounty hunter? No doubt killed by Indians."

"Morgan killed a man, but he did not commit murder. That man in Muddy Springs was one of the men who slaughtered his family."

"What does it matter now? All this killing. It's all in the past. Jacob was right. He came from a ghost town and his past is nothing but death."

Rubén picked up the medicine pouch.

"The past is never all bad, Esther. You have to sift through it, and know enough to hold on to what is valuable."

Danny pressed himself against the barn wall, contorted so that he could see the yard through a crack. He watched the cabin window, watched Millie's mother and Rubén, or at least their shadows in the candle light.

"They're still trying to save that son of a bitch. Tell me again, Millie. What did he say about the knife?"

Millie had snuck out of the house while her mother slept and now sat playing with a piece of straw, looking tired and bored. "I don't remember. Something about a knife. He's sick. He didn't know what he was saying. It didn't make any sense and we could hardly hear him anyway."

Danny grabbed his blankets out of the straw and started rolling them up.

"What're you doing?"

He shoved his belongings into his saddlebags. "What does it look like? I'm gettin' the hell out of here."

"But why?"

He wasn't about to tell her he needed to go before Braddock told everyone who had tried to kill him. He didn't want that marshal hauling him off to jail. It was a shame. His plan was all messed up now and he'd have to make a run for it. Millie looked so pretty sitting there in the dark. He wanted to do things to her and now he never would. He'd be on the run.

"I don't want to leave you." He dropped his saddlebags and reached for her. "I'm gonna take you with me."

"Take me? Where?"

"Just away. Maybe Colorado where it ain't so stinkin' hot."

"I can't up and leave." She pushed him away.

"Yes, you can. You're always sayin' nobody appreciates all you have to do. You want to spend the rest of your life working in that cook tent? Or taking care of Mary?"

"Mama needs me."

Danny grabbed her arm and threw her onto her back in the hay. She landed hard, grunted, and Danny threw himself on top of her. She struggled, tried to push him off but with one hand he pinned both of hers above her head.

"You ain't nothing but a fuckin' tease."

She looked scared. If she could get a breath she would probably scream. He pressed his other hand against her windpipe. All she could do was whisper, "Let me go."

"Prancing around in front of me, lettin' that yellow hair brush against me. You let me in that kitchen in town. You come out here to the barn. Followin' me around and letting me kiss you? And then you push me away?"

He lowered his head and stuck his tongue deep into her mouth until she was choking.

"And you let me do this." He grabbed at her breast through her dress and apron, squeezed it until she cried out, then slapped her. Blood ran down her chin from her lip.

"You'd best be quiet." He released her breast and took out his knife. "You know whose knife this is? It was my Daddy's. You know how I got it? I pulled it out of his dead body."

"Stop it, Danny! You hurt me! You're scaring me!"

He twisted her hands until she started to cry out but he raised the knife and she shut up. She tried again to wriggle away but he was heavy on her, pinning her legs with his body and her hands still in his grip. He put the knife beside her face and fumbled with his trousers. He pulled up her skirt and shift and spread her bloomers apart.

She didn't even scream, just whimpered as he thrust himself inside her until he lay still upon her, satisfied. Seeing the revulsion on her face turning to anger, he said, "Now look what you done. What would your Mama say about this, you out here in the barn with a man like this." He laughed, but stopped at the sound of a horse approaching. He yanked up his trousers as he jumped to his feet, then dragged her up beside him. She tried to pull down her skirts, straighten the bloomers tangled around her legs, but he pinned her to him and clamped a hand over her mouth.

"It's your bootlicker brother. Shit." He put his mouth by her ear. "You say one word and I'll kill everybody, you understand? Your Mama, your brothers, that pretty little sister of yours. I'll kill every one of them."

She nodded and he lowered his hand, dragging her back into the stall. He picked up his knife.

"Now you listen, what you did out here was shameful. And I ain't gonna tell anyone. Or kill anyone. But say one word, they're all dead and you're gonna watch."

She nodded. She wiped blood off her chin

and tears from her cheeks.

"Now, now, don't cry." He smoothed her hair and smiled at her. "You know I love you."

"You love me?"

"Now, why you looking so confused?" He turned her loose. "Of course. Since the first time I saw you. Why do you think I been hanging around here all this time?"

She stumbled across the stall and leaned against the wall of the barn, gagging.

"You sneak on into the house and get some things together. Not much, now," he cautioned. "I'll get my stuff ready and later, when everyone's asleep, I'll come get you." He slid the knife into its sheath and finished buttoning his trousers. "Go."

Millie looked into the darkness at the barn door. She looked for Roy and Al, then ran across the yard to the house, easing past Richard's horse tied to the porch railing. She waited in the shadows, listening to her mother and Richard and Rubén through the open window.

She glanced at the barn. He was near the door, watching her. She crouched into shadow as Richard came out and led his horse toward the barn. She waited a few more minutes and then snuck inside and up the stairs to her pallet.

■ ■ ■ ■

Rubén spread the square of buckskin on the floor. From inside the medicine bag, he removed small pouches made of soft kid-skin, untied them, and placed them beside the buckskin.

"What's wrong?" Esther asked, from the chair next to the bed.

"Perhaps this is not a good idea."

"You must try."

He twisted around from where he sat at the foot of the bed and looked at her. He'd insisted she stay in the chair. He couldn't let her watch him paint because she was not *Diné.* It was bad enough that she, a white woman, would hear the sing. He thought about making her go outside, but he didn't want to be alone.

He was afraid.

"What if I do it wrong?"

"My God, Rubén. If he dies, it won't be you who killed him."

Rubén sighed. He was almost sorry he had confided in her about the medicine bag. Once he'd told her the story, what had happened at the stockade and afterwards, told her about the ancient medicine man, there was no turning back. She had latched onto

325

the idea like a dog with a bone.

He knelt in front of the buckskin, the open pouches arrayed beside it.

He was Roman Catholic, had been for a decade past a half century. But since the day he fell through the floor at the ruins, fate directed him toward the *Hataalii.*

He took some corn pollen and sprinkled it awkwardly, all the while silently praying that Jesus Christ would not take offense. The pollen scattered aimlessly across the buckskin.

The words of the sing would not come. Panic knotted his stomach. He had been too young when he left *Diné-tah.* He tried to sing, then stopped. Tried again. Esther whispered prayers of her own, her eyes closed. He stretched for his saddlebags on the floor by the bed. He took out his rosary beads, made the sign of the cross, bowed his head, and put his hands together.

He prayed the only way he knew how.

He prayed in Spanish.

"Jesus, my lord, help me. I beseech thee. Show me the way."

The room filled with haze and he blinked to clear his clouded vision. The adobe brick walls faded into walls of logs and mud. He was no longer in the cabin but in a large, dark hogan that smelled of dirt, sweat, smoke. Smelled of sickness, blood and vomit. A man lay on a blanket. Two women, one grey-haired and the other younger, knelt beside him. The younger woman cried softly. Beside her two small children slept on the floor. Through the doorway more people watched and waited. The sick man's clan. Beating drums filled the air.

The *Hataalii* appeared before him. He sang the Coyote Way.

The *Hataalii's* face, painted white, filled the hogan. His eyes glowed, pulled Rubén until he was inside the *Hataalii,* until he became the *Hataalii.*

The rosary beads fell to the floor.

In the hogan Rubén sang and danced and instructed assistants in the dry painting; this shape, that color, use the pollen here. The drums beat louder; the room spun. Rubén twirled and sang.

The hogan blurred and he found himself on his knees, kneeling before a piece of buckskin, in Esther's cabin.

He began to sing the Curing Way.

He opened a pouch and poured sand into his palm. He knelt over the buckskin. With great care, pinching tiny amounts between his forefinger and thumb, he sifted the contents of the pouch onto the buckskin. He took the bag of pollen and did the same.

He sprinkled finely ground bark into the design that took form.

Carefully, he chanted. His voice strengthened and his hand steadied. His memories returned now that he had opened the door, as the ancient *Hataalii* had promised. These were not the memories of a child who had watched such ceremonies with wonder, but ancient tribal memories from the beginning of time, from when the *Diné* first emerged into the fourth world. As he sang, he envisioned the story of creation. He saw Changing Woman and White Shell Woman and the holy Insect People.

The old *Hataalii* appeared before him, as Grandmother had appeared at the ruins. The *Hataalii* nodded approval and guided Rubén's hand and voice.

Rubén sang and made the dry painting until it was finished, until his voice gave out. He sat on his heels, leaned his back against the bed. A deep silence fell. When he opened his eyes, embers glowed in the fireplace, and the pouches lay scattered on the floor. He picked up each one, tied it tightly and tucked it into the medicine bag. When he was done, he scraped the dry painting into a mound in the center of the skin. He scooped up a fistful, held it. With his other hand he pulled himself up beside the bed.

He sprinkled the painting over Morgan. He placed some in Morgan's hand and closed the fingers over it.

Esther watched with tired eyes.

He wrapped up the rest of the dry painting in the buckskin and shuffled outside. Esther followed as far as the dooryard.

In the moonlight, in the middle of the yard, he laid the buckskin on the ground and unfolded it. He picked up some of the painting and, holding a pinch between his index finger and thumb, pressed his lips against his fingers. With quick, hard breaths, he sent the pollen to each of the four directions. He picked up more and blew another pinch of the sacred sand up to the sky, another pinch down to the ground. Only a few grains remained in his hand. The night breezes had dispersed the remaining dust into the desert.

With a great sense of relief, he muttered a quick prayer of thanksgiving. He prayed to God and Jesus and Mother Mary and Changing Woman and White Shell Woman, even to the *Hataalii,* to whatever holy being was in power.

He shook the small amount of sand remaining on the buckskin into his hand. Returning to where Esther stood, he poured the very last of the sacred painting onto her palm. She closed her fingers tightly. He asked her to take the buckskin and burn it in the fireplace.

"Morgan walks in the spirit world. It will be up to him, to return to us or not. Go now and sit with him."

Esther watched Rubén walk toward the barn. His grey hair brushed his bony, sagging shoulders. Stiff legs dragged boots through the dust. She seldom thought of him as a very old man, but at this moment it was evident. He had been gone for only two days, but from his story about the old Navajo and the medicine bag she knew that he had been on a long, hard journey.

She went back inside and rested her hand for a moment on Morgan's chest, willing the beats of his heart to steady. She turned up the lamp, looked for her sewing kit, and cut a small square from the buckskin. Sewing it into a tiny sack, she put the grains of sacred painting inside, stitched it shut, and tied it to the rawhide hanging from her neck, next to Rubén's crucifix.

For a long time Morgan drifted, not knowing where he was, not caring, happy that the pain was gone and the nightmare over. There was no more red; there was only blackness, only emptiness.

In the distance a small light appeared, wavering like a candle in a breeze. The tiny glow spread and grew larger. It sparkled, like new fallen snow in bright sunlight.

The light spiraled toward him, then over him, enfolding him in warmth and filling him with peace. Shapes appeared within the light. As they approached they grew more distinct. A terrible fear gripped him when he realized the shapes were his wife and children. He didn't want to see their mutilated bodies covered with bloody mud. He turned away, he closed his eyes, but the light remained, and the figures came closer. Shaking, he accepted that he could not escape them.

His family emerged from the light, whole and alive as they had been before Miller and his vicious gang had attacked them.

He opened his arms to them and embraced them all. The light flowed around them, soothing, warm, bright. When it dissipated, he was with them in their hogan, sitting near the fire pit, his toddler son on his lap. The baby nursed at his mother's breast. Logs, fragrant with sap, peeled smooth and chinked with mud, formed a dome around them. Elk hides softened the dirt floor; pots hung on the wall; the central fire pit released a lazy twirl of smoke toward the hole in the roof; savory meat bubbled in a crock. Blankets and animal skins lay piled in their sleeping area. His daughter ran to him, laughing, arms filled with wildflowers. He ran his hands down her black braids, looked into her mahogany eyes. "What have you brought me, my precious little one?"

She laughed and flung the flowers into the air, scattering them throughout the large room.

His wife finished nursing the baby and placed him in his cradleboard. She went to the flap in the doorway.

Morgan moved his son from his lap and leaped up.

"No! Don't open it. The others. When I rode up . . . I don't want you to see them."

"The others are gone, my husband. They have been gone for a long time."

"Gone? No, they're — where did they go?"

He realized his family had been all alone all these years. He had held them in his heart. A feeling of great sorrow welled up within him. "I kept you from joining them. I'm sorry."

"We chose to wait for you. You said you would come to us."

Faint sounds, familiar voices, came from outside. "What's that?" he asked. "Do you hear it?"

"I hear nothing, my husband."

The sounds grew louder. Singing, chanting, praying.

No, Rubén. Don't wake me.

CHAPTER TWENTY-SEVEN

Danny waited in the barn and watched the moon sink toward the horizon. Soon the eastern sky would begin to lighten. He'd been waiting almost the entire night for that crazy old Injun to quit his ranting. He figured by now everybody was asleep, even the boot-licker over there where Roy and Al usually bunked. They weren't in the barn because they were still out guarding the farm, keeping their eyes out for all those murdering renegades. Danny wanted to laugh.

When he heard Rubén snoring out at the ramada, he went to the corral and saddled two horses in painful slowness, keeping everything quiet. By the time he finished, a pale light glowed along the eastern hills. He checked to make sure his Winchester was loaded before shoving it into the scabbard on his saddle. He hummed softly to keep the horses quiet and led them to the cabin. He tied the reins to the porch railing and eased the door open.

Smoke hung in the air from the dying fire and the one candle that burned on the kitchen table, casting meager light throughout the room. He looked to the top of the stairs. Millie sat huddled under a blanket, eyes red from crying, her swollen lip trembling. He held a finger to his lips and raised the knife in his other hand. She tossed the blanket aside, grabbed a satchel she had hidden underneath it, and quietly descended. He followed her as far as the door.

"Go," he whispered. "Wait by the horses."

Richard had awakened when he heard Danny walking around in the barn, but stayed still and listened to the horses hooves thump softly across the yard before he got up. From the barn doorway, he watched Danny go into the house and Millie come out.

By the time Millie had tied her bag behind the cantle and mounted her horse, Richard was beside her, startling her. She gasped. "Be quiet," she whispered. "Please!"

"What do you think you're doing?" He grabbed her horse's bridle. "Don't you think Ma's got enough to worry about right now?"

"Let go!"

"What happened to your face?"

"Nothing."

"Where is he?"

"In the house. Be quiet."

"What the hell is he doin' in there?"

"Richard, please! Don't go in there!"

He was through with whispering. "You ain't goin' nowhere with that weasel." He ran into the cabin, saw a shadow by the bed. Candlelight flashed on the knife blade Danny had raised over Mr. Braddock.

Richard charged. He slammed into Danny and grabbed his arm. It took all his strength to pull Danny to the floor. The bedside table crashed to the floor and his mother cried out. Richard fought hard to reach Mr. Braddock's holster and keep Danny pinned to the floor.

"Ma, push the gun to me!" He held his hand toward her, pointed to the gun on the floor, but with one loud grunt Danny threw him off and ran. Richard leaped to his feet, pulling the pistol from its holster.

Danny, his hands on his reins, stopped when he saw Richard. "You gonna shoot me? I ain't even armed!"

"I'm taking you to jail." Richard raised the pistol. "You tried to kill Mr. Braddock. I'd guess you're the one that shot him, too."

Danny laughed. "I ain't goin' to jail for

that. As a matter of fact, there's people that'll pay me for killin' that squaw lover."

"You can tell that to the marshal." Richard put his thumb on the hammer and pulled until it clicked.

"He ain't gonna do nothing."

Richard hesitated. What Danny said was true. Uncle Jacob did know all about it and would do nothing. He lowered the pistol.

"I promised my pa I'd kill Braddock and he'll be dead soon enough if he ain't already." Danny started to untie the reins.

"Shoot him! Shoot him!" James screamed, bursting through the doorway. "He killed Mr. Braddock!"

"I stopped him," Richard said.

"No! Mama's in there crying," James said. "Mr. Braddock's dead!"

"James, look out!" Richard pushed the boy away.

"He's bad! He killed Mr. Braddock!" James grabbed the gun.

His wife stood in the light, holding the cradleboard with the baby in it. Glowing tendrils of light floated past her, glided across the floor like wisps of fog and surrounded him where he sat holding his son on his lap. He wrapped his arms around the boy, pulling him closer until he could rest his cheek on the boy's shining black hair. His daughter hung on his neck. She laughed and kissed him. He closed his eyes and reveled in the touch of her little lips on his face, sweet, innocent, full of love and life.

"Come." His wife beckoned. "We must go."

Morgan let his little boy wriggle free and wobble away. His daughter hugged and kissed him one more time, then she, too, was in the doorway, holding her little brother's hand.

His wife held the blanket aside, letting more of the sparkling fog drift in, and the radiant light surrounded them. The cloud of light that had floated around him was dissipating and slipping toward the door, leaving him in encroaching darkness.

"It is time to go." His wife held out a hand.

His family was ready to join the others who left so long ago. They would have done so years ago if he had not so relentlessly held them in his heart.

"Tji' na Kai. 'A doodaii' to' niiyidíchííd." His wife held out her hand to him.

You must come with us. Or you must let us go.

His heart filled with love and peace. His beautiful wife, his children, stood before him, waiting for him to fulfill the promise he'd made all those years ago, as he'd raised the pistol to his head. He got to his feet and walked toward the doorway. A gunshot rang out. The beautiful image of his family shattered as he turned toward the sound and darkness snatched him away.

The first shot penetrated Rubén's fitful sleep. He awoke, alarmed, not sure what he had heard but recognizing Mary's high-pitched screaming. For a moment he felt himself falling through darkness again, as he had at the ruins, but he forced himself to consciousness. He rolled over so that he could see the cabin. Danny lay in the dirt. James held a smoking pistol with both hands, and Richard fought to get it away from him. Millie struggled to control the horse she sat, sawing the reins. A second horse snorted and bucked, tossing its head against the reins that bound it to the porch railing.

Rubén thought he was awake, yet this nightmare appeared before his eyes. It made no sense to him.

Danny rolled over and got to his knees. Blood flowed from his side; he touched his fingers to it and brought them close to his face.

Rubén tried to force his aching body to its

feet. He got to his hands and knees. He could move no farther.

Danny grabbed the railing and pulled himself up. He waved his bloody fingers at Millie. "Look what the little bastard did." He yanked his rifle from the scabbard, levered a cartridge into the chamber and pointed it at the boys. Richard wrenched the pistol from James and stepped in front of his brother.

"I'll kill the little bastard. Get out of the way," Danny yelled. "I'll kill all of you!"

Rubén wrapped his arms around the ramada's corner post and dragged himself to his feet. Once up, he willed his stiffened limbs toward his rifle but when he let go of the post his hip gave out and he fell.

Cursing, he crawled toward the rifle.

Esther appeared in the dooryard with the scattergun and pushed Mary back into the house.

"No!" The blast of the shotgun drowned out Millie's screams and slammed Danny to the ground.

The recoil of both barrels flung Esther into the cabin wall. She pulled her fingers from the triggers and shook them.

Danny writhed in the dirt. A bloody bone protruded from shreds of flesh at his shoulder, and his arm lay a foot away.

Rubén's fingers touched his rifle.

Mary's face appeared again in the doorway. "Get in the cabin." Esther's voice was calm, quiet. "Richard, get everyone inside."

Richard took hold of James and Mary and pushed them through the doorway.

Danny used his rifle to drag himself to his knees, then dropped it and pulled his pistol. Rubén took aim but Millie jumped off her horse.

"Move, *mija,* move!" The girl heard him and looked toward the ramada. But she didn't move.

Then Morgan was in the doorway, holding Danny's knife in one hand. At first Rubén thought he saw a ghost, Morgan's drained face framed with matted, tangled hair, white bandages falling away. But the ghost held to the doorway, next to Esther pulling spent shells from the scattergun with shaking hands. Morgan stepped into the yard, grabbed the railing and stood between Esther and Danny, holding the knife before him like a shield.

"No, no, do not do this." Rubén tried again to get up.

"It ends here," Morgan said.

Danny laughed. "You gonna stop me? Come on, squaw man, let's see how good you are with that knife."

"I won't let another man come home to what I found."

Danny pushed Millie away and Rubén quickly aimed. Before he could pull the trigger, Morgan stepped toward Danny, holding the knife out. The clear shot was gone.

Esther's shotgun snapped shut. Both barrels blasted Danny's chest open in an eruption of noise and blood and Millie, splattered with red, screamed and kept screaming.

Roy and Al ran up and helped Rubén to his feet.

"Where have you been?" he shouted.

"We heard the gunfire but we thought it was Indians," Roy said.

"We run all the way to the wagon road lookin' for —" Al stared at the scene by the house.

Rubén limped across the yard, a hand pressed against his hip. His friend sat on the ground, his back against a post. Rubén stood over him and swore an ugly oath. "*Que chingados estas accindo!* Are you trying to kill yourself?"

"I heard a shot, the children —"

"Do not talk. I worked hard last night to keep you alive. Now you must cooperate."

He held out his hand and Morgan gave him the knife. Rubén turned it over, looked

341

at the name engraved on the hilt. "Is this not the name of the man you killed? This is the very knife you found that day?"

Morgan nodded.

Rubén held the knife gingerly. A dark aura seemed to surround it. "It is over now. The circle has been closed."

He motioned to Roy and Al. "Carry him back to bed. And do not hurt him." They seemed happy to have an excuse to escape the grisly scene in the yard and hurried to the task, helping Morgan up and into the cabin.

Esther stood over Danny's body, reloading her shotgun with shaky hands, while her daughter leaned against her, sobbing, her face buried in her mother's shoulder.

Rubén put his hand on the shotgun barrel. "No need, *mi amiga.* No need."

Esther, dazed, let him take the gun from her. "I killed this boy. I'll serve time in hell. But I kept my children safe."

"I am sorry I could not do it myself. I doubt you will go to hell for killing this guttersnipe."

"Thou shalt not kill." Esther put an arm around her daughter and they went inside.

Thou shalt not kill, Rubén thought. Indeed, but I am the Lord thy God, Thou shalt not have false gods before me was the first commandment, and he had broken that one. He had turned his back on the Holy Roman Church and begged help from pagan gods and performed superstitious rituals to save his friend. Perhaps this bloodshed was God's punishment. Because of him, punishment wrought against this innocent family. And he, forced to watch, helpless to stop it.

Si, there were sins worse than murder. But he, too, was willing to serve his time in hell, because his friend was alive.

CHAPTER TWENTY-EIGHT

Rubén marveled at the stillness of the yard. No cicadas hummed, no quail cooed, even the chickens and goats were quiet. Only the buzz of a few flies.

Richard, pale and shaken, came to the doorway. Behind him James and Mary hovered, their big eyes staring from flushed faces.

"Keep the children in the cabin," Rubén directed, and the boy pulled the little ones inside and closed the door. Rubén gathered up the pistol, scattergun, and Danny's Winchester. When Roy and Al came out of the house, Rubén nodded toward Danny's body. "Take him to town and tell the marshal what happened."

"Okay," Roy said.

"Mr. Rubén?" Al asked. "What did happen?"

"Just tell him his sister killed the boy. I am sure *Señor* Tillinghast will not be too concerned about that. Also tell him everyone is safe. Wait." He slid the knife back into its scabbard on Danny's belt. "Tell him that this knife is to be buried with the boy."

They each grabbed a leg and dragged Danny toward the corral. Al ran to the barn and came back with a shovel. He scooped up the severed arm, walking a crooked path to the corral as he kept the arm balanced on the blade.

The door opened. Esther came out, leaned over the railing, and threw up.

"Ma?" Richard called from the doorway. "Will you be in trouble for killing Danny?"

"Good God, no!" She wiped her mouth with her apron. "Why would I be?"

James pushed past Richard. "Mama? Am I in trouble? For shootin' Danny?"

"Nobody's in trouble."

James eyes filled with tears. "I thought Mr. Braddock was dead."

"We'll explain it all to Uncle Jacob. Don't worry." Esther wiped the tears from his face. "Now don't cry anymore, okay? I can't

344

stand to see any more crying today."

"Okay, Mama." He went inside.

Rubén said, "Perhaps you should hitch up the wagon and take the children back to town."

"Yes. Richard, go hitch up the wagon. You can take them back to town."

"Ain't you comin', Ma?"

"Later, dear. I'll come later."

Esther sat on the bench and watched Roy and Al tie Danny's arm on top of his body. "I wish they would throw a blanket over him."

"Throw a blanket over him!"

"Yes, sir, Mr. Rubén."

Rubén sat beside Esther while Roy and Al headed toward town with Danny's body. Richard followed in the wagon with the children sitting in the bed, jolting and rocking down the rutted path to the wagon road.

Esther got up and kicked dirt over her vomit and then over Danny's blood. Some of the blood had sunk into the dirt but the rest was turning black and drawing flies. They buzzed and scattered when the dirt flew at them.

Rubén went in to check on Morgan and it wasn't long before Esther also entered. She went directly to the cupboard, got a glass and Rubén's brandy, poured herself a drink

345

and took a big gulp, looking out the window toward the road.

Rubén came to stand beside her. He kept his voice low. "Don't put it away." He took down a glass and poured himself a drink.

"How is he?" she asked.

"Better. Go see for yourself. He is feeling badly about what happened here."

"He should feel bad. God knows nobody got killed in the front yard before you two came along. You should both feel bad."

"We do. And we apologize for bringing all this trouble to your doorstep, *Señora*."

She swallowed another mouthful of brandy. "Do you think the ceremony healed him?"

"I do not know. It is not like Jesus saying 'take up your bed.' He is still sick and weak. Not exactly a miracle."

"But you said he would be dead before morning. He isn't dead."

Rubén smiled. "No, he is not dead. And I do not think he will die."

"If he hadn't distracted Danny, I don't know what would have happened."

"If he had not gotten in the way, I would have shot the guttersnipe myself."

"He came here looking for Morgan, didn't he? This was all over that bounty."

"No, not for the bounty. He saw Morgan

346

kill his father."

"Danny's father? He was the one?"

Rubén nodded.

"Jesus Christ," she whispered. "Danny would have been no older than James."

Rubén took the glass from her hand. "Go. Talk to him."

Esther sat on the edge of the bed and watched Morgan breathe, watched the steady rise and fall of his chest. It was a miracle — no matter that it didn't qualify as such in Rubén's mind. Rubén had not laid his hand on Morgan's still chest that morning; he had not held fingers against breathless lips. She had taken his hand and it had been cold. Cold as death. James had been at the bottom of the stairs. He had seen what she saw, knew why she had cried.

"Morgan?" She touched his forehead, warm again but not with the raging fever of the day before.

He turned his face away from her.

"If it hurts you to speak, we can talk another time."

"All this trouble. For you and the children."

"It's over now. The children are safe." She brushed his hair back from his forehead and knew there was nothing this man could do that she wouldn't forgive. He took her hand and held it against his chest. She felt his heart beating. "It wasn't your fault that boy sought revenge."

She blinked back tears and stroked the dark hair on his forearm until his hand released hers. He slept. She touched his face and kissed his forehead, then she went outside.

Danny's horse stood by the railing, flicking its tail at flies.

She gathered the reins, climbed into the saddle and went to be with her children.

CHAPTER TWENTY-NINE

In the warmth within the cabin, Rubén nodded off, but at any slight movement from the bed, his head popped up and his eyes opened. He provided whatever was asked for or needed — a drink of water, a sheet pulled up or down. He was happy to do it.

When Morgan slept, Rubén tried to do the same. But instead of restful sleep, he sank into ugly and fragmented dreams filled with snatches of childhood memories. Images of his recent imprisonment or the bloody conclusion to Danny's life. Awake, the realization that his body had betrayed him was worse than the dreams. Even thinking about his helplessness that morning made his hip throb and his back tighten in painful spasms. He looked down at his hands, at raised blue veins like snakes crawling under spotted skin. Crooked fingers. He was heartsick. His life was nearing its end and, except for Morgan, he had no one. If Morgan had died, he would have been completely alone once again.

That first night spent in Esther's ramada, when he'd gone to the spring for water and seen her family through the window, he'd regretted for the first time that he had no family of his own. It was something he had never pursued, something that had never occurred to him, due to circumstances, he supposed, and because of his own family's betrayal, a betrayal that he now knew had never happened. A whole life of bitterness for no reason.

The door opened a crack and Al called his name. He turned in the chair. "What is it?"

"We dropped Danny off at the jail."

"What did the marshal say?"

"He said he weren't gonna arrest his sister."

"Of course not. Ah, gracias, Al. You two can go back to work now."

"You don't need anything in here?" Roy

craned his neck, looking toward the bed.

"We have all we need. Do not worry."

Then he sat and worried. About Morgan, about himself. He was moving on to worry about Eleven and the old Navajo medicine man when a knock at the door brought his head up again.

"I thought I told you to get to work." He turned to glare at the doorway.

"I am working. I came to check on my patient." A layer of dust covered Captain Dugan's uniform. Dark stubble rimmed his drawn face and gray circles accentuated tired eyes. "How is he?" He leaned to one side, offsetting the weight of his medical bag, as if it were more than he could manage. He came toward the bed, his boots heavy on the floorboards.

"He is much better."

Some of the tiredness left the Captain's eyes. "I couldn't get away any sooner. My hospital is full of injured Indians."

"*Si*, come in. Look for yourself." Rubén motioned for the captain to sit and pulled another chair over from the table.

Dugan sat for a moment looking at his friend, then laid a hand on Morgan's forehead. He smiled a little as he bent down to pull his stethoscope from his medical bag.

Rubén felt a twinge of envy, at this friendship that had preceded his.

"Does he sleep well?" Dugan asked.

"He wakes often. Sometimes coughing."

Dugan inserted the stethoscope's ivory tips into his ears, then held the bell against his friend's chest. "Morgan? Are you awake?" Morgan opened his eyes, and Rubén forgot his jealousy at the sight of his friend's familiar half smile.

"I am now."

Dugan turned to Rubén. "I'll leave you some quinine and laudanum in case you need it. He needs to stay right here in bed and rest."

"Gracias, Capitán."

Morgan coughed and pushed the stethoscope away. "J.C., you look like hell."

"I'm not surprised." Dugan rolled up the stethoscope and put it back in his bag. He placed the bottles of medicine on the bedside table. "You need to stop talking. You look like hell, too." He turned to Rubén. "He needs to sit up more so he can breathe easier. Are there any extra pillows?"

Rubén started to get up, but Dugan put a hand on his arm.

"Tell me where they are. I'll get them."

"Check the trunk upstairs. I think that is where the *señora* keeps extra bedding.

351

Dugan came back down with two pillows and they helped Morgan to sit up.

Dugan loosened the bandages and re-arranged the splint. Before he secured the bandages, he took a hemostat from his bag and poked it against Morgan's fingers. "Do you feel that?"

"No."

"Well." Dugan dropped the instrument into his bag. "Let's hope that's a temporary problem. It's too soon to tell. The swelling could be pressing on a nerve."

Rubén took a deep breath and asked the question he had wanted to ask since Dugan arrived. "*Capitán,* what happened to the —"

"The prisoners?" Dugan pulled a flask from his blouse. He unscrewed the top, lifted it to his lips, and swallowed. "They had the hanging first thing this morning. After the trial, of course." He gave a harsh laugh. "The major let that go on for about five minutes."

"Eleven was executed?" Rubén asked.

"He and five of his men. Lucky for the rest of them there were some politicians from back east at the fort, or the major would have hanged them all. Women and children — all of them."

"But they were innocent!"

"They were innocent of stealing the horses

352

— I know that. But they were renegades and two of the soldiers they shot died. Nobody could've justified that to the major." Dugan took another swallow from his flask and held it out.

Rubén drank gratefully.

"It's our fault," Morgan said. "If they had —"

"Didn't I tell you to stop talking? And how could anything be your fault?"

Quickly swallowing, Rubén said, "He means because they were caught with a string of horses. They were delivering them to us. It was our horses the army thought they had stolen."

"Your horses?" Captain Dugan looked from Morgan to Rubén. "That's where you got the horses? From the renegade Indians?"

Rubén quickly put the flask back in Dugan's hand.

"Here, *Capitán,* have another drink. And, *por favor,* tell me what happened to the old Navajo medicine man."

"Who?"

"That old Navajo medicine man. You know, he was in the stockade. He rode beside me on the way to the fort, by the river."

Dugan shook his head. "I don't know who you mean."

Rubén described the *Hataalii*.

"No, I don't recall seeing anybody like that."

For a moment, an all-encompassing confusion disoriented him. Had he dreamed all of it? The ghostly old man? The whole debacle in the yard? The healing ceremony? He wished it to be a dream, but the images' crystal clarity dashed his hope.

He scraped his chair across the floor in his hurry to get up. Looking around for the medicine pouch, he found it on the floor on the far side of the bed. When he bent to pick it up, he saw his rosary beads behind it.

"I think the Holy People are teasing me." He put the rosary beads in the pouch, closed it and held it tightly against his chest. At the sight of Dugan, he laughed. Poor *Capitán.* So dusty and tired and now so confused. "There was a ghost among the prisoners." Rubén held out the medicine pouch. "He gave me this. He told me what to do to bring Morgan back from the spirit world. Otherwise he would have died."

"Rubén, how long has it been since you ate anything? Or got any rest?" Dugan asked.

"I was in the spirit world." Morgan said it quietly but it had the effect of silencing the *capitán.*

Dugan took another drink. "You were dreaming. It was the fever."

"I believe you," Rubén said. "Last night, the veil was very thin in this little house."

"The veil?" Dugan asked.

"*Si*, between this world and the next."

"I don't understand any of this." Dugan took a hypodermic needle from his bag. "I'm going to give you some morphine to help you sleep." He rolled up Morgan's nightshirt sleeve, injected the morphine, and put the needle back in his bag. "I have to get back to the fort." He stood and picked up his medical satchel. "Morgan, do not get out of bed. I'll be back in a few days to check on you."

"Thanks. You get some rest, too." Morgan's eyes were already drifting shut.

Rubén walked outside with Dugan. The setting sun cast a rosy glow across the hills, the day's last light. Roy and Al stood by the corral, smoking. They looked guilty, caught slacking, but when Rubén ignored them, they went back to their conversation, leaning on the fence. Goats bleated from the spring and the old buck banged against his enclosure.

"I think Morgan will recover," Rubén said.

"I think so, too. You've done a good job of

taking care of him."

"It is not a job. He is my friend."

"And mine."

A low vibrating tone resonated from inside the cabin, followed within seconds by another.

Dugan's smile spread across his entire face. "Snoring."

Rubén laughed. "He is resting well!"

"He should sleep through the night. I hope you're able to get some rest as well."

"*Gracias* for all you have done."

Dugan rode away, becoming only a dark shadow silhouetted against the red sky. He stopped and looked back, raised his arm. Rubén waved, then went inside, not bothering to light candle or lamp, and quietly arranged his blankets on the floor by the bed. He eased himself down and stretched out on his aching back, folding his hands on his chest.

"I am glad you chose to come back from the spirit world. What a shame if the only white man I can tolerate had died." He listened to his friend snore. "Although *el Capitán* is not a bad sort."

He yawned and soon drifted into sleep.

Chapter Thirty

Esther pulled her shawl close around her shoulders. She welcomed the cool, early morning air that promised summer's end. Once again she had awakened before dawn. When this happened, which was often lately, it was useless to try to go back to sleep. She would get up, dress, and — as soon as the sky lightened enough to reveal the road — walked to the edge of town to stand by the wooden fence that enclosed the cemetery. The rocky ground and piles of dusty stones covered miners, drifters, any unfortunate person who had come to an untimely end, either through illness or violence, which was pretty much everyone who died in Chasm Creek. In all the years that she had lived in the Arizona Territory, she had not known one person to die of old age.

One grave lacked an accumulation of dust.

She tucked her arms inside the shawl. Her mother had given it to her many years ago when she and Howard left Rhode Island. A triangle of knitted wool, made with the pastel colors she had loved as a child — yellow, light blue, lavender and white — even though she was a married woman with a couple of children when her mother gave it to her. She felt closer to her mother when she wore it than she ever had in her presence. It was a loving gift, now that she thought about it — something to protect her from the chill.

The first week after the shooting she had gone out to the farm a few times. She found Morgan always sleeping, and she wouldn't let Rubén wake him.

"No, let him sleep. He needs his rest." Each time she sat by the bed for a while, watching him breathe. Then she got up quietly and went home, to Jacob's house.

The last time she went out, Rubén had come out to the wagon. "He was angry when I told him you had been here. He said when you came back I was to wake him up or he would put me out of my misery."

"I think he'll let you maintain your misery a little longer."

They both laughed, but then Rubén became serious. "He wants to see you, Esther."

"Yes, well, we don't always get what we want, do we?"

She didn't want him to wake up while she was there. She didn't want to talk to him or look into his eyes, she didn't want him to reach for her hand. She didn't want to feel what she felt. She didn't want to want him. She never got out of the wagon that last time. She left and then she stayed away.

She missed her conversations with Rubén. It pleased her when he revealed more of his life to her. How he had felt betrayed and lost and homeless when the Mexicans told him his family had sold him. How he came to believe his visions spoke the truth. The truth had given him happiness, in one way. But such sadness came with it, knowing he had based his whole life on a belief that turned out to be a lie.

"And now Morgan also knows the truth," she'd said.

"*Veritas liberabit vos*. The truth will set you free."

They may have been set free, but the truth of her own life did nothing but imprison her.

She went to work each day, came home, did chores, cared for her children. Then she sat on the porch and watched the road to the west until dark. Most nights she lay awake until before dawn. Then she would get up and walk to the cemetery.

When she'd ridden Danny's horse to Jacob's house after the shooting, after she had killed Danny, Millie met her at the door. The girl's swollen face was red and wet with tears. She fell into her mother's arms, sobbing. Esther held her for a while, guided her to the sofa, sat with her until the sobs slowed, then she had asked her daughter why. "Why could you leave us, your family, to run off with Danny?"

She'd been shocked, then horrified, at what Millie told her. She sat on the sofa holding her daughter all through the night, glad that she had killed that boy. A guttersnipe, as Rubén always called him. A horrible, evil young man who had put his hands on her daughter. Violated her.

But now, weeks later, with the heat of anger gone and the danger to her children past, she thought about Danny and felt sorrow. Maybe not because she'd killed him — she wasn't sorry she killed him — but that any of it had to happen at all. So much sadness.

She hoped that with time she would feel better, that she would find solace in having done the right thing. Killing Danny had been the right thing. She'd had no choice; of that she was sure. Yet it grieved her. There was no reason for what he had done to Millie, other than his own mean spirit.

She would think about Danny, the same age as James. Finding his father dying in the street, a man gone mad holding the bloody knife. He'd been so young. There was no excuse for what he did to Millie, but she could understand he felt he had cause for what he did to Morgan.

Her thoughts always came back to Morgan.

She sat in the wet grass outside the cemetery fence and leaned her head against one of the pickets.

How could she love a man who had caused such pain for her family? If she had never met Morgan, she might have lived her entire life without killing anybody. Millie would not have been raped and then willing to sacrifice herself to save her family. Her ten-year-old son wouldn't, with murderous intent, have shot a man. Who would show up next, waving a wanted poster with no regard for innocent people who happened to be nearby? Or some other person from his past with a grudge, from whatever he'd been doing for the intervening ten years.

Jacob agreed with her. He said to stay away from those two. She smiled, picturing Jacob's earnest face as he repeated his advice every time he saw her, usually with a finger wagging.

The knot in her stomach loosened, the ache in her heart diminished. She breathed.

Then she looked up. Who would be riding into town at this early hour? The abrupt hard ache in her belly told her she knew the answer.

He rode slowly, leaning, his arm in a make-shift sling and pressed against his side. He reined to a stop and sat for a long moment before easing down from the horse to stand by the picket fence, close enough she could see the dust on his boots. He faced the rock-covered mounds and swatted his hat against his leg.

She wanted to tell him come to the house, come inside, lie on my sofa, rest. I'll bring you cool water to drink, I'll take care of you, please smile again.

Instead she stared at his boots.

"Rubén and I are leaving."

"Oh." She waited for the sudden blow of his words to ease into a hollow, sinking emptiness. "When?"

"This afternoon."

"Oh." It came out as a gasp. She pulled her shawl closer and wrapped her arms around herself, struggled to keep her voice steady. "When — when did you decide this?" She forced her eyes upward.

The side of his mouth turned up, but there was no smile in his eyes. "It was decided for us. J.C. came by last night. Seems Major Whitehall is wondering what Jacob is doing about his prisoner. If he sends someone to check, they'll know Rubén isn't in jail. The major will chase him down to stand trial for his part in the renegade's crimes."

She knew what that meant. Major White-hall would hang Rubén.

"You're not well enough to travel."

"There's no reasoning with the *Bilagáa-na's* hatred."

"You can't leave. Not so soon." She wasn't even aware she had spoken aloud, but he answered her.

"We've been here too long."

Forever would not be long enough. "Where will you go?"

"It's a big country, Esther."

She wanted to fill the silence that fell between them, but what was there to say? Her mind was blank except for a sudden image of a great, expansive void. Wide tree-less plains stretching in all directions to vague horizons, nothing but space and two distant riders with a mule.

"We paid Roy and Al two months in advance. They'll keep on taking care of the farm so you can stay in town. By then your husband'll be back."

"Couldn't you wait a day or so?" she whispered.

The sad smile returned. She noticed his

lip had almost healed, the stitches were gone, a stubble of mustache replacing them.

"The children — I know they would want to see you before you leave. They'd want to say goodbye to Rubén."

He put his hat on and pulled himself onto his horse.

"I'll tell that to Rubén. It'll make him feel better."

"Will you come to the house and tell them goodbye?"

"You know he can't come into town." He looked down at her. "And they don't need to see me again. Not after what happened. Tell them goodbye for us. Tell them I'm sorry."

She stood, searched for something to say, some way to delay him, and brushed the wet grass from her skirts. When she straightened, she asked, "Your hand's not any better? Is it painful?"

"No. But I can't move my fingers." He looked down at the splint and bandages. "Maybe that's good. I used to hold on to things too tight." He turned his horse away. "I am sorry, Esther."

"Morgan." She grabbed the bridle to stop him. Her heart broke when she saw the look on his face. Did it hurt him that much to leave her? "Let us come out to the farm to say goodbye. I don't want it to be like this, in the street, here. Please?"

He bent down and gently pulled her fingers away, his hand lingering on hers for a moment. Look at me, she thought. Look at me as you looked at her, and I will never let you leave. But when he looked at her there was nothing in his eyes but suffering.

"We'll see you out at the farm. Today. Don't delay. We can't wait long."

She watched until he was out of sight.

She turned her back to the cemetery and walked to town, into the sun's first rays breaking over the top of the mountains, letting her shawl fall around her arms.

When Esther and the children got to the turnoff on the wagon road, they found Roy, sitting his horse, smoking. He touched his hat brim. "Ma'am."

She reined to a stop. "You're not still worried about Indians, are you?"

"No, ma'am. I'm keepin' a lookout for soldiers a'comin'."

Esther pulled on the ribbons, turned the wagon off the road, and drove down the rough tracks to her cabin.

Morgan leaned against a porch post, watching their approach. He raised his hand to his mouth, and a curl of smoke drifted from under the overhang. Captain Dugan must have left some cigars when he was there last night, she thought, when he was warning them to leave.

They rode up to the barn. Two horses were standing outside the corral, their reins tied to the fence, saddles, blankets and bedrolls slung over the top rail. Beside them a mule awaited the load of panyards and supplies that lay on the ground nearby.

She glanced into the wagon bed at James and Mary. Their little faces were portraits of misery, all frowns and sad eyes. Mary was sniffling.

"Don't you children carry on now. It'll make them feel worse. They don't have any choice in this, any more than we do. I explained it."

"Yes, Mama," James said.

Mary began to sob. James put his arm around her. "Don't cry, Mary. Be a big girl."

"I don't want Mr. Braddock and Mr. Rubén to go away."

Morgan walked across the yard to meet them. Mary and James jumped from the wagon and wrapped their arms around his legs.

"Mr. Braddock, are you really going away?" Mary looked up at him with tear-filled eyes.

"We don't want you and Rubén to go." James appeared to be the next to burst into tears.

Esther climbed down from the wagon. "Children, let loose of his legs before you trip him and he hurts his other arm." She pulled them away.

"They're okay." He tossed the cigar away, crouched down and hugged each child.

At that show of affection, Mary wailed, and Morgan pulled her closer.

"Don't cry, precious. Please don't cry, little one." He rested his chin on the top of her head and closed his eyes tightly. "Will you promise me something?"

She stopped crying and nodded. "What?"

"That you'll be a happy little girl. And grow up to be strong and smart like your mother."

She rubbed her eyes with her fists. "Okay."

Morgan smiled at her. "You promised, so start now. Come on." He touched her cheek. "No more crying."

Mary smiled. "I will be like my Mama!"

"I want to be like you, Mr. Braddock," James said.

"You might could pick a better model, son."

Esther was about to pull the children away when she spotted Rubén at the far corral.

She waved to him. "Is that Richard in the round pen? Is he going to try to break that horse?"

"Yeah!" James said. "We can watch him get throwed off!"

He and Mary tore away. Millie climbed down from the wagon and followed them. She stopped for a minute and looked back. "I'm sorry, too, Mr. Braddock. That you have to go."

The children ran to the corral. They greeted Rubén and climbed onto the railing, hoping to see their brother get thrown into the dirt. Esther wondered if she should go over there with them. Morgan was watching her. She didn't want to meet his gaze. Or didn't dare. She stared down at her hands, clasped and unclasped them.

"This is hard for everyone," she said.

He came up beside her, took one of her hands, squeezed it. "I'm sorry."

She pulled her hand away. "Sorry doesn't help much."

"What would you have me do?"

"You must know what I'd have you do. If you must go, then take Rubén somewhere safe and come back."

"Look at me." He pulled her around so she was facing him. "Each time I woke up, you were there, taking care of me. When I remembered what happened to my family, you were there. You never left me. I know I should tell you I would do anything for you, anything you ask. But I can't."

"Morgan, please — I love you."

The words hung between them. She could almost see them shimmering in the morning sun.

"What are you saying?" His eyes searched her face. "You'd leave him?"

Her heart thudded and a sudden flash of images filled her mind's eye, the way dreams happened in a few seconds, images showing her what her life could be. She wanted to speak but the words wouldn't form, her lips wouldn't part to let them out.

He looked away from her. "No, of course you won't leave him. I was married — I know what it means."

The pain in his eyes when he mentioned his marriage broke her heart. He still grieved for the wife he had loved so much. He loved her still. He would always love her.

"I'm sorry. I'm so very sorry." She would never see him again. The tears ran down her face unchecked.

"You say you love me but you won't leave your husband. A husband you don't even want."

His sudden flash of anger surprised her.

She didn't care if he still loved his wife. She was dead. They were alive. Obviously he cared for her. Unable to restrain tears, she said, "I can't imagine you not in my life. I want you to come back."

"And if I did, you would have me settle for scraps? While you sit at the table with another man. I can't, Esther. Even to think of his arms around you, of you lying next to him —"

"Do you think this is easy for me?" Her voice broke. "I didn't ask for any of this."

He took a deep breath and, when he spoke again, the anger was gone from his voice. "I know you didn't. None of us did." He watched the tears stream down her face. "Please don't. I can't — I can't take it."

"Then say you'll come back."

She saw, for the first time since she got out of the wagon, the paleness of his face, the circles under his eyes, the hollows beneath his cheekbones, the way he clenched his jaw. He was still recovering from his wounds and the knowledge of his family's fate. He was mourning them for the first time. And she, instead of comforting and understanding, added to his torment.

"Come, let's sit on the bench in the shade." She slipped her arm around his waist, and he put his arm over her shoulders. "I've been unfair. I've been selfish, wanting to have everything."

They sat on the bench. He held her hand. "You're not selfish. You're beautiful. I will never think of you without thinking how beautiful you are."

This was all there would be. From this moment on. He would think of her. She would think of him. They would have their memories of each other and nothing else.

"Stay one more night," she said.

His hand tightened on hers.

"We could talk." She choked back the sob that caught in her throat, and blinked back her tears. "I want you to hold me."

She awaited rejection as the tension grew between them, then it suddenly dispersed.

"I'll send Roy to the fort," he said. "To see if J.C. can keep the major away 'til tomorrow."

He lifted her hand to his lips.

CHAPTER THIRTY-ONE

Esther was plucking a chicken for the evening meal when she looked up to see Roy in the cabin's doorway, a folded paper in his hand. "Got a message from Captain Dugan, ma'am. It's for Mr. Braddock."

"He's resting." She nodded toward the bed. "I'll give it to him. He's been waiting for it."

"Yes, Ma'am." Roy left the note on the table.

She wiped her hands, dropped the towel over the chicken, and went to touch Morgan on the shoulder. When his eyes opened, she handed him the paper and stood by the bed so she could read along. He unfolded it. Captain Dugan wrote in small, neat script.

The major is busy — minor uprising by the Pimas on the Gila. No orders for any other scout to look for renegades. No orders for anyone to check on Jacob's prisoner. Have a good night's rest, my friend, and God speed to you both in the morning. J.C.

"I'll tell Rubén." He handed the note to Esther. She put it on the table, returned to plucking the chicken. When he went outside, she watched through the open door.

Rubén was loading supplies onto the pan-yards. He stopped and leaned against the mule, a hand on the pack saddle, and listened to Morgan, nodding, then turned to look toward her.

She finished with the chicken and threw it in a pot with some water, took it to the fire ring outside. Time to find the children and tell them they would spend the night at the farm. There'd be one last family dinner, all of them together. She would even include Roy and Al, since they'd be staying on. But all she could think of was getting everyone fed and out of the house, and sending the children to bed so she could be alone with Morgan. She wondered if he thought the same when, after they ate, Morgan told Roy and Al they could have the night off.

"You don't need us to stand guard?" Al asked.

"We'll be fine for tonight."

"We'll be in the barn if you need us," Roy said.

"And why don't you children head up for bed." Esther was glad they were tired enough to go without an argument, kissing her goodnight before climbing the stairs to their loft.

Richard hugged her and headed for the barn. "Roy and Al play poker a lot of nights," he said. "And they're not very good."

She laughed with him, gave him another hug, then gathered the plates and carried them to the sideboard.

"I'll get some water for the dishes," Morgan said.

"You don't have to do that," Esther said, but he was already out the door with the bucket.

Rubén drained his coffee cup and brought it over to her. "Come and sit down." He pulled out a chair for her. "I hate to see you looking so sad. I feel as if your sadness is all my fault. 'Tis because of me we must leave."

"Well, you do have the option of staying and hanging."

"That is true, *mija*." He smiled a little. "But I am hopeful that you do not desire that outcome."

"I wish you didn't have to go."

"We all wish that. But since we must, I thank you for all your kindnesses, to me and to Morgan."

"I haven't done anything."

"Yes, you have, *mi amiga*. There is no way to repay you. But perhaps there is a small thing I could do for you, to make tonight a little less sad."

"I don't know what you could do."

"I would like to stay in your house tonight."

"Why, if that's what you'd like, certainly." She had thought Rubén would spend the night out at the ramada, as usual. Having him in the house tonight wasn't exactly what would make her less sad. She'd been looking forward to time alone with Morgan. She tried to hide the sudden disappointment she felt but knew she'd done a poor job of it when Rubén laughed softly.

"You will find two horses ready for you and Morgan. I tied them out by the far corral. I will stay here and keep an eye on the children. And clean up the dishes for you as well."

Morgan came in with the water. He put it down by the sideboard and held out his hand to her. Before she took it, she hugged Rubén, and his arms tightened around her before he let her go.

The sun, below the golden horizon, etched bright pink into the bellies of scattered clouds. They rode away from the ranch, slowly, silently. Esther felt time running out. Riding slowly made it seem to take longer to get to town. She wanted everything to take longer, wanted nothing to hurry this night. Quail fluttered through the scrub as the horses walked toward Chasm Creek. A jackrabbit leaped into their path, froze for a second, then bounded away.

The leather reins were rough in her hands; the air, thick in her lungs; her body, heavy against her bones. Everything appeared brighter, louder, coarser — the saddle rubbed through her thin dress. Small, cactus-studded hills surrounded them with long shadows that faded as the sky turned grey.

A coyote emerged on the crest of a ridge. When it saw them it hung its head low to the ground. The last rays of sunset cast a reddish tinge on its fur. Then the coyote raised its head and turned, disappearing into the desert.

They continued toward town, riding past the cemetery. They rode past the jail. A light burned inside.

"Will Jacob come to the house?" Morgan asked.

"He's been staying close to the jail. He got word the Yuma prison wagon is on its way, and he doesn't want to miss it."

Jacob slapped the cork on his mescal bottle and slid his feet off the desk. Otto was straining to see out the window.

"What the hell you looking at, Schmidt?"

"Your whore of a sister and her boyfriend."

Jacob jumped up and looked out the window in time to see his sister and Braddock passing by, heading toward the house.

"I'll be a son of a bitch," he muttered.

"That you are, and your sister is a fast

piece of baggage. Left her children somewhere and headed —"

"That's enough." Jacob picked up the
shovel handle. "Enough out of you."

Esther lit the parlor lamps while Morgan
got glasses and Jacob's bottle of whiskey.
He poured them each a drink, sat back on
the sofa, and stretched his legs.

"It's so quiet here without the children
around. Oh! I'm sorry!"

As if he could read her mind, he said,
"You don't have to walk on eggshells around
me. It's not like I don't know you have
children. And I don't."

"I'm sorry."

His mouth turned up in his half-smile,
and the creases around his eyes deepened.
"And stop being sorry."

"I don't want to say the wrong thing."

"What would be the wrong thing? Something to remind me my wife and children
are dead? As if otherwise I would forget?"
His words were painful to hear but gently
said, his eyes were kind.

"No, of course not."

He put his glass down and took her hand.
"You're worried that if I think about what I
found in my hogan that day, I won't be able
to bear it."

"Yes."

"When I think of them now, it's their spirits I see. I don't know, I don't pretend to understand it, but I know they're all right. They're whole again, they're happy. I'm not saying those other memories are gone. But when they start to come into my head, I think of them as they are now, and that is what I see. They live in my heart, the way Ida lives in yours."

"I don't understand. As they are now?"

"I saw them. I saw them in the spirit world." He stared into space, his face as peaceful as she had ever seen it. "That morning, when you thought I was dead, I was with them."

Could that be true? Had he really been in some other world, a spirit world, where his family lived on like they had been, before — ? Her thoughts went to Ida. Where was her soul? Was she a spirit, surrounded by others? Playing? Happy? "I want to believe that."

"It's true." But a shadow crossed his face, and his eyes were shining.

"And yet . . . what is it? Something bothers you."

"All these years I thought someday I would go home to them." He played with his ring, pushing it with his thumb, then he raised his hand to cover his eyes.

She touched his shoulder.

Then the door crashed open and Jacob walked in, holding his arm out, blood smeared on his palm.

"Good God, Jacob! What happened to you?" Esther rushed to him.

"It's nothing. I broke what was left of that shovel handle on the cage. Saw your horses so figured I'd come and get you to take care of it."

Morgan got up from the sofa and quickly pulled out a chair at the table, motioning for him to sit.

A sliver of wood, the size of a pinky finger, was jammed into Jacob's palm.

"What did you do, kill him with that shovel?" Esther asked.

"Nope. Not that I didn't want to."

"Did he escape?" Morgan asked, darkness in his eyes.

"For Christ's sake, he's in the cage! He ain't going nowhere. He needed a lesson in manners. I banged on the bars, that's all."

"We'll have to pull that out," Esther said. "I'd offer you some whiskey for the pain but it seems you've had enough."

"Mescal. And what else is there to do? I can't go out prospecting until that prison wagon gets here.' "

"Looks like it better get here soon," Morgan said.

"Amen!" Jacob looked around. He looked at Esther. "So where are the children?"

"At the farm."

"Alone?"

"No, they are not alone. Roy and Al and Rubén are there."

"So what are you two doing?"

"Visiting." She pulled the splinter out.

"Ouch! Jeez, Essie!"

"Okay, you're all set. You can go now."

"Don't I get a bandage? Okay, don't worry. I can take a hint." Jacob wiped his bloody hand on his pants and inspected the wound, then he inspected her and Morgan through narrowed eyes. "You two look like you've had a hard day."

"Most days are hard, Jacob."

"Yeah, well, get some rest." He snorted and left, slamming the door as he went out.

She and Morgan went back to the sofa. He poured more whiskey into his glass and took a sip.

"Morgan, tell me about that morning. I want to know what you saw — in the spirit world."

He told her about being with his wife and children, surrounded by a bright, sparkling light. How they stood in the doorway, beckoning to him, and his wife told him he had to choose.

"You didn't choose them?"

"I did. I chose them."

"But you came back."

"There was a gunshot from the yard. The children were screaming."

She sat forward, her elbows on her knees, and rested her head in her hands. "We made you come back."

His hand touched her back, rubbed her knotted muscles, squeezed her shoulder.

"Nobody made me come back. Your children were screaming. Mine were safe."

She raised her head to look at him. "It's our fault you're not with your family. You must be angry with us."

"How could I ever be angry with you?"

He pulled her close and his arm went around her. She was content to sit there, with him holding her. She sank against him, and there were no more words between them.

Her eyes were drifting shut when footsteps on the porch brought her back to life.

"That better not be Jacob." She pushed herself up and looked through the window to see a man on the porch, holding a tray covered by a towel. She had seen him around town, one of the miners that wandered around and occasionally had business in the mining office. She opened the door.

"Your brother? The marshal?" He waited for her nod. "He paid me to get this food from Will at the cook tent and bring it up here. Said there was two people stayin' at his house looked half-starved." The man held his arms out, gave the tray a little shake.

She caught a whiff of spices and hot peppers. The man shook the tray again, and she realized she was supposed to take it from him. "Thank you!" She placed it on the table and, when she turned to close the door, the man was already halfway to the saloon. The towels covered two plates of beans and sliced pork, a couple of warm tortillas laid over the top. "I guess Will has a Mexican working at night. Looks good. Are you hungry?"

Morgan came to the table. "Your brother is a surprising man."

"True. You never know sometimes, with Jacob."

They ate in silence for a while. Then Morgan said, "It really is quiet here tonight."

"It's the stamp mill. Mr. Snapp stopped running it at night."

"Things are slowing down? What will happen to the town if the mines play out?"

"I have some ideas."

"Tell me."

He wants to know what I'll be doing after he's gone, she thought. He wants to be able to picture it when he thinks of me.

"I don't know. I think maybe people will turn to cattle. And the town will become a real town. Maybe it will need a post office, or a school, or a stage stop."

"You sound like J.C. He's always talking about the future, too." As he spoke, his fingers softly caressed her hand. He lifted it to his lips and kissed each finger.

"I shouldn't send these plates back to Will without washing them." She pulled her hand away, got up and started to clear the table. "Don't you ever think about the future?" A hopeless look came into his eyes. He was still a fugitive and now the army was after Rubén. What future did either have, except being on the run?

"This moment is all I want to think about." He drew her onto his lap. "I want to hold you." His voice was hoarse, close to her ear, his lips brushing her skin.

She rested her head against his shoulder, felt his breath on her face. She touched his cheek.

"You're warm. I think you should lie down and rest for a little while. Come."

She guided him to the bedroom. He sat

on the edge of the bed.

"Here, let me help you." She lifted the sling over his head and hung it on the bedpost. "Lie down."

He stretched out on the bed. She pulled his boots off, then opened a drawer in the bedside table, got a match, and was about to light the lamp when he reached for her arm and stopped her.

"Rest with me."

She sank onto the bed beside him.

He ran fingers gently along her arms, leaned over her. His lips found hers. She wrapped her arms around his shoulders, pulling him closer, until the urgency was more than she could stand.

She got up and stood next to the bed.

"I don't want to have any regrets. After you're gone."

"I understand," he said.

"No. I don't think you do."

Then, one button at a time, she removed her clothing. And between caresses and kisses helped him remove his.

He was heavy, half on top of her, half beside her, still, his breath slow. She smoothed damp hair from his face and looked over his shoulder to the window. Only blackness.

Hot tears mingled with the perspiration

on her face. She slipped out of bed and opened the window. When she came back, Morgan shifted, made a space for her. He buried his face in the crook of her neck and, with a deep sigh, fell back to sleep. In each other's arms like this, she was finally close enough.

The night air cooled them. While he slept, she touched his face, his body, filled her nostrils with his scent, trying to burn it all into her memory. Sleep eluded her. After a while, she felt agitated. Not wanting to wake him, she eased out of the bed and got dressed.

In the middle of the deserted street, she listened to the creek washing over the rocks and looked up. One by one, stars faded as dawn crept into the sky beyond the canyon walls, beyond the cemetery until its white picket fence became visible in the early light.

She went back into the house to wake Morgan.

It was time to ride back to the farm.

Her memory of the leave taking: bright morning sunlight and long shadows, crying children and stoic adults. Morgan and Rubén, their heads down, reining their horses and the mule away from the family gathered by the corral . . . disappearing behind a hill. Out of sight even before they reached the wagon road.

She would never know which direction they took.

The children had drifted away, still sniffing and rubbing their eyes, as if they knew somehow she had nothing left in her with which to soothe them.

She turned toward the cabin. The coyote that had been hanging around all summer appeared between the barn and the chicken house and trotted into the yard. She picked up a stone but the coyote changed direction and ran toward the wagon road to disappear over the same hill as Morgan and Rubén.

They were gone.

Her arms and legs ached from her night of clinging to Morgan. She looked down at the stone she had meant to throw at the coyote. Round and smooth, a river rock. How nice it would be, to be impervious like this rock. Hard. Solid. Unbreakable. No place for pain to enter. She prayed, Let the waters tumble over me, Lord, and polish me as smooth as this rock.

She walked to the dooryard and lowered herself onto the bench. Warmed air floated softly against her skin. Cicadas whirred, quail cooed, and the goats bleated from down by the spring. The children shouted to each other from the barn and the garden. The sounds flowed over her.

She touched the crucifix and the pouch of sacred painting that hung from her neck. She had pulled them out from under her bodice and tried to return the crucifix to Rubén but he refused it. She was to keep it, a gift, so she would remember him.

As if otherwise I would forget.

She went inside the cabin. She lay on the bed where Morgan had almost died and, with her hand wrapped around the amulets hanging from her neck, fell asleep.

CHAPTER THIRTY-TWO

Jacob dragged Otto from the strap-iron cage and used his pistol to direct him out to the street and into the waiting prison wagon. The driver locked him in, climbed back up and slapped the reins. Miners in the street turned to look, some called out to Otto, but the big man sat with his head hanging, for once nothing to say. Jacob was happy to see him go.

Good riddance, Jacob thought, touching his bandaged hand. Now things could get back to normal. His thoughts were already turning to the hills and some prospecting when he remembered the driver had dropped off a young woman, now waiting for him in the jail.

The young woman stood when he went inside. Soft yellow hair cascaded down her back and framed the prettiest face he had ever seen, even though sunburned and peeling. She raised a gloved hand and extended it to him.

"I'm Victoria Burnham, Marshal Tillinghast. I'm very pleased to meet you."

For a moment he considered bowing and raising that dainty hand to his lips, but instead held her fingers for a moment and let go. "What can I do for you?"

"I'm looking for Howard Corbin, my fiancé."

Jacob sank into his chair behind the desk.

"He sent me this letter quite a while ago." She rifled through her reticule and produced a well-worn envelope. She took out a piece of stationery which she spread out on the desk for him to see. "This letter says he was on his way, but he never showed up. You must know him — he's conducted a lot of business here in the Chasm Creek area."

The envelope was in Howard's handwriting, addressed to the Palace Hotel in San Francisco. Jacob tilted his head back and studied the ceiling beams for a few moments. He felt the slight bulge in his vest pocket where the letter this girl had written to Howard was tucked way down where he could forget to give it to his sister. He pressed a forefinger and thumb against the bridge of his nose and closed his eyes for a moment, but she was still there when he opened them.

"Yes, I know him." He took in a deep breath which exhaled as a loud, heavy sigh.

"Do you know where he is?" Her voice quavered and her eyes grew damp.

Jacob had spent most of the last five years wishing Howard Corbin would disappear. Now that he may have done so, Jacob would have given his eye teeth to be able to put his hands on the man. Specifically, on the man's throat.

"He left town well over a month ago, maybe two months. Haven't heard from him since."

What little color was in the young woman's face drained before his eyes and she sagged a bit. He jumped up and helped her over to the cot inside the cage.

"You really came all the way from San Francisco to look for that — him?"

"On a steamer to Yuma and then on that horrible prison wagon."

Jacob gave her his handkerchief to stem the flood of tears.

"I'd run out of money, but an officer at the prison took pity on me." Her voice was soft, quiet, and sweetly sad. "I know something terrible's happened to him."

Jacob could hardly believe Howard had inspired such tenderness.

"Now that might not be the case, Miss. Maybe he got sidetracked by some business." How many little fiancés had Howard scattered across the countryside? Look at this poor girl! Barely older than Millie. Howard! Gambling and carrying on with this young girl, living a plush life while Esther and the children struggled to recover from Ida's death and keep the farm running. And where the hell was Howard now? Jacob supposed it was his duty as marshal to find out, even though he couldn't have cared less personally. But how to go about it was a puzzle.

First thing was to get rid of the girl before she crossed paths with Esther, a thought that made his stomach cramp. Not that Howard didn't deserve to be caught, but Esther had already suffered enough. He needed time to figure out how to tell her, how to handle all this. He'd have to convince this Victoria woman to go to Phoenix and await word from him there.

"Mr. Tillinghast?" She came out of the

cage clutching the wet handkerchief. "I think you should organize a search party."

Jacob pressed a hand to his forehead.

"This letter," she picked it up from the desk, "said he would be leaving for California in a few days. Isn't there a possibility that he never left the Arizona Territory? That something —" Her words caught in a sob, "could have happened before he even left?"

If nothing had happened to Howard, Jacob would make sure something did. "I think, Miss, that you ought to go to a hotel in Phoenix. This ain't no place for a young lady like yourself to be, alone as you are."

Neither is Phoenix, he thought, but at least she'd be away from Esther who, if she happened to see her, would surely ask about such a pretty stranger. And if he lied, she'd know it. She would get the truth out of him. No, Esther must not get one glance at Victoria Burnham.

The perfect, porcelain-doll face with its peeling nose took a stubborn turn, and a delicate blue vein throbbed at her temple. "I'm not leaving until I know what happened to Howard."

"Believe me, we all want to find out what happened to Howard." He directed her toward the chair behind his desk. "But since he ain't here to take care of you, I feel it's my responsibility to see that you are safe, okay?"

She opened her mouth to protest, but Jacob took her hand and filled it with coins he'd pulled from his pocket. "This should be enough to pay a driver and get a hotel room."

She nodded, her eyes filling with tears again. "Are you a relative?"

Jacob sucked in air so fast, dust caught in his throat and he coughed. "Yes, in a way, you could say we're related. I'm going to find a wagon and a driver. I promise I'll send word by the end of the week. Would that be okay?"

She nodded again. "But if I don't hear from you by then, I'll be back."

Later, he watched from the boardwalk as the wagon in which she rode disappeared around the bend at the far end of town. With a satisfied sigh, he took off his hat and gave his head a good scratching, savoring his feeling of relief at getting her out of town. Then he spotted Esther, working her way through the crowded street toward him.

"Who was that girl, Jacob?"

Chapter Thirty-Three

Esther sat in the shadows on Jacob's porch and listened to the town grow quiet. The sounds from the saloon were always the last to fade. Gradually the yelling and singing became sporadic and fewer horses traveled between the mines and the main part of town. By the early hours of the morning, not too long before dawn, silence descended over Chasm Creek. A storm threatened. Humid air muffled the banging of the stamp mill. The town hogs wallowed beside the creek, staining themselves with red mud which looked black in the moonlight, then waded into the water which washed the mud away and exposed the whiteness of their legs. They drank, making loud snorting sounds, before returning to the street to forage for more food.

She tried to lighten her gloom by thinking of happy moments, but she couldn't remember a happy moment no matter how hard she tried. Thunder rumbled far beyond the canyon walls. It sounded like low, throaty laughter. God laughing at her, enjoying this joke, torturing her with tales of Howard's adultery. She had no claim to righteousness, no entitlement to moral judgment. Her own sin diminished her anger even though she felt she was due the anger, but it didn't diminish her resentment.

In the morning she woke stiff and damp to the bone, still in the chair on the porch.

"Mama?" Millie was shaking her shoulder. "Mama?" James and Mary also stood near. She could feel the warmth of their bodies even though they seemed to float in wisps of fog.

"Millie, go ask your uncle to get our wagon from the livery."

Esther pushed herself from the chair, went inside, and began packing up their belongings, all the while aware of the younger children hovering in the cloudiness that enveloped her. They started carrying their stuff out to the wagon.

"Leave room for the goats. We're not coming back here."

James stopped midway across the living room, arms full of blankets, and looked at her. "What about our jobs? Me and Millie —"

"I don't want to talk about your jobs right now. Your job is get the wagon loaded."

They piled everything into the wagon, then drove the goats up a make-shift ramp to climb upon the household goods, balancing themselves as the rocking wagon made its way through the street, Esther cursing under her breath at every wagon, miner, hog that got in her way.

Jacob's goats scattered when she pulled up in front of the jail.

Jacob came running into the street.

"What are you doing?" He saw the children and household items piled in the wagon. Then he noticed the goats. "You've got all your stuff — even the goats!"

"I'm going home." She left him to stand in the street and watch her drive away.

When she got to the farm, she found the barn door had been smashed. It hung by one hinge and hay was scattered all over. She reined to a stop. "Richard!" she yelled.

He was at the round pen, working a horse. He snubbed it to the center post and ran over.

"Soldiers," he said. "They showed up after dark last night, about a dozen of 'em. Came pounding down the trail straight to the house. Said they were looking for renegade Indians and tore everything up. Broke down the door to the barn and rode right inside."

"Looking for Rubén," Esther said.

"They didn't say no names, but it looked that way. They went in the house, too, but they didn't hurt nothin'. Then they left."

"Oh, God, are they tracking them?" The men barely had a day's head start and they couldn't travel quickly.

"I don't think so, Ma. I heard 'em talking and they said it was too dark to follow a trail and their only orders was go to the Corbin farm and bring that old Indian back. They asked us where he went but me and Roy and Al said we didn't know what they was talkin' about."

Thank God for Captain Dugan's warning or Rubén would be hanging from a gallows at Fort McDowell this morning.

"They broke the buck goat's pen, too. He run off but he come back this morning." Richard grinned. "He's too used to being handed a flake of hay. Bet there'll be lots of kids come the new year, though."

They both looked toward the wagon road as a rider approached. Captain Dugan reined in at the wagon. "Ma'am," he said.

Esther climbed down. "You children bring that stuff into the house."

The captain dismounted and Esther led him away from the cabin. "Captain Dugan, thank you for all you've done."

"The soldiers came back without a prisoner."

"Yes, they had left yesterday morning, thanks to you."

"I regret I didn't get to say goodbye to them."

"You saved Morgan's life and now Rubén's."

"I don't know that to be true, but I wanted you to know I was able to discourage the major from sending a scout to look for them. It's a big country; they could've gone in any direction."

Any direction. She could do nothing but nod while he looked at the broken barn door and the goat shed. "Let me help with some of these repairs." He rolled up his shirtsleeves. "Ma'am, please send for me anytime you need anything. I know Morgan would want me to help out. At least until your husband returns." He went over to the goat shed and Richard handed him a hammer.

Rain pounded the roof. Wind shrieked through the trees by the spring. Esther crawled out of bed, felt her way in blackness to the window and shut it. Her feet touched a puddle beneath the sill and another one in front of the chest at the foot of the bed. She got a pan from the kitchen and put it under the leak, then went up to the loft to check on the children and put extra bedding over them. She came downstairs and pulled a blanket from the chest and threw it on her bed. She climbed in and

397

curled up, clutching the covers around her and listened to the water dripping into the pan while her mind raced.

If she left Howard, what else was there for her to do but go back east? Isn't that what women did — go back to where they came from? But she didn't want to take the children back to Providence, where grass, trees, and cobblestones smothered every inch of ground. Damp and heavy air. Leaves that blocked out the sky. How could she live again in such closeness? And how could her children bear it, having been gone so long or never having seen it, in James and Mary's case.

She thought of the night, not so long ago, when she clung to a fast horse and galloped across the desert, under clouds sparked with lightning in a vast night sky, Morgan riding at her side.

She could not leave this place.

Why should she? When Howard returned, she would tell him to leave, and she and the children would stay.

What a story she'd wrung out of Jacob. That poor young girl — traveling all this way looking for a man who had betrayed her. Business trip, indeed! In whose arms was he spending this summer?

But every time she felt outrage boiling up

over Howard's behavior, her sweet night of stolen love with Morgan stopped her. The memory that brought aching loneliness. She couldn't remember the joy without a terrible longing. What a fool she had been to think the memory would sustain her. Instead, it would be her punishment — a joke she had played upon herself. The only way she could be released from the pain would be to forfeit the memory.

Remembering was all she would have left of him, even though each time a memory rose up, it brought with it the sharp pang of loss.

He would never come back. He had asked her to leave her husband and, at that moment, she had not spoken, afraid to take a chance for herself. Afraid of making the wrong decision for her children. Afraid to break the rules.

Had she known then about Howard, she could have answered Morgan. And her answer would have been worth nothing, because she still couldn't drag four children across the country, running from bounty hunters and soldiers. He would always be a fugitive.

She wanted to be washed smooth, like the rocks in the creek bed, so these sad thoughts and unanswerable questions couldn't find purchase. She curled herself up into a ball and let herself weep until exhaustion overcame the whirling in her mind.

Her eyes opened to the dull grey of a wet morning. She got out of bed and wrapped the blanket around herself, startled to see the children already at the breakfast table, quiet, their big eyes following her as she walked past them and through the door.

Outside, fat drops of cold rain plopped on her hair, dripping through to her scalp, seeping down to her shoulders. By the time she reached Ida's grave, she was soaked. She sat by the grave, drew her knees up and wrapped her arms around them. A soft mist hung over the trees surrounding the spring. Leaves shook under the heavy raindrops. She breathed deeply of the cold, clean air and looked at the pooled water. It reflected saguaros shrouded in mist, the faint hint of mountains in the distance swathed in thick tendrils of fog.

She took no joy in the beauty; she could see it for what it was. An illusion.

Somewhere beyond those misty mountains was a man who had betrayed them all, including a girl hardly older than his own daughter. And out there somewhere — in a place she couldn't even imagine — the enormous emptiness of the world had sucked up the man she loved with all her heart and the man she had come to think of as her friend, Rubén.

She turned her eyes from the illusion in the pond to Ida's grave.

Beneath the ground lay the decomposed body of her daughter. She tried to picture her as a spirit, happy and whole, the way she used to be, the way Morgan said he saw his family in the spirit world. But all she saw was her daughter's moldering bones. And then the moldering bones of the young man she herself had killed. She began to hit her head, trying to drive out the images. Soldiers breaking her barn door, looking to hang one of the best men she'd ever known. Howard in bed with the young yellow-haired girl. She looked again at the grave. At a skeleton, shreds of rotted flesh, worms and beetles crawling over the decomposing remains of her baby.

No spirit world. No heaven. Only hell.

The rain stopped. She pulled herself in tighter, until her chin rested on her chest, and from somewhere far away she heard her children calling to her. Soft hands patted her head, shook her shoulders. She dared not look up. Something deep inside made her protect them, shelter them from what she knew. She was afraid of what they would see in her eyes if she looked up, afraid of what they would hear in her voice if she spoke, so she kept her head down and her body held tight.

Jacob blew out the flame on his miner's lamp. A thin spiral of smoke curled toward the ceiling of his dugout from the blackened wick stuck in a bowl of sand and bacon grease. The rain had stopped and all along the canyon miners were taking advantage of the cool weather to fire up their retorts. The hot little fires cast red reflections on the low-lying clouds clinging to the hillside.

He had already spent a couple of hot days working his arrastra, his goats patiently pulling large boulders around and around the stone-lined hole while he shoveled in the rocks from his mine. This morning, at dawn's first light and despite a lingering hangover, he gathered up the pulverized ore like the treasure he hoped it would be and carefully mixed it with mercury. Only gold would adhere to the mercury; worthless stone was left behind as he poured the mixture into the covered metal container. A hot fire heated the mercury to vapor which was captured in coiled metal tubing to be used again. All those little flakes became a nugget of pure gold sitting in the bottom of the retort.

He stood and stretched. No more work this morning. He had to wait for the mercury to cool. He put the nugget in the cinnamon can, turned to put the can back in his saddlebags and saw Richard at the foot of the hill, climbing toward him.

"What's wrong?"

"You need to come to the farm. Ma's sick. Like she was after Ida."

When they got to the farm, he found Esther as Richard had described. James and Mary stood over her by the grave with gloomy faces while Millie, over at the ramada, tended a fire. She lifted a pot onto the flames.

Jacob crouched beside his sister. "Essie?" He tried to take her arm but she pulled herself tighter.

Mary made a whining sound, her mouth downturned and tears filling her eyes under pinched brows.

"Millie!" Jacob yelled. "Come and get these children. Take them somewhere for a while."

"Where, Uncle Jacob? Everything's soaking wet."

"I don't care. Take them under the ramada

403

with you." He waited until they were out of earshot and leaned in close to his sister. "Essie? It's just you and me here now. Please tell me what's wrong."

Her shoulders began to shake with sobs. She let him unwrap her arms from around her legs and raise her pale face, swollen from crying.

"Oh, Jacob. Everything is such a mess."

He let out his breath and almost laughed. She recognized him and had announced an accurate assessment of the situation. Richard was wrong. This was not the same as after Ida. She was not mad. She would be all right.

"Let's see if we can't clean things up a little," he said.

He scooped her up and carried her into the house, the muddy blanket flapping from his arms. Inside, he let the blanket drop to the floor and sat her at the edge of the bed. He toweled her hair as dry as he could, found a dry nightgown for her, then made her lie down under the covers.

"I'm going to get a fire going. Take the chill off this place." He threw a handful of kindling into the fireplace and got a small fire going, adding bigger sticks and finally a good-sized log. A cheery fire filled the hearth.

All that time Esther had said nothing. She turned her back to him and pulled the quilt up to her ears.

The children came quietly into the house. Millie had the pot she'd been heating, nothing in it but water. "I thought Mama would want to wash up."

Jacob put his arm around her. "That was nice of you, Millie, but I think she's asleep. Maybe you could get some dinner ready?"

"Okay, Uncle Jacob."

He carried a chair over to the bed and watched his sister sleeping. Mary came and sat on his lap for a while, until the food was ready.

Before he went to eat, he touched Esther's forehead to make sure she wasn't feverish, and she stirred.

"Morgan?" She sat up.

"It's me. Jacob."

After a moment she said, "Oh."

Jacob reached for the box of matches. "Shall I light the lamp?"

"I was dreaming." She looked over at the children, around the table, waiting. "No. Leave it dark."

He blew out the match. "Where is Braddock? And the old — Rubén?"

"They left."

"They left? Then why did you —"

She rolled over, turning her back to him again.

"Essie . . ."

"Leave me alone. Please."

He waited for her to fall back to sleep before he joined the children at the table.

After dinner, after the children were asleep in the loft and Richard had gone out to the barn — where he said he was more comfortable now, out there with the other men — Jacob checked on Esther one more time. She was still sleeping, so he went outside. The ramada was, indeed, deserted. The old Indian's belongings, the panyards and tack for their mule, everything, gone.

He spread a blanket in the barn for his bed. In the morning, he opened his eyes to bright sunlight streaming in through the spaces in the roof. Cursing quietly for oversleeping, he went to the doorway and stretched. Goats churned up the muddy yard, going back and forth to the spring and milling around the milk stand where they stood bleating. The children went to and fro intent on their morning chores. At the far corral, Roy and Al worked to get a saddle on an uncooperative mare. Richard banged boards and nails into a broken fence section. It seemed like all was right with the world again and his mood brightened until he went back inside the house and saw Esther's breakfast on the bedside table, untouched, and she was still in bed, her back turned to everything.

He said her name but she didn't move. He said her name louder. No response. "Well, okay, then," he said. "I reckon I'll have to send for Mother to come and care for these children. I can't do it. I've got a job and a mine and —"

A pillow flew against his head. He whirled and caught it.

She was sitting up and he handed her the pillow.

"Eat. You'll feel better."

Under Jacob's watchful eye, she picked at the cold biscuits and eggs.

"They say our trials make us stronger," he said.

Coffee was still hot by the fire and he poured them each a cup.

"I feel like a vase that's been broken. You glue it back together, but it's never watertight again."

"If you weren't feeling watertight, it was a poor choice of weather to go sit in the yard and refuse to move."

"I know." A tear ran down her face.

"Look at you. You've cried so much lately,

it's become your natural state." He picked up his handkerchief and dried her cheeks. "This can't be over Howard. How many of these tears are about Braddock? At least you had the sense to finally send him packing."

"I begged him to stay."

"You what?" His sister was a fool. He, on the other hand, was not. He knew full well what had taken place at his house that night. Even Otto had figured it out. And now, after compromising his sister, the man had packed up and left town.

"Don't look so angry," she said. "There's no point."

He got up and paced from the bed to the window and back again. He sat on the edge of the bed and leaned forward, elbows on his knees, clenched his fists and tried to keep the rage from his voice.

But his anger wouldn't allow him to stay calm. He heard his own voice grow louder and could do nothing to stop it. "For God's sake, Essie, you spent the night with him and then he up and leaves you?"

"He had to leave! Oh, God, Jacob. If only I had known." She blew her nose. "And here I thought the reason Howard never touched me was because he was mourning Ida."

Jacob cringed a little inside, his fingers touching the letter in his vest pocket. But as much as he hated Howard, he didn't want his sister with Braddock either. "At least now you know you can divorce him. I'm sure he'll go along with whatever you want."

When Jacob finally left her alone, Esther pulled back the quilt on the bed. Howard's Civil War revolver, an old Colt Navy, powder can, balls, and caps were scattered across the sheet.

She tried again to load the pistol properly. She had trouble with the percussion caps but eventually managed to complete the job. She slid the gun under her pillow. Yes, now she could divorce Howard. But if he tried to get back into her house, she would be ready for him.

She lay back and imagined she again stood against the cabin, lifting the loaded shotgun. She pulled both triggers but this time, as she watched the close-range buckshot open his chest and throw him under the horses' hooves, the face was no longer Danny's but Howard's. She began to understand what Morgan meant, how a new image could replace the old and bring ease to one's heart.

CHAPTER THIRTY-FOUR

Jacob's feet rested comfortably on his desk, a bottle of mescal rising in his hand, when Victoria threw open the door and came in, dragging her battered portmanteau.

"Have you learned anything about where Howard might be?"

Had it been a week already? Jacob dropped his boots to the floor and slid the bottle into its drawer. "I asked around a bit. Everybody says he left town."

"Then you'll be sending out a search party?"

"Let's be reasonable, miss. It's not unusual for people to disappear in these parts once in a while. Maybe he's gone prospecting. He'll turn up."

"He already owns a gold mine. Why would he be prospecting?" Those blue eyes began to fill.

"He didn't happen to tell you where that gold mine was, did he?"

"Who cares? He's missing! He could be hurt or —"

Jacob leapt from behind the desk in time to catch her before she fell to the floor. He carried her to the cot inside the cage and laid her down. When she opened her eyes, she turned away from him, curled up into a

410

ball, and let out a desperate wail. "Where is he?"

"Now, now." He patted her shaking shoulder. "I'll see what I can do. You stay here and rest."

Saturday night brought miners from their claims and to congregate at Will's. A fiddle appeared, soon joined by an out-of-tune guitar. Instruments screeched, feet stomped, singing ensued and Jacob smiled. This was his favorite time of night, when the music played and everyone was happy and not yet drunk enough for the fights to start.

Through his mescal haze he recalled there was a reason he had come to the saloon. "Shit! Howard!" He pulled out his sidearm and banged it on the bar until folks settled.

He faced the customers and cleared his throat, only because it seemed any important speech he had ever heard started with throat clearing. For good measure, he spat on the floor. "This won't take long — just a quick announcement. It has come to my attention that Howard Corbin might be missing." He paused, leaning with his elbows on the bar, and waited for the hoots and exaggerated sounds of concern to subside.

He continued in his most official voice. "It has been reported that he never arrived in California, where, as we all know, he was headed when he left town. If any of you have an idea what became of him, or if he mentioned any change in plans to anybody, I'd appreciate it if you'd let me know. Otherwise, whoever's willing can meet me at the jail at daybreak for a search."

He turned and tossed down a shot. The miners resumed their revelry. Jacob drank and danced and laughed, and drank some more, trying to forget the young woman at the jail. Then a small thought insinuated itself into his foggy brain, a memory that squirmed its way eventually into a full revelation.

"What's wrong?" Will leaned across the bar, waving a bottle of mescal. "Need a refill?"

"No. Probly don't need a search party, either." A large flock of black buzzards flapped through his mind, from a ridge high in the mountains. He recalled mentioning those birds to Essie not too long after Howard had left town. The buzzards followed him out of the saloon and down the street, flapping and screeching and hissing in his mind. He stumbled to the jail. Inside, he struck a match and yelled, dropped it, and yelled again. Victoria was sitting at his desk, in the dark, wide awake. "Jesus!" he said. "Why are you sittin' there like some kind of spook?"

"What did you find out?"

He waved her out of his chair and away from the desk. He sat down and waited for his heart to slow from the fright she had given him. "We're gonna check the hills northwest of here in the morning."

He held a shaking match to the lamp on the desk, illuminating her pale face, the dark circles under her sad eyes, the lips quivering. He didn't mention his suspicions about Howard's whereabouts. If he was right, she'd find out soon enough that she was on her own.

"Too late to head to Phoenix and there ain't no hotel here. You can sleep there in the cage."

He left her there. Not so drunk that he didn't know he was drunk, he worried about climbing the hill to his mine in the dark. Instead, he went to his house where he stripped and fell onto the bare mattress in his bedroom, first time he'd ever lay down on it, and slept fitfully until a loud banging on the door awakened him.

"Marshal! You in there?"

"Oh, God." He pressed his aching temples. The banging persisted while he pulled on his trousers and shuffled barefoot to the door. He pulled it open, shielding his eyes against the early morning sunlight. "What the hell?"

"You said daybreak. We been looking all over for you 'til we saw your goats out front here."

The man standing there pointed up the road to the jail where about a dozen miners waited with their horses, one of them holding the reins to Jacob's horse, fetched from the livery, saddled and all ready to go. Some men had brought their mules, packed up as if they expected a long expedition. The goats were weaving in and out among the riders, nibbling on a stirrup or worn chaps until kicked away. It looked like most of the self-appointed posse had stayed up all night drinking and were eager for an adventurous ride into the hills.

They clattered out of town in a cloud of dust, whooping and waving their hats, but soon had to settle down and pay attention to their horsemanship as Jacob led them off the wagon road, cut across the desert and headed straight to his destination. In a couple of hours, they were gathered in the foothills northwest of Esther's farm, at the bottom of a steep incline, looking up at the ledge where Jacob had seen the buzzards earlier that summer.

"We can go the long way around on horseback, or leave the horses here and climb straight up. It's not far," Jacob said.

"Lot of cactus," one of the men said.

Half of the men followed him and the goats up the hill while the others stayed below, holding the horses and mules. Jacob's head crested the top of the ridge. Straight ahead, at eye level, lay a pile of bones. Lots of bones. He scrambled up the ledge and stood over the saddle that sat on top of the horse's skeleton.

Several of the men climbed up behind him. "How long would ya say this has been here?" one asked.

"Early summer." Jacob removed his hat and ran his fingers through his hair. "Now that I think on it, 'twas probably a few days after Howard left."

"Yeah, it's his saddle," another man said, a miner who liked to play cards in the saloon. "Who else's would it be? All fancy stitched with tassels and such while little James wears them raggedy clothes." The man who said it looked embarrassed that he had spoken such tender thoughts aloud, his eyes shifting among the others, until he saw they were nodding.

A few feet away, dead branches had fallen away to reveal a cave-like opening in the side of the hill. Jacob took a deep breath. Time to get this over with, he thought.

He walked over with the others following.

One of the men kicked at the branches. "Looks like somebody tried to hide this entrance." He pushed the dried sticks away with a boot. "Who'd want to hide a cave?"

"It's not a cave," Jacob said. "It's a mine. Look."

"Hole-eeeey shit," someone said.

Inside, the walls were excavated, shovel and pick marks evident, and wooden beams made out of mesquite trunks served as supports over a tramped hard floor. It was hard to tell how far back the tunnel once went because most of it was blocked. The shaft of sunlight slanting through the entrance pointed directly to a human skull, face down, half buried. A stretch of bony spine and broken ribs protruded from a mound of rocks, dirt, and broken wooden posts. A dung beetle crawled out from under the skull and scampered into the shadows. The men held their bandannas tight against their faces, some of them groaning and turning away.

The rest of the body lay buried in the rocks and dirt where buzzards and other scavengers couldn't reach it, but the worms and beetles had. They'd found Howard

Corbin's tomb.

Jacob found the sudden silence to be properly respectful and a little touching. After all, Howard was his sister's husband, but when he turned to fully appreciate the sight of his posse, standing with hats removed and heads bowed, he saw what had caught their reverent attention was not the rotted body of Howard Corbin, but the outstretched arm and the sack beyond the finger bones: a sack loaded with quartz stones so thickly laced with gold that they glittered even in the gloom of the mine.

Jacob picked up one of the rocks and the men behind him crowded closer, straining to get closer to the lustrous stones.

"Son of a bitch hit a vein." Jacob picked up the rest of the stones, put them in the sack and hefted it in his hand.

"There must be gold all through these here hills." The voice came from outside the mine entrance. At that, everybody bolted for the opening, pushing and shoving to get outside first.

"Hey!" Jacob yelled, following them out of the mine. "Hey!" Already some of the men were pacing out distances and ripping their shirts into rags to flag their claims. He walked to the edge of the cliff and pulled out his flask. He was in no hurry to get back

417

to town. He didn't relish the chores ahead of him, telling two women that Howard was dead. While he was pretty sure one of them was going to collapse into hysterical tears, he had no idea how his sister would react.

Someone yelled up from the bottom of the hill. "What the hell's goin' on up there?"

"Go on back to town. Somebody ride out to Howard's farm and tell my sister to come into town."

"You found him?"

"What's left of him. Don't break the news to Esther, though. That's my job. Just say I need her to come to town right away."

The men at the bottom of the hill rode away.

Jacob slid back down the hill, grabbed a shovel and a tarp from one of the mules left behind, and climbed back up. It was his sister's husband after all. Some respect should be shown. The men finished measuring and staking and, with some looking embarrassed and others impatient, watched while he headed back to the cave to shovel out Howard's remains.

Jacob took his flask out one more time at the bend in the road, knowing once they passed this point Chasm Creek would be in sight. The mule had balked all the way and now Jacob had fallen behind everyone else. He'd be the last one to ride into town. He rounded the bend and saw Esther's wagon in front of the jail. He almost panicked, then relaxed a little when he saw the whole family was actually in the wagon. Still, too close to the jail. What if that girl came outside? He hadn't thought this through. He should have gone out to the farm. Any sane man would know enough to deal with one woman at a time.

Esther spotted him coming and climbed out of the wagon. She paced back and forth in the street, waiting for him, while the riders ahead of him stopped and bunched up in the street.

The men stared down at the ground, inspected their horses' manes, looked up at the one lone cloud hanging in the northern sky, while they waited for Jacob and the mule to catch up.

"Well? What is it?" Esther demanded of one of them.

One of the men said, "It's about Howard, ma'am."

"No!" Jacob yelled.

"What about him?" Esther asked.

"Well," the man removed his hat. "He's dead, ma'am."

"Shit." Jacob pushed the flask back into

his shirt.

Jacob urged his horse onward, nudging through the crowd until a path opened on either side, like an honor guard. He drew closer to his sister, then the mule balked again. Jacob watched with growing horror as his sister's gaze landed on the mule and the canvas bundle, not more than three feet square, tied onto its back.

The mule gave out a loud bray and shook itself. It was a long shake, starting at its nose, down its neck, along its back, skin rippling over prominent rib bones, ending with a flick of the tail. Flies buzzed up from the canvas and one corner shook loose, allowing a couple of bones to slide out and plop onto the dusty street. A goat walked over and lowered its head, sniffed, then jumped back.

"I'm sorry, Essie." Jacob dismounted and rushed to her side. "That's all that was left of him. Seems he's been dead all summer."

Esther stared at the bones in the street. She raised a hand to her lips and pressed shaking fingers hard against her mouth.

Richard climbed onto the wagon seat and sat next to Millie, whose face had paled. She clung to Richard's arm. "That's Pa?"

James and Mary leaned out of the back of the buckboard near where their mother stood, straining to get a look.

One of the miners dismounted. He removed his hat, approached Esther. "We're sorry for your loss, ma'am."

"Thank you." Esther muttered around fingers still pressed against her lips. She hadn't taken her eyes off the bones in the street.

"And we was wondering, ma'am, do you think the mining office is open this afternoon? Some of us have new claims —"

Jacob shoved the man. "For God's sake! Go find Snapp if you want to file a claim!" He pulled his flask out of his shirt and held it toward his sister but she shook her head.

"Someone pick them up, for Chrissake," he yelled, pointing at the bones. He took a big swallow and noticed Victoria's face in the jail window. A couple of the men jumped down, shoved the bones back inside the canvas and retied it, flapping their hands at the flies. When Jacob looked again, the face in the window had disappeared.

He leaned toward his sister and whispered. "Guess you won't have to shoot him after all."

She pressed both hands harder against her mouth. Her eyes watered and her shoulders began to shake. Jacob put an arm around her, and she leaned heavily against him. It

421

didn't sound like she was sobbing. He bent closer, his lips at her ear. "Essie? Are you laughing?"

Mary poked James and pointed at their mother. "See? She ain't even mad!"

"Shut up," James said.

Esther headed for the jail. Jacob tried to steer her back to the wagon but she pushed against him and then broke away.

"Let us through, let us through," Jacob yelled, trying to catch up with his sister. "Can't you see she's overwrought? Hysterical!"

Jacob was still trying to grab her when she reached the jail door and pushed it open. She stopped dead and screamed. Victoria hung suspended from the top bars of the strap-iron cage, her face the same color as the dark blue pattern of the scarf tied around her neck, her arms and legs thrashing, eyes bulging.

Esther fell against the wall and screamed again.

Jacob rushed past her. "Jesus!" He pulled out his knife and sawed at the scarf, trying to hold the girl up with his other arm. The scarf fluttered apart and Jacob guided her flailing body to the cot. She landed hard and lay coughing, her hands at her neck, her mouth open wide in a red face.

"You're okay now, you're okay." He loosened the scarf and pulled it from her neck, then heard the wagon rolling away. "Stay right here."

He ran to the window. Esther and the children were headed out of town. The posse had disappeared. The mule stood in the middle of the street, flicking its tail at the hovering flies, surrounded by Jacob's goats nibbling at the canvas.

When she got back to the farm, Esther spent the afternoon doing chores and trying not to think. Not thinking about Howard. Not thinking about being a widow, whatever that would mean. She put Roy and Al to work in the garden.

"Looks like it's gonna rain." Al studied the sky.

"And when it rains, you can quit," she said.

They began plowing under the dead summer garden so the winter planting could begin. Richard was assigned to the barn: fix the door, clean up the hay, repair the buck goat's pen so he can't get out again. Yes, she knew he was not inclined to do so, do it anyway. She assigned Millie to clean out the chicken house, rake up the manure and haul it by the bucketful to Roy and Al so they could spread it in the garden before any rains came. She didn't know where the two youngest were. Off somewhere playing, which was fine with her.

She lit a fire in the outside ring, heated the tub of water, washed everything in the cabin she could get her hands on. She scrubbed the kitchen chairs, the table, the bed frame. Then she took all the towels and rags outside. It felt good to rub everything against the scrub board, her hands immersed in hot, soapy water to her elbows, not minding the lye soap on her skin. She wrung it all out, hung it on the line, and propped the line up with the pole they used.

She went inside and started sweeping but in a pause between passes with the broom she heard muffled sobs coming from the loft. She went up the stairs. James was sitting on his pallet, his face wet with tears, but it was Mary who was sobbing.

"I'm sorry, Mama. I'm sorry."

The girl was on her knees, her rear end sticking up, her face buried in her pillow. She said something but the pillow muffled her voice.

Esther pulled her away from the pillow and made her repeat what she had said.

"We did it, Mama! We're sorry."

"You did what?"

"We killed Pa. Me and James."

"What on earth are you talking about?"

"Remember the day Pa left?" James asked. "When you spanked me and Mary for going into town?"

Esther nodded. "Go on."

"We didn't go into town. We followed Pa. He went across the fishin' creek and up in the hills."

"He never saw us," Mary chimed in. "He went up this steep hill, so we climbed up and followed him inside."

"He went in a cave." James talked faster. "We snuck in and hid and he was comin' out and when he saw us he jumped and he banged into a piece of wood against the wall and it all fell."

"Fell?"

"On top of him."

Mary looked at her mother with big round eyes and nodded her agreement.

"He was all squashed under that piece of wood and stuff and yellin'," James said. "And we started to run out but he yelled even louder."

"Yeah." Mary made her voice low and mean. "Get back in here, you little brats!"

"I told him, Mama," James said. "I told him I was gonna get some help, but he said no — you get back here! He said he didn't

425

want nobody finding his mine. He called us names —"

"Bad names," Mary said. "Little bast . . . bastids!"

"All the time he was tryin' to pull himself out from under them rocks. I tried to help, Mama. I tried. Honest."

The children fell silent.

"Well? Then what?"

"We heard noises coming from over our heads and we got scared so we ran out."

"Oh dear God."

"More fell down. Rocks. Dirt," James said.

Her littlest ones had seen this?

"All that stuck out was his one arm."

"And his head, James." Mary wrinkled her nose. "There was blood comin' out from his mouth."

"Oh, God," Esther moaned. "Why didn't you tell me?"

"I wanted to, Mama." Mary crawled over and snuggled into her mother's lap, clinging to her, and looked up with tear-filled eyes and trembling lower lip. "Pa said not to tell where he was. He said if we told he'd make us sorry! We'd be in a lot of trouble just for being there. I was scared he was gonna get me."

Howard had been the monster in Mary's nightmares?

"And I was afraid you'd get sick again, like when Ida died." James burst into tears and she pulled him close, wrapped her arm around him. He cried into her neck.

"Oh my God."

"When you cried so much after Ida died, Pa said he was gonna send you to a place for crazy people," James said. "I was afraid, Mama! I didn't want you to go away. Not to no place for crazy people!"

She pulled them closer, hugging and rocking them.

"Listen to me. You didn't kill your father." She wished with all her heart that she had killed him — a long time ago. "The rocks fell on him, and he's dead. That's all. You didn't kill him." Oh, God, how she wished they had told her. "And I'm not going to get sick. I'm not going to a place for crazy people." She kissed their cheeks and made them say they believed her.

The children cried themselves into exhaustion and fell asleep, one on each shoulder. She eased them onto their pallets and went downstairs. She slipped outside and sat on the bench by the door. The sky had grown overcast and the air smelled like rain.

Richard came out of the barn carrying a saw and a hammer. When he saw his mother, he came toward her, smiling, but when he got closer his expression became serious. "Ma? Are you okay?"

"I'm fine, dear. Go on back to what you were doing. I need some time to be alone, to be quiet."

"Are you that sad about Pa? Because none of us is."

"Richard! That's harsh."

"May be." He shrugged. "But we never liked the way he treated you or us."

He peered at her with his grown-up concern. "I'll be at the goat pen if you need anything. Roy and Al went into town for supplies, I don't know what, and Millie's helping me."

"Thank you, son."

Then she was alone. In the quiet yard, only a few horses left in the corrals, the goats off somewhere foraging for grass, even the chickens were still. And the thoughts came, the ones she'd tried to crowd out of her mind from the moment she had heard about Howard. Seen his bones lying in the dirt. Regrets. She buried her face in her hands but no tears came. She leaned back against the cabin. "I might not go to hell," she whispered to herself. "At least not for committing adultery."

The commandments didn't even address the worst sins anyway. Nobody ever said thou shalt not be a fool. Thou shalt not live thy life making stupid decisions. She wiped the tears that finally came, cried not for Howard but for her own stupidity. She took in a deep breath and looked up to see a rider approaching. A man in uniform, riding a grey dun horse with a pretty gait.

She stood up, smoothing her hair and running her hands down her apron before stepping out into the yard.

He reined to a stop and dismounted, smelling of cigars and soap and saddle leather. He removed his hat. "Ma'am."

"Captain Dugan, what brings you out here again so soon?"

"I heard about your husband. I wanted to offer my condolences."

Esther knew she was supposed to say something, but all she could do was look at the compassionate face, the concerned eyes. This officer stood in front of her offering sympathy. This kind hearted man.

She brushed her hair out of her face. "Thank you."

"I understand your husband served in the war."

"He did."

"I'd like to offer a military funeral, at the fort. With all the appropriate honors."

A harsh laugh burst from her lips, and she

clapped her hand over her mouth. She studied the captain's dusty boots and felt her cheeks redden. Light drops of rain pattered into the dirt. "I'm sorry, it's been a hard day."

"I understand." He stood straight, as if he were at attention, both hands holding his hat at his waist.

"We'll bury him in the cemetery in town. That'll be good enough."

"Ma'am?"

"I mean so the children can visit, bring flowers, you know."

"Of course." Captain Dugan nodded, his eyes friendly. "They'd want to do that." He mounted his horse.

"It was kind of you to offer, though." The captain didn't seem in a hurry to get back to the fort. He sat his horse, looking past her to the house. A smile came to his face and she glanced back to see Mary and James had come out onto the porch.

"I know I said it before, ma'am, but if you need anything please send for me."

"I won't need anything."

"I hope you won't mind if I stop by now and then, to be sure."

She put a hand on the horse's neck. "Do you hear from Morgan?" It was what she had wanted to ask from the moment she saw the captain riding in.

"No." The smile left his face, but the kindness lingered in his eyes. "I don't expect to." He put his hat on and touched the brim. "Mrs. Corbin." He reined his horse around and rode away.

She awoke in the night and went to the window. In the dark sky a line of peach-colored light glowed behind the hills to the east. She pushed the window sash open. Cold air rushed in. The rain of the previous afternoon had extinguished every trace of summer as suddenly and completely as a heavy blanket slapped on a fire.

Pulling her nightdress closed at the neck, she touched the rawhide strip that held Rubén's crucifix and the pouch of dry painting. She lifted the cord over her head and held them in her hand. She ran a finger over them.

Through the window, the glow spread across the horizon, turned golden, swallowed the stars one by one.

She left the window and knelt at the trunk at the foot of the bed, coiling the rawhide around the amulets, and dug into a spot underneath the bedding and extra shawls and Howard's flannel shirts. She tucked the bundle into a deep corner. She layered

everything back over it and lowered the lid.
The latch clicked into place.

She threw on her shawl and went out to
milk the goats.

Chapter Thirty-Five

They traveled hard for several days after
leaving Chasm Creek, Morgan pushing
them on despite Rubén's pleas for a slower
pace and more rest. But Morgan said J.C.
could delay Major Whitehall for only a
while, and there was no way to know how
long nor if there would be a pursuit. So
Morgan pushed them along. Rubén paid
little attention to the direction of their flight
or to anything except his concern for his
friend, who was still sick and in pain. But
after several days he took notice of their sur-
roundings.

He said, "This is not the way to California."

They passed the San Francisco peaks and
the land opened up, awash in pinks and
greens in an early morning light. They
stopped at the crest of a hill, sat their horses.

Rubén's eyes fell upon *Diné-tah* for the
first time in over sixty years. Through his
sudden tears a vast landscape wavered and

the word — *querencia* — had come to his lips.

"What do you mean?" Morgan had asked.

It was a word from his young days in Mexico City, from the bullfights, the place the bull went to in the ring to draw strength before facing the toreador again. "It is where one feels safe, where one's power is drawn, restored. It is home, you could say, but more." He did not know how to put it into English for his friend.

They rode more slowly through tawny grasslands frothed with seed, past hummocks of gray rock encircled with white horizontal stripes in the shadow of red sandstone cliffs. As they traveled through the unearthly landscape, the days grew shorter and the nights colder. Several mornings, while he stirred the fire back to life, Rubén saw herds of elk or antelope in the mist, moving ghost-like across the painted plains.

When first they came upon hogans, the family emerged and stood watching with wary expressions. Once they heard the name Morgan Braddock, wariness disappeared. The *Diné* had their stories, stories of a white man who stood up to the *Bilagáana* at the Bosque Redondo and later had taken revenge for the massacre at his ranch, and they welcomed Morgan. Then Rubén introduced himself as *haltsooí din'é,* born to *bit' ahnii.* When they realized he was a stolen child returned after so many decades, the children rode on fast horses to spread the word, and nearby families gathered to celebrate.

This pattern repeated each time they reached a new cluster of hogans. Rubén and Morgan lingered for days at each stop, allowing the singing and feasting to feed their souls and heal their bodies.

Rubén's presence comforted many families still searching for stolen children. He learned that, after signing the last treaty, the *Bilagáana* promised to arrange the return of Mexican and New Mexican captives, but those promises remained unfulfilled. Several times headmen had traveled all the way to Washington and spoke with the President of the United States — to no avail. They were told to pursue their claims in the courts, but judges running the local courts still held their own Navajo slaves.

Families of those slaves, mothers and grandmothers, sought Rubén out, asked him to tell his story over and over again, content to sit near him and occasionally reach out and touch his arm.

He grew ashamed that he had ever denied

or disparaged these people. How much they had accomplished in the ten years since their surrender and imprisonment!

In the last year alone over a half million pounds of wool had been sold to markets back east, they told him with great pride.

They said the *Bilagáana* told many lies, claiming to have defeated the *Diné,* but that had never happened. In Canyon de Chelly alone, hundreds avoided capture by hiding on top of Fortress Rock, and were never removed to the Bosque Redondo. They even saved saplings of the cherished peach trees, and now the orchards flourished again, they told Rubén. At mention of the peach orchards, his heart and eyes filled.

More *Diné,* those who lived in the western areas, thousands, escaped capture. And those that had been removed eventually returned and flourished. They had survived, persevered. Never defeated.

He and Morgan slowly made their way through the reservation, to hogans spaced to leave plenty of grazing for each family's stock, and they rode sometimes for days before being greeted by a new family. At each stop, Rubén's respect for these people grew. He witnessed their industriousness and enjoyed their sense of humor. They had worked their way back from complete devastation to prosperity. They made jokes about the often missing treaty allotments — they did not need them.

Eventually, Rubén and Morgan came to a trading post, a long, low structure of rocks and dried mud in the middle of the high desert, run by John Lorenzo Hubbell. Colorful blankets hung from stunted trees surrounding the building.

They dismounted by a water trough and, after the horses slaked their thirst, Morgan and Rubén stretched their legs by wandering around the trees, looking at the wares. Morgan touched a woolen saddle blanket with tightly woven stripes of black and red and cream. "This would make a nice replacement for that ratty thing you've got now."

"*Si*, that is a fine piece of work. Hand it to me, *por favor*, and I will ask its price."

Morgan lifted the blanket from the tree branch.

"Be careful. Do not snag it!"

Inside the trading post a warm fire crackled in the fireplace and Hubbell stood behind a wooden counter. Shafts of sunlight streamed in through several windows, illuminating more blankets and paintings covering the walls. Piles of silver jewelry covered the counter, and shelves held bags of flour, canned goods, and other items needed for life on the reservation.

Señor Hubbell's gaze fell upon the blanket in Rubén's hands. He smiled. "You have excellent taste," he said. "Anaba Nizhoni is one of our most talented artisans."

Rubén clasped the blanket to his chest. "Anaba?" he whispered.

Morgan leaned toward him. "Are you all right?"

"My childhood friend. She was there the day the Mexicans came."

Rubén held the blanket tighter, sank his face into it, closed his eyes. He saw again that morning when the Mexican rider had grabbed him, hauled him onto his horse and rode away. Rubén had twisted with all his strength to look back and saw his little friend running, screaming, through the scattering sheep.

When he felt he could speak, he asked, "Where does this Anaba Nizhoni live?" and prayed for a good answer.

"Canyon del Muerto," Hubbell said. "About forty miles north of here."

Rubén lifted his head and looked at Morgan. "We could be there tomorrow!"

The next day, their horses' hooves tramped softly in the sandy soil and mud beside a trickle of a stream meandering through the center of the canyon. They rode between towering red sandstone formations that grew taller and steeper as they entered the depths of the gorge. Ravens took flight from their perches among the rocks, caws echoing high above as their black shadows slid down the sides of the cliffs.

Rubén shivered. Overhead the sky was blue but the yellow sunlight illuminating the upper canyon walls did not reach them.

The ravens disappeared beyond a turn in the path and all fell silent except for saddles creaking and jangling bits. Sheer rock loomed above them, a thousand feet high. He raised his eyes toward the sky and saw, nestled in an overhang more than halfway up the sheer walls, buildings similar to those on Haunted Hill. Homes with windows, doorways, round towers, smaller separate buildings. He had paid little attention to these structures when he was a child, but now he stared at them with wonder. Where had those people gone? How could they abandon this beautiful canyon? Wherever they were now, did they still think of this place? Perhaps their souls remained. Ghosts. Or in the people themselves, in his own blood, in his own heart.

Rubén marveled at the sight and the rush of memories caused by all of the scenery they rode by. He recognized each tree, each rock. They spouted forth vivid images of his childhood. This tree he had climbed. That rock he hid behind. The trees had grown larger and the rocks smaller, but he knew them. The juniper plains above the canyon had been his last sight of *Diné-tah* but here, within its sheltering walls, he had spent most of his young childhood.

He looked at Morgan and saw that his friend was also lost in reverie. He reached over and patted Morgan's arm, smiled at him. He wished all memories could be happy ones.

"They say the ancient ones could fly," Rubén said. "That's how they got up to their homes so high in the cliffs."

Morgan looked up at the cliffs and smiled. "They could fly, you say. I like the idea."

Where the canyon diverged, they turned to the north, entering Canyon del Muerto. The passageway narrowed, the cliffs loomed higher. They moved in and out of shadow, depending on the direction of the winding trail. Trees and brush forced them to ride close to the narrow stream until the walls widened and opened onto a field to the left of the path. Cattle and goats and sheep grazed on the thick grass. Bright yellow cottonwoods shimmered against towering rock walls that glowed purple in the morning light and enclosed the field on three sides.

Farther back, nestled against the rock walls, were the peach trees.

"I know this place!" Rubén put his heels to his horse. At a fast trot he rode straight toward the hogans beside the orchard.

He called her name as he rode. "Anaba! Anaba!"

A hand pushed aside a blanket in the doorway of a hogan as Rubén approached. Anaba emerged. Her eyes peered out from dark copper skin and, although sunken in scars and wrinkles, they still sparkled like stars in the night sky as Rubén remembered.

She raised a hand to shield her face from the sun. "Who calls my name?"

"It is your friend Yiska!" He reined in his horse. "I found your blanket at Hubbell's. He directed me here. My heart bursts to find you alive and well after all these years."

Her aged face lit up. She opened her arms as he climbed from his horse.

He embraced her, rested his cheek against her white hair.

She welcomed him and his friend into her family.

They provided a hogan for him and his friend, and a celebration larger than any previous took place for many nights. They stayed for weeks that turned into months, and he and Anaba told each other the stories of the long lives they had lived since fate had ripped them apart. Rubén learned her husband had died on the Long Walk, and a newfound anger toward the white men with whom he had lived surged within him. This new family saw his anger and regrets grow until the husband of Anaba's oldest daughter brought him to the sweat hogan and taught him the ceremonies. He spent many hours there until his judgments and resentments washed from his pores. He no longer held hatred toward his people or the *Bilagáana*. His heart held only gratitude.

When he realized this, he went to Anaba and told her.

"Now you are again *Nabahiidiné,*" she said. "A child of the Holy People."

On this morning he dribbled more water onto the rocks and offered a prayer of thanksgiving for the good fortune of his people and himself. Inside the cone-shaped hogan, he held the gourd ladle over heated rocks, tipped it and let water drip and burst into a cloud of sage-scented vapor that would carry his prayers through the smoke-hole to the Holy People. The rough wooden beams added the scent of juniper, and all of it smelled like home. He remembered the day he'd ridden up to Anaba's home and the broad smile upon Morgan's face. His friend had brought him here. To have a friend like that was truly a blessing. Morgan had known where Rubén needed to be, and it was not California!

He came out of the hogan, blinking in the bright sunlight, and stretched. Fluffy white clouds in the sky above the canyon rims mirrored the herds of sheep that grazed along the stream flowing at the base of vermillion cliffs. He bent and scooped handfuls of fine red sand to rub over his body until he was dry.

After he dressed he followed the well-worn path leading back to the family lands. The peach trees extended their leafless branches to form a canopy over his head. Along the banks of the stream, the white, boney branches of late autumn cottonwoods clacked against each other in the cool breeze.

Rounding a bend, he neared the hogans of Anaba and her three grown daughters, Sitsi, Yanaba, and Yazhi. Anaba worked at the huge outside loom. Morgan sat on the ground nearby, the carding brushes in his hands, the smaller grandchildren and great grandchildren climbing all over him in their play.

Rubén loved to watch Anaba's patient hands dance around her loom, the flying shuttle weaving through the colored yarns, creating a design that already existed in her mind. The movements and soft sounds mesmerized him, wrapped his bones with a feeling as soft as the wool fibers that clung to the wooden frame.

And while Rubén was healing his heart and soul, his friend had also been healing. It pleased Rubén to see how Morgan had lost the gauntness that had ridden with them when they left Chasm Creek. Tsohanoai, the Sun Bearer, had painted healthy color on Morgan's face, and not one headache since the healing ceremony in Esther's cabin. Still, Rubén worried about the sadness that sometimes lingered in his friend's eyes.

Morgan saw him coming, pulled a few children off and stood. Together they walked away from the family.

"The men are returning." Morgan nodded to the south where riders drove herds of horses before them to join the sheep and goats. The family's stock would spend the cold months in the shelter of the canyon far below the windswept piñon and juniper plains.

Morgan lifted his face up to the sun, eyes closed.

Rubén felt a chill in the breeze. "Soon it will be winter." Sandstone cliffs glowed in sunlight. Silhouettes of the men and their herd of horses disappeared against desert varnish that stained the walls black, then reappeared. "I am looking forward to snow again."

Morgan smiled. "I kind of miss the warm weather myself." He pulled close the woolen tunic Anaba had made for him.

Rubén thanked the spirits again as Morgan held the tunic tight with the hand that had been crippled. Shortly after they arrived, Anaba said she wanted Morgan to help her with her weaving.

"He can't help you," Rubén had said. "He is still too sick."

"I need my wool carded so my daughters can spin it. Mr. Hubbell is waiting for more blankets."

Rubén shook his head. "He cannot even hold onto a piece of wool. His fingers do not close! Let me help you instead."

Anaba Nizhoni frowned. "No. I want your friend to help me."

When she asked Morgan, he said he could

444

not refuse her anything. He would try. She used strips of soft leather to tie the injured hand to a carding brush. At first, his attempts were awkward but after several days and some adjustments to the method of wrapping the leather ties, the results improved.

For days, Morgan sat silently beside the old woman while she worked her loom. He brushed and brushed. One day, he began to talk. He talked all day. The next day, and the next, he continued to talk.

Once, when Rubén and Anaba were alone, he asked if she knew that Morgan spoke of the dead.

"You know I do not speak the language of the *Bilagáana.*"

"He should not speak of the dead. He will disturb *hozho.*"

"He is our friend, but he is *Bilagáana* and has different ways. He needed to speak of these things." She smiled. "I needed my wool carded. I am weaving his words into the blanket."

Each week Anaba had used fewer leather strips to tie the brush, and each day Morgan spoke less of his lost family and more of other things. His hand became strong and healthy again.

Rubén thought of all this as he stood

445

beside his friend.

"What are you smiling about?" Morgan asked, pulling Rubén into the moment, away from memories.

"I was thinking about how things that seem lost forever can be found again."

"You've found your place," Morgan said. "It's good to see you so peaceful."

"And what about you? Have you found peace?"

A wintry gust blew Morgan's hair across his face, and he brushed it away. "Hell, it took you sixty years. I know you say this is my home, but I'm not sure."

"You are not thinking of leaving?"

"I don't know. Maybe."

"There are always answers if you seek them. Maybe you should go into the desert with no food or water and ask for a vision, like Jesus did."

"Is that a ritual of the *Diné* I haven't heard of?"

Rubén laughed. "No self-respecting Navajo would wander around in the desert without water. We prefer the sweat hogan when we seek answers."

That night Morgan slept in his hogan and dreamed of going into the desert. He walked for days, to where the canyon opened up into a vast plain of swirling colors splashed and spread across the flat ground, on the hills, up the sides of the sandstone monoliths that jutted abruptly and cast dark shadows across the land. Yellow lichen speckled the smooth walls of the canyon.

He found himself on a promontory. He sat and watched shadows grow long. Darkness fell and brilliant stars studded the night sky. Towering shadows etched black designs on the valley floor as the glittering moon sailed from one horizon to the other, and the beauty of the land filled his heart with peace.

Sun Bearer appeared on the horizon and Morgan closed his dreaming eyes. The red haze behind his eyelids faded to sparkling white. It's snowing, he thought. It's snowing and Rubén is missing it.

The white light turned to a crimson mist through which two eyes approached. The eyes grew closer and larger. Silhouetted against the red of a sunset sky, a coyote panted, blurry and transparent, shadowy paws barely touching the ground, eyes like golden nuggets. It turned, then stopped and looked back over its shoulder. Its eyes had melted and were streaming like tears, leaving golden streaks across its muzzle. Then it dashed away and dissipated into the red sky.

■ ■ ■

The next day, Rubén listened to Morgan recount the dream. They stood by a fire ring outside their hogan, hands held toward the warmth. Brown grass spiked through a thin dusting of snow.

"A dream like that has meaning," Rubén said. "Let us talk to Anaba Nizhoni."

At the old woman's hogan the fire crackled. Sweetened smoke pirouetted up through the smoke hole.

"Leave it to a white man to have such a foolish vision." She grunted as she settled herself more comfortably on a pile of blankets. "Coyote is nothing but a trouble-maker. You thought he had eyes of gold, but it was only pine sap. The coyote cannot see what is right before him. Neither can you. You let your dreams melt in the sun." She shook her head sadly. "You must learn to listen to your heart. That is what will guide you."

"Damn it, Rubén. Why did you make me tell her?" Morgan spoke in English. "Now I look foolish to Anaba Nizhoni."

But Rubén replied in the language of the *Diné*. "You are a white man. You always look foolish to her."

448

Anaba laughed. "Do you want me to tell you what to do? I do not need a vision to see the way." She sprinkled a bit of dried sage into the fire. "All you have to do is ask."

"Tell me," Morgan said.

"You dream of coyotes that run away because it is time for you to go."

Morgan got up abruptly and went outside.

"No!" Rubén cried out. "How could you say that to him? He is my friend."

"And you are a good friend to him. That is why you will let him go." Anaba got to her feet. "He has spirits in his heart that are calling him. Spirits that long for him as much as he longs for them."

"What are you saying?"

Anaba shook her head. She shuffled to the other side of the room. "You see the sadness that hangs around him like a cloak. It will always be so with him."

Did she know of his walk in the spirit world? About the choice he made at that time? When he opened his mouth to ask, she laughed. "I understand more English than you know." She picked up the blanket Morgan had helped her with. "Give this to him. It is his."

Rubén joined Morgan outside the hogan. Clouds heavy with snow filled the sky. "It does not seem the right time to me. Stay."

449

Morgan folded his arms across his chest and hunched against the chill wind. "You've found your place, Rubén. I need to find mine."

"My family is your family. Your place can be here if you choose to make it so." He hugged the blanket to his chest. "You already knew what Anaba would tell you."

"It's time. I've already packed to go. I was ready early this morning."

Rubén looked away. "Go then, *si kis*." He used the *Diné* word for friend. "I know too well what it is like to be in a world that is not your own. You have been like a son to me. For that, and for many other reasons, I will always be grateful to you."

"I am your son, Rubén."

Rubén nodded. His throat closed with sudden sadness. He held the blanket out to his only friend. He wanted him never to leave, but Anaba was right. Morgan was right. "Will you come back someday?"

"A part of me will always be with you, with the *Diné*. And you, *shizhe'e*, my father, my friend, will always be with me."

He tied the blanket next to his bedroll, then removed his silver and malachite ring and placed it in Rubén's hand. He closed the gnarled fingers around the ring before releasing his grip.

450

Rubén pressed his fist to his heart, and tears ran into the crevices of his face. "Go," he said. "Find your home. Your *querencia.*" His friend swung into the saddle and reined his horse away. Its hooves broke through the thin ice covering the shallow stream as Morgan rode toward the narrow canyon path. The clouds broke apart and a bright shaft of sunlight descended into the canyon, turning the dull brown leaves clinging to a cottonwood to shimmering copper. Four ravens took flight from the rock wall, circled above, called out, and Morgan looked up toward the sound. Rubén watched the ravens until the wind blew the clouds again, thwarting the sun. The ravens' shadows faded before they reached the canyon floor. Rubén's eyes again sought his friend, but he was gone.

Chapter Thirty-Six

"What're you doing here, boy?" Jacob tucked his flannel shirt into his trousers and pulled his suspenders up. He'd emerged from his privy to find James scrambling up the rocky hillside. "Does your ma know where you are?"

"She was still asleepin' when I left." James pulled his shirtfront out of his trousers and let the small sack he had hidden there fall into his hands. He held it out to his uncle.

"What's this?" Jacob pulled open the drawstring. The sack was full of eagles, half eagles, silver dollars. "Where'd you get this?"

James pulled himself up to his full four-foot height. "It's my sweepin's. And my winnin's. All the money I made last summer at the saloon. Mr. Will bought all the gold dust and was holdin' this for me."

"You made this much? Why, it's a small fortune!"

The boy nodded. "I know. I was gonna use it for Christmas, but I thought maybe you could go to Prescott."

"Did you want me to take you there? To shop for Christmas gifts?"

James shook his head. "I want you to hire a detective to find Mr. Braddock. That would be better than Christmas presents, wouldn't it?"

Jacob hefted the sack of money in his hand. "You want to spend all this money to bring Braddock back?"

"I think Mama misses him."

Jacob stared down into the earnest eyes of his nephew. Such compassion in that little face, and barely ten years to accumulate it.

"Yes, I suppose she does, James." He

shoved the money inside his own shirt.

"Don't tell Ma, okay? Let it be a surprise."

He doubted that James would get what he wanted, but he wasn't opposed to taking a ride to Prescott, for his own reasons. And he wasn't going to tell Essie about that either.

When Jacob got to Prescott, he made inquiries among the law enforcement officials regarding a young blonde woman. He'd heard Victoria had gotten an offer of a job in Prescott — that was all he knew. That and she was gone from Chasm Creek and she wasn't in Phoenix either. He figured she was working in one of the saloons but none of the lawmen knew of anybody recently hired, and they kept pretty close track of the whores, especially the pretty ones.

Then a deputy recalled a pretty young lady who had gone to work for the Tone family, in a big house on Marina Street.

"There's a whore house on Marina?" The sheriff was obviously shocked. "Since when?"

"Hell, no. I don't know what she's doin' up there, but she ain't whorin'."

Jacob had been expecting to pay out a couple of dollars and have a nice time with a pretty whore, figuring that must be what she had been doing when she threw in with Howard. In fact, he'd been dreaming of it since he heard she'd quit Phoenix for Prescott, and James had given him the perfect excuse to make his dreams come true. But she was no whore, as the deputy had said. He hadn't planned on paying a call on a lady. Not at the home of an influential family.

Maybe next time he'd wear better clothes.

The next day he went to the Pinkerton office, and received more disappointing results. When he talked to them about searching for Braddock, they informed him they had neither the time, manpower nor inclination to embark on such a fruitless endeavor, at least not for the amount of money being offered. By Jacob's own admission, Braddock could be anywhere on earth. The agent also pointed out that, according to Jacob, the man had no roots, no family ties, and had given no hint as to which direction he was headed when he left. The chances of finding him were millions to one, and Jacob should be grateful the company was too conscientious to steal his money.

He'd left their office, intending to head for home. The goats followed as he led his horse from the livery, ducking his head against the cold wind blowing down Montezuma Street, whipping up dry leaves and scattering them across the courthouse square. He passed the Depot House on Whiskey Row and happened to glance through the window. A fire roared in the big stone fireplace. One drink to warm up before he headed south, back to Chasm Creek, wouldn't hurt anything.

Inside, he leaned against the bar and enjoyed his drink. Behind him boots tapped on rough floorboards in time to a piano, glasses clinked and whores laughed. Outside the wind whined through naked tree branches and rattling shutters. One drink turned into another as he contemplated his wasted time in the territorial capital.

He had another shot of mescal to push away the vision of James' disappointed face, the face he would encounter when he got home. He appreciated the Pinkertons not taking the boy's money when they knew the search would be fruitless, and he hadn't wanted Braddock found anyway. The man was no good for Esther. After all, she had begged him to stay and he still rode off.

The wind shrieked outside and heavier clouds darkened what little midday light managed to squeeze through the sooty windows. He didn't relish the trip back to Chasm Creek in this weather. It was too early for snow, not even Thanksgiving yet, but maybe he should wait a day or two. Just one more drink, then he'd take the animals back to the livery. His thoughts drifted toward Marina Street. He could call on her, the way you called on a lady.

The door banged open in a flurry of dried leaves. A tall man in a dark oil-cloth duster, hat pulled down over his eyes, pushed the door shut. The customers at the tables grumbled at the blast of cold air before resuming their drinking and card playing. But Jacob felt a lingering chill as he watched the man brush dust off his clothes.

"Jesus Christ," Jacob muttered as he whirled around to face the bar. Within seconds a hand closed on his shoulder.

"Jacob? I saw the goats outside —"

"There's plenty of goats in Prescott."

"Not with pack saddles and panyards. They were drawing a crowd."

"Someday people'll see the sense of it."

Braddock eased up to the bar and ordered a whiskey. He took a sip, then asked, "How goes it in Chasm Creek?"

"You mean how's Esther, don't you?"

Braddock finished his drink and did not reply.

"You'll be pleased to know the ditches you and Rubén dug work fine — good winter

456

crop planted. Roy and Al are still there —
they make better farmers than they did
wranglers. Things are good, real good."

"Well, I am pleased to hear it." Braddock
held up his glass. This time the bartender
left the bottle. "I take it her husband is
back."

"Oh, yes, he's definitely back. Since
shortly after you left, as a matter of fact.
'Twas his gold mine that paid off the farm."

"She's happy, then?"

"Oh, yes, I would say she's happy. Very
happy, indeed." Jacob glanced over and
caught the look that flashed across Braddock's face.

"You weren't on your way to see her, were
you?"

Braddock cleared his throat. "I'm on my
way back east. I thought I'd head down to
Maricopa and take the train."

"Take it where?"

"I don't know. Maybe back to Vermont."

Jacob pushed his glass away. Perhaps he'd
had too much to drink. When he looked at
Braddock all he could see were his sister's
sad eyes. Oh, she tried to hide it, but he
knew. And James' hopeful face, asking him
to find Braddock for his Mama. Even when
that Captain Dugan had come into town,
he looked unhappy. In fact, every time he'd

457

seen Captain Dugan out at the farm helping out, the man appeared unhappy, more
so whenever he looked at Essie. All those
people, who in Jacob's estimation seemed
normal otherwise, sulking and pining because of this jasper. He shook his head. May
as well make everyone happy. Essie, you are
going to owe me for this.

"Maybe you should stop by. She might
want to buy your horse."

"I can sell the horse to J.C." Braddock
twirled the empty glass between his hands,
then refilled it. "I don't know if I could take
another goodbye."

Jacob looked up at the ceiling and sighed.

"You'd be passing practically right by
Chasm Creek. The children would want to
see you."

Braddock smiled a little, but it faded
quickly. "It wouldn't be a good idea . . .
with her husband there. I don't want to
cause her any more trouble."

Jacob leaned closer. "Well, Howard isn't
exactly there — at the farm, I mean. Okay,
actually, I have somewhat sad news about
Esther's husband."

He waved the empty mescal bottle at the
barkeep. When a full bottle was placed in
front of him, he filled his glass and took a
big gulp.

"Turns out he had a little girlfriend in California the whole time." Jacob launched into the whole story about Victoria. By the time he got to the part about the attempted hanging in the jail, Braddock had slipped his pistol from its holster, checked each chamber, and threw some coins on the bar.

Jacob grabbed Braddock's arm. "Wait! Where're you going?"

"Chasm Creek." Braddock pried Jacob's hand loose. "It's time I met this Howard."

"You intend to kill him!" Jacob started to laugh, and then laughed harder at the confused look on Braddock's face.

"If it comes to that."

Jacob tried to keep a straight face. "Like I said, he's not actually out at the farm."

Braddock was halfway to the door. He stopped and turned. "Where is he, then?"

"Oh, he stayed in town." He waited a few seconds, the better to enjoy the look on Braddock's face. "In the cemetery."

High in the Bradshaws, Morgan pulled his hat down as far as he could. He could barely see five feet ahead as the snow blasted sideways across the trail. The weather had taken a turn. When they got into the mountains the temperature had dropped and the rain showers they'd headed out in had turned to flurries. And now this, much more than flurries. The whiskey was wearing off. He realized they had gone off without proper provisions and thanked God he at least had gloves. Maybe they could find a shelter or cave or someplace where they could rustle up enough dry wood for a fire and tomorrow get out of the mountains. He twisted around to peer at the trail behind him. Somewhere behind the curtain of snow, Jacob and the goats followed. Maybe Jacob had a tarp they could use for a shelter.

Then the wind suddenly diminished, died down completely, leaving still air that smelled clean and a world soft and quiet. He didn't think there had been a time when he'd been enfolded in such deep silence. Not even his horse's hooves penetrated the powdery snow. The flakes, big and fluffy, clung to his clothes like a thick blanket.

He settled into the saddle, relaxed.

They came to a steep, downhill section of the trail. His horse stumbled. Morgan tightened his legs and pulled on the reins but the ground was icy, and the horse lost its footing again and pitched forward, then twisted and fell sideways.

The horse's frightened whinny tore through the silence. The illusion of softness shattered in a flash of excruciating pain when Morgan hit the rocky ground. Pain so intense he couldn't cry out quickly faded and he felt nothing. His horse struggled to its feet and stood over him, blowing vapor from its muzzle. Morgan tried to get up but nothing moved. Flakes of snow whirled down onto his face. Snow clung to everything, turned it all a glistening white — juniper trees, sage brush, prickly pear cactus. Boulders. His horse snorted and walked away, silently disappearing into the falling flakes.

He shivered. His teeth chattered. He thought again about trying to get up. He thought about moving his arms, his legs, but pain had returned, quickly becoming so unbearable it took his breath away. Where was Jacob? He yelled Jacob's name but it sounded like a groan.

He tried to lift his head, to look for Jacob, but he couldn't do it and his breath quickened and he panted with a sudden terror. Pressure bore down on his legs, making them heavy, pushing them into the ground and then he couldn't feel his legs at all. He sucked in air, held it, fearing the excruciating pressure rolling up his body with agonizing slowness would reach his lungs and squeeze the air out of him. Then he stopped breathing. He stopped shivering. He marveled at the quiet and blinked snowflakes from his eyelashes.

In the total stillness, he thought of all the pain he had known in his life and what he would give now to stop the relentless, crushing pressure. He thought of pain he'd inflicted, men he'd killed. All who suffered in the past, of all the harm done — one man to another. To women, to children. The war, the killings that had nothing to do with war. Evil, hateful, dark and disturbing — the images of death filled his mind. The smell of blood filled his nostrils. He saw a crimson river pouring down an icy path, saw the sadness its spilling caused and then he was glad he felt nothing.

Only tired.

The bloody images faded.

Shafts of golden light broke through the clouds. Sunset. The whiteness surrounding him grew brighter. Silver and gold.

A shape grew closer and more distinct. His daughter. Her bright eyes, her smile. He wanted to touch her. He lifted his hand and reached for her. She called to him and he answered, *"Shi yózhi."* She waved, indicating he should follow her. Yes, it is time, he thought. *K'ad naa nísdzá.* Now I come to you. His daughter smiled and held out her hand. Behind her waited his wife, his son, the baby.

A shadow fell and a face hovered over him. As if coming from afar, he heard Jacob's faint voice calling his name. He tried to speak but his jaw fell slack and the air floated out, forming a cloud of vapor that hung before him and obscured Jacob's face. The cloud grew, sending gleaming wisps of fog curling upwards.

Silver light permeated the air, soaked into him, flowed through him, until he was full, until he was glowing, and then the light pressed outward and shattered the quartz-like chrysalis that had been his broken body, and he followed his family into the spirit world.

When Jacob saw Braddock's horse emerge from the curtain of snow, he caught the reins and gave his own horse a nudge to move faster. He hurried to close the distance that had opened between him and Braddock and, if not for the red stain in the snow, might have ridden right by. He tied the horses to a shrub and skidded over to where Braddock lay. He fell to his knees.

"Jesus Christ." He brushed the snow away from Braddock's face. "Braddock!"

Braddock's glazed eyes focused somewhere beyond, it seemed beyond the trail, beyond even the mountains. He spoke words Jacob didn't understand, then his mouth fell open and the light extinguished in Braddock's eyes.

By the time it was full dark, Jacob had a good fire going. The storm had stopped. The wind had calmed. Travel would be easier tomorrow. The sun would come up and melt the Goddamn snow.

He'd slung Braddock over his horse, wrapped in a blanket that had been tied next to his bedroll. While looking for some rope to tie his body to the saddle, Jacob made the joyful discovery that the bottle of mescal from the Depot was in his saddlebag, even though he had no memory of putting it there, and now he pulled the cork with a flourish. The horses and goats watched him from the edge of the circle of light, ghostly disembodied faces with their bodies hidden by the gloom of the night.

Through a mescal haze he realized that this might possibly be his fault. He'd encouraged Braddock to make this trip; at the very least, he hadn't tried to stop him. But accidents will occur. It could've easily been himself that fell off a horse onto a pile of rocks — these things happen! "Oh, Jesus," he said. What am I gonna tell Essie?

Lifting the bottle, he held it toward the blanket wrapped body draped over the horse. "Here's to you, Braddock. Sorry son of a bitch." He took a long drink.

He sat against smooth rocks and basked in the fire's warmth, the bottle braced between his outstretched legs. A nebulous glow behind a distant peak climbed higher and fused into a perfectly full moon. The animals puffed clouds of vapor. The hushed peacefulness of the night and glistening snow reminded him of winter nights back east, brought his thoughts to childhood Christmas eves, when he and Essie would try to stay awake until midnight so they could sneak out to the barn and wait for the animals to speak.

The shadowy goats and horses bobbed their faces in and out of the circle of light. "You ain't got nothin' to say, have you?" It began to appear as if their lips were about to move, so he stopped looking at them and took another drink. He didn't need their opinions; he'd get opinions enough from his sister.

The moon rose higher, transcending the few scattered wisps of clouds remaining.

He tried singing, "God rest ye merry gentlemen, let nothing ye dismay," but his throat tightened and tears welled in his eyes.

He slapped the cork onto the bottle and crawled into his blankets.

Strange dreams of dust devils howling and screaming like rabid coyotes haunted Esther during the night. As she lay awake between dreams, her thoughts traveled over the past few years. She'd lost her baby, her husband, and a man she loved. She'd been attacked by one man and she'd killed another. The memories spun around in her head, nightmare images even though she was awake.

She slipped out of bed and opened the window. The chorus of frogs from the spring did not soothe her, and they were silenced by the forlorn hooo-hooo of a great horned owl.

She was alone.

Far away thunder augured a storm coming. She could smell rain in the air. That meant snow in the high country. She hoped Jacob did not get caught in bad weather if he was on his way home. She wondered what his important business had been that made him leave her and the children to run off to Prescott. Maybe that's why she couldn't sleep — why she felt so alone — Jacob off somewhere for days, the first time since summer.

Yet, here she stood in her own cabin, on

her own farm. She had survived all that happened in the last two years. She kept her children safe. She took care of them. She didn't need Jacob to be here holding her hand.

She looked out at the yard, past Ida's grave, past the ramada and chicken house, to where the winter garden already did well. Bright leaves on the pumpkin and squash vines were shining in the light of the full moon. She expected carrots, beets and turnips would be ready in time for Thanksgiving dinner.

Gold from Howard's mine paid off the farm. She had enough now, no need to worry. Funny how Howard, dead, provided so well, especially since his intent had been to desert them entirely.

She got back into bed but thoughts of Howard lingered. His betrayal was hard to forgive. At least she knew there were good men in the world. Jacob, usually. Of course, Morgan and Rubén. Captain Dugan.

The emptiness and regret she always felt when she thought of Morgan was not as sharp as it used to be. In a way, it was sad how little sadness she felt. It was a moment in her life. She had lived it fully.

She dreamed no more that night.

■ ■ ■ ■

On a morning days later, past dawn, she kept glancing toward the wagon road as she milked the goats, wondering if Jacob was on his way back from Prescott yet. He'd said he was running an errand for James, which was ridiculous, of course, and James denied it anyway. She turned out the last goat and sat on the milking stand. Smells of coffee and bacon came from the house and stirred a hungry rumble in her stomach. Richard, Roy, and Al, working in the garden, must have caught the aromas because they kept looking up toward the house.

The chickens erupted into a frenzy of squawking and flapping, banging against the walls of their enclosure and the swinging gate, and a shadowy shape darted across the side yard.

Esther knocked over the milking stand in her dash to the house for the scattergun. She stood by the kitchen table and broke it open to check the chambers. She snapped the gun shut.

"What, Mama?" Millie asked, lifting her floured hands from biscuit dough.

"A damned coyote. I believe it's the same one that hung around all summer." She cocked the hammers on each side and turned to go out, but Mary was in the doorway.

"I don't see no coyote."

"Any," Esther said.

"Ma." James' voice carried down the stairs. "How can you be sure it's the same one?"

"I recognize the gleam in his eye. And the way he comes right into the yard because you keep leaving the chicken house door open." Esther looked up to where the boy peeked over the edge of the loft. She glared at him until his head disappeared.

"Mary, get out of the way, please." Esther stepped out into the dooryard and raised the gun. The coyote, holding a limp chicken in its jaws, stood in the middle of the yard, staring at her. He wore his winter coat, his fur thick and full. He was fat and healthy, no doubt due to his easy diet of fresh chicken!

She raised the gun, sighted along the barrel. She could not pull the trigger. The coyote slowly turned and walked away. He looked back at her from the edge of the yard before trotting off into the desert.

She eased the hammers down with her thumb. "James, get out here and round up those chickens."

Millie came to the doorway. "Someone's coming."

Esther looked toward the trail. A rider, indeed. And goats with panyards.

Jacob tied his horse at the corral and walked across the yard. "Essie," he said. "You don't look well."

"It was a hard trip back. Snow in the Bradshaws."

"Well, come on inside. A hot cup of coffee will revive you."

"I need to talk to James first."

"Oh, right, about your business in Prescott. I'll send him out. When you're done with him, remind him to round up those chickens."

Jacob walked toward the barn, around back past the buck goat pen, his nephew following. When they were out of sight of the cabin, he crouched down and pulled the sack of coins from inside his shirt.

The look, the one he'd been picturing for days, appeared. "I'm sorry, James."

The boy took the sack with both hands. "You didn't hire the Pinkerton man?"

"I tried, son. They said —"

He'd left Braddock's dead body at Fort McDowell and pondered all the way from there to here on what to tell anybody about it and still didn't know until this minute,

470

looking at his nephew's sad face.

"They said there weren't no point in them taking your money because they knew Mr. Braddock had gone somewhere — somewhere far off. It would be too hard to find him and bring him back."

James hung his head and scuffed his boot in the dust.

"Uncle Jacob? Did Mr. Braddock go to live with his other family? Those Indians?"

"What do you know about that?"

"I heard Ma and Mr. Rubén talkin' when Mr. Braddock was sick. You remember, back when we killed Danny."

"James, you all didn't just kill —"

"I heard Ma sayin' Mr. Braddock wanted to be with his other family. So, is that where he went? I reckon that would be far away. There ain't no Indians left around here."

Jacob took a deep breath and stood up. He put his hand on the boy's head and looked up at the blue sky and off at the distant hills. "Yes, James. I expect that is where he went."

"Well, okay then. But let's not say nothin' to Ma. I'll get her somethin' else for Christmas."

"Say nothing about what?" Esther was standing at the corner of the barn.

"Mr. Braddock. Uncle Jacob tried to find

him but he says he went to live with his Indian family. I'm sorry, Mama."

She searched Jacob's face. One hand covered her mouth, the other reached for the barn wall.

"I'm sorry, Essie." He took his hat off. "It happened up in the mountains, the night it snowed —"

"The night the moon was full. You were with him?"

Jacob stared at his scuffed boots. He nodded.

"He was coming here?"

When he dared to raise his eyes she had turned away, leaning against the barn, looking toward the wagon road. Jacob slid his fingers along the rim of his hat. The sharp air held the scents of wood smoke and creosote. A horse whinnied in the corral. Chickens clucked on the far side of the yard. A breeze kicked up, blowing dust across the yard, in front of the barn, toward the chicken house. Esther brought the hem of her apron to her cheek.

"Mama?" James' eyes filled. "Is Mr. Braddock's other family in heaven?"

She didn't speak right away. Then she nodded. "Go now, James. Go and lock up the chickens." When he hesitated, she said, "It's all right."

472

Jacob wanted to tell his sister about that look in Braddock's eyes at the end, right before he died. Braddock had seen something before the life went out of them.

He said, "I think he was okay with it, Essie. With the dyin', I mean."

She turned to look at him. "How can you say that?"

"He was talkin' Indian. Right before —"

She stepped away from the barn. "I came out to tell you breakfast is ready."

"Essie —"

"Go inside with the children. Have something to eat."

She would go inside and tend to her children, but right now she wanted to be alone. As was her habit of late, she went to Ida's grave and sat beside it. The cottonwood had shed most of its leaves, and she brushed them away from the grave.

She remembered the anguish she had once felt, thinking of her daughter's body beneath the dirt. Better to feel that, better to feel sadness, or longing, even hatred or grief, instead of this emptiness.

Resting her forehead on her knees, she could understand being okay with the dying.

She thought she heard Mary crying. Of

course, James would have told the others, and Mary would be sad. Her little girl had taken to Mr. Braddock. She started to get up. Her hand brushed the fallen leaves and sunlight glinted from a bright object. She cleared away more leaves at the edge of the grave and uncovered a small stone, laced with gold ore, pushed into the dirt at the base of the cross. She picked it up and brushed it off. It looked like the stone Mary had carried around most of the summer.

Footsteps approached and, out of the corner of her eye, she saw military boots topped by the blue trousers with the yellow stripe of the cavalry. Captain Dugan, holding his hat in both hands at his waist, stopped at the edge of the grave. She kept her eyes on the dried leaves as they shifted in the slight breath of air his approach had stirred.

"I hope I didn't startle you, ma'am," he said. "Your brother said I'd find you back here."

"What brings you here this morning?" She looked up, sighed. "Never mind. I know."

He swallowed hard before he could speak. Something stirred deep within her. This good hearted man had lost his friend.

"There'll be a funeral at the fort tomorrow. Full military honors. For Morgan."

She leaned forward and pushed the stone back into the small indentation its removal had left at the head of the grave.

"Mrs. Corbin, if you'd like, I can arrange for Major Whitehall's carriage to come for you and the children. I'd be honored if you'd allow me to escort you." A moment passed. "Actually, I'd be grateful."

She fought the tears that threatened to spill over. Tears not for herself but for the sadness she saw in Captain Dugan's eyes. Tears for the sadness they now shared.

"Morgan thought most highly of you and your family."

She nodded. "And of you."

He helped her to her feet. She held onto his hand and waited while he struggled to keep emotion from his face. "I liked thinking he was out there somewhere. I reckon he was like a hero to me."

He was heroic. He'd saved her, saved her children. He even saved Rubén before he was free to go. "He's with his family now."

The captain smiled a little and nodded.

"We were about to have breakfast, Captain. Won't you join us? It's a long ride back to the fort, and you shouldn't go on an empty stomach."

"I reckon there's no need to hurry back." He took a deep breath. "Thank you, ma'am."

He pulled her hand through his arm and walked with her to the doorway.

"Millie," she said as they entered the cabin, "please set another place." She pointed to a chair.

"Captain Dugan, please. Take a seat at the table."

CHAPTER THIRTY-SEVEN

A sound awakened Rubén from a fitful sleep. He opened his eyes to the blackness and listened. Anaba's steady, quiet breathing. A mouse scratching near the cook pots in the corner.

What was that?

The wind. He tried not to grunt as he rolled over, seeking a softer spot for his old bones, closer to the warmth of Anaba's body.

What was that?

A sound. From outside.

His eyes adjusted to the darkness. Slivers of moonlight limned the blanket hanging in the doorway. The blanket moved, just barely. A shadow blackened the shafts of light, just for a second. Something was out there.

He rolled away from Anaba and creaked to his feet. After pulling the covers up over his wife, he went to the door and held the blanket aside.

A coyote! Not five feet from the door. Looking right at him. It opened its mouth in a smiling pant, as if in greeting. It turned and trotted a few feet away, stopped and looked over its shoulder at him.

Rubén slipped out of the hogan.

He followed the coyote through the family enclave and into the open spaces beyond. The full moon, still low in the sky, cast a silvery sheen on the leafless cottonwoods.

His bare feet sank into red sand as he followed the coyote to the south, winding through the canyon, following its curves and bends. Now and then the coyote glanced back. Rubén saw its eyes glowing yellow. Drops fell from them as it trotted through the brush. Rubén found a trail of golden nuggets. He picked them up until his hands were full.

The coyote disappeared down a wash lined with scattered boulders, brush, and occasional piles of flood-tossed juniper branches. Rubén could no longer see the coyote. He followed the trail of golden teardrops, running now, the nuggets he had gathered falling from his thrusting fists, his lungs sucking in the sage-perfumed air. He ran on, rejoicing in the pumping of his legs, feeling each muscle as his legs propelled him along effortlessly.

He rounded a bend in the wash. No more nuggets on the ground. He raised his eyes. High above, a light glowed from a cleft in the rock, from deep within its shadow.

He left the wash, stepping into shadow, guided only by the light ahead. His feet left the ground. He rose higher and higher, the wash below sinking into darkness. He ascended to the glowing light and found a small cave. Resting his hands on the edge of the opening, he peered inside.

Gold lined the cave, covering walls, the ceiling, the floor, so bright it took minutes for his eyes to adjust from the darkness outside. Then he saw the coyote. It lay curled up, resting its head on its encircling tail, eyes closed.

"Ah, *si kis,*" Rubén whispered.

The coyote slitted open one eye. Rubén laid a hand upon its head, stroked it. The coyote looked at him, and a small golden tear slipped from its eye, ran down the side of its muzzle. Rubén caught the golden drop. "I miss you, my friend. But you have found your home. I am happy for that." The coyote settled back into its sleep, and Rubén gently drifted away into the dark night.

Deeply burrowed into his blankets, he

awoke to Anaba's arms around him, her voice in his ear.

"You must be having a pleasant dream, to look so happy in your sleep."

"Asleep or awake, I have much to be happy about."

He closed his fingers around the golden nugget.

ABOUT THE AUTHOR

Patricia Grady Cox is a member of Western Writers of America and Women Writing the West. She lives in Arizona, which is the setting for most of her writing, and enjoys the opportunity to visit and conduct research at the actual locales of her stories. Her love of southwest history, culture, and landscape combine to infuse her writing with authenticity. Her goal is to entertain and touch the hearts of her readers while transporting them to another time. Visit Patricia at www.patriciagradycox.com

The employees of Thorndike Press hope you have enjoyed this Large Print book. All our Thorndike, Wheeler, and Kennebec Large Print titles are designed for easy reading, and all our books are made to last. Other Thorndike Press Large Print books are available at your library, through selected bookstores, or directly from us.

For information about titles, please call:
    (800) 223-1244

or visit our website at:
    gale.com/thorndike

To share your comments, please write:
    Publisher
    Thorndike Press
    10 Water St., Suite 310
    Waterville, ME 04901